THE TRUCEKEEPER SAGA

BOOK ONE

THE BLOOD CRYSTAL

BY

MATT TWINLEY

First published in 2022 by Twin Bee Books

First edition

British Library Cataloguing-in-Publication Data
A catalogue record for this book is available from the British Library

ISBN 978-1-7399856-0-8

Printed and bound in Great Britain

Cover design by Book Beaver

www.matt-twinley.com

For Sophie,

who showed me the magic that's hidden in all life throws at us.

'The scariest monsters are the ones that lurk within our souls.'
Edgar Allan Poe

The Blood Crystal - Character List

Hannah Moreland — *Human*
Daegan — *Trucekeeper*

Truceleaders

Caedric Asterson — *Trucemaster*
Lord Bertram Byron — *Vampire*
Drakkar Wynter — *Warlock*
Aarava Dragos — *Centauride*
Aleesia Sarkas — *Elf of the Ethyr Tribe*
Eldrin Naeris — *Elf of the Mythlon Tribe*
Braddock Leadshield — *Dwarf*

Arcadian Staff

Axis Crawford — *Librarian, Half-Elf*
Lena Frostgem — *Healer, Faerie*
Sophie Gleamthistle — *Head of Blood Crystals, Faerie*
Talos Stonham — *Quartermaster*
Mantir Iskiros — *Arcadian Army General, Minotaur*

Trucekeeper Trainees

Niall Adams — *Human*
Tanitya Varin — *Mermaid*

Fennrock Leadshield — Son of Braddock, Dwarf
Celeste Norvaris — Elf of the Mythlon Tirbe
Luminon Theras — Elf of the Ethyr Tribe
Asti Melotos — Satyr
Rideo Felixon — Faun
Natala Montis — Oread Nymph
Limara Perata — Leimakid Nymph
Mimi Rivera — Limnad Nymph
Nathan Jenkins — Human
Amber Carter — Human
Jason Hammond — Human

Thule

Kori Kasumi — Queen of Thule, Yuki-Onna
Gondei Pascal — Guide, Barbegazi

Etheria Allies

Ansel Dalton — Former Arcadian Spy, Werewolf
Marina Adrielle — Mermaid

Arningham School

Luke Crawley — Pupil
Zack Reeves — Pupil
Veronica Wright — History Teacher
Maxim Barlow — Headmaster

Familiars

Dex — Hannah's Familiar, Kamaitachi

Kiko — Niall's Familiar, Kitsune

Zephyr — Caedric's Familiar, Caladrius

Raji — Daegan's Familiar, Raiju

Willow — Sophie's Familiar, Unicorn

Carex — Nathan's Familiar, Furi

Malia — Jason's Familiar, Mujina

Hunter — Amber's Familiar, Inugami

Echo — Fennrock's Familiar, Yamabiko

Randy — Mimi's Familiar, Ramidreju

Mikoa — Limara's Familiar, Tanuki

Callie — Natala's Familiar, Carbuncle

Otis — Asti's Familiar, Keukegen

Arlo — Rideo's Familiar, Jackalope

Caelan — Celeste's Familiar, Jaculus

Silas — Luminon's Familiar, Muscaliet

Cordelia — Taniiya's Familiar, Kawauso

Willow — Sophie's Familiar, Unicorn

Chapter One

An Old Friend

HUNTING werewolves is always a dangerous affair. Especially during a full moon.

The man was well aware of this as he listened intently for any sound that could help him decide his first move. He could hear nothing, save for the wind whipping his face, the waves crashing against the cliff walls and the rapid beating of his heart.

He stepped back to examine the rough walls of the castle ruin, studying every crevice and point of access. After securing his wide-brimmed hat atop his head, he leapt. The man crawled up the wall, his hands and feet propelling him upwards as his dark brown trench coat flapped about him. He paused at the top, his hands gripping the ledge. There was only a distant shuffling far off in the ruin. It was safe to crawl inside.

He took care to make as little noise as possible and withdrew a strange-looking weapon. It looked like a dagger: a thin blade about ten inches long that flashed in the moonlight. A small hole the size of a pin lay above an ornate crystal embedded in the sapphire-coloured handle, a curious R etched onto its surface.

Clasping the weapon, he squeezed his thumb against the hole. A needle obediently thrust up and pierced his thumb, forcing a small drop of blood to squeeze out as he pressed it against the crystal. When it made contact with his blood, it glowed dimly. He flicked the weapon with a slight gesture and faint red footprints appeared on the floor, as though made by ultraviolet lights. They were terrifyingly large—at least twice the size of a normal man's. He touched his bloodied thumb to the crystal again. His whole figure darkened as he became one with the shadows.

A gust of sea air hit his face, causing him to pause. The sound of teeth gnashing on bones reached his ears. He took a moment to collect himself. His orders were to discover any information and eliminate any threat—that did *not* mean kill, or so he hoped.

He peered around the corner. Crouched on its hind legs, next to a pile of bones, was a creature feasting on a carcass. A gust of wind blew in through the window it faced, and the man smiled. He knew it was best to approach a werewolf from downwind, scent hidden; he had learned that the hard way.

The man crept into the room, and his boot landed on a bone, his breath catching in his throat. The werewolf looked up, sniffing frantically. Its face was long and thin, with razor-like teeth stained with blood. Fierce yellow eyes searched for the intruder. But even with its night-vision, there was little chance of spotting him hidden in the shadows.

Still, the man had to hurry. Piercing his thumb and pressing it to the crystal once more, he waved his weapon towards the far corner of the room. A brick rose a few feet and clapped back down, making a sound that drew the werewolf's attention.

It jumped into the corner, sharp claws loudly scraping against the wall. The man raised his weapon again, and a spark of fire shot like a bullet, striking the wall just inches from the werewolf's face. It slowly turned and gave a low, fierce growl. The man kept his weapon raised.

He knew the werewolf recognised him. His face was concealed beneath the brim of his hat, but his dark stubble and greasy long dark hair gave him away. The werewolf's eyes narrowed.

'Trucekeeper,' the werewolf growled.

'You know my name, Ansel. Don't pretend we're enemies,' the man replied.

'So, they sent *you*… Can't say I'm too surprised, Daegan.'

Daegan smiled sadly. 'You can guess why they sent me.' He hesitated, afraid he might aggravate Ansel. 'You are partly responsible, by the way.'

Ansel growled. 'I'm not solely to blame. There was a war. I wasn't the only killer.'

'Neither was I.'

Ansel bent his snout to resemble something like a smile. 'Oh, I'm not so sure. You were one of the best. You can't call me a killer, Daegan—not compared to you.'

A twinge of guilt soared through Daegan, but he refused to let it show. He nodded towards a pile of bones. 'Are you sure about that?'

'Animals,' the werewolf replied. 'I don't kill humans.'

'Not if you can help it.'

Ansel grinned, his teeth protruding from his mouth. 'It's been some time, Daegan. What brings you to me now? I assume it's nothing good.'

Daegan held his aim at the werewolf.

'The War's over,' Ansel continued, 'and things are back to the way they were. Lower your weapon and leave me be.'

'I just want to talk,' Daegan reassured him.

'That's what you said last time. I trust you remember how that ended?'

'As I recall, that was your fault.'

Ansel turned away. 'My memory's fuzzy.' A silence grew between them. 'Why tonight? A full moon isn't the wisest time to approach a werewolf.'

'*Corvus oculum corvi non eruit.*' Daegan smiled.

Ansel frowned. 'You can't be implying we're the same. It's been too long for that.'

'Perhaps. But it wouldn't matter when I came. You've been in this form for some time. When were you last human? Two, three years ago?' Daegan asked.

Ansel kept frowning. 'How can you tell?'

'A werewolf's need to feast is stronger during a full moon. They lose the human side of their mind to the werewolf's and can't stop themselves. Only when they've… fed on humans can they revert to their normal self at the next sunrise. I know you, Ansel—you hate killing as much as me. I think you've controlled your werewolf form. You've refused to give in to your urges, and now you're stuck like this. Hence the pile of *animal* bones.' Daegan smiled again. 'I'm impressed.'

'It's not easy. Do you have any idea how it feels? Hungry all the time? Constantly craving meat—raw, wet…'

Ansel's eyes gleamed, and Daegan saw a dangerous look he had seen too many times. 'I'm glad you've changed, Ansel, but—'

'I've done nothing to warrant a Trucekeeper's contract,' he barked. 'No werewolf this hungry deserves that.'

'I've just come to ask you a question.'

'Then speak,' Ansel snapped.

'We haven't forgotten your role in the War. We're still grateful. If there's anything the Trucekeepers can do for you—'

'Is that all you came to say?' Ansel roared.

'No,' Daegan said, his breath quickening. 'We remembered how much you did for us, how you supplied information from the enemy—'

'I'm not doing that again.'

'But there's—'

'No,' Ansel growled.

'There's a mole,' Daegan pleaded.

'A mole?'

'Yes. A spy, double agent—call it what you will.'

A vague grin appeared on Ansel's face. 'It's finally happened. I suppose it was only a matter of time… How did you find out?'

'There have been several Leviathan targets that either evaded or assassinated us. We were sure someone warned them ahead of time. Do you know who it is?'

'No.'

Daegan grimaced.

'I don't know *who*,' Ansel continued, 'but there was a plan—to place a mole in the heart of the Trucekeepers. Right in Arcadia.'

'Who could it be?'

'I just heard its aim was to progress all the way up to the Truceleaders.'

Daegan fell silent, trying to take it all in. 'A Truceleader? One of them—'

'—is a traitor, yes,' Ansel finished for him. 'No idea which one, but be careful. They're there for only one reason.'

'To end the Truce.'

'From the waves we rise,' Ansel said. 'The very motto of the Leviathans.'

Daegan was stunned, his guard slipping as he lowered his weapon.

'I'm sure it hurts, Daegan. All those Trucekeepers dying. They're not all your fault, you know. Astraea was—'

'What happened to her was my fault,' Daegan snapped.

Ansel gazed back at him 'You didn't say how many Trucekeepers had been killed,' he said delicately. 'How many, Daegan?'

Daegan closed his eyes, but Ansel broke his reverie with a roar; one of hunger and anger. He knew he shouldn't tell him; it showed a weakness in the Trucekeepers. But Ansel deserved an answer.

'I'm the only one left,' Daegan told him, gritting his teeth as he tried not to show any emotion.

Ansel sighed. 'Then, my old friend, you've already lost.'

Daegan holstered his weapon and readied himself to leave. Ansel was no threat.

'Thank you, Ansel. I wish you well. If you need anything, any favour, you're always welcome at Arcadia.' With that, Daegan turned to leave.

But a low grumble came from behind him. 'You're not leaving, Daegan.'

Daegan stopped, his head dropping in disappointment. 'You don't need to do this.'

'No, Daegan… I do. I have my orders, same as you.'

'Orders to kill me?' Daegan asked.

'If you were the last Trucekeeper, yes.'

'Then pretend you never saw me,' Daegan said, his thumb pressed against the pinhole, blood dripping down.

Ansel growled and shook his head. 'I'm sorry, old friend.'

It was the last thing Ansel said. Daegan pressed his bloody thumb to the crystal and cast a dazzling light that stunned Ansel in the middle of his attack.

He pricked his thumb again as Ansel charged. Daegan reacted, firing a shot of flame. The werewolf dodged it, but he cast the spell again, immediately, this time hitting Ansel on the shoulder. The Trucekeeper sidestepped, using the sharp edge of his blade to cut the werewolf.

Ansel screamed and swiped a bloody claw at Daegan's face. He dodged and unleashed another flash of light as he punched and slashed.

Ansel recovered his sight and lunged. Daegan danced away and shot a quick spell that blasted the werewolf across the room. He crashed into the wall, and cold bricks fell from the ruin to the dark sea below.

Ansel lay still next to the collapsed wall.

Daegan crept forward, bracing himself for any movement.

In an instant, the werewolf's bright eyes snapped open. Daegan's reaction was automatic; he fired another spell, propelling Ansel backwards—but it was too late. Ansel grabbed his leg, and they were both dragged out of a hole in the ruined wall.

Wind rushed past Daegan as they fell. Ansel dug his claws into Daegan's leg, who responded with two sharp punches and a slash of his weapon. Ansel released his grip with a grunt, and Daegan let out a kick, putting distance between them as they continued to plummet towards the sea.

The cliff was tall, but Daegan had a matter of seconds until his body hit the ground. He pressed a small button on the strap around his chest. With a firm line trailing behind, an arrow shot from the strap and embedded itself firmly in the cliff-face.

His fall slowed until he was left dangling against the cliff, grimacing as the strap dug into him. As the Trucekeeper fiddled with the device, the line uncoiled, carrying him gently to the shore below.

Once at the bottom, he pressed a button. The arrow fell from the cliff, the device automatically curling up the wire and resetting itself.

Daegan surveyed the rocky beach. The moon was bright enough to reveal any werewolves lurking in the shadows, but there was no sign of Ansel.

A splash sounded, and he raised his weapon.

But, as the figure from the sea revealed herself, Daegan holstered his weapon. From the deep waters emerged what appeared to be a woman. Auburn hair clung to her shoulders, dripping with water as she leapt onto a rock. She spotted Daegan and beamed. Daegan couldn't help smiling back.

The mermaid pushed her hair behind her ear with one hand and stroked her long fishlike tail with the other. Emerald-green scales ran down to a multi-coloured fin.

'Long time no see,' she said, her voice melodic.

'It's good to see you too, Marina,' Daegan replied. There was a pause, an unspoken tension between them. 'How are you?'

'Better now,' the mermaid replied, gesturing at the castle above. 'Ansel's been trouble.'

'For you?'

'For my tribe.'

Daegan raised his eyebrows. 'How so? He caused trouble from time to time, but—'

'We used to be a large tribe, happily swimming around the ocean and not harming a soul.'

Daegan smirked. 'Not all mermaids can claim not to hurt anyone.'

'That may be the case,' Marina snapped, unamused, 'but we're peaceful. But Ansel—' Marina looked up at him, her voice trembling. 'You noticed he wasn't eating humans? I suppose *we* were the next best thing.'

Daegan clenched his fist. 'He told me they were animals.'

'And that's what we were to him—animals. Enough like humans to satisfy his craving. As far as he was concerned, we were animals for him to...' She fell silent.

Daegan didn't know what to say. It was his job to stop incidents like this from ever happening, and he had failed without even knowing it.

Marina took a deep breath as she composed herself. 'It's not your fault. It's over,' she said, an emotionless edge cutting into her voice. 'He landed in the sea. I doubt even a werewolf could survive that. Now...' She looked at him gently. 'Give me your arm.'

'My arm?'

Marina noticed his hesitation. 'Not all Etheria are monsters. Let me heal your arm.'

'No.'

'You can trust me, Daegan. You know that, don't you?'

Daegan smiled briskly. 'Good to see you, Marina. I'm glad I could help. Sorry it was too late.' He pulled his hat down, shading his eyes from the moonlight. 'Until next time.'

Marina let her arms fall to her lap and watched him leave before vanishing into the sea with barely a splash.

The waves rippled gently. It was almost as if there had never been werewolves or mermaids. Almost as if the world hid no secrets at all.

Chapter Two

A Friend and a Fiend

THE bell roared. A unanimous groan came from the unruly mob of teenagers as they trudged up the stairs into Arningham School.

One pupil remained. At first glance, there was nothing extraordinary about Hannah. Her blonde hair was often more unkempt than she wished, and she looked perpetually tired, despite the make-up she dabbed around her eyes each morning. She was proud of her eyes, though; they were mostly green, but one was half-blue, and she did her best to show them off with her make-up.

She stood in the school's courtyard a while longer as she surveyed the playground; it was mostly empty, save for a few late-comers frantically copying out each other's homework. She delayed making her way to class for as long as she could, every ounce of her being telling her to go home, nap, take the day off. *No one will notice if I miss just one lesson… will they? Not in sixth form…*

Hannah stroked the bannisters as she wandered up the stairs, praying for her hand to rebel, to grab the banister and refuse to go any further—any excuse would do… But her hand continued up with her.

A small group of her classmates were already huddled in the hallway outside the classroom. She stayed a few steps back, holding her books and awkwardly waving hello to the others. Waiting for any other lesson, she'd be quite happy to chat with them, but not History—not with Zack there. Already she could hear the whispers and giggles from one group as she took out her equipment, pricking her finger to test her blood sugar level.

Just a bit high, she thought with a grimace, retrieving a pump from her pocket to give herself insulin.

'The robot needs a new battery,' someone chuckled in a whisper so loud you could hear it a mile away.

She turned away in a vain effort to hide her pump from the others. She hated her diabetes; hated how it made her stand out, hated all the needles, hated how weak it made her feel. No one had ever thought to comment on it before Arningham. It was only when she got on Zack's nasty side that things went wrong.

It was in the first term after she started at the school that Zack asked her out. It wasn't an interesting date, as Hannah had been to that café too many times for it to be at all memorable. But Zack was one of the "cool kids," and Hannah understood the more they liked her, the easier life at school would be in the long term.

Sadly, it hadn't gone the way she expected. Hannah had tried to bolus subtly, her insulin pump held under the table, but he was too nosy. She assumed it would just be easier to explain how it wasn't a weird-looking phone. She *thought* she'd be able to trust him; she *thought* he'd be okay with her telling him; she *thought* it would be "no big deal."

'You mean you used to be really fat?' he asked. His eyes appraised her body with a mixture of disgust and humour.

'No,' she said, her tone clipped as she picked at her nail, doing her best to stay calm. 'I've never been overweight.' She paused, suddenly insecure. 'I said I'm *Type 1* diabetic. It's genetic.'

'But fat people have diabetes.'

'Being overweight can sometimes cause *Type 2* diabetes, yes. But Type 1 is about genetics.'

Zack just scoffed, suddenly keen to end the date and get away. Before Hannah got home, he had removed her from the group chat with him and his friends and, by the time the new school week started, the entire school knew. Some thought it was "hilarious." When she used her pump to give herself insulin in class, some stricter teachers accused her of texting. Zack's snort could always be heard over the other giggles from his entourage.

Not that school was all bad. On paper, she ought to have had no trouble at all. She was bright, got on well with most of the pupils— at least when she could be bothered to talk—and more or less excelled in all her classes, though this didn't dissuade teachers from insisting she could do better if she tried harder.

At least she had Luke.

Where the hell is he? she thought. *He should be here by now.*

Luke and Hannah had been inseparable since their first day at Arningham, and he, too, had been subjected to the same unpleasantness from Zack and his friends. When she had told him about her diabetes, he didn't even blink. Seeking solace in each other had seemed the best defence.

Hannah stood patiently outside the classroom, trying her best not to listen to the inane bragging of Zack Reeves and his planned party later that night. She felt relieved he didn't even try to invite her. He hadn't invited her to anything since their date.

'Boo!'

Hannah didn't jump.

'You never fall for that anymore!' Luke complained with a sarcastic pout.

'Because I'm not five,' Hannah retorted. 'You need to come up with something better.'

'Sorry I'm late,' he said as he glimpsed his reflection and fiddled with his messy brown hair.

'Where were you?' Hannah asked, trying to ignore the wolf-whistling from behind them, Zack's jealousy hid behind a veneer of jibes.

Luke rolled his eyes. 'Have they been like this all morning?' he asked, blowing a kiss in the hopes it might wind Zack up.

'Don't change the subject. Where were you?' Hannah saw a glint in his eye.

'Just—just doing homework in the library,' he stammered.

'Who with?'

Luke looked to his side for support. 'Kate,' he admitted.

'Kate Hewitt?'

'Yeah.'

'Oh.'

Luke shifted his feet, fiddling with a pen to pass the silence. 'Something wrong with that?'

'No,' Hannah replied, too quickly. 'Of course not. She's lovely… some say. I just wish you'd been here so I wouldn't have to deal with *them* by myself.'

'Fair enough. Sorry, sir. Won't happen again,' he said with a salute. 'Hey, check this out!'

He withdrew a strange blue object from his bag. It was made from porcelain and looked shockingly like a ray-gun with holes. Luke placed his mouth to a hole and blew, making a high-pitched sound like a flute.

'What the hell is that?'

'An ocarina!' he announced, oblivious to the judgemental stares around him. 'Cool, isn't it? Another one to add to the collection.'

Hannah made a non-committal smile. 'You might want to double check the definition of "cool."'

Luke frowned. 'Something up?' he asked.

Hannah cocked an eyebrow but looked away. 'I heard back.'

'From…? It couldn't be the charm school.'

'About that archaeology course.'

Luke's eyes lit up, as if he were the one with good news. 'Oh, finally! And?' He squeezed his eyes shut and crossed his fingers.

'I got in,' she told him, her voice remaining monotonous and bored.

Luke leapt into the air, his fist raised in triumph. Zack whispered something to his friends, who jeered in response.

'You don't look excited,' Luke commented. 'That's what you wanted, right?'

Hannah nodded, her body tense. 'Yes. It's all I wanted for as long as I can remember. Since I was a kid. But now…'

'Now you're fretting because you'll miss me.'

'Sure,' she joked, letting the corner of her mouth curl into a smile.

'Come on. What is it really?'

'I need an A,' she sighed.

Luke paused. 'So? You're predicted an A.'

'Yes—predicted. It's not guaranteed. And neither is my place on that course until I get an A.'

'So you'll just have to work hard, and make sure you get an A. Simple.'

'Ha, simple! Of course! Easier said than done, you know that.' She paused, staring hard at the floor, wishing life would go easy on her. 'All I've wanted and planned for is so close—my dream career, a chance to escape home, a route to a job I'd love… and all that stands between me and that plan is an examiner and a few essay questions. What if I don't revise the right topics? What if my essay style doesn't get me the A? What if I—'

Luke put his hand on her shoulder. 'Hannah, listen. You're the smartest person I know. If you can't get an A in the subject you love, no one can. I have complete faith in you. Having said that, I suck at this consoling thing. Could I interest you a song on the ocarina?'

At that moment, Miss Wright invited them in, and Hannah took the opportunity to avoid the onslaught of the ocarina. Once in the classroom, Hannah sat in her usual seat next to Luke, her thoughts still picturing Luke and Kate together. She shook it from her mind but stared hard at her pen when Kate walked through the door, mumbling a feeble apology for being late, her cheeks red and her manner flustered.

The clock ticked away the seconds. Minutes seemed like hours and the hour an eternity. Miss Wright was an engaging teacher, and at least Hannah found History interesting—but she was still itching for it to end.

She heard a snigger from behind her. Zack—the arrogance in the laugh was unmistakable. Miss Wright gave him a warning glare before she turned to the board.

Zack seized the opportunity and flung a crumpled piece of paper. It landed right in front of Hannah. He cursed, having just missed the intended recipient.

'Hey! Blondie!' he whispered loudly.

She turned to him and frowned. Zack grunted and beckoned for her to pass it on.

Instead, she peered inside but couldn't bother reading the whole thing. After the words "behind the bike shed at lunch", she could guess the rest. She slowly turned to face him, her eyes gleaming above a mischievous grin. Zack grumbled and sank in his seat, dreading what she was going to do.

Hannah hummed under her breath as she folded the paper into a point and formed two flaps. Zack had been immensely proud of the paper plane design he had apparently 'patented' back in Year 9. After the number of times he had sent them soaring into the back of Hannah's head, she knew his design fairly well herself.

'Go fetch,' she muttered beneath her breath as she flung it forward. It took wing and deftly shot across the room before crashing beside Miss Wright, who jumped slightly. After a quick glare at the class behind her, she snatched it from the ground and unfolded it.

'Mr Locke will be on duty there during lunch break,' Miss Wright warned the class. 'I sincerely hope *this*—' she held up the note before tossing it in the bin '—is just a joke.'

Zack's face turned red; out of embarrassment or resentment, Hannah couldn't tell—but she enjoyed it. She faced the front, unaware of his furious glare and his hands balled into fists as the lesson went on.

Chapter Three

Shattered to Pieces

MISS Wright tried desperately to be heard over the commotion of the class packing up as soon as the bell rang. Hannah stayed sitting, preferring to leave the room last. She stole a glance behind her. Zack still sat there, hatred spitting from his eyes, daring her to move first.

She calmly gathered her books and moved her foot beside the table, ready to push off in a sprint at a moment's notice. She counted to five, pushed with her leg and raced towards the door. Hannah could hear an exasperated Miss Wright reminding them not to run, but she was drowned out by Zack's heavy footsteps as he gave chase.

Luke trailed behind as Hannah sprinted away, almost getting to the stairwell before Zack caught up. With an almighty slam, his hand slapped the folders tucked under her arm, sending papers flying everywhere.

She turned to face him, trying yet failing to look intimidating. 'What was that for?' she snapped, angrier than upset.

Zack shoved her shoulders, and she stumbled towards the stairs.

'Hey—' Luke interjected.

But Zack grabbed Luke by the collar instead and shoved him hard against the bannisters. His upper back arched and dangled over the high drop. Zack shook him roughly until his ocarina slipped out of his bag and soared helplessly to the ground, smashing to pieces.

Luke let out a whimper—out of fear or disappointment, Hannah couldn't tell.

'Zack, what are you doing?' She struck him on the back, desperate to slap some sense into him. 'You're overreacting! Just leave him alone!'

'Overreacting?' he repeated, seething through gritted teeth. 'You've been trying to humiliate me, kick me out of school for years. All because I told everyone—'

Hannah had heard enough. 'Leave him alone!' she begged, more forcefully this time. She wouldn't put it past Zack to push him over the railing; all it would take was a small shove… 'Leave him alone!' she yelped again.

But Zack's grip was firm, and he shoved Luke further and further, his face a picture of fury.

Luke turned to Hannah, a look of determination on his face. 'Hannah, don't. He wouldn't dare.'

'Wanna bet?' Zack growled.

Hannah couldn't bear just standing there. She looked from Zack to Luke, screaming at herself to do something, anything.

What? Save Luke? Stop Zack?

With a grunt, she shoved her own weight against the pair. Zack's grip slipped from Luke as they toppled over in a heavy heap, bodies slamming to the ground.

Hannah winced as she staggered to her feet and rubbed her arm. She felt a panicked tapping on her shoulder and turned to see Luke, mouth agape, pointing down the stairs.

Zack lay at the bottom, unmoving. His eyes were closed, and a pool of blood had formed a halo around his head. Hannah's eyes widened, and she cursed silently.

'We have to leave,' she said.

'Leave? Shouldn't we help him?'

Hannah gripped Luke's shoulder and turned him sharply to face her. 'Would he stop to help you?'

Luke looked down, unable to hold her gaze. 'No… It's not right…'

'We *need* to,' she urged. She wrenched her shoe from her foot and slammed it against the CCTV camera in the corner. Bits of glass and wire fell to the floor, and Luke gasped. '*Now!*'

A scream broke out from beneath them, followed by a stampede of footsteps hurtling towards the unmoving body.

'Run!' Luke gasped, flying down the corridor, with Hannah rapidly following suit.

They didn't know if they were being chased or if anyone had even seen them. But they ran anyway; they would run as fast as they could until they lost their pursuers and then—

'In here!' Luke blurted out between heavy breaths. He grabbed her wrist and tugged her into a room, slamming the door.

Crammed in a cupboard, they pushed past an array of mops and buckets and stood perfectly still. Hannah's lungs threatened to burst from her chest, but she held her breath and felt Luke do the same as the pursuing herd stampeded past.

'I think they're gone,' Luke whispered after an agonising wait.

Hannah didn't respond, her mind instead focusing on the consequences. *There's no way I'm getting away with this. I know what they'll say when I get home. And then what if I—*

'Hannah, it's—' Luke started, interrupting her thoughts. But he didn't know what to say. He knew what was going through Hannah's mind. 'Mr Barlow hates Zack as much as you do. He'll understand and go easy on you. He'll probably…'

His words trailed off as Hannah wrapped her arms around him. Luke's body stiffened at first, but after a beat, he hugged her back. Hannah gazed up at him. She felt her breathing quicken and her heart race. For a second, she wondered if it wasn't the thrill of the chase but something else entirely.

Soon, the silence of the closet became awkward, and they separated. Hannah pushed her hair behind her ear, her face a picture of confusion, as Luke gave an uncomfortable laugh.

'Not that it isn't delightful in here,' she whispered, 'but it's probably safe to leave now.'

Luke nodded and muttered something in agreement. With a cough, he opened the door to find their headmaster, Mr Barlow, leaning against the wall, his arms folded in triumph.

'Found you,' he hissed.

Chapter Four

The Punishment

HANNAH had bitten her nail down to her skin but still picked at it—not that it helped calm her nerves. It wasn't something she had done since she was young.

It had started as soon as she realised how angry she had made Zack, and only got worse once Mr Barlow found her and Luke. She had feigned an air of innocence at first but couldn't lie to herself.

A giggle caught her attention, and she looked up. Zack's friends were peering through the door's window; some laughing, some glaring at the one who had "attacked" their friend. After a few choice gestures with her hand, they left Hannah to brood bitterly.

She spared a thought to Luke, who was with Mr Barlow right now. There was no shouting, but a twinge of guilt still reared at the back of her mind. It was her fault—Luke wouldn't have been in any trouble if it weren't for her. But she couldn't have let Zack get away with it. She had to do *something*… but maybe not what she actually did.

The door opened, and Luke shuffled out. He grimaced stupidly in a vain effort to make Hannah laugh.

'Good luck,' he whispered with a pathetic thumbs up.

'Hannah!' boomed the headmaster's ominous voice.

For a second, she considered staying in her seat—or leaving completely. Perhaps if she just walked away, it might all disappear.

'Hannah!' he called again, louder this time.

With a sigh of resignation, she waited at the doorway; Mr Barlow expected absolute obedience. He loathed it when pupils sat down without being invited to do so. As much as it was in Hannah's nature to push boundaries and flout rules she didn't agree with, she hoped some self-restraint might save her skin.

Mr Barlow sat at his ornate desk, carefully studying a pile of papers. His room was disconcertingly dark, the only source of light a weak, green-tinted beam from his desk lamp. The blinds behind him were firmly closed and, with no computer in sight, Hannah wondered how he got any work done in here at all. She could vaguely make out some strange-looking pictures adorning the walls but could barely see them through the cloak of darkness. Other than that, the room was bare; no photos of home or family, no bookshelf.

'Destruction of school property, hiding in a room that is out-of-bounds to pupils, fighting and injuring another pupil… Had a good day?' Mr Barlow looked up over the papers he was reading, his eyes piercing deep into Hannah's. She could see it in his eyes: disappointment, anger, frustration. She looked down. 'Look at me,' he said, his voice quiet but with so much malice she shuddered.

'Sir, can I just—'

Mr Barlow held up a spindly, pale hand. She stopped immediately.

'What's wrong with you?' he asked her simply. 'It's a tragedy how much of a waste you are.'

Hannah opened her mouth to respond but found no words.

Mr Barlow stared at her before continuing. 'On paper, you're an exceptional student. Athletically inclined, I'm told—but you gave it up. Very academic—with a particular penchant for History, as I understand. And an offer for an archaeology course that many in your situation would kill for. So, what went wrong?'

There was a pause, a long one.

'Er… I don't know, sir,' she replied.

'It was a rhetorical question, Miss Moreland,' said Mr Barlow, exasperated.

Hannah cursed herself. She wanted to make him like her enough to let her off, just the one time. But she'd never mastered the art of charming people.

'Is it home?' he asked.

Hannah snorted. She left her response as that. A proper reply would come with a string of questions. Once people learned she didn't live with her parents, they always assumed that was the root of every problem. It was true that she didn't get on with her aunt, but there was more to it than that.

'Stress of exams?' he tried. 'Friend troubles?'

'Sort of,' she said.

'In what way?'

'Zack.'

'What about him?'

'He's a bully.' She regretted her words as soon as they left her mouth.

'A *bully*?' He spat the word. 'How old are you, Miss Moreland?'

'He ridicules me, he laughs at me—and Luke too! Zack threatened him. He was going to—'

'Hannah…' he sighed.

'He didn't like that I snitched on him in History, so he threw my folder to the ground, shoved me, so Luke tried to defend me. He shoved him too and nearly pushed him over the bannisters…' her voice trailed off as her eyes met his. She knew what he was thinking.

'Were there any witnesses?'

'No,' Hannah whispered. 'Apart from Luke.'

'So no actual third party?'

'No, sir. But the CCTV camera—'

'You mean the one you destroyed?'

Hannah bit her nail. Mr Barlow sighed and rested his hands on the desk.

'Hannah, I'm sure you're not surprised to hear how disappointed I am. You show the potential to be an incredible member of this school's community, yet you repeatedly disrupt classes and argue with your classmates. You take matters of justice into your own hands, resulting in a pupil being rushed to hospital. The doctors believe he has a concussion and broken bones but will be on the mend before too long. I highly suggest you visit the hospital as you owe him an apology.'

Hannah opened her mouth to protest, but he held out a sickly white hand to stop her before she could even start.

'I'll have to bring your aunt in to give her the news formally. But I'm afraid I can't allow you to remain at this school at the moment. Therefore, until we decide whether a more permanent punishment would be appropriate, you will be indefinitely suspended. Please collect your belongings and vacate the premises immediately. Thank you.'

He waved his hand towards the door, gesturing for her to leave. Hannah was glued to her seat.

'You what?' She didn't know what else to say. Her mouth hung agape. 'You can't do that.'

Mr Barlow frowned. 'Yes, I can.'

'I mean, I know you *can*. But… but I need to stay here. I need to get an A so I can—'

Mr Barlow shook his head. 'You'll still be able to take your exams, but you may not remain a pupil and attend lessons here.'

'But there's still so much on the syllabus! Seriously? I'm *expelled?*'

'Indefinitely suspended,' he corrected her. 'For now, at least. Good day.'

Hannah marched out of his office, slamming the door as she left. She continued to storm down the school, slamming her fist into the lockers that lined the corridor. She had worked so hard every day of her life for the chance to escape home, to get the chance that had been so close to her. And now her dreams lay in tatters.

Luke approached her, a caring look in his eyes and shards of his broken ocarina cradled in his hands.

'What happened?' he asked.

Hannah barged past him, wiping her eyes. She didn't know what to say to him. She only knew she regretted everything as she pushed her way through the doors and left the school, and Luke, behind her.

Chapter Five

Here Be Monsters

HANNAH stood at the bus stop, still picking bitterly at her fingernail.

Her meeting with Mr Barlow replayed in her head. The moment that had ruined her plans and pushed her life off course. She wished she had gone about it differently. She knew she was to blame, but she was still angry; angry at Barlow, angry at Zack, angry at herself.

And now I feel sick and thirsty. Great.

She recognised the feeling and rummaged in her bag for her test kit. She was still fuming, her heart beating like a drum when she primed her lancet device and shot the needle into her finger.

Her eyes widened as the blood squirted up. She cursed under her breath as she touched her finger to the glucose monitor, excess blood dripping down her hand.

High. I knew it.

It was only when she got her pump out that she saw it. A slight glimmer grabbed her attention. Nearby, a crystal lay on the ground, about the size and shape of a large coin, only thicker. She frowned and looked around her at the deserted street, wondering if someone had dropped it. She picked it up and brought it to her face, examining it intently. She admired its red tinge and how it refracted the light as it moved, emitting a rainbow. Upon closer inspection, she noticed a strange symbol resembling an *M* at its centre.

She was so wrapped up in the crystal she barely noticed the man who approached her.

'Excuse me,' he said.

Hannah jumped and instinctively pocketed the crystal as she faced him. The man she saw was handsome; tall and dark, with polished stubble and a twinkle in his eye. A white streak of hair ran down the middle of his head, and he nodded amiably.

'Yes?' she replied.

'I'm sorry to bother you. Do you know how long it might be until the next bus?'

Hannah glanced at her phone. 'About five minutes.'

The man smiled, the twinkle in his eye shining brighter. 'Thank you.'

'Where are you headed?' Hannah asked after a brief pause, preferring to keep her thoughts at bay.

'Nowhere in particular,' he replied. 'You?'

'Home,' she said, making sure not to give any specific details.

'And where might that be?'

'Not too far.' She smiled politely and turned away.

Yeah, that was a mistake. Trust me to talk to a creep. You're on fire today, girl!

Hannah gazed into the distance, feeling the man's gaze burn the back of her neck. She stole a quick glance at the man—he was grinning at her, his eyes gleaming as they stared. Luke usually accompanied her on the bus back home from school, one of the few things she hadn't argued with her aunt about; without him, she felt uncomfortably vulnerable. She prayed for the bus to come. But it was nowhere to be seen, nor were there any cars or passersby. She was utterly alone, aside from the man who still stared. Without moving her head, she slipped her hand into her pocket and clutched her keys between her knuckles, hoping desperately that she was overreacting.

His footsteps approached her, loud and determined. She turned her back and moved away, her heart hammering against her chest, her keys digging into her fingers as she clutched them even tighter.

But then he stopped. Though her back was towards him, she could still spy his shadow. Ever so gradually, it changed, as if his entire body were transforming into something different.

Hannah turned and gasped. The man was nowhere to be seen. In his place stood something quite different. At first glance, it looked like an oversized wolf, growling as saliva dripped from its open mouth. Its hair was dark and spiky, its eyes yellow, with sharp claws and sharper teeth. Spikes ran down its back and its tail, whipping from side to side. But what chilled her the most were two wings that sprouted from its back, each one bigger than its entire body. They flapped aggressively, their spiked edges scraping against the pavement. If it weren't for the white streak across its head, Hannah would never have guessed this monster had once been the same man.

She wanted to scream, but no sound came. All she could do was watch as the monster approached her with hungry eyes. As it leant back on its hind legs, Hannah knew what was coming. Without a second to spare, she leapt to the side. The creature pounced, landing where she had been a second earlier.

It faced her, its growl furious, before leaning back again. Hannah instinctively fell back, stumbling into a thick blackberry bush that lined the street. She gasped as she tumbled down a slope, thorns cutting her face and arms as she hurtled to the bottom.

With a wince, she rolled out from the bush, wiping her bloodied hands on her skirt. Soon, a familiar shadow blocked the light. High above her, the winged wolf hovered, its colossal wings flapping rhythmically. Hannah felt its gaze lock onto her, and she rolled out of the way as it began its rapid dive. The ground thundered as it thudded to earth, narrowly missing her.

She looked around, desperately searching for anyone or anything to help her survive. All she could find was the crystal, having fallen from her pocket and now lying beside her.

Hannah didn't know what made her do it, but the crystal seemed to call out to her. As the monster growled once more, she crawled backwards. The wolf howled and charged. She shut her eyes and clasped her wounded hands over the crystal.

At once, a flash erupted, so bright she could see it through her closed eyes. Then, there was a thud and a whine.

Hannah slowly opened her eyes.

The monster lay on its side, apparently hurt, its wings flapping weakly. A few steps from the creature stood a man with a long knife.

Though not as bizarre as the monster, the man also didn't seem to belong. He wore dark clothes with a dirty, long leather coat, knee-high boots, and a wide-brimmed hat he kept tilted over his eyes. A golden badge pinned to his lapel shone brightly with the letters *T* and *K* overlapped in a kite shape.

'Who are you?' the man asked.

'Who are *you*?' Hannah repeated, her voice loud and high-pitched.

But the man ignored her as the creature crawled to its feet.

'Stand back,' he instructed.

Hannah didn't have to be told twice and moved behind him. He flicked his wrist and an oblong-shaped object assembled itself on his forearm, a blue wolf emblazoned on the front.

'What is that?'

'Shhh,' he insisted. Hannah would normally object to being shushed, but she decided today she'd make an exception.

The wolf charged. Hannah readied herself to leap out of the way, but, with a determined gesture, the man raised his knife and a flash emitted from the tip.

Hannah shielded her eyes in time. But the wolf, stunned by the light, altered its course, and ran to their side. As it did, the man lashed out with his knife.

The wolf let out a venomous roar as it swiped with its claw; the man dodged. It swiped again and, once more, the man dodged. The wolf leapt with its mouth open, but the man had expected this move—in one gesture, he avoided its snout, grabbed its neck and pulled himself onto its back.

Hannah couldn't believe what she saw. The wolf furiously jumped about, trying to knock the man off, but he grabbed its fur tightly and sat precariously between the spikes on its back. With a roar, the wolf took flight, soaring into the sky with the man still holding on.

Hannah stood rooted to the spot as she watched, unable to tear her eyes away. As the beast raised its wings, the man slashed with his knife. The more he slashed, the lower it flew until they were just a few metres from ground. The wolf rolled upside down until the man lost his grip and fell with a thud.

The wolf gave him no time to rest. The man staggered wearily to his feet as the wolf landed and prowled its way towards him.

Hannah looked for anything to help. Then she saw it—the man's knife lying on the grass. She knew fully that if she left now, she had a better chance of surviving. But this man had saved her— she couldn't leave him to die.

Gripping the knife in her hand, she ran towards the wolf, and with a grunt, she plunged it deep into the monster's side. It howled in pain as it turned on her, its once yellow eyes now a deep red. She sank to the ground, paralysed with fear. She shut her eyes as the wolf opened its mouth, ready to sink its teeth into her neck.

This is it...

But nothing came. Just a whistling sound and a quiet thud.

Hannah opened her eyes to see the wolf lying lifeless on the ground, an arrow sticking from its neck. Finally still and unthreatening, its once horrific eyes were nothing but an empty void. The man had his arm stretched out, another arrow loaded in a device hidden within his wide sleeve. She took it all in. The monster, the man, the crystal, the knife, his hidden crossbow…

The man grabbed her hand and tugged, but she pulled back.

'Let go!' she shouted, not sure whether she should shout or thank him for saving her life.

The man let go instantly but continued to gaze at her with curiosity. He took her hand again, less forcefully this time.

'You need to come with me,' he told her. 'Please. It's important.'

Chapter Six

Too Few Answers

THE sky darkened, and the clouds became heavier as Hannah zoomed past the barren fields.

She stretched and sat back in her seat. As odd as the man looked, at least he had good taste in cars. As luck would have it, they found a parked car a short walk from the field where the dead monster lay. He expertly broke into it and hot-wired the engine, which spluttered to life.

They had barely uttered a word since starting the journey, but Hannah summoned enough courage to ask some questions. She had no idea who this man was or even where they were going. But this man, whoever he was, had risked his life to save hers; he was no threat to her.

At least, that's what she told herself.

'So… considering I've never met you and I'm now in a random car with you, I think I'm entitled to ask some questions,' she said.

He studied her for a moment. 'If you must,' he muttered.

Doesn't act like a knight in shining armour, she thought.

'Okay. First, what the hell was that thing?'

'What thing?'

'You're kidding, right? The *thing* that tried to kill us. What was it, a wolf?'

'I suppose you could call it a *type* of wolf.'

'But it had wings.'

'Very astute. You're a shrewd one.'

A few sarcastic replies of her own came to mind, but she held her tongue. After all, he *did* have a lot of weapons.

'It wasn't just a wolf, was it?'

The man looked at her curiously again, as if he wasn't sure if he could trust her. 'There's not much I can hide at this point. You've already seen him. I can't deny he exists.'

'Who—*what* was he?' she asked again.

'Zelom,' the man answered simply.

'Bless you.'

The man grunted.

'His name was Zelom. He was a zburător.'

He said no more, as if that had been a sufficient answer.

'Can you explain to me what a… what was it called?'

'A zburător,' he snapped.

'Right. What is a… zburător?' Hannah silently congratulated herself on pronouncing the word.

'They're exceedingly rare, from Romania originally. I assume you know what *that* is.'

'It might surprise my old Geography teacher but yes.' She couldn't help the snappy edge to her voice.

For the first time, the man let out a small smile. 'It means "flyer" in Romanian.'

'Okay. Not really helping me to understand what's going on but alright. Can you tell me who *you* are?'

The man shifted, apparently reluctant to answer much more.

'My name's Daegan.'

'Daegan,' Hannah repeated. *At least it's easier to say than zburător.* 'I'm Hannah,' she said, to fill the silence.

Daegan smiled. 'Pleasure.'

Doesn't sound like it, she thought bitterly.

Hannah became fed up with trying to squeeze answers from Daegan, so settled back and watched the countryside fly past. She ignored the voice in the back of her mind that screamed at her to run away. She needed answers, and it seemed the only way was to trust Daegan—whoever he was.

Chapter Seven

Location Unknown

'GET out,' Daegan barked.

Hannah obeyed as Daegan hid the car beneath the branches of an overhanging tree. She stretched and surveyed the surrounding countryside; she was certainly far from home. Daegan had driven the car off the road and into what appeared to be the edge of a dense forest. Aside from a road sign for nearby towns and villages she had never heard of, there was nothing but fields and forest. The heavy clouds had broken open and a light rain fell, forcing Daegan to shrug his coat over himself a little more.

'This way,' he commanded as he marched off.

'Where are we?' she asked.

'Do you ever stop asking questions?'

'Would you like me to?' Hannah grinned, but Daegan stared straight ahead, continuing to push through the forest.

It soon grew dark, and the trees blocked out whatever light remained. Daegan withdrew the knife he had used earlier, and a bright light illuminated the forest.

'What is that? Some kind of knife-torch?'

'No,' he replied curtly.

Hannah stopped dead in her tracks. Daegan walked a few more paces before he realised she had stopped.

'What's wrong?' he asked. Hannah was sure this was the first time he had actually shown her any concern since the fight.

'I need some answers,' she said. 'This is insane. I seriously appreciate you saving my life—but I don't even *know* you. I came with you because I was scared of that… zburător thing. I didn't know what else to do. But this is creepy! You've driven me into the middle of who-knows-where, and now you're leading me into a secluded forest with a knife!'

It was only when she told the story out loud that she realised how mad the situation was. She felt a tingle down her spine, and her breathing quickened. She took a step back.

'And all you've given me is your name and the name of that thing you slaughtered in front of me. I want to know what it really was, why you saved me, what that knife is, and where you're taking me. Until then… I'm not moving.' She folded her arms and frowned, ignoring the quiver in her voice.

Daegan looked at her, dumbfounded, before regaining his composure. 'Okay. You want answers? Fine—but you're not supposed to know *any* of this.'

'Why not?'

'*That* wasn't one of the questions. You can't add more now.' He took a breath. 'Right. First, that "thing" was a zburător called Zelom. Zburătors come from Romania—'

'You already said that—'

Daegan raised his hand. 'Don't interrupt, or we'll be here all night. Zburătors are… Well, I suppose you'd describe them as half-wolf and half-dragon.'

Hannah let out a laugh. 'You realise how ridiculous you sound, right?'

'Says the one who was nearly murdered by that "ridiculous" thing.'

Hannah wrinkled her nose and looked away.

'Second, I wasn't intending *to* save you. The crystal you had… I'm not sure where you got it, but *that's* why I'm here. I don't know how it worked for you, but it did, and you should be grateful. That's what brought me to you.

'The knife in my hand—think of it as a magical tool I can use as a dagger and many other things.

'And finally, I'm not allowed to say where I'm taking you… but since you have to be taken there and you're so stubborn, I'll tell you it's a secret location where people like me live. I need to ask them what to do with you. Any more questions, your highness?'

Hannah realised her mouth had dropped open.

'You're mad,' she said. 'I feel even less safe with you now.' She paused. 'I'm leaving. I'm sorry, but you're a whack job and I—'

Daegan didn't let her finish. Before Hannah knew what was happening, he had grabbed her, pinning her arms behind her back. She tried to scream, but all that came out was a feeble, terrified groan. She kicked and elbowed him, but he took every hit she lashed out. Somehow, he tied her arms behind her back. Hannah shook her entire body, trying desperately to escape. As a blindfold covered her eyes, the world became black.

She fought against the fear and the tears that threatened to flow. She refused to let him see her like that. At least the zburător just wanted to kill her—she had no idea what this crazy Daegan wanted. Hundreds of theories flooded her mind, each one more terrifying than the last.

Daegan guided her around the trees, paying no attention to her muffled pleas. Even when she tripped over what she assumed was a tree root, he dragged her to her feet and continued. She tried counting her steps and noting which direction they turned—just in case she ever had a chance of escaping but soon lost count.

Before too long, Daegan released his grip. Though she could see nothing, she could hear his footsteps and the sound of something scraping. *A key?* Whatever it was, she then heard stone scraping against stone.

A door, Hannah assumed.

Daegan gave her a soft nudge, and soon the spongy forest floor became hard. She heard the clipped sound of footsteps on stone, and the chilly winter breeze vanished.

They walked through what felt and sounded like a corridor. A million thoughts ran through Hannah's mind. *What is this? Some kind of cult? Am I going to be sacrificed to some weird zburător God?*

To her relief, after a flight of stairs, the ground became quieter as her feet walked on what she guessed was carpet. Daegan stopped her, and she heard muffled voices, some calm, others loud and animated. There were three stern knocks on a wooden door, and the voices ceased their bickering immediately.

The door creaked open, and Daegan guided Hannah through the doorway. She held back a whimper, sensing a room of eyes on her.

'Take that blindfold off, Daegan. I'm sure she means no harm,' a gentle but commanding voice said.

'But sir—'

'Off,' the voice repeated.

Daegan fumbled with the blindfold until it dropped and revealed a grandiose room. Hannah saw the high ceiling held up by golden pillars and resplendent with paintings of creatures she had only ever read about. She was in the centre of the room next to Daegan, standing on a marble floor. She felt tiny, surrounded by towering platforms that were topped with seven ornate golden chairs with red velvet cushions. Upon them sat seven bizarre looking figures.

Hannah stole a quick look around, glancing at the figures who studied her. Some looked normal, some looked a little strange, but there was one who beggared all belief. Hannah was sure she was dreaming.

Chapter Eight

The Girl with No Past

'WHO is this?' inquired the first voice, booming jovially.

He was a fairly short, elderly man whose shiny mound of baldness on his head was flanked by grey hair that curved down his face into an impressive moustache. Over his circular, wide-framed body he wore loose-fitting blue robes that hid his protruding belly, but what struck Hannah most of all was his arched eyebrows. They possessed the ability to look either friendly or the complete opposite at the drop of a hat.

'Her name is Hannah,' replied Daegan.

'Hurry, Daegan!' said another voice. 'Her name's not important. We're in the middle of something here!'

This voice belonged to a tanned, handsome man with azure eyes and golden hair combed into a ponytail. At first glance, he looked only a few years older than herself, but the more Hannah looked, his eyes told a different story, giving the impression that he was even older than the first man.

Beside him was a sun-kissed, regal-looking woman, also beautiful. She had darker hair with a reddish tinge that was almost purple. Her eyes were lighter but colder.

Hannah struggled not to stare at their long ears that broke through their hair and rose to a point.

The woman spoke next. 'Are we supposed to know who this is?'

'I don't know,' said Daegan. 'That's why I brought her to you.'

'She's not a Leviathan. Far too pretty. Looks mean enough though.'

The owner of this voice was the polar opposite to the couple with pointed ears. While they were tall and beautiful, this man was old, with messy red hair and a tremendous beard covering his weathered face. But his most striking feature was his height; or, rather, lack of height. The elderly man who seemed to be in charge looked like a giant in comparison. Were he twice the size, he'd be a formidable figure to come across.

'No,' Daegan responded. 'She doesn't even know about Etheria.'

This statement caused a murmur in the room.

'Why is she here then?' another voice sounded, the tone of which unnerved Hannah. 'I trust, Daegan, you haven't flouted our most sacred law?'

This man was almost revolting, resembling a walking corpse; deathly pale, with greasy black hair that reached his shoulders. Still, there was something captivating about him. Perhaps it was the way his eyes gleamed, as if he held a secret he would whisper if only you gave yourself to him.

'Not at all, Sir,' Daegan said, remaining calm. 'I wasn't expecting to run into her at all. A blood crystal summoned me.'

'*Summoned*, you say?' growled another voice. 'Few crystals will summon one of us.'

This man was harder to see than the others. He wore a cloak that ran the length of his body, with a hood that covered his face. Beneath the hood, though, Hannah could still make out his face; dark and bearded, his eyes glinted with a red light.

'That's what I thought, Sir,' Daegan told him. 'As I recall, there is only one crystal unaccounted for.'

'But this girl,' said the last voice, 'is not Astraea.'

The owner of this final voice was the most surprising. The others all looked relatively normal. If they walked down the street, there would be double-takes but no screams or frantic phone calls. This last one, however, would cause alarm. She had beautiful dark skin, cascading brunette hair, and wore a strange type of armour with bronze bands around her arms. It was what was below this that caused the most shock. While her top half was human, her bottom half belonged to the body of a horse with chestnut fur.

Hannah was convinced she was dreaming. *Either that or on drugs.*

'No,' said the hooded man, 'but that does not mean we should immediately dismiss her.'

'He's right,' chimed in the man with greasy hair. 'Crystals have a tendency of finding new owners if not destroyed.'

'So, this girl is just a minor inconvenience?' asked the blond man.

'If she needs to die, can we just get on with it?' moaned the woman beside him.

'No!' Hannah shouted.

The room was silent. They stared at her in wonder.

'Who are you?' asked the short, hairy man.

Hannah gulped. 'I'm no one,' she stammered. She took a moment to regain her composure. 'Hi,' she started. 'Nice to er… meet you all. My name's Hannah, Hannah Moreland. I go to Arningham School and—I don't know what else to say.' She trailed off, feeling hope drain from her.

'Your parents,' said the horse-lady. 'Who are they?'

The sight of the horse-lady was astonishing, but Hannah still gazed at her own feet, too terrified to look up.

'You got me there,' she whispered. 'No one ever told me. I tried to ask but…'

'Interesting,' said the short man.

The oldest man shook his head and walked towards Hannah, giving her an encouraging smile. Hannah attempted to return one, smiling through her fear.

'This girl is no threat. Not to us, not to anyone,' he addressed the room, his voice booming with confidence. 'She is not Astraea; I think we can be sure of that. As Byron said, blood crystals have indeed found new owners in the past. It's unusual but not unheard of. What were the circumstances of your meeting?' he asked Daegan.

'Zelom,' Daegan said, causing another stir throughout the room.

The old man held up his hand. The talking ceased.

'You found him?'

'I wouldn't say that,' Daegan said. 'He found *her*. Tried to kill her. Luckily, I was assigned to the crystal that found its way to her. If she hadn't grabbed hold of that, I wouldn't have been able to find him.'

The old man gazed first at Daegan, then again at Hannah.

He turned to the room. 'We all know about Zelom and how dangerous a Leviathan he has proven to be. For whatever reason, Astraea's crystal found its way to this girl. I had assigned Daegan to that crystal, and it was quite a turn of fate that he could save her in time. She has done nothing wrong—she's an innocent victim.'

'So, we're not executing her?' yawned the regal woman.

'Of course not,' snapped the horse-lady.

'Don't be ridiculous, woman,' the short man rasped.

'If I may, Sir.' The hooded man rose to his feet. 'Daegan blindfolded her, but she's still seen too much.' The room nodded in agreement. 'May I?'

The old man sighed and nodded before settling back in his chair and sipping from a cup and saucer.

'No!' gasped Hannah. She tried to wrestle herself from

Daegan's grip, but he held firm. 'I've barely seen anything! I don't even know what's going on! Please…' Her legs crumpled, and she fell to the floor. 'Please don't kill me.'

The hooded man approached and from his wide sleeves withdrew a long dagger similar to Daegan's. She made a last effort to free herself, but it was no use. She was too weak, too scared. All she could do was watch as he aimed the dagger towards her. Soon, there was nothing but darkness. The room, the daggers, the strange figures… they all disappeared into a distant dream.

Chapter Nine

Trapped but Not Forgotten

HANNAH lay in bed, staring up at the ceiling and following the cracks and stains on the off-white plaster. The uncomfortable IV drip strapped to her hand and the constant beep of the heart monitor was driving her mad. She was desperate for someone, anyone, to relieve her of the monotonous blips and distract her. She lay there, still and silent, trying to remember how she ended up in hospital in the first place.

She remembered leaving the school, ignoring Luke—something she still felt guilty about—and waiting at the bus stop. She had a vague memory of a man talking to her—but that was it. The next thing she knew, she was in this plain white room.

The police were considerably more understanding than her aunt, wanting only to ask a few questions. Who was she? What did she remember? Did she see anyone? Could she give any descriptions? Hannah gave them all the information she could, all the while feeling embarrassed and small beneath their stares.

She begged them to explain what had happened, but they knew as little as she did. Someone found her close to midnight, lying face down next to the bus stop. The ambulance took her away to hospital where the doctors just put it down to a lack of control over her diabetes. Hannah had just scowled—*I can tell when my blood sugar's going high or low.*

The police told her they were investigating it just in case, though they didn't seem too interested.

'All a little strange, but I don't think you need to be too worried,' Constable Higgins said with a half-hidden yawn. His partner whispered in his ear. 'Oh, yes. We also found this on you.'

From his pocket he withdrew a plastic wallet with a strange-looking crystal, round and thin.

'Does it look familiar?' he asked.

He handed it to Hannah, who let the crystal tumble into her hand. She gazed at it, frowning. It looked oddly familiar, but she couldn't quite figure out where she knew it from.

'Is it yours?' Constable Higgins asked.

Hannah nodded slowly and cautiously.

'Right. We'll be off then.' Constable Higgins and his partner gave a casual wave before heading out the door, leaving Hannah to stroke the crystal with her thumb.

Understandably, Hannah was left shaken after everything that had happened. Her aunt displayed no such emotion. As soon as the police had phoned, she rushed over to the hospital to yell at Hannah at the top of her voice. She had convinced herself Hannah had been drinking herself silly after her suspension from school. Her punishment was the usual one—to be locked in her room when she returned home.

If I return.

She frowned and sat up. That one thought ran through her head, and the blips of the heart monitor quickened. *Why not? I could just not go back. They're not my proper family, they don't care about me. I'd be better off anywhere else.*

It was with that thought in her mind that she turned to the IV drip, its tube nestled into the top of her hand. She wrinkled her nose and grimaced as she took hold of it and slowly, ever so slowly, pulled it out. Her stomach flipped as she felt the tubing move and squeezed her eyes shut before she yanked it out. Her hand darted to apply pressure to the wound. She quelled the blood that immediately oozed out and reached with the other hand to grab cotton wool and a bandage from a nearby cabinet.

With a poorly tied bandage wrapped around her hand and a drop of blood dripping down her arm, she slipped out of bed. She shrugged on the school uniform she had been wearing when they found her and picked up her rucksack. She flipped through the contents, wishing she had packed some toiletries instead of just schoolbooks and keepsakes… although the shell from that time she and Luke had gone to the beach last summer brought a sad smile to her face.

She surveyed the room to make sure she had everything. That's when she saw the crystal lying peacefully on a cabinet. Her bloodied hand reached forward to pick it up.

A flash of light shone from the crystal, illuminating the room in dazzling white.

She remembered.

The man, Zelom, turning into a zburător; Daegan appearing just in time; the hideout with all those strange people. Memories flooded her mind like a whirlpool. She jumped, expecting to see Daegan again—but he was nowhere to be seen.

It doesn't matter, Hannah smiled to herself. *I know where to go now.*

Hannah held her breath and bit her tongue as she crept towards the door and opened it. She grimaced at the creak and squinted her eyes at the bright fluorescent lights of the corridor. Even more heart monitors sang out, an orchestra of soft, repetitive beeps. There were no other sounds, apart from the occasional sniffle of the night nurse at her desk.

Her feet crept along the teal linoleum floor as she tiptoed down the corridor, praying the nurse wouldn't look up and wondering if she could just leave the hospital without getting into more trouble.

As she rounded a corner, a sudden but familiar snore stopped her in her tracks. Hannah's eyes widened as she saw her aunt, head tilted forward onto her chest, fast asleep.

She's still here, Hannah thought, amazed. She couldn't remember the last time her aunt had put Hannah first. She refused most of Hannah's requests and, over the years, Hannah had assumed that she just hated her. But here she was, staying at the hospital, making sure she was okay.

A twinge of regret surfaced inside, and she considered not leaving. But the crystal inside her pocket was a reminder; she had nothing left here, but who knows what would happen with Daegan. There were too many questions left unanswered. With one last glance at her aunt, Hannah sneaked down the stairs and out of the hospital into the fresh night air.

/ <h1>Chapter Ten</h1>

Change of Plans

THE internet café she found was quiet and the coffee surprisingly good. Hannah hadn't expected to find one so easily, but someone pointed her in the right direction. There was a perfect volume of noise in the background, a relaxing blur of talk and music lulling her into a sense of calm. She sipped her coffee as she settled down to figure out her next move.

She started by writing everything she remembered.

Everything I Know:

- *I'm suspended (possibly expelled?) from school.*
- *I hate my aunt and the twins, and I think they hate me too (not sure…)—there is nothing keeping me here.*
- *I'll probably be happier away from them—so it's good to leave.*
- *I got Luke into a load of trouble, and he might hate me now.*
- *I'll run out of insulin in two days. I'll need some to change my pump.*
- *A man/monster-thing called Zelom attacked me.*
- *Monsters exist—at least "zburători" do (wolf-dragon things).*

- *This weird crystal summoned a man called Daygun (is that how it's spelled?) who saved me.*
- *He drove me for a few hours into the countryside.*
- *The last sign I saw before he stopped the car said that we were "4 miles from Bury" and "8 miles from Arundel"— wherever that is (there were other signs too; what did they say?)*
- *He blindfolded me and walked me through a forest.*
- *We turned left after about 200 metres and then down a hill. Then, after about 400 metres, we turned right.*
- *When we got to wherever he took me, I heard a sound of rock scraping against rock (maybe I should look for a clump of rocks with a secret doorway?)*
- *Problem—I don't know how he found the door or how he opened it.*
- *Another problem—I have just £51.43 to my name.*
- *Correction—I have £44.93 after the coffee and internet. Can't survive without caffeine.*
- *I'll be in more trouble if I go home and will stay unhappy. I'm probably not allowed back at school; but I have no one to help me, no job and nowhere to live.*
- *Solution: There are only two people who could help me—Luke or Daygun.*
- *Luke might hate me after all this and would probably just try to convince me to go home to my aunt or tell me I was crazy— Daygun's my best bet.*

Hannah sat back and read through her list. She still struggled to understand the events of the last few days. Part of her was convinced she had made it all up. Maybe she had been drugged; it could have just been a hallucination. Though that didn't explain why one moment she had no memory of it and the next, after touching that crystal, it all came flooding back.

She found a map online and looked up the location of the two towns from the sign she remembered. She searched for a forest nearby and measured eight and four miles to triangulate a position that would match the clues she had. She spent close to an hour intently pouring over hundreds of photos of the area, taken by enthusiastic hikers.

Her hand paused on the mouse, and her heart skipped a beat. There was a photo of two people, an elderly man and woman, adorned in walking gear and grinning. But Hannah barely noticed them. Instead, she gazed behind them, at a familiar roadside lined with trees she half-recognised and a familiar car—the one Daegan had stolen.

She checked the date of the photo—uploaded yesterday. Hannah clicked the mouse a few more times, hoping she might find the specific location where the photo was taken.

'Bingo.' She grabbed a pen beside her and scribbled down the photo's geotag.

She knew where to find Daegan.

Chapter Eleven

An Impossible Search

HANNAH reluctantly handed the money to the taxi driver, sure he had overcharged her, and watched the car drive away, leaving her alone.

Already, the area looked familiar. She knelt near where Daegan had parked the car. It had been wet that day and the ground was softer. She saw the imprint of the tyres still in the mud, and her eyes followed the tracks until she saw the car, still hidden under a tree. Confident she was in the right place, she headed off in the same direction Daegan had led her.

Hannah blinked her eyes to stave off her fatigue—she hadn't slept since she left the hospital. Unsure of how safe the forest was, she decided against napping by a tree. Still, as the rising golden sun shone through the branches and early morning mist, Hannah felt contented. She drank in the forest's beauty and relished in the crunching sound of the autumnal leaves beneath her feet.

Soon she slowed and sighed, knowing this would happen eventually. This was where Daegan had blindfolded her. She fought through her disorientated memory and was pretty sure they had continued straight on; at least, she hoped so.

She counted every step, turning left after a few minutes and carrying on. A thick tree root stood in the middle of the pathway. She remembered it from last time, rubbing the bruise it gave her then.

Getting closer, she congratulated herself.

Hannah paused at a junction, doubting her memory. She was sure Daegan had deviated from the pathway. The expanse of trees and ferns ahead of her was so thick it was difficult to see far, but she spotted a trail of pushed down ferns, about big enough to have been made by a deer—or a human.

She pushed through the trail, raising her arms to protect her against the ferns, which still slapped her face. It was an effort, but she soon came to a small mountain of rocks a couple of feet taller than her. There were about five, all standing upright and leaning against one another with moss covering the cracks between them. They were mostly smooth to the touch, with almost an otherworldly quality.

Exhilaration coursed through Hannah's veins as she explored the rocks' hard surface. *Now, where's that secret door?* She jumped back when she heard it emit a gentle hum. She stroked another rock; once again there was another hum, slightly louder this time. But soon frustration overtook her excitement. Try as she might, there were no latches, secret handles, or buttons—no sign of any door.

She glanced upwards; pinks, reds and oranges tantalised the treetops as the sun rose higher in the sky. Panic began to set in. The later she left it, the more likely she'd run into someone walking through the woods, someone who might be on the lookout for a girl who ran away from hospital. The police were already suspicious about her. How would they react to this?

Hannah gritted her teeth and clenched her fist, desperation creeping up her spine. She'd been so close, but now... Her fist crashed against the rock, forcing a pitiful whine from it. With a grunt of frustration, she leant back and slid down the boulder.

Now what?

She dug her heels into the forest floor, hoping to distract herself from a growing headache. *I can't stay here. And who knows if I'll see Daegan any time soon. I can't go back; I'll be in so much trouble for leaving.* She smacked her lips slightly and swallowed, her mouth suddenly dry and thirsty.

She knew this feeling too well.

Hannah knew having milk in her coffee earlier had been a bad idea, even as she ordered it—milk always made her blood sugar rise. It wasn't unusual for a small internet café not to have almond milk, but she needed the caffeine to stay awake and couldn't stand the bitterness of black coffee. In hindsight, though, the risk of having milk when she was already running low on insulin had been a bad call.

She pricked her finger with a lancet and squeezed out a drop of blood as she brought out the glucose monitor.

That's when she sensed it. A heat emanated from her thigh.

Hannah frowned and dug into her pockets to find the mysterious crystal giving off a gentle warmth. She took it out, her eyes widening in surprise. It was glowing dimly, humming the same sound the rocks had.

With a sense of relief, she waved her arm and noticed how the crystal glowed brighter and hummed louder when closer to the rocks. She continued forward, her heart beating rapidly. The humming raised in pitch, and the crystal tugged her hand. She allowed it to guide her, taking a few steps forward, arm still outstretched until—SNAP!

A jolt shot through her, and Hannah let go. The crystal had lodged itself into a hole in the rock—a perfect fit. She smiled and reached forward, her bloodied finger pushing the crystal like a button. It dropped obediently into her hand, and she heard the familiar sound of rocks scraping against one another.

Hannah stood with bated breath as the rocks moved upwards like teeth parting, giving way to a dark pathway hidden behind them. She took a deep breath and stepped into the mouth of the rocks, her body already feeling better. The rocks shuddered as they closed and trapped her inside.

Chapter Twelve

A Familiar Figure

ECHOES along the corridor, clattering on the stone floor, the flicker of the torches on the wall—Hannah remembered these sounds from the last time she had been there. At the end of the corridor stood two identical wooden doors, heavy with rusty handles. Unsure which to choose, she heaved open one of the doors at random. She squinted her eyes to adjust to the dim light, but soon they widened with shock.

Lining the cobweb-strewn walls were several glass vats containing a thick maroon liquid, its metallic scent unmistakable. Hannah felt her stomach heave and turned to escape. But a figure blocked the doorway, beady eyes glowing in the low firelight of the torches.

Hannah gasped, instinctively stepping away from the dark figure who, with a smooth gesture of his hand, brightened the room.

As the shadows died, Hannah relaxed. Despite his broad shoulders, he was not nearly as intimidating as his silhouette had been. The figure that been so imposing just seconds ago now revealed himself to be the elderly man she had seen last time; the one in charge. A bright blue bow tie stood proudly amongst his tweed suit that struggled to contain his bulging belly, only just contained by the flowing dark blue robes. Like Daegan, he too had a golden badge on his lapel, only with the letters *T* and *M* overlapped in a square. Unlike Daegan, this man came across as more of a caring uncle; the sort of man you could find in a country village reading poetry by a fireside with a hot cross bun and a cup of tea.

'I'm sorry to frighten you,' he said, his booming voice less gentle than his words. 'I promise you that wasn't my intention.'

The man stood still, a half-smile planted on his face. But that was not enough for Hannah to forget the vats of blood in the room. A shiver ran down her spine.

'What is this?' she whispered.

His smile did not waver. Instead, he stepped to one side and waved a hand to the door. 'Please. Let's get some fresh air. The scenery down here is so morbid.'

Hannah followed him through a maze of stone corridors, too nervous to break the silence. He shuffled forward confidently, his head bent forward as if too heavy for his neck and his bald patch shining in the flickering light of the torch lamps. Eventually, the man opened a door, bigger than the rest, and stood aside for Hannah to enter first. Hannah beamed as she finally stepped into a room whose architecture did not resemble a dungeon.

This room was a large, open space, ornately decorated as far as the eye could see. Intricate drawings and maps adorned the towering ceiling, held up by golden pillars. She glided across the white marble floor and admired the bright statues standing between the pillars. They were of several creatures Hannah had only ever read about, some next to bizarre-looking plants Hannah could scarcely have imagined. A red carpet led from a colossal door at one end to wide marble steps at the other.

A small chuckle awoke Hannah from her reverie, and the man smiled proudly. 'Quite something, isn't it? I remember the first time I saw it.'

'What is this place?' Hannah asked incredulously.

'*This* is just the entrance hall. Quite wonderful, but come this way.' The man beckoned Hannah onwards to the large door at the end.

Hannah hurried after him, keen to see what could be more impressive.

With a click of his fingers, the mammoth doors creaked open, and sunlight poured through.

'Welcome to Arcadia.'

As Hannah stepped outside, a gust of wind sent her hair flying. She whipped her head up, and her mouth dropped. A dragon—*or perhaps a wyvern*, she thought—soared past, its majestic wings flapping gracefully to maintain its speed with a rider on top who tugged the reigns in one direction. The dragon leaned to the left and soared higher until it was out of sight.

She stood on a hill outside a castle, complete with animated gargoyles flying from tower to tower. From here, she saw everything: the luscious green meadow and the murky forest beyond. The forest's wild mass of trees stretched to the horizon and ran through two titanic mountains with snow-capped tips, one of which led down to a lake. Its waves lapped up a golden beach that lay beyond a dock that housed wooden ships with grandiose figureheads. Above this magnificent sight was a cloudless azure sky, populated by a host of stunning winged creatures.

'Woah,' was all Hannah could muster. For the first time in her life, she was speechless.

'I know,' replied the man. 'This view never gets old.' He turned to Hannah. 'I know how keen you must be to explore, but Arcadia is a big place and—'

'Arcadia?' Hannah repeated, still amazed.

'Come. I promise you can explore later. But for now, there is much to discuss.'

As Hannah turned, she halted dead in her tracks. In front of the castle were white stone steps that led down to an area Hannah expected to find a moat. Instead, it was like a small, bustling town full of people and creatures. They carried weaponry Hannah didn't even know anyone used anymore. People with pointed ears tested swords and bows on dummies; short men with beards bashed battle-axes and shields. A small group of people around Hannah's age stood listening to a man who gestured to the weapons as he lectured. The man had a long, dark coat and a hat that covered his face. Hannah's heart leapt.

'Daegan!' she called.

The man looked up, and despite the distance, their eyes met. Hannah knew he recognised her and felt her cheeks blush as the group turned to stare at her. But Daegan ignored her and continued his lecture. Crestfallen, Hannah turned away.

'Please,' the man said once again. 'Come this way and I'll explain everything.'

Chapter Thirteen

A Bold New World

THE trek up the castle was exhausting. They journeyed through corridors lined with suits of armour and plush carpets, climbing higher and higher up the castle, through spiral staircases, until her legs begged to rest. The man, however, was hardly even breaking a sweat beneath the heavy tweed suit. Hannah was astonished that a man of his age and stature could manage such a climb with so little difficulty.

But by the time they reached the top, she soon forgot her aching limbs. Like the rest of Arcadia, this room took away what little breath she had left. Delicate lights floated around a curious tree in the room's centre; the edges of the circular room were adorned with bookcases stuffed to the brim with thick tomes and cabinets containing peculiar objects. The key feature, however, was the white bird, similar to a heron, perched on the tree.

'I apologise for the mess,' the man said as he sat down and encouraged Hannah to do the same.

She hesitated before doing so. She was becoming increasingly aware of how little she knew of this man. 'That's okay. It's not as bad as my room.' She paused. 'Who are you?'

With his confident smile still firmly in place, the man responded, 'Caedric.'

'Caedric?'

'I know,' he replied with a slight laugh. 'I didn't choose it. Tea?' he asked as he poured steaming hot water into a mug.

Hannah shook her head, instead taking her glucose monitor out to test. She didn't want to go low now; she needed to keep her wits about her.

'No need to bother with that,' he said.

'It's not a phone,' she snapped back, a little too defensively.

'I know. But it won't work.'

Hannah looked down at her monitor as she pressed the button again and again, panic setting in.

'It's not broken,' Caedric said, as if reading her mind. 'Electric devices don't tend to work in Arcadia.'

Hannah took a breath, making sure to stay calm. 'Okay, but I need this. I'm a Type 1 diabetic and…' She trailed off, confused at Caedric's amused smile.

'And do you feel high or low?'

'No, but—'

'You'll continue not to. Arcadia's a special place—you'll experience no hyper- or hypoglycaemic events while you're under our care.'

Hannah didn't know how to respond. She couldn't believe something so ridiculous but couldn't quite hide her eyes lighting up at the thought of ridding herself of all needles, pumps and highs and lows.

Caedric just sipped his tea before filling a long wooden pipe. 'I thought that'd excite you, but I'm sure you don't believe me. And you're wise not to. I distrust people who leap to believe something that's too good to be true.' He lit his pipe and let out a puff of smoke that gave him the look of a sleeping dragon. 'Just wait and see. The proof is in the pudding, after all! It's just one of the many wonders of Arcadia.'

'And what is it you do here… in Arcadia?' she asked.

'I'm the boss, I suppose. Officially, I'm the Trucemaster—a traditional title I don't much care for, but that's my job. Now…' Caedric leaned back in his seat, mug of tea in hand. 'Your last visit here must have been confusing.'

Hannah let out a snort.

Caedric nodded. 'I'd be interested to hear what you remember. Or, more precisely, what you understand.'

He leaned forward with a plate and offered her a cake. Hannah refused with a polite smile.

'Okay.' She paused, clearing the fog in her mind, and decided where to start. 'Well, monsters exist apparently.' She looked up; Caedric said nothing. 'Right?'

'Well, I wouldn't put it quite like that,' he said matter-of-factly as he helped himself to some cake. 'And I'm not sure I'd label them as *monsters*. Careful not to say that here—some might get upset! I believe some in your society use the word "cryptids." We prefer Cryptoetheria, although we mostly just say Etheria.'

'Etheria?'

'I won't bother you with the etymology, but it's a nicer word than monster, creature, beast… Not all are as ruthless as Zelom.'

The memory of Zelom shot through her mind. She winced. 'You sure about that?'

'Take Zephyr, for example.' He pointed towards the bird on the tree, who loyally flapped its wings and landed on Caedric's outstretched arm. It leaned forward and snatched up some crumbs that had fallen onto Caedric's robes. 'Zephyr is no ordinary bird, as I'm sure you've guessed.'

Hannah nodded.

'He's an Etheria known as a caladrius. Unlike many birds, a caladrius has the ability to heal. I'm not sure I'd be sitting here now if it weren't for my dear friend.' As Caedric stroked the bird, it closed its eyes in delight and cooed. 'Etheria live all over the world, although many live in settlements like Arcadia. You'll see many, but some live on the outskirts—they prefer to be left alone.'

'So, which ones are real? There are loads of monsters—sorry—Cryptoetheria. Which ones are actually real?'

'Sometimes the same species has different names in different cultures, but…' His eyes glistened. 'They're all real. From vampires to dragons; chupacabras to leprechauns. Where do you think the myths came from? We were the ones to make sure you humans thought them mere stories. Were you to discover the truth, the Truce would be broken.'

'And what type of Etheria are you?'

Caedric simply smiled and spread his arms. 'Does it really matter?'

Hannah frowned, unsure. 'And Gods…?' she asked curiously.

Caedric sighed and looked out of the window. 'Ah, the age-old question of deities. I don't think so. There are some that think *maybe* they might exist. But I'm not sure. You have some species thought to be deities by some, but they're just Etheria. Sometimes stories are just stories. But I'm not convinced either way.'

'But how is this all hidden? How come no one has ever stumbled on Arcadia before? Or flown over it in a plane?'

Caedric nodded understandingly. 'Because, strictly speaking, it doesn't exist—at least, not in the same dimension as the world you're used to. Think of it like branches on a tree. By going through the entrance to Arcadia, it's as if you fell from one branch to another.'

Hannah frowned and itched her head, struggling to get to grips with all this. 'But there must be some *normal* humans who know about this.'

'Of course. There are some, but others assume they're mad. Then there are others who pose more of a threat. Thrunters, who hunt and slaughter Etheria whether they're innocent or guilty; for sport, for money, to eradicate them from this world. They see them as monsters. And Pyres—those who want to become Etheria themselves, no matter the cost.'

Caedric shook his head solemnly before inhaling and moving on. 'So, you're aware of the existence of Etheria; what do you know about *that*?' he asked, pointing to the crystal she cradled in her lap.

'The crystal? It's magic?'

'I suppose. The crystals give us abilities we wouldn't be able to perform otherwise—much like magic.'

A smile crept onto Hannah's face. 'Now you're talking. What "abilities" does it let us do?'

'Oh, the possibilities are endless. We have used blood crystals for…' Caedric waved his hand, 'millennia. Perhaps we've only scratched the surface of what's possible. We only teach a select range of spells. Some are needlessly complicated, even dangerous. Even most warlocks stick to our recommendations.'

One word stuck out in Hannah's mind. '*Blood* crystals?'

'Yes. Touch your blood to any other crystal, and nothing will happen—these are special. You didn't notice? Without blood, it's just a crystal, but when you make an offering…'

Hannah thought back to each time she had used the crystal. The fight with Zelom—she had just tested her blood sugar; when she ripped out the IV, blood had run down her arm; she had tested in the forest outside Arcadia too.

'Convenient, isn't it?' Caedric leaned forward. 'Every time you've truly needed the crystal's magic you happened to have offered blood to make it work—without even knowing! Quite extraordinary. These priceless gems come from there.' Caedric pointed to the opening of a cave nestled in the bottom of the mountain, opening out to the lake, guarded by a clump of trees. 'The Melissani Cave. Only there can you find blood crystals.'

Hannah turned the crystal over in her hand and noticed the shape carved inside.

'A rune,' he answered before she could ask. 'Many find it helpful to enchant blood crystals with runes befitting to each individual's character.'

Hannah raised her eyebrows. 'Sounds difficult.'

'It is, but you're not bound to one for life. People change; they develop. Even I'm not the same man I once was. One rune doesn't sum you up for your whole life.'

'What if you have the wrong rune? Will it kill you?'

'Of course not! Your abilities are just less responsive, weaker.'

'But what do you use these for? Why don't more people know about them? They could be used for... everything!' Hannah felt her spine tingle, and she clenched her fist around the crystal.

As ever, Caedric remained calm. 'In many ways, Hannah, I agree with you. Yet that would be in breach of the Truce.'

Hannah groaned. 'What Truce?'

As if on cue, a knock sounded from the door. 'Enter!' called Caedric.

The door opened, and a girl entered. She was slightly older than Hannah, with long auburn hair and emerald eyes. Hannah smiled politely, but her eyes soon darted away. The girl's left cheek was flaky and pink, like a burn scar, with an infinity sign carved at its centre.

'You can look,' the girl said, adding, 'I don't mind. I'm proud of it.' Her straight face showed no signs of such pride.

Hannah shifted in her seat.

'You're not the only one. Most feel like that around us.'

'Us?' Except for the mark on her cheek, the girl looked perfectly normal.

'She's not human, Hannah,' Caedric explained.

Hannah blinked. 'I'm sorry... What are you?'

The girl made a small bow with her head. 'My name is Yvette. I'm a faucherêve.'

Hannah stared at her blankly, then looked to Caedric for clarification.

'Faucherêves may look human, but they're Etheria. They have…
abilities.'

'What sort of abilities?'

'I control dreams,' the girl stated, staring at Hannah. 'I put you
in a coma and create a dream for you. If I wanted, I could keep you
there—forever in that dream-world. I can make it mundane or fun
and exciting, heaven or hell. It's up to me.'

Caedric must have seen the worry in Hannah's eyes, for he
placed a reassuring hand on her shoulder. 'It's okay, Hannah. Yvette
will not cause you any harm. I give you my word.'

'Then why is she here?' Hannah asked, holding back a quiver in
her voice.

'You asked about the Truce.'

'Then just *tell* me. Come on—explain it to me, give me a book.
This seems a little intense.'

Caedric softened his voice. 'I promise nothing will go wrong.
Yvette will show you the Truce as it happened. You'll learn the
hidden truth that so few know. Simply telling you the facts won't let
you understand properly. Do you trust me?'

Hannah wrinkled her nose, her eyes fixed on her shoes. But
when she looked up, she saw genuine concern on his face.

She nodded. 'Sure.'

'Thank you,' said Caedric, as he guided her to an armchair.

Hannah leaned back and concentrated on breathing as Yvette
drew up a wooden chair. She cleared her throat and, with a simple
stroke along the lines of her scar, it lit up and emitted a low buzzing
sound.

'So, what do we do n—'

But Hannah didn't have time to finish. With one hand stroking
her glowing cheek, Yvette touched Hannah's head with her other
hand. Hannah's body went limp, and the room became dark as she
fell into a deep sleep, all control given to the faucherêve.

Chapter Fourteen

The Truth of the Truce

HANNAH felt like she was in a deep sleep—only one she could not awake from. As far as she was aware, there was nothing but an empty blackness.

She tried speaking. Nothing. She tried shouting instead. Still, she heard and saw nothing. With panic setting in, she tried moving her arms, legs, hands, toes—she felt nothing.

'Hannah,' came a soft voice, 'Hannah, it's me.'

'Caedric!' Hannah tried to shout. She couldn't feel her mouth move, let alone hear anything. She tried again.

'It's okay,' she heard Caedric say. 'You're doing fine. Everything is normal. This will be a strange experience, but I implore you just to relax.'

As though the sun were rising, flowing hills and fields emerged; a natural landscape populated by all manner of creatures—animals she had seen in real life and zoos living side by side with griffins, mermaids, giant wolves and flying horses. It was a surreal sight.

'What you see now was Earth,' said Caedric's bodiless voice. 'Many thousands of years ago, humanity evolved alongside all creatures. Some will be familiar to you, some will not. Earth was home to humans, animals and Etheria. Today, Etheria are reduced to myths, legends and folklore, but they all stem from reality.'

The view blurred slightly, and shapes moved as if in fast-forward. Once it stopped, time had passed. A simple village stood before her, complete with primal huts with humans working, playing, cooking, talking. Around them were animals; horses being ridden, cows being milked, sheep being sheared, chickens laying eggs. This was the world she knew.

But there was more. Short, squat men with beards next to tall, beautiful human-like beings with pointed ears. Minotaurs and centaurs worked together, laughing at each other's jokes. Flying creatures soared through the sky above, dropping meat and fresh fruit. Behind her were deer and rabbits in a meadow, grazing peacefully beside fauns, nymphs and muscaliets. Giants were visible in the distance, constructing more huts. It was a strange sight but a joyous one.

'For centuries, humankind lived in harmony with animals and Etheria, the boundaries of which have always been blurred. But some Etheria didn't agree with the status quo.'

Once again, the image faded and changed. Hannah found herself in a large hut, privy to what appeared to be a secret meeting. Centaurs, dwarves, minotaurs, elves, vampires—a variety of Etheria gathered around a warm fire, whispering.

'As is their way, humans used Etheria and animals for work, establishing their dominance. But there were Etheria who believed they should be superior; that humans should be their slaves. Many Etheria rallied together, but humans refused to become subservient.'

The world blurred and returned Hannah to her spot, overlooking the village. She was witnessing an argument; a large group of humans and a handful of Etheria on one side, and an even larger group of solely Etheria on the other. In the middle-ground between the two groups were two men, one who looked pale—*a vampire*, Hannah thought. The argument grew heated as both sides joined in. Angry shouts reached Hannah's ears, but she couldn't make out the words.

Suddenly, the human drew a sword and pointed the cold metal towards the vampire. The vampire remained calm and unmoving, while both groups crouched, weapons at the ready. In a flash, the vampire moved so fast Hannah barely saw what had happened until it was over. The human lay lifeless on the floor, his body beside his detached head, eyes still wide with shock. There was a pause before both groups screamed and charged towards one another.

'And so, war broke out; a war that ravaged the world for years. Its destruction left no one untouched.'

The landscape faded to reveal a battleground. There were limp corpses of every species scattered as far as the eye could see. An icy shiver ran down Hannah's spine.

'After a time, it seemed all was lost for the humans. They were planning to surrender, praying they would not be massacred.'

Hannah found herself in a dark cave, the only light coming from the entrance above. A group of men came cautiously into the cave, two of them carrying another who was badly injured.

'An elite group of human warriors made a startling discovery. After losing a battle against a band of Etheria, the humans fled. They carried with them their injured commander. He was a brave and honest man they could not bear to leave.'

Hannah watched, captivated, as the men made their way down the cave. A flame sparked, and one man held out a torch. As the flames flickered, the cave lit up with orange and yellow light. Hannah gasped along with the men as the torch's light sparkled in the crystals surrounding them. The stalagmites and stalactites, like spears, and the floor beneath, were all made from crystal.

'These men hid in this cave, admiring the crystals as they laid their commander on the crystal ground. They stayed silent, hoping the Etheria would not find them.'

The commander groaned and grasped his wound. Hannah held her stomach in sympathy when she saw just how badly he was injured. Blood pushed through his fingers and dripped onto the cave floor. The crystal floor beneath pulsed as though alive, glowing a dim red light.

'Imagine their surprise when, just minutes later, what had once been a fatal wound was nothing but a scratch.'

Hannah watched as the men celebrated their commander's miraculous recovery and waited for the scenery to finish its transition. Still in the cave, time had worn on; she saw make-shift beds and the remains of meals scattered on the ground. The men worked in the corner; some scrawling on parchment, some hammering away as they put all their force into each swing.

'The warriors remained here for some time, tediously experimenting with the crystals they had discovered.'

Before she knew it, Hannah was now on top of another hill, overlooking an enormous field in which a battle was fiercely raging, both on ground and in the air. Even the nearby sea foamed as an equally savage fight ravaged the deep. Griffins grabbed humans, piercing them with their sharp talons and dragging them up to the sky. Dwarves swung their battle-axes towards ogres as elves moved elegantly, each of their arrows finding their mark between the eyes of humans. Vampires slashed their opponents and feasted on the remains. Minotaurs charged through warring crowds as werewolves ripped their enemies to shreds. It was a horrific scene, but Hannah couldn't tear her eyes away.

'One day, during the final battle of the Great Etherian War, the warriors emerged from their cave with weapons and tools made from these crystals.'

The battle below soon changed. Even from a distance, Hannah could make it out. Fierce, bright lights shot around the battlefield from the band of human warriors. They wielded all types of weapons—swords, bows, hammers, maces—all imbued with blood crystals. What was once a slaughter of humans soon became a slaughter of panicked Etheria, clueless how to defend themselves from this new threat.

'The Etheria didn't stand a chance. They fought valiantly and may even have emerged victorious if it weren't for the crystals. But they were defeated.

'Soon after, representatives of both Etheria and humanity met to ensure a war like this would never devastate the world again. And so, the Truce was born.'

The surroundings faded to the top of a cliff where a human and an elf shook hands in front of a large, rectangular slab of stone engraved with writing. Cloaked figures surrounded them, all holding blood crystals and wearing golden badges. *Trucekeepers*, she noticed.

'The Truce stated humans had won the war and the right to be the dominant species. They would, however, show mercy to the surviving Etheria and let them be free. However, to prevent another war, their existence was to remain secret, and they were to remain out of sight from humans. This part of the Truce gave birth to Trucekeepers, trained warriors sworn to eliminate any threats and ensure the Truce was never breached.

'The Truce was carved in stone and Trucekeepers protected the peace. Humans lived with Etheria as a distant memory, soon so distant they became myths and legends passed from generation to generation. For the most part, Etheria remain hidden. Occasionally, an Etheria appears before a human or leaves traces. But humans are cynical, and these minor incidents only fuel the myths. Amazing how much easier Photoshop has made our job.'

Again, the environment changed. Hannah was now among the training grounds where she had seen Daegan earlier, Arcadia Castle towering proudly above. Around her stood numerous cloaked figures firing blasts of light at dummies.

'Trucekeepers are trained warriors who protect the Truce from a multitude of threats, punishing any breach of the Truce. There were still skirmishes and battles; the one with the Tuath Dé Danann in Ireland was infamous. For centuries, they ruled with an iron fist and Etheria have feared their wrath.'

The light dimmed, and Hannah found herself in a dark room lit by a roaring fireplace. In the centre was a rectangular table surrounded by various Etheria.

'A band of rebel Etheria known as Leviathans threatened this reign. They were angry, seeing the Trucekeepers as unjust and dictatorial. They believed themselves superior, convinced Etheria should have won the war, and thought the tides were turning. Humans had had their time; now was the age of Etheria. Humanity would be doomed to remain hidden or, more likely, made extinct. Executed.'

A tall man with an angular face stood at the head of the table, long white hair framing a pale, youthful face. He slammed his fist on the table. It shook wildly, and goblets wobbled.

'And with their fanatic leader, Sigurd Thornwood, at the helm, the extinction was likely. He housed the Leviathans in the Etherian settlement of Scholomance. With the Wild Hunt supporting him, the Leviathans gained power and the support of many Etheria.'

The Leviathans around the table raised their right fists and cried in unison, 'From the waves we rise!' Their motto reverberated through the room like a knell.

'But they also gained opposition—many Etheria were content with the way things were and wanted to maintain peace; they understood that the Truce was a necessity to avoid bloodshed. If humans were to discover the existence of Etheria, war wouldn't end until either was extinct. The Etherian community was split. Every act from the Leviathans cause a ripple; these ripples grew to become waves, and eventually tensions gave birth to the Leviathan War.'

Hannah expected another horrific battle scene, the sort of sight she was sure would give her nightmares for weeks to come. But there was nothing.

Caedric ended his tale. 'Many lives were lost. It decimated the Trucekeepers. Only a handful of us remained. Some even defected to the Leviathans. Etheria have now spread throughout the world, many no longer living in the lands they originally called home.

'Although the Trucekeepers were victorious, the War did not die. An uneasy peace returned, and the Truce remained… but so too did the Leviathans. Though now just a small band of radical Etheria, they have posed a threat ever since, one that has risen in recent years.

'We need to strengthen the Trucekeepers. The tides are indeed turning—that's why we need you, Hannah.'

Caedric's last words became hollow, echoing around the black expanse surrounding her. She felt light-headed and struggled to breathe. Hannah cried out for help, but still her voice refused to be heard. She scrunched her eyes up and screamed, desperate to be awoken. But no one could hear her.

Chapter Fifteen

Daegan's Protests

HUSHED voices became frustrated whispers which soon turned to unimpeded shouts. Hannah awoke, eyes blinking as she tried to remember where she was. The first thing she saw was a white bird who looked at her curiously before whistling and fluttering its wings as it flew around the room.

Beside her sat Yvette, fast asleep with the scar on her cheek still glowing. She wondered if she was dreaming too, or if she even could dream.

'… and her safety ought to be our priority. Besides, I don't have time for this. There's a traitor in our midst that we must sniff out. *Aquila non capit muscas.*'

'An eagle does not catch flies…' Caedric mused, translating what Daegan had said as he considered his words. 'I wouldn't compare this matter to a fly. It's far more important. Especially since—'

The voices quickly stopped as they spotted Hannah waking up. She looked over and saw a riled Daegan standing next to a calm Caedric, happily smoking his wooden pipe.

'You're back,' Caedric noticed. 'I trust you had a pleasant sleep?' he said, half a smile hidden beneath his moustache.

'Hardly restful but certainly educational,' Hannah replied.

'Excellent!' exclaimed Caedric. 'A positive reaction.'

'To a reckless activity,' muttered Daegan.

Hannah frowned. 'What's up with him?'

'Daegan is more old-fashioned than myself. He prefers books to practices—'

'Practices, which are downright dangerous,' spat Daegan.

'Oh, don't be so childish!' Caedric chided him.

'You told me it would be safe.'

'I did. And did any harm befall you?'

'No,' Hannah admitted. 'But that's not the point!'

Caedric removed the pipe from his mouth and busied himself with refilling it. 'With the amazing abilities of faucherêves,' began Caedric, 'always comes a certain amount of risk—as with everything. Yvette has never let anyone come to harm while under the influence of her dream-weaving. Daegan once had an unfortunate experience with an unpractised faucherêve.' He turned to Daegan. 'But that was a long time ago.'

He turned back to Hannah. 'I'd like it if you could trust me, even if Daegan refuses to do so.'

Daegan scowled as he examined Hannah through narrow eyes. 'You think she'll trust anyone? She questions everything we tell her—'

'This is a new world to her, Daegan,' Caedric reminded him. 'Were you so different all those years ago? Don't you remember that feeling of seeing an Etheria for the first time?'

Anger sparked in Daegan's eyes, but he held his tongue.

'Remember who you're talking to,' Caedric warned, unfazed, as he relit his pipe.

Daegan hid his face beneath his hat and muttered an apology under his breath.

Caedric turned back to the dazed girl. 'Do you understand now?'

Hannah thought back to school—all the hours she had spent studying; the countless books she had scoured over and essays she had written. She wished she had had a faucherêve to help her then.

'It's not too complicated. I know what the Truce is and the deal with those Leviathan guys. But I've heard of a leviathan. I assumed it would be an Etheria too.'

Caedric nodded. 'Nowadays, the word "leviathan" just refers to a group of Etheria. But there was once *the* Leviathan that the group took their name from.' Caedric released a plume of light blue smoke from his nostrils. 'I'm not the expert though.' He turned to Daegan with a coy smile.

'It's a long story. Don't worry about it.' Daegan huffed. 'It fought against humans in the Great Etherian War, but no one even knows which version of the story is real. It depends whether you think Gods ever existed.'

'Just like the many mysteries in human history,' Caedric said, 'we have debates about Etherian history too.'

Hannah nodded slowly, trying to take everything on board. 'Okay, so there are Leviathans… and Thrunters and Pyres too.' She smiled, proud to include all those new terms. 'But it seems a little unfair that Etheria have to remain in hiding.'

Daegan rolled his eyes while Caedric smiled sagely. 'It's understandable to question the ethics of the Truce. Some do—the Voiceless Dawn, for example, though you need not concern yourself with them for now. But, as it is, humans are more likely to go to war for supremacy than Etheria—except for Leviathans, naturally.'

'But how did they decide what was Etheria and what was an animal?'

'It was too long ago for anyone to know now,' Caedric replied. 'Although, as is still the case, I imagine it was in part influenced by the fear of that which is different.'

'*Timendi causa est nescire*,' Daegan whispered. He caught sight of Hannah's confused look and translated. 'Ignorance is the cause of fear.'

'Hannah,' Caedric said, 'I have instructed Daegan to be your mentor. He will teach you about the Truce and all documented Etheria. He will also train you how to fight, defend yourself, investigate Etheria-related events and use your blood crystal.'

'Wait—' Hannah interrupted. She couldn't believe all this was happening. One moment she was running away from home, now she had been recruited into a secret organisation to fight and protect monsters. 'You want to recruit me into your little cold war? Do I have any choice?'

'Of course,' replied Caedric. 'I know nothing of the life you led before. There could be people, commitments, hopes and dreams you'd rather return to. I would understand that.' Hannah remained silent. 'Should you choose to join us, Daegan will be your mentor and you his apprentice. He will teach you all you need to know, and you will accompany him on missions until you are ready to take the Trials.'

'Trials?'

'Just a test of sorts to see if you're ready to qualify to become a proper Trucekeeper.'

'And if I refuse?'

Caedric casually waved his hand. 'I shall confiscate your crystal and wipe your mind of all memories of Etheria once more; permanently this time.'

Hannah winced.

'The blood crystal you possess came to you and summoned Daegan—that's not something that happens to just anyone.'

Hannah looked to Daegan. Even he nodded in agreement, though reluctantly.

'Besides, when you regained those memories, you persevered to find Arcadia. You've earned this chance, Hannah, but in the end, the choice is yours.' Caedric leaned forward and looked her in the eye. 'What do you say?'

Chapter Sixteen

The Trucekeeper's Apprentice

'STICK close to me. Don't wander off,' snapped Daegan as they left Caedric's office.

'Obviously,' replied Hannah. 'I'd get lost. I'm not an idiot.'

'Good,' he said as he hastened down the stairs.

'Where are we going?' she called out as she sped down a corridor after him.

'The library. A dream can't teach you everything. There's more you need to know.'

'Can't you just give me the gist?' Hannah pleaded. The last thing she wanted was a hefty history book; she needed rest. 'Or, better yet, wait a while? I'm tired.'

Daegan stopped dead and turned to face her. 'You're *tired*?' He spat the word.

'Yeah. Some of us need to sleep. Especially when they get all this dumped on them.'

'We haven't *dumped* anything on you. There's no time to be tired! As a Trucekeeper you have to keep going—even when you're *tired*.'

Hannah groaned. 'That's going to be one hell of a lesson to learn.'

At the end of the corridor, Daegan heaved open a door to reveal the most incredible library Hannah had ever seen. There were varnished oak bookshelves taller than the house she grew up in. In the rafters above flew winged Etheria, clutching books between their claws. On the ground, at long tables littered with parchment, were backs hunched over tables as wizened Etheria studied manuscripts. The room was unnervingly quiet, every footstep an echo.

'*This* is your library?' Hannah asked incredulously.

'Yes. You'll find most things you're looking for—eventually. *In libras libertas.*'

Hannah wrinkled her nose. 'In what?'

Daegan cocked an eyebrow. 'It's Latin. Freedom in books.' Seemingly oblivious to both Hannah's confusion and the surrounding wonders of the library, he walked off, soon lost amongst the bookshelves.

Hannah glanced at the table next to her, covered with countless open books. One caught her eye; despite the tiny handwriting and runes Hannah could barely decipher, she recognised two large pictures: one of a tall and handsome ghostly-looking man; the other was of a fierce wolf, fangs bared with scaly wings.

She looked up to see two red eyes staring back at her. 'You're the girl,' the man gasped.

Hannah said nothing in reply, too captivated by his stare.

'The one from the other day,' he went on. His eyes narrowed as his stare became more intense. 'How are you here? I cast the Oblivion spell myself. I wiped your mind!'

'I—' Hannah didn't know where to begin. She tried to reply but found herself unable, hypnotised by the man's eyes. All she could do was hold out her blood crystal as an explanation.

He looked at her open hand, and his eyes gleamed even brighter. 'That crystal...'

'Drakkar!' Daegan called as he strode up to the table. 'If you're quite finished with my pupil...'

The man wrinkled his nose, and the red gleam in his eyes dimmed. Hannah blinked and took a deep breath, as if she had just come out of a trance. She stepped back towards Daegan.

'*Pupil?*' Drakkar repeated. 'Is this not the girl you brought to us barely three days ago? The one whose memory the Truceleaders unanimously agreed to erase? How dare you—'

'I had nothing to do with her return,' Daegan interrupted. 'The girl has a natural affinity with that crystal. Summoning me during her fight with Zelom was no freak accident. She found her own way back, and, well, I suppose that's all Caedric needs to decide she's one of us.'

The two men shared a look, one that made Hannah decidedly uncomfortable.

'Preposterous,' muttered Drakkar.

Daegan frowned and leaned forward to peer at Drakkar's open book. 'Interested in her fight with the zburător?'

Drakkar slammed the book shut. He picked it up and, with a mutter of, 'Good luck to the both of you,' turned on his heels and stormed out of the library.

'A friend?' Hannah asked as she watched him leave, his back hunched.

'Hmph,' Daegan replied. 'I wouldn't call him that. He's a valued Truceleader though. I've always felt a little sorry for him. He's had a great deal of trouble in his life.' Daegan beckoned to Hannah. 'This way.'

She followed him begrudgingly to the maze of bookshelves. Hannah was dreading the sort of books Daegan would pick out for her.

'Here,' he said.

A thick book dropped into her outstretched arms. She stumbled as she caught it, struggling with the weight.

'You don't have this on audiobook?'

'Another one!' he called.

Another book, even heavier than the last, fell into place. Hannah gasped.

'Is there a trolley I can put these in or…?'

Daegan soared up a ladder and disappeared onto the ledge above.

'Is this really necessary? Yvette already showed me how the Truce started. Do I really need to read all this?'

'*Nullus est liber tam malus ut non aliqua parte prosit,*' he called out. 'No book is so bad it's not profitable!'

What's with all the Latin? Hannah pondered as she looked down at the books he had given her. *The Moral Compass: Morality and Ethics of the Truce*—by Montgomery Nero. *Gilgamesh and the Trucekeepers*—by Sîn-lēqi-unninni. *Trucekeepers and Blood Crystals: A History*—by Theodore Clarendon. *The Leviathans and the Leviathan War*—by Daegan.

Of course, he gives me his own book, she thought, rolling her eyes. *And why only one name? He's not Madonna.*

Hannah grimaced, already dreading the long, sleepless nights she would have to spend pouring over books. She looked at some on the shelves beside her. *The Most Dangerous Etheria Known to Man*; *Blood Crystal Magic Vol. 1*; *The Truth in the Myths*. For a moment, Hannah considered substituting the books Daegan had given her for some more interesting ones.

'Incoming!'

Hannah's thoughts evaporated as another book fell towards her. It hurtled down and slammed onto the stone ground with an almighty slap. A multitude of pages scattered the library.

Daegan peered over the ledge. 'That book was over three hundred years old, Hannah.'

She didn't know whether to feel guilty or angry. Seeing an ancient book bound with so much knowledge shatter before her was heart-breaking, but it wouldn't have happened if Daegan hadn't been so careless.

'From where I was standing, that was your fault, Daegan,' said a voice behind Hannah.

She turned to see a tall, slim girl with wavy red hair and high cheekbones. Pointy ears poked out from beneath her hair—an elf—though she looked unlike the other elves in Arcadia. She certainly had the beauty and ears; but the way she held herself betrayed a lack of confidence that most elves displayed. She turned to Hannah and smiled warmly.

'I warned her,' Daegan said as he climbed down, but his confident demeanour soon wavered. 'But perhaps I should have been more careful… Do you think you could fix it?'

'I can add it to my ever-increasing to-do list,' the girl sighed as she gathered up the book and its scattered pages. 'You can collect it tomorrow morning,' she told Hannah. 'I'm Axis.' She held out a slender hand.

'Er, Hannah,' she replied, shaking her hand.

'Put those books down, Hannah,' Daegan interrupted. 'We need to collect some more.' He grabbed her arm and pulled her after him.

But she snatched her arm back. 'No!' she snapped.

'What?'

'I said no. I've only just arrived, and you're piling all these books into my arms and blaming *me* when *you* drop them and—'

She saw Axis listening in. She was pretending to read the book in her hands but couldn't hide a satisfied smile.

'*The Moral Compass*? Trucekeeper history books? Really? How much of this am I really going to need to know?'

Daegan pursed his lips. His eyes shone with frustration, but he stayed silent.

'Teach me something *practical*. Teach me about the monsters—'

'Etheria,' he corrected under his breath.

'Teach me how to be a Trucekeeper, how to find Etheria, how to fight!'

Hannah realised how loud she had been talking and held her tongue, blushing as she noticed several people enjoying their argument.

'You want to learn how to fight?' Daegan asked. 'Fine. Follow me.'

He stormed off. Hannah followed, waving at Axis who gave her an encouraging wink.

At least someone's on my side.

Chapter Seventeen

A Hard Lesson to Learn

HANNAH followed Daegan through several corridors before he ushered her through a door. At first, she thought they were in a huge circular sandpit, but as she looked at the rows of seats, she realised they were in an arena similar to a coliseum. She could hear calm waves from the lake just beyond the walls and the distant sound of everyday life in Arcadia; shouts, laughs, the occasional clash of metal on metal.

'Why do you have an arena? Am I going to be fed to lions? Or a sphinx?'

'It's for training. In the past, there were games where we fought Etheria to prove ourselves, but that's been banned for a long time now. It was barbaric killing for entertainment.'

'Isn't that what Trucekeepers do anyway? Kill dangerous Etheria?'

Daegan shot her a disdainful look. 'It's not that simple. There may be dangerous Etheria, and they may break the rules of the Truce—but we do not simply kill. We offer them a chance for redemption; we talk things through—even offer an alternate punishment. Death is the *last* resort and never one I enjoy.

'Fighting is strictly forbidden in Arcadia,' he continued. 'It goes against our commitment to peace. However, this arena is an exception. Trucekeepers need to know how to defend themselves.'

Hannah smiled. 'Finally. Learning to fight—more useful. Do I need my crystal?'

Daegan cracked his knuckles. 'Not now.'

Without another word, Daegan sent a fist flying towards Hannah. She doubled up, pain burning through her stomach. She gasped for breath and staggered.

'Reflexes are slow—makes sense. Zelom was fierce but clumsy. If you had been alert and ready for an attack, you'd have had a better chance.'

'Hey!' Hannah protested. 'I didn't exactly see you having an easy time against him. I helped *you*!'

Daegan gazed at her, a smile teasing the corner of his mouth. Without warning, he leapt forward with his fist again. Hannah was ready this time, and moved to dodge it—but, as if expecting this, his leg swept her feet from under her. She hit the sandy floor with a thump.

'Slap the ground when you're thrown,' he instructed as he walked away. 'It'll help to absorb the impact. Now, you showed promise,' he droned on, 'but to be a Trucekeeper you need more than that.'

Hannah staggered to her feet. 'If you're going to beat the hell out of me, maybe I don't want to be a Trucekeeper.'

Daegan circled her, his heels clipping against the shallow sand. 'Why weren't you at school when Zelom found you?'

Hannah thought back. It was strange how it already seemed so long ago. 'I got expelled,' she muttered.

A glint flashed in Daegan's eyes. He stopped. 'Why?'

Hannah shrugged. Daegan's open palm slapped her cheek.

Hannah screamed. 'Why did you—?'

'Why?' he barked.

He went for a slap again, but Hannah jumped backwards, narrowly missing his speeding hand.

'I took my anger out on someone, okay?'

She was desperate for this to be over. *What's he expecting? For me to instantly become an expert fighter?*

'How?' he asked, calmer this time.

'I pushed a guy down the stairs. He had to be hospitalised.'

'And what did your victim do to warrant such… heinous behaviour?'

Hannah's face dropped, all traces of a smile evaporating as memories of Zack came back to her. 'He's a… you know,' she mumbled.

'There are many people like him,' he replied, knowingly. 'I doubt you hospitalise all of them. Why this one?'

He threw another punch; she dodged. Then an outstretched palm came for another slap; her hand blocked it. His leg moved to curl around hers; she pushed him away.

Daegan beamed.

'He hurt me,' she told him simply.

'Is that all?'

'And he threatened my friend.' Suddenly, she realised she hadn't even told Luke she was leaving. Guilt washed over her.

'Standing up for your friend…' Daegan mused. 'Very noble. Noble can get you killed,' he snarled.

He lunged forward, a kick aimed at her stomach. Hannah backed away and turned, tripping over her feet as she did and landing face first on the ground. She felt blood trickle from her nose and mix with the tears running down her face. For a fraction of a second, Hannah thought she saw Daegan pause, concerned.

'Why are you here?' he asked, apparently no longer worried.

'To learn about Etheria?' she replied, getting to her knees.

'Are you asking me or telling me?' Daegan grabbed her shoulders and threw her back. 'Why are you here?' he asked; louder, angrier.

'To become a Trucekeeper!'

'Liar. You only just learned about Trucekeepers today!'

It was unrelenting. Daegan gripped her arms.

'Once more!' he warned. 'Why did you come here?' He raised his hand.

Hannah felt the heavy beat of her heart. She thought of school, of Luke, of her fight with Zelom. She knew the answer and didn't care if it was the one Daegan was looking for.

His hand came down for a slap, fast as lightning—but Hannah was faster. Still on her knees, she ducked before jumping back to her feet.

Daegan's fist flew towards her stomach; Hannah knocked it away and grabbed his wrist. She curled her leg around his and threw him to the ground. His hat flew to the side as his body hit the ground with a thud. She gripped his collar, her arm raised in a fist.

'Because I have nothing to lose,' she said. That was it; her answer—the truth.

Though winded and hurt, Daegan grinned. 'You can let go now.'

Hannah let his collar go and walked away. She made sure he wasn't looking as she wiped her face with the back of her hand. A salty, red mixture smeared across her arm. She heard Daegan chuckle as he dusted his hat and returned it atop his head.

'Was there a point to this?' she spat.

'Of course.'

'I'm going off this Trucekeeper idea,' she muttered. 'Tell me why you… did you break my nose?'

'Lena can fix it easily enough—'

'Why?'

'To prove a point.' Daegan gave away no emotion. 'When you refused to face the truth, you couldn't protect yourself. But when you were honest, when you *understood*—that's when you could fight back.'

'I—' Hannah stuttered.

'If you understand what you're fighting for, you'll stand a chance at surviving. You'll have a clearer mind. It'll save you from getting killed.' With that, he turned on his heel and left. 'And if you end up dying, you're just wasting my time.'

Chapter Eighteen

New Recruits

CAEDRIC didn't seem particularly fazed when Hannah told him what Daegan had done, but he agreed to have a word with him.

So too did Lena, the faerie in the medical wing. As soon as Caedric brought Hannah in, the full-sized faerie, wings larger than her whole body, audibly gasped in outrage. As she patched Hannah up, she kept muttering how unacceptable Daegan's behaviour was. Hannah sensed a feisty side to her—something she was sure came in useful when patching up wounds sustained in battle.

'I wasn't expecting faeries to look so…' She didn't know how to finish her sentence.

Lena smiled knowingly. 'We're not all aos sí. That's a catch-all term. So many words for so many Etheria; humans often end up lumping a load of us together. You lot use the word faerie for everything, but ones like us still exist. Though we don't all have wings, I'll give you that. We're not too far removed from elves, you know. Certainly related to the same descendant, but I think we're better. I mean, we can change size. What can they do?' She sighed. 'Sometimes I want to just break the Truce to set the record straight once and for all. I wish we all just called each other Etheria and be done with it. We don't need to distinguish, give out labels. Heck, even humans do it, too. It doesn't matter what we're called—we're all citizens of the world, no matter the plane of existence of dimension we live.'

Hannah smiled through her winces as the faerie continued to talk and patch her up. She told her about life in Arcadia and even about her skirmishes into the human world. She loved sneaking into theatres, particularly into productions of *A Midsummer Night's Dream* to laugh at the different interpretations of faeries.

The next morning, the sun shone through the thin white curtains, waking Hannah up and lighting her sparse room. She hadn't had time to decorate her new room in Arcadia's castle just yet. She turned her back to the window and shrugged the duvet over her head. No school—no reason to wake up.

Then came three hard knocks.

'Breakfast is in thirty minutes,' called out Daegan. 'Be there.' There was a pause. Hannah could imagine how difficult it was for him to be polite. 'It's delicious, so you'd be missing out…'

Hannah begrudgingly kicked off the duvet and rolled over to her bedside table. She looked for her glucose monitor before realising she didn't need it anymore. She smiled giddily, a feeling of freedom washing over her before she swivelled her legs out of bed. She grimaced as her bare feet touched the ice-cold stone floor and hurried them to the fur rug, wiggling her toes in its delectable warmth. She wondered if it was real fur. *Is it an animal or Etheria?*

She opened the shabby wooden wardrobe and saw a bleak choice of outfits; a plain, dark blue dress hung limply next to a dirty white shirt and light brown trousers; crumpled at the bottom was a brown jerkin on top of black sandals and sturdier, but uncomfortable-looking leather boots. On the dresser by the window was a mirror and small collection of headbands. She decided not to spend too long getting dressed and pushed aside thoughts of what had happened to her clothes from yesterday. She shrugged on the ugly dress and sandals and selected a headband to tame her wild bedhead.

Hannah dusted off the cobwebs and examined herself in the print-stained mirror. She direly needed a shower and a few extra hours of sleep—not ideal for her first full day in Arcadia—and noticed a bit of blood still sticking determinedly to her face. She splashed herself with the freezing water from the basin and looked again. Still not perfect, but it would have to do.

At least the headband looks good, she thought.

Ignoring how self-conscious she felt in the dress, she made her way down into the entrance hall, marvelling at the intricately decorated tapestries waving calmly in the morning breeze.

'Lost?' came a voice from behind, more a statement than a question.

Hannah whirled around to see a man she recognised from her first visit to Arcadia. With ghostly pale skin, charcoal black hair and alluring eyes, Hannah was both repelled by and attracted to him. He leaned against the bannisters, his clothes almost comically gothic. *Vampire*, she thought. She didn't expect them to fit the stereotypes so accurately.

'Erm, breakfast,' was all that came to mind.

The man regarded her with a serious expression and beckoned her to follow him with a bony finger. 'This way,' he commanded. He led her back up the grand staircase and down a different flight of stairs.

'Byron,' he stated simply.

'I'm sorry?'

'My name is Byron. Lord Byron, if you will.'

The man looked straight ahead and gave away no emotion.

'Byron… like the burgers or the poet?' She laughed at her own joke.

Byron did not. Instead, a look of disgust appeared on his face, the first emotion he had displayed.

'As in the so-called *poet*.' He spat the word and fell quiet once again.

'A relative?'

He did not respond, and instead opened an ornate door and stepped inside.

Hannah had always loved breakfast, but she had never had it like this. The dining hall was decorated similarly to the entrance hall, with tapestries, statues and pillars adorning the walls. In the middle were more Etheria than Hannah could name huddled around several long tables. Elves sat next to dwarves, and minotaurs shared meat with fauns. There were others Hannah didn't recognise and plenty not even sitting at tables. In the corner were griffins, enfields and centaurs sharing food.

From just a whiff of the food, Hannah's stomach grumbled; she didn't think she had ever eaten nearly as well as they did in Arcadia. All parts of a full English breakfast were piled high; stacks of sausages, bacon and black pudding, mounds of eggs, tomatoes and hash browns, bowls full to the brim with beans. There were all variety of eggs, bagels, smoked salmon, croissants, potatoes, fruit. She could even smell the stirring aroma of ground coffee and freshly squeezed orange juice.

She searched for a spare spot to perch herself and enjoy breakfast. To her relief, a hand shot into the air and waved. She followed the hand down to a boy's face, laden with freckles and a dishevelled mop of red hair. She returned his smile as he gestured for her to sit with them.

'Hi,' she said nervously.

A chorus of "hello," "hi" and "good morning" echoed among the group at the table.

One girl with a round face, piercingly narrow eyes and olive skin caught her eye. 'Nice headband,' she said.

'Oh.' Hannah touched it absent-mindedly. 'Thank you.'

The girl leaned forward and asked in a hushed whisper, 'What are you?'

Hannah blinked. 'I'm sorry?'

'Elf?' prompted the girl.

'Nah, she looks more like a dwarf,' said one of the others—a faun, she recognised, with light brown skin that emphasised his white teeth as he grinned. The others giggled.

'I don't know,' said another girl with long black hair and golden skin. 'It's not just the eyes. She's pretty pale, so I'd say vampire. But they don't like breakfast.'

'Why not?' asked Hannah.

The group stared at her.

'Seriously?' asked the boy who had waved, sounding confused. 'Vampires aren't too fond of daylight. Obviously, they avoid breakfast—'

'—and lunch,' chimed in the girl with the overly round face. 'You rarely see them until dinner time. Apart from Byron, of course.'

'So come on, tell us,' said the boy with red hair. 'Some of us haven't been studying Etheria for very long, and there're loads of humanoids. What are you?'

Hannah frowned. 'Do I look, what, *inhuman*?'

'Well, yeah. Your eyes…' said the girl, her finger pointing at Hannah.

She lowered her face as they all stared, waiting with bated breath for her to reveal her species. Even here, amongst fauns and centaurs, without her diabetes to worry about, she still felt like an outsider. 'Sorry to disappoint. I'm human, same as you guys. Well, some of you.'

'Oh,' said the girl, disappointed. She continued to stare at Hannah's eyes and held back a laugh.

'Unfortunately for us, we're the only other human trainees,' explained the red-haired boy, gesturing to the girl and a bigger boy with puffy pink cheeks who looked like he was used to such feasts.

'Why "unfortunately?"'

The boy sneered. 'Don't you feel like a loser? Being human while all these Etheria can do so much more than us?'

Hannah nodded, preferring not to argue about the Pyres Caedric had mentioned and hoping this boy wasn't one. 'What brought you all to Arcadia?' she asked as she helped herself to a generous portion of scrambled eggs, blushing under everyone's stares.

'Oh, it was all *their* fault!' squeaked the girl. 'I was sleeping in some house—no one lived there, and I needed somewhere to stay…' She shifted, as though reluctant to go into much detail. 'Then these two come in and awaken this demonic spirit thing…'

'We got cursed,' mumbled the larger boy through a mouthful of food. 'Byron couldn't lift it, so he brought us here.'

'Name's Nathan,' said the boy with red hair through a mouthful of eggs and bacon. Flecks of food flew across the table. 'That's Amber and Jason.' He pointed to the girl and boy whose plate was now so loaded there was no sign of an actual plate beneath the mountain of food. They limply raised their hands in greeting.

Hannah leaned forward and saw the others at the table—they were all laughing and chatting excitedly. The humans rolled their eyes at them, and Hannah grimaced. She regretted sitting at this end. The Etheria looked far more inviting than the humans.

'So—what are you doing here?' asked Amber.

'She's one of us obviously,' interrupted Nathan. 'That's why I told her to sit here.'

'One of you?' Hannah wasn't sure what they were talking about.

'You're a Trucekeeper trainee, right?'

'Yeah.'

'Why's she so late?' asked Jason through a mouthful of at least two sausages.

'I don't know,' replied Nathan. 'She's one of Daegan's.'

'That explains it,' mumbled Amber. After a beat, she turned to Hannah, excited again. 'Have you got your blood crystal yet?'

'Mhm,' Hannah nodded.

'Oh!' she exclaimed. 'What rune did you choose? I spent *ages* choosing mine. It was such a tricky decision. I mean, how could you possibly pin down your personality when it's constantly evolving—'

Hannah soon stopped listening. So too apparently did Jason and Nathan, judging by their expressions. Amber didn't seem to understand the concept of grammar; she was a constant babble of words, a running commentary on every thought she had.

'I have the one that looks like an M,' Hannah interrupted to quieten her.

'Oh, wow!' Amber seemed far too enthusiastic. 'What made you choose that one?'

Hannah shrugged. 'It just came with the crystal already.'

Once more, Hannah felt herself shrink as they stared.

'You mean you didn't forge yours yourself?' asked Nathan.

Hannah shook her head.

'You just… what, found it?'

Hannah nodded, feeling foolish. She had never been happier to see Daegan appear.

'Why are you sitting here?' he snapped.

'They're new too and I thought—'

'Come with me. I'll introduce you to the Truceleaders.'

'Can we come?' asked Nathan, standing up before Daegan had a chance to reply.

Daegan paid the others no attention. 'Come, Hannah.' And with that, he turned away.

Hannah stood up and forced a smile. 'See you guys around?'

None of them said a word, just glaring at her. Eagerly, Hannah chased after Daegan and ignored the looks that followed her.

Chapter Nineteen

The Truceleaders' Greeting

'THANK you,' Hannah whispered once they were out of earshot of the table.

Daegan said nothing, only nodding his head in recognition.

'How many Truceleaders are there?'

'There are always seven Truceleaders on the Council, including the Trucemaster.'

'Caedric.'

'Exactly; they're not all complete strangers.'

She followed him up to the long table on a platform at the end of the dining room. She kept her head down and ignored the glances.

Around the table were seven people. An eclectic mix, all whom she recognised from when Daegan had brought her to Arcadia for the first time. Like Daegan and Caedric, they also wore golden badges; the letters T and L overlapped in a circle.

The warm smile Caedric flashed soothed her nerves.

'Truceleaders,' Daegan announced with a polite bow. His thumb held his middle finger to his palm, and he moved his hand to his chest.

Some kind of salute, she guessed.

'Allow me the pleasure of formally introducing our newest recruit—Miss Hannah Moreland.'

All heads turned, and her cheeks blushed.

'A pleasure as always,' Caedric said.

'You already know Caedric,' said Daegan. 'The vampire over there is Lord Byron.'

'We've met,' said Byron, nodding his head politely. He took a deep gulp of a red liquid from a jewel-encrusted goblet, before dabbing his lips with a silk handkerchief.

Daegan gestured to the female centaur, a centauride, next to Byron. 'This is Aarava.'

Aarava was the Truceleader Hannah remembered most vividly. After all, it wasn't everyday she saw a centauride. She didn't quite know where to look; her hazel hair cascaded down her brown, scarred body to the chestnut-coloured body of a racehorse.

'Please,' Aarava said, 'don't feel uncomfortable. I know some Etheria can be unusual to see for the first time. Imagine my reaction when I first saw a human!' She chuckled to herself before grabbing a sausage and sitting on the ground, her legs tucked under her body.

'Here,' continued Daegan, 'we have the elves, Eldrin and Aleesia.' They looked how Hannah expected elves to look, although Eldrin was startlingly pale compared to Aleesia's golden skin. They both had majestic postures and athletic bodies but barely gave any notice to Hannah. Instead, they gazed at her momentarily before continuing their breakfast.

The squat man with a beard the size of his entire body confidently waddled to Hannah, his large red cheeks blending in with his pink skin. 'Miss Hannah,' he said in a shout, clicking his heels together as his stomach protruded. 'Me name's Braddock. The only dwarf on the Council. Pleased to meet ya,' he said in a thick, almost comical accent.

'And finally,' Daegan went on, 'our resident warlock, Drakkar.'

The man from the library looked up. His rugged face contorted as his scarlet eyes narrowed. He smiled a toothy grin, erratic teeth pointing in various directions. Drakkar reached for her hand and brought it to his lips.

'I believe we met yesterday. Yet too briefly and far too informally,' he said.

He planted a kiss on her hand, spots of saliva sticking there. Hannah held back a grimace and tried to retract her hand, but he gripped her like a vice.

'I apologise for my behaviour,' he said. His voice sounded different, almost as if he were making fun of her. 'I am in the middle of some very tiring research. Perhaps you'll aid me some day? I hear you have a knack for blood magic.'

'She does indeed,' Caedric called out, beaming. 'She'll make a fine addition, make no mistake.'

'Maybe you're Etheria yourself. Your eyes... A sorcerer, perhaps?' Drakkar hissed, excitement taking hold of him. 'Tell me girl—who are your parents?'

Hannah looked to Daegan and Caedric, hoping they might step in so she could avoid the question. But they too waited for her answer with curious looks.

'I don't know,' she admitted, eyes fixed firmly on her feet.

'Fascinating,' Drakkar whispered.

'Hannah,' whispered Daegan. 'We take our leave.'

She contained her relief as Daegan made their excuses. He brought his hand to his chest, saluting the Truceleaders once more. He gestured for Hannah to do the same.

'United we stand,' he said with a curt bow.

Hannah muttered the same, trying to ignore the flush that crept across her cheeks as she did so.

'Not a people person, are you?' he whispered as they walked back down the dining hall, leaving the Truceleaders to their breakfast.

'Not really,' she replied. 'You don't seem like one either.'

'Absolutely not,' Daegan laughed. 'By the way, what did you think of them?'

'Who? The Truceleaders?'

Daegan nodded.

'They're fine, I guess. Some seem friendlier than others.'

'Did any seem—how do I put this?—less trustworthy?' he asked. 'I'm interested in first impressions,' he muttered as explanation to her questioning look.

Hannah shrugged. 'I don't think the elves like me. Or Byron. Drakkar seems a bit creepy. Why?'

Daegan merely nodded, not answering her question. They stopped near the table she ate at earlier. 'General training has already begun for new recruits,' he said. 'You're to be put on a fast-track course; I'll give you one-on-one lessons until you catch up. Since you showed particular—shall we say, talent—during our encounter with Zelom, you'll also be put through further intensive training.'

Hannah's face heated, aware of the sneers from Nathan, Jason and Amber at the table.

Why did he have to tell me all this here? Please, shut up!

'You have potential, Hannah. You owe it to yourself to fulfil that potential.'

He paused, expecting questions or protests, but Hannah stayed quiet. He raised a surprised eyebrow. 'Excellent. I'll meet you out in the main hall in half an hour. Enjoy breakfast with your friends.'

With that, he left Hannah to the jeers and giggles from her fellow new recruits.

'Ooh! Chosen one.'

'Daegan's special ickle girl.'

'How's she better? She didn't even make her own crystal! She stole it!'

Hannah wasn't hungry anymore. She preferred an empty stomach to spending another moment with them. She bowed her head and walked swiftly out of the room, feeling no different to how she had at school.

Chapter Twenty

Training in Blood Magic

THE next few weeks zoomed by. Daegan wasn't lying when he said their one-on-one lessons would be intensive. For nearly a month she woke at sunrise, getting to bed at sunset and only able to enjoy a couple of hours away from his exhaustive training.

For the first few days, Hannah was confined to just Daegan and a classroom. The stone walls were drab, and it was colder than the rest of the castle, with only a chalkboard and a handful of desks decorating the depressing room.

Still, what Daegan taught her was far from boring. She had expected lessons on history, theory—anything other than what she wanted to learn. Instead, Daegan went through every Etheria found in Arcadia. Afterwards, they looked at the most common Etheria living amongst human society and what Trucekeepers usually had to deal with. He was impressed by the number of species she already knew.

Come day two, he explained more about the specifics of the Etheria she would encounter; their weaknesses and strengths and how to turn them to her advantage.

On the third day, he started a crash course in blood magic that continued for the rest of the week. Hannah had been looking forward to learning about magic as much as Etheria but never realised how arduous it would be.

'Stand there,' he instructed as he pushed the desks to the edge of the classroom. 'Now, show me your blood crystal.'

Hannah retrieved the crystal from her pocket and held it out. He inspected it briefly and nodded.

'Good. It's fairly standard.'

'In a bad way?'

'No, it makes things easier.' Daegan opened a chest and rummaged around before bringing out a grubby dagger and handing it to her.

'Here.'

Hannah took the weapon and raised an eyebrow. 'Haven't got a nicer one?'

Daegan grinned. 'I know. I had the same reaction to that one too. Don't worry, it's just a training one. You can upgrade once you master the basics.'

'I don't understand. You said we were doing magic. Why do I need a dagger?'

'Trucekeepers rarely use blood crystals with their hands. Sorcerers—witches and warlocks—don't even *need* blood crystals, but it helps them channel their magic; makes it easier to control. Without this dagger, your magic is weaker, less focussed. Plus, how else are you supposed to give the crystal your blood?'

Hannah glanced down at the dagger, keeping her fingers away from the rusty blade. She wondered when she got her last tetanus shot.

The handle was scratched and showed signs of use, but what Hannah noticed most was a small hole, perfectly sized for her crystal and, just above, a minuscule hole the size of a pin.

'I put my crystal in here?' Hannah pointed to the larger hole.

Daegan nodded.

The crystal slotted in with ease. She tipped it upside down, her hand ready to catch the crystal, but it stayed in securely.

'Blood crystals are amazing, aren't they? It won't come out unless you want it to.'

Hannah prodded it with her thumb, and as promised, it slipped out obediently. She laughed, impressed with how easy it all was.

'Okay! Tell me what to do next. Just point and shoot?' she asked, aiming the tip of the blade at Daegan's face.

Daegan ducked down and ripped the dagger from her.

'First, *never* point this at anyone you do not intend to harm. Second, we call this a telum.'

'More Latin?'

Daegan nodded.

'Okay… So, point the *telum* and shoot?'

'For now, just point it. *Only* point it.'

She did so, trying not to grin too much.

'Alright. Now what do I say?' she asked.

'You *say* nothing—unless you're a moron.'

Hannah let her hand drop and pouted. 'But then how—?'

'Sorry to break it to you, but there aren't magic words. I want you to picture this in your mind,' he said as he drew a simple pattern on the chalkboard.

She stared at the pattern and swallowed her disappointment. 'Nothing's happening.'

'Because you're not doing it right!'

'Well, teach me instead of shouting at me!'

Daegan paused, then said, 'Alright, I'll slow down. When you touch your blood to the crystal, you're connecting it to your… soul, your life-force—whatever you want to call it. It can sense your feelings, hear what you hear, see what you see. Make sense so far?'

Hannah slumped back in her chair and jotted it down in her notebook. This was just the basics—if she couldn't nail this, then she doubted she would last long.

'So, if it can—' she started, but Daegan held up a hand.

'Questions later.'

Hannah grunted. *Why couldn't Aarava teach me?*

'We do not use words to command blood crystals. There can be language barriers, associations with different words or images—it can get lost in translation. What we use is much more effective.'

'And that is…?' she asked, desperate to get to the point.

'Glyphs,' he told her, pride in his voice.

'Like runes?'

'Similar. Runes were originally used as letters but are carved into blood crystals and some telums themselves—it can give them certain properties. These glyphs are different, created solely for magic. You prick your thumb with the telum—'

'I prick my thumb?'

Daegan's mouth curved in a slight grin. 'The small pinhole just above where the crystal goes. Put your thumb there, and a needle will pop up to pierce your skin and release some blood.

Hannah tilted her head. 'Don't worry. I'm pretty used to that. I can't seem to escape needles.'

Daegan nodded, satisfied. 'You'll be one step ahead of the other recruits then. Press your blood to the crystal—and when you feel truly connected—see the specific glyph in your mind. Some like to wave the telum in the glyph's pattern. Understand?'

Hannah nodded. 'I think so.' She picked up the telum and threw it from hand to hand. 'So, I press my blood to the crystal, look at *that*,'—she pointed to chalk drawing of a glyph—'and abracadabra?'

'Precisely. But don't say abracadabra.'

'Okay,' she sighed. 'Let's give it a go.' She took her position again.

'Legs wider apart,' he insisted. 'Some spells recoil. Best get used to this stance.'

'What does this glyph do?'

Daegan's mouth curved coyly. 'You'll find out,' he purred. 'Nothing too explosive.'

Explosive? Hannah thought. She could be clumsy at the best of times. She didn't want Daegan to regret having to train her more than he already did.

Hannah placed her thumb over the small hole. The pin leapt up and pierced her thumb—she barely winced; it was gentler than a lancet. She pressed it to the crystal and felt it glow beneath her rosy thumb, feeling the connection. She stared at the glyph on the chalkboard.

'It's not enough to just look at it,' she heard Daegan say. 'See it in your mind.'

Hannah tried—nothing happened.

She tried again. Still, the telum was unresponsive.

She let out an exasperated sigh. 'I can't do it,' she huffed, collapsing onto her chair.

Daegan sat opposite and studied her closely. 'What makes you happy, Hannah?' he asked.

'Honestly? Food and sleep.'

'That might work…' Daegan mused. 'Anything else? A person or a special memory?'

Hannah's mind went blank. She had forgotten everything that had ever happened to her. Then, from nowhere, came a familiar face, smiling with a mop of mousy hair and warm eyes.

'Luke,' she whispered.

'I'm guessing he's the boy you were defending at school?'

Hannah shrugged, trying to appear nonchalant.

'That ought to do. Think of a memory with him—any memory.'

Hannah closed her eyes. The first memory that came to her was a recent one—the two of them hiding after the incident with Zack, seconds before the headmaster found them.

'You see it?' she heard Daegan say.

She nodded, choosing not to tell him the range of emotions running through her mind.

'Good. Now, stand up and aim your telum again. This time, close your eyes and picture that glyph the same way you pictured your memory. Wave the telum if it helps.'

Hannah was surprised to see him give her an encouraging smile.

I can do this, she thought.

She took her place once more, spread her legs wider, anticipating Daegan's criticism, and pricked her thumb. She pressed it to the buzzing crystal and closed her eyes.

In her mind, she was hiding with Luke. So vivid, she could even see the dimples in his cheek as he laughed, feel the pressure of his hands on her back as she looked into his eyes… She glanced down and saw, etched into the closed door, the glyph. She drew it in the air with her telum.

The crystal vibrated, and she opened her eyes. The tip of the telum had lit up and a white light shone, dazzling her. She removed her thumb from the crystal and the light gently detached itself from the blade and hung in mid-air.

She jumped in triumph and turned to Daegan who gave her a rare, genuine smile.

'Fantastic. Now, this is the Illumination spell—very useful in the dark. Hold on to the crystal for less time and it would just be a flash—perfect for startling enemies. We call that a Stun spell.'

Hannah watched the ball of light moving after her, like a helium balloon chasing a toddler.

She took her stance again and pricked her thumb. She concentrated on the connection between blood and crystal, saw the glyph once more and opened her eyes. Once more, like she hoped, a white light blared from the tip of the blade. She let go of the crystal, and the other ball floated to join the first that promptly faded.

'Stop,' Daegan insisted. 'I'm proud of you—but sit down.'

'Why?' she protested.

'I'm surprised you lasted this long. Don't you feel it?'

At first, Hannah had no idea what he was talking about—but then it hit her. A sudden weakness, her head becoming light, like the ball of light floating above her. Her knees buckled, and she fell into Daegan's arms.

'Careful,' he warned her. 'Magic takes a lot out of you. Drink this.'

Without giving her time to protest, he poured a vial down her throat. It tasted like mould and moss. It made her cough, and she pushed back the urge to vomit.

'What was that?' she asked, her tongue stuck out in disgust.

'We call it aqua vitae. Blood crystals drain your blood and energy. Until you're used to it, you'll only be able to do a couple of simple spells like this. You'll have to drink aqua vitae to regain your stamina.'

'It... *drains* my blood?' she asked, horrified.

'Less than you would give if you donated,' he responded simply, 'and more than just blood—your energy. Still, for your first time you've achieved more than most people.'

'I guess I'm more used to using my blood,' Hannah mumbled.

'You can lose a lot in long battles. I've needed a few days to recuperate sometimes. But with any luck you won't face those sorts of battles.'

Hannah nodded, trying to stay conscious even after the vile liquid. 'Are there other spells beside weird light tricks?'

'Of course. You'll need to practice a variety; if you're predictable, someone can match your spell, and the crystals connect.'

'What happens then?' she asked, aware that he would probably have to explain this again when her head didn't feel so empty.

'Crystal convergence. You'll suffer that draining sensation to an intense degree. Whoever gives up first has to suffer the power of both spells hitting them. Some Trucekeepers use that to duel and practice. I don't recommend it; if you think one light spell was draining, convergence would knock you out—or worse. It'll take a couple of years of training for you to survive that.'

Hannah yawned in response.

'Bed,' Daegan insisted. 'You said sleep made you happy. Consider this a reward.'

'Was that a compliment?' Hannah mumbled through a foggy head.

'They may be rare, but I give them.'

Hannah couldn't remember how she climbed to her room. She was vaguely aware of jeers from Nathan, Jason and Amber as she passed them on the stairs. She didn't have the energy for a comeback, though. Instead, she crawled into bed and slept through the afternoon only to be woken by a sharp knock on her door.

'Breakfast!' called Daegan.

Hannah grunted and pulled the pillow over her head.

Chapter Twenty-One

Hidden Truths

BEFORE long, Daegan developed a more structured, varied approach to her lessons. In the morning, she studied Etheria theory and history, which swung between either fascinating or downright boring. The afternoons were combat and magic training in the arena. Unlike her first lesson with the magic, Hannah had no trouble with the combat.

Before Daegan taught her to fight with a telum, he insisted she be competent with hand-to-hand combat. For Hannah, it was a cinch. At school, the other girls had made fun of her for preferring martial arts, but now she was immensely thankful she hadn't quit too soon.

Daegan's moves were lightning quick; his blows hit hard, and his throws were firm. Hannah knew he was holding back but was still glad she could cope well enough, landing a few heavy hits and throws of her own.

'You're quick,' he praised her, each of his punches defended by a firm block. 'Use it to your advantage. Dodge as well.'

She did so, ducking the next two punches but missing his kick. His boot whacked her stomach, and she went flying.

'See? If you had dodged, that wouldn't have happened.'

Hannah swallowed a bitter reply and jumped back to her feet.

Daegan moved to the centre of the arena. He whipped back his coat and took his telum from the holster around his waist, like a cowboy toying with a pistol.

Hannah admired how ornate his telum was. The blade was a dazzling silver with golden edges and runes in the middle. The sapphire handle also had a golden rim where the crystal was lodged.

'When do I get one like that?'

'You've got a way to go yet. Maybe not until you get your badge.' He pointed to his diamond-shaped golden badge proudly.

'How long will that take?'

'In the past, Trucekeepers were trained rigidly for ten years—at least.'

'Ten years!' exclaimed Hannah, distraught at the thought of dedicating ten precious years of her life to this monotony.

'Things are different now,' Daegan told her. 'Recently there's been, let's say, a lack of Trucekeepers. Especially after the War.'

'What do you mean? Trucekeepers have been—what, killed off?'

Daegan nodded. 'In a way.'

'When?'

'It started during the Leviathan War—oh… fifteen, sixteen years ago.'

'What happened? Caedric glossed over that part.'

Daegan looked around, as if hoping for someone else to answer the question. 'I gave you a book about this.' He shot her a look but sighed.

'There was a leader,' he began. 'A Leviathan leader. Very persuasive; powerful. He caused a surge of support for the Leviathans among the Etheria community. It all led to a huge war. Many were killed, and it devastated us. Them too—we put up one hell of a fight.'

'The leader—you mean Thornwood, right?'

Daegan had to bite back his rage. 'He was a crossbreed. A blend of vampire and warlock blood. A ruthless combination. He led a Leviathan army against the Trucekeepers. We emerged victorious—but at a cost.'

'How many Trucekeepers survived?'

'A few,' Daegan nodded. 'But in the last couple of years…' Daegan looked her dead in the eyes. 'I'm the only one left.'

A shiver ran down her back, and a silence fell between them.

Hannah shifted on her feet, awkwardly. 'I'm not supposed to know this, am I?'

Daegan shrugged. 'It's not a secret per se, but we're not supposed to tell you until the Trials. Still, the more you know, the better prepared you are.'

He shook himself as if trying to forget. 'Anyway, that's why we're training you all so much. We need more Trucekeepers. Bring out your telum.'

Hannah did so, checked the crystal was secure and took her stance.

Daegan had her go through some of the combat glyphs she had learned already: the Stun spell—a dazzling flash of light that stops targets in their tracks; the Blast spell—a gust of energy that propelled a target backwards—and the Strike spell that felt like a hard punch. Together, she mastered the art of stringing spells together, eager for him to move on to Flame, Bolt and Ice spells.

'This isn't usually done!' Daegan called out, concentrating on protecting himself from her volley of spells. 'Trucekeepers rarely need to fight other blood crystal users. It's good to master, though. Not that you've managed to—'

Hannah expected a criticism, so cast the Stun spell, forcing Daegan to blink and shield his face. With his defences down, she launched a Strike and a Blast spell. He flew off his feet and landed with a heavy thud.

'Well…' he said, dusting himself off, 'you learn quickly.'

'I know,' said Hannah, hiding her cocky grin.

The lessons didn't stop there. For weeks, Daegan insisted Hannah continue a strict regimen of magic, combat and Etheria lessons. Her favourite spell was the Tracker spell that lit up recent footprints. Once she had mastered that, Daegan hid somewhere in the labyrinthine castle, leaving Hannah to find him as fast as possible with the spell. It was even harder when he hid in Sotera, the quaint Etheria village behind the castle, but Hannah managed to find him eventually, chugging skaldmead with a red-faced shōjō who was struggling to stay on his feet. She had taken much longer than she was supposed to, instead delighting in the bustle of Etherian urban life; window shopping and eavesdropping while trying some skaldmead of her own. She had had to swear a cheeky clurichaun to secrecy though; she had mistaken him for a leprechaun—*honestly, what's the difference?* she thought bitterly to herself—and he had threatened to tell Daegan she had been drinking skaldmead without permission. She couldn't wait to be able to explore Sotera herself.

Hannah adored wandering through Phulakopis, the busy avenue beneath the castle. Arcadia Castle towering over the avenue was a constant reminder of the Trucekeepers protection, but it had a different atmosphere to the castle. It felt more peaceful and relaxed like Sotera, only stocked with everything required to keep the Trucekeepers running; armouries, blacksmiths and crystal huts.

Her combat training soon progressed to weapons, mainly sword-fighting and archery.

'What's the point of learning to fight with a sword if I use my telum?' Hannah asked.

'I love your curiosity, Hannah, but do you always have to challenge the status quo?'

Hannah was only partly listening. Sword in hand, she was concentrating more on hitting the dummies as quickly as possible.

'You could just as easily use your crystal with a sword-telum. Some Trucekeepers have done.'

'Because they're smart cookies like me!' she shouted, landing a killer blow in the neck of a dummy, before a quick horizontal swipe saw its head fly across the arena.

'There's not an infinite supply of these,' he scolded her, throwing the now decapitated dummy on the heap of others. 'Why settle for one weapon when you can have two?'

Saying no more, Daegan pricked his thumb and pressed it to the crystal. With a slight flash, the telum grew until it looked nothing like his telum at all. Instead, there was a red handle with intricate carvings on the hilt and ruby patterns running up the blade.

'Woah!' exclaimed Hannah, her eyes wide with astonishment. 'That's one bad-ass sword, Daegan. Compensating for much?'

He ignored her and, with a smooth motion, cleaved the head off a dummy summoning a thundering tremor beneath their feet. Small clouds of sand and dust floated from the arena floor.

'Is that an earthquake?'

Daegan chuckled and waved his sword. 'It's this. Swords aren't always mere instruments of war to cut and stab. Some are imbued with special properties. Not all of them—the ones that exist are rare. This one I picked up during a little expedition.'

'Fancy,' Hannah commented.

'It's called Groundbreaker. We're uncertain of its origin, but we have theories. It glows red when I'm in danger and causes earth tremors. Handy for when a scrap gets vicious.'

'Can I?' she asked, reaching out her hand.

Daegan looked at her with a glimmer of amusement and handed her the sword. Once in her hand, she was dismayed to see it revert to Daegan's normal dagger-telum.

'What happened?'

'Weapons are bound to the crystal itself, not the telum. It requires a constant supply of the user's blood to summon the sword—my blood for Groundbreaker. Sorry,' he said with a satisfied smirk.

Hannah gazed at her own crystal. She was learning more and more each day and couldn't help wondering what secrets might already be hidden within her own crystal.

Chapter Twenty-Two

Trucekeeper Toys

HANNAH had asked for a sword to bind to her crystal every day for a week, and every day Daegan refused. 'Not until you're ready,' he would tell her. At this rate, Hannah feared she never would be. However, Hannah was soon given more to train with.

After picking her up from a lonely breakfast, Daegan guided her deep underground into the heart of the castle, the walls becoming damp and the temperature cold.

'You're improving with combat and magic,' he said as they descended a spiral staircase. 'You've nearly caught up with the other trainees.'

'Does this mean the faeries will bind a sword to my crystal?' Her heart thumped in her chest.

As expected, Daegan gave her a tired look. 'We've been over this, Hannah—summoning a sword so early in your training is unwise.'

'At least let me *try*!' she pleaded.

But it was no use. 'I'm afraid I can't allow that, Hannah,' he said, 'but there is something I wanted to give you.'

By now, they had reached the bottom of the seemingly never-ending staircase and entered a room unlike the rest of Arcadia. Most of the castle and its grounds were old-fashioned and traditional; Gothic and Victorian, or stuck in the medieval ages. This room seemed far more advanced. There were countless worktops, each with one or two men in long dark coats, masks secured to their faces, busy working on a variety of technological projects. Hannah saw as many weapons here as she had at the blacksmith, but there were more than just blades: bubbling vats of viscous liquids, large containers labelled 'nitro-glycerine' and tall posts pulsing with azure electricity.

'Don't move!' shouted an angry voice.

Hannah halted just in time as an arrow whistled past her face. Her eyes darted to watch the arrow fly into its mark, a straw mannequin that promptly burst into flames.

Hannah laughed out loud. 'Now *this* I didn't expect!'

'Ah, Talos!' Daegan called as he approached one of the men.

This man's coat had a green tinge, but his face was a mystery, hidden behind an off-white mask. It had black opaque circles for eyes and a protruding nose resembling an enormous bird. It immediately reminded Hannah of plague doctors.

'Hannah, meet Talos. Talos, my newest trainee.'

'Bit young, isn't she?' chided Talos in a thick London accent.

'But eager, I think you'll agree, and quite the capable little fighter.'

A frown crossed her face. She resented being referred to as "little", regardless of the context. Her mind wandered as she watched two men suck up a purple liquid in a pipette and drop it on a sheet of metal. In seconds, the metal crumbled away until it was nothing but dust.

'Talos is our technological weaponry expert,' Daegan told her, his eyes sparkling with boyish excitement. Hannah's curiosity peaked; she had never seen Daegan like this.

'I won't keep you. I'm sure you're almost as busy as I am,' Talos snapped as he gestured to a worktop. 'Laid out before you is the standard equipment for Trucekeepers. You may select alternative equipment depending on the mission. From left to right, you have your belt-rope, wrist-bow, throwing knives or shurikens, selected poisons and shield gauntlet. Understand?' He gazed at her through the thick circles where his eyes should be.

'Er, bits,' she replied. 'Shurikens—they're like ninja throwing stars, right? Throwing knives are self-explanatory. Poisons...' She looked up questioningly.

Talos tutted. 'Shurikens injure, stun—whatever you want. Poisons are used with throwing knives. Select the poison you desire, coat the blade and—throw. Anything else?'

'Yeah. I don't understand the—what was it? Wrist-bow?'

'Which part do you not understand?' he asked patronisingly.

'What it is.'

'Obviously, it's a bow that one wears on the wrist,' he explained, as if she were a child. He grabbed her hand. 'Like so.' He wrapped a heavy piece of leather round her wrist and tied the straps. 'Now, if you wouldn't mind flicking your hand back...'

Hannah wasn't sure what was about to happen, so her whole body tensed up. 'Like this?' She kept her arm horizontal and flicked her hand upwards.

A clunky box of metal from beneath sprang to life, and Hannah pulled the trigger without a second thought. An arrow shot out at incredible speed, embedding itself into what looked like a painting of Talos—or at least someone with the same mask.

'I gather these are like firearms used in *your* world,' he said with a touch of disdain.

'Yeah, we call them guns,' Hannah said, a brow furrowed in confusion. 'Why don't you just shoot Etheria with these?'

Daegan coughed, embarrassed. 'Aside from only killing as a *last resort*...'—his eyes gazed into hers, trying to solidify the importance of those words—'you must remember that Etheria are unique, and we need to keep the Truce. We make our weapons from adamant, a specific but rare metal—one that can actually harm them. A simple steel-sword or lead-bullet is less effective. We don't have enough adamant to fire countless arrows. And besides, we can't allow human scientists to discover adamant. Furthermore,' he coughed, 'we have not yet been able to fire adamantine bullets with gunpowder. They don't react well together.'

'There's only one metal you can use against Etheria?'

'Four actually,' Talos chipped in, 'but we don't use iron as its mere presence can be dangerous to faeries, or silver as that's also poisonous to many Etheria. We mine adamant from our own Cave of Melissani. Alternatively, you can use orichalcum, but...'

'But what?'

'Sadly, orichalcum can only be mined from Atlantis,' Daegan explained, 'but they're now independent and not open to trade negotiations.'

Hannah shrugged, bored already by the politics. 'That sucks.'

'Quite.' Talos took over. 'Remember these arrows have a range of up to twenty yards.'

'That's it?'

'If you don't appreciate the technology, leave it *here* and risk your life out *there*,' he snapped. 'She's worse than you used to be, Daegan. Is there anything else that requires further clarification?'

'Yup,' she said, untying the wrist-bow and replacing it on the desk. 'Belt-rope?'

'Standard belt worn around the waist or across the body—however you want. Small compartments for extra arrows, potions or poisons. On the buckle here,' he demonstrated, 'is a lever. Press that, and a rope will extend.' As promised, when he pressed the lever, a rope fell from the belt, dangling at their feet and coiling neatly on the ground. 'Press the button, and it will shoot out at speed. The end is magnetised to loop around objects. Used for a variety of purposes, the possibilities are endless.'

He pressed the lever once more and, like a tape measure, the rope shot back into its housing within the belt.

'Impressive,' she conceded, holding back a smile. She felt like a kid in a toy shop. 'And the last one?'

'As I said earlier, a shield gauntlet. Attach it to your other arm, like so.' He attached the leather wrapping to her left arm. Hannah noticed how it was heavier than the wrist-bow.

'Where's the shield?'

Talos ran a gloved finger along a thick metal line running down her forearm. 'Here. Whereas with the wrist-worn firearm you flick your hand up, this time you flick your hand *down...*'

As per his instructions, Hannah curled her hand downwards. The gauntlet clicked, and the metal expanded on top of her arm, revealing a dark grey, oblong shield that ran the length of her forearm.

'Very useful,' Daegan commented. He activated his own. Hannah remembered it from his fight with Zelom and took a moment to admire it. It was black with a picture of a blue wolf and a lightning bolt. 'Particularly helpful when fighting an opponent with a sword.' He nodded towards the exit. 'There's a shortcut to the arena that way.'

Daegan bade farewell to Talos, telling him she would take the shield gauntlet now to train. The rest of the equipment would remain in the lab, but Hannah couldn't resist sneaking a toy for herself. She quickly cast her eyes over the equipment and pocketed the belt-rope before heading into the arena.

Chapter Twenty-Three

Play Time

HANNAH enjoyed training with the shield. She found it easier than dodging and considerably less painful than deflecting punches with her bare arm. She quickly learnt to use it when fighting with her telum too, and before long, she was as adept with the shield gauntlet as she was with everything else.

Having caught up on all the Etheria theory, the final week of training was predominantly physical. As Daegan explained, she wouldn't often find herself battling crystal against crystal, sword against sword, or even fist to fist.

'So,' he said, 'we put them *together*. Fighting with your fists, telum, magic and any other equipment you have.'

'Like a sword,' she muttered bitterly.

'There's more to magic than just summoning a sword.'

She soon found her imagination light up, imagining various combinations to blend the fighting styles together.

'It's the best way to fight most enemies, be they Leviathans, Pyres, Thrunters,' he continued, substituting his own telum for a training one.

'Why are you doing that?' she asked hesitantly. 'We're not fighting each other, are we?'

'Of course! No better way to learn.'

'But if we're using everything I've learnt so far won't that be a little… full on?'

She didn't want to admit to feeling nervous. She could take in one thing at a time, but putting it all together and facing Daegan at the same time…

'*Dulce periciulum*—danger's sweet. Show me what you've learned!'

With that, he took a stance and raised his telum to her chest. He always recommended going for the body; it was the largest area and able to cause a lot of damage.

Hannah carefully manoeuvred herself into the same stance and cracked her knuckles. As soon as she raised her telum, Daegan quickly cast a spell. Hannah flew back, thudding to the ground in a cloud of dust.

She knew Daegan wouldn't miss the opportunity, so rolled out of the way, narrowly avoiding his boot as it crashed into the ground.

Crouching on the balls of her feet, she swiped at his legs with her own. He crashed to the ground as well, firing a Strike spell as he did. It hit her in the face and pushed her onto her back. She wasted no time in rolling to her feet, just in time to dodge a fist.

Hannah pierced her thumb on her telum, but it was too late. With a flash of light, he stunned her, senses only returning when she felt a thump in her stomach. She fell to her knees, disappointment surging through her veins. *I lost!*

'That would have been it,' he growled, his telum against her throat. 'Dead.'

'Not if you're gloating,' she hissed through gritted teeth as she flicked her left hand down, and the shield slid into place.

She swiped his telum away with her shield and leapt up, launching a kick that hit its mark. Then a punch, slap and throw in one smooth motion.

Daegan jumped back up.

'That's more like it,' he told her, a smile breaking through. 'Let's crank this up a notch.' He pressed his thumb to his crystal, and Groundbreaker formed in one hand. On the other, his own shield clicked into position.

Well, that's not fair.

His sword crashed down, and a tremor shook the arena. Hannah fought for her balance, only just managing to dodge as he swiped with his sword. She raised her arm as his sword crashed against her shield. She grunted against the thud, unable to see his other hand punch her face.

She tasted blood and spat it out. *Time to fight dirty.*

She punched; he dodged. She kicked; he dodged again. A punch, a block. He lunged with his sword and missed her by inches. The earth quaked in terror as it hit the ground.

Then Daegan lost his balance—that was all Hannah needed. Like lightning, she let out a firm slash with her telum. Even with her blunt blade, it sliced through Daegan's coat.

He paused and looked down, touching the wound and pulling away bloody fingers.

Hannah's heart pounded, adrenaline coursing through her veins. Pressing her thumb to the crystal, she fired a blinding flash. As he blinked away the light that scarred his vision, she punched him in the gut and kicked his hand. Groundbreaker flew away, returning to a telum as it clattered to the ground. She fired a Strike spell that hit him full in the face and a Blast spell that propelled him backwards.

She let out a laugh as he fell to the ground, lost in a cloud of dust and sand.

Daegan staggered to his feet and made his way to Hannah, every step a struggle.

'Sorry,' she said sheepishly, flicking her hand downwards and sending the shield back into the gauntlet.

'Early finish today,' he told her with a grimace. 'I might need to go to the medical bay.'

He looked at her with a blend of jealousy and pride. '*Ad astra per aspera.*'

'Meaning?'

'Through hardships, to the stars… You weren't a bad one to train.' He shook her by the hand. 'Congratulations. I think you're ready to join the others. They won't know what's coming.'

Hannah smiled and shook his hand, before bringing her arms around him in a hug. His body stiffened immediately, and he tried to pull away.

'I'm still your training officer though,' he told her through the suffocating hug.

'I know,' she said, her smile beaming into the coat she had sliced open just seconds earlier.

I wouldn't have it any other way.

Chapter Twenty-Four

No Place Like Home

IT had only taken a month of Daegan's intense training regimen for Hannah to catch up with the others. He had taught her from sunrise to sunset, whereas the other trainees only had a few hours of training a day—although they were expected to retreat to the library afterwards and pour over a mass of books. Needless to say, very few trainees ended up in the library at all.

To Hannah's surprise, there were many Etheria trainees, all assigned to different Truceleaders as mentors. They had lived in Arcadia their whole life but were still getting used to living in the castle instead of dwellings like Sotera and Phulakopis.

There was a mermaid, Taniiya, who for obvious reasons mainly attended meals and lessons by the lake. There was a dwarf, Fennrock, who was the son of Braddock, something he was eternally proud of. Celeste and Luminon were two elves, distant cousins of Eldrin and Aleesia respectively, and just as cold and impersonal. Asti, a satyr, and Rideo, a faun, had been best friends since childhood and spent most of their time joking together and pulling pranks on the others. And finally, there were Natala, Limara and Mimi, happy-go-lucky nymphs who preferred drinking, dancing and flirting than studying. Natala was a mountain-based oread nymph, with smooth dark skin and bright eyes that never failed to enchant the satyrs; Limara was a meadow-loving leimakid nymph, her golden skin and straight black hair always immaculate; Mimi was a limnad nymph, often found skipping around a lake, her tanned skin constantly wet.

Unlike Nathan, Jason and Amber, Hannah got on with all of them very well, conscious of the irony that she was more friendly with Etheria than her fellow Humans. Although they had lived in Arcadia their whole lives and were set in their ways, they were ever welcoming to newcomers. Still, Hannah struggled to feel like one of them.

After Byron's seemingly endless lesson on Vampire History—*How can anyone make vampires boring?* she wondered—Aarava's lecture on the importance of runes and Braddock's enthusiastic talk about his preference for battle-axe telums, Hannah made her way to the library, hoping to avoid Nathan, Jason and Amber at all costs.

As expected, the library was empty, save for a wizened elf studying an old parchment and Mantir, the minotaur general of Arcadia's army, frantically scribbling notes from a dusty book.

Hannah's attention turned to a hushed but heated debate. She turned to see Drakkar hissing threats to Axis who adamantly refused to look him in the eyes.

'Listen, you half-breed, I *need* this book!'

Arms crossed and eyes fixed to the wall, she shook her head. 'Absolutely not. You may be a Truceleader, but that book is classified—even to you.'

'Then what's the point of having the damned thing here?' he snarled.

'For the only ones who *are* authorised,' she answered simply.

Drakkar tapped his foot. 'And pray tell, they are…?'

'That's also classified.'

With a frustrated grunt, Drakkar swept his hand and threw the papers on Axis' desk over the floor before storming out of the library.

Hannah rushed to help Axis.

'No need,' she said in a hushed voice. Hannah could scarcely believe she stood up to someone like Drakkar.

'It's fine. I'm surprised at how you dealt with him. He's not my favourite person here.'

'Nor mine,' she admitted, peering over her shoulder to make sure he had left.

'What book did he want? Is *Fifty Shades of Grey* locked up somewhere?'

'I'm afraid I can't tell you.'

Hannah hid her disappointment behind a smile.

'What did he mean when he called you a half-breed? You're an elf, right?'

Axis shuffled her papers and avoided Hannah's gaze. 'In a way,' she said, 'but only half-elf. In fact, I'm only half-Etheria; my father was a human—like you. At least, that's what I was told. I never met him. My mother was frightened to death that if I grew up in the real world, I might inadvertently break the Truce… You know how kids talk. So I was taken here. Most accept me for the strange mystery I am, no questions asked—that's the beauty of Arcadia. But some like Drakkar…' She shrugged.

After making her excuses, Hannah left the library, preferring not to be the only trainee there; she had plenty of books from Daegan in her room anyway. Even after a month, she struggled to see Arcadia as home. Who was she to live in the same castle as mythical creatures and the brave Trucekeepers who protected them?

She trudged up the stairs feeling sorry for herself, her fingers running along the marble banisters, stroking the pillars, and locked herself in her room. She tried reading one book but failed to focus her mind. Instead, she flicked through the detailed pictures or stared out the window.

She had quickly fallen in love with the view from her room. It almost made the arduous climb up the tower worth it. High in the castle, she could see all of Arcadia; from the Cave of Melissani to the forest and the dwelling within where nymphs, satyrs and fauns lived with other Etheria who preferred to live amongst the trees rather than a house in Sotera; from the lake to the mountains where wild Etheria Hannah hadn't seen yet lived peacefully. Etheria roamed free—laughing, loving and living. It was a good place, a *cheerful* place; so why wasn't it home?

Chapter Twenty-Five

Put on Pause

HANNAH sat at her usual spot in the dining hall, making sure to be as far from the trainees as possible. Given the chance, it wouldn't take long for Nathan, Jason and Amber to turn them against her. Fortunately, they hadn't succeeded just yet, but the whispers and giggles were audible. Hannah glared at them and, afraid of being noticed, they swiftly looked away.

Hannah sighed. *Why stay here?* she wondered. She had given it a go, but it was no different to school—not that going back there was an option.

'I have a small announcement for the trainees,' a bored-sounding Byron announced in a monotonous voice.

'Oh, is it time for the Trials?' shrieked Amber, jumping in her seat with excitement.

Hannah couldn't help rolling her eyes. Amber glared at her, but Hannah just glared back. She bit into a sausage and let the juice flow down her chin. Amber looked away, revolted.

'I'm afraid not, Miss Fawcett,' replied Byron, exasperated to be relaying the message at all. 'As you should be aware, they only occur during eclipses—of which one will not occur for some time.

Fortunately, I might add, as I don't think anyone here is capable of passing yet.' He sniffed with disdain. 'My announcement is simply that today you shall meet with your own personal trainer rather than group training. That is all.'

And with that, he disappeared. Hannah turned round, craning her neck to see where he went.

'Looking for someone?' called another voice.

To her surprise, Daegan sat opposite Hannah with as much of a friendly smile as he could muster. It didn't suit him; he looked more awkward than amiable. Still, she was pleased to see him. She had to hide a smile when she spotted the polka-dot piece of material Lena used to patch up the hole she had cut in his coat during their fight.

'Long time no see,' Hannah said, spearing another greasy sausage.

'It's only been a couple of days. I've been on a job.'

'Ooh, exciting. Do tell,' she said, munching through the sausage.

'Afraid I can't. Some jobs I can talk about. But this one…'

'Oh, go on!' Hannah pleaded. She leaned forward and whispered, 'I won't tell anyone.'

He sighed and peered around. 'Well, without going into too much detail—because I *can't*—I was in Italy, near the Alps.'

Hannah whistled. 'Very nice. I suppose this job comes with some perks. Where did you stay? Five-star hotel?'

'Nothing like that. Drakkar makes travel too easy to warrant accommodation.'

'How so?'

'He can create portals—a quick way to travel. Warlocks are wonderfully rare. We're lucky to have him.'

Hannah grimaced. *Even a bully like him is great. Everyone here is so great. And then there's me…*

'What were you doing there?' she asked.

'Talking to a badalisc.'

Hannah frowned and took another bite of sausage. 'Don't think I know that one.'

'Imagine a sort of—demonic goat.'

Hannah held back a laugh, and even Daegan grinned.

'Well, it's a little more than that. He's not usually much trouble. In fact, the people of Andrista have a whole tradition focused on him, and most sightings are assumed to be part of their festival. But he's been causing more trouble than we allow recently. I just had to calm him down.'

'Did he put up a fight?'

Daegan tightened his lips. 'No. We had a peaceful, diplomatic... chinwag.'

'So if he's not a danger to anyone, why not just leave him be? The Truce doesn't seem fair sometimes.' She frowned and pushed a bit of egg around her plate.

'Careful. You're starting to sound like the Voiceless.'

'The who?'

'The Voiceless Dawn.'

'Caedric mentioned them a while back. Who are they?'

Daegan pinched his lips together. 'You should have read about them by now. I do give you a reading list for a reason, you know.'

'Yeah, yeah.' Hannah preferred not to dwell on the pile of books in her room—a pile that never seemed to diminish.

'The Voiceless Dawn are a group of revolutionaries. They don't believe the Truce is necessary for peace and think Etheria and humans could live together. So, they're against the Trucekeepers, but even more against the Leviathans.' He narrowed his eyes. 'They've been quiet since the War, actually. I suppose it proved that the Truce is the best way to avoid bloodshed—for now at least.'

Hannah raised her eyebrows. 'It almost sounds like you admire them.'

'I do a bit.' Daegan nodded. 'Is that a surprise?'

'Sort of. I thought you were more a ride or die Trucekeeper.'

'I am, but only out of necessity. If we could all live side-by-side without spilling blood, I'd join the Voiceless Dawn at the drop of a hat.'

'Not your hat though,' Hannah said. 'I can't imagine you'd ever choose to drop that.'

Daegan smirked. 'What the Voiceless want is a beautiful dream—but a naïve one. Trucekeepers may not be ideal, but it's the best way to keep everyone safe. Anyway...' He sighed and tapped the table to change subjects. 'I just came to say hello—'

'Hello,' Hannah replied.

'Lessons going well?'

'I guess,' she grumbled. 'But I wanted to ask—'

'Jolly good. Anyway, I know what Byron told you all, but I'm afraid I can't train you this week.'

Hannah nearly choked as she felt her elevated mood drop.

'What?' she hissed. 'I've finally caught up with *them*,'—she tilted her head towards the other trainees—'and now they're going to overtake me again!' She ran her hand through her hair, resisting the urge to tug on it. 'Do you realise how much they're going to love this? I bet the Voiceless don't have this problem. Maybe I should join them instead.'

'I'm sorry. Really. But something's come up that needs my attention. It might do for some time.'

'How long?'

Daegan shrugged. 'I can't be sure. Perhaps a month— approximately.'

'A month? You're my personal *trainer*, and you're refusing to *train* me for a *month*?'

Daegan didn't reply. His face remained hidden beneath the brim of his wide hat, and he avoided her gaze.

'I'm sorry,' he told her in an earnest tone. 'I won't ignore you for the *entire* month and will try to call in occasionally. And, excluding today, you'll still be taught by others like normal. I believe Mantir's giving a lecture on battle formations. I saw him prepping in the library—he's very nervous. For today, get through your reading list. That's an order.'

Hannah shovelled the remaining contents of her breakfast into her mouth, ignoring the thought at the back of her mind that wondered how a fierce minotaur could be nervous of a group of teenagers.

'Fine,' she muffled through a mouthful of food. 'See you in a month.'

Chapter Twenty-Six

No Longer Special

HANNAH delighted in the gentle breeze that caressed her cheek and blew her hair across her face. Daegan wouldn't approve of her sitting precariously on the windowsill, her legs dangling down the side of the tower and her toes wiggling in the cool breeze—and that thought made it even better. She ran her finger across her right thumb, feeling the gentle bumps the telum had given her as it constantly pricked her thumb for blood. She had become so used to it before Arcadia; she wondered how the other recruits were getting on with it.

Arcadia could be difficult: the lessons, the trainees, sometimes Daegan… But the view from high up was worth it. It all looked so peaceful, idyllic even. Not needing her insulin pump made it even better; it had been such a relief when she had slid it out and given it to Lena, hoping never to need it again. She couldn't help but feel naked without it, though certainly wouldn't choose to go back to wearing it if she could help it.

She glared at the intimidating pile of books in her room. *Later*, she thought as she turned her back to them.

The sun shone high in the sky, and a couple of baby dragons played with each other above the treetops. Mermaids dove in and out of the sparkling lake as hippocamps raced across the surface. Nymphs, satyrs and fauns lounged in the meadow, playing flutes and drinking wine. Closer to the castle, elves and dwarves were having a heated debate about philosophy while Mantir trained the armour-clad Etheria of the Arcadian army.

Part of Hannah wanted to join in and be part of the happy every-day life; but she didn't dare. Daegan gave her strict instructions to get through her reading list. It wasn't worth being caught disobeying him. Instead, she surveyed the beauteous surroundings, happily procrastinating.

A small cloud of dust from the arena caught her eye. She frowned. There was no combat training scheduled for that day, and no one was supposed to be in there.

Unless a couple of trainees had sneaked off by themselves.

With a smirk, Hannah leapt from the windowsill and pulled on her shoes. This was too good an opportunity to pass up. As Daegan had told her, fighting was strictly prohibited in Arcadia unless in authorised training sessions. Perhaps it was a couple of overly energetic trainees keen to show off. And if it was Nathan, Jason and Amber... Hannah's eyes sparkled as she imagined Caedric leading them out of Arcadia, wiping their minds and shaking his head in disappointment.

Hannah hurtled down the castle and whistled through the maze of corridors until she came to the arena. She strained her ears, hearing grunts and punches. They were men, no doubt about that. Hannah felt a twinge of disappointment; she had hoped it was Amber—she was the worst. Perhaps it would be Nathan, their ringleader.

She hugged the corner of the wall and peered around. The sight that greeted her, however, was not one she had expected.

The one exchanging punches and blocks was not Nathan, Jason or Amber, nor any other trainee. Through a cloud of dust, Hannah saw Daegan exchange fists with someone else—a boy, more or less her age, with close-cropped hair and dark skin. He was quite handsome, Hannah thought, save for the wisp of hair on his large chin, but that didn't change her reaction.

She felt a hole in her stomach, as if someone had punched her gut. That was *her* trainer! Not his—whoever he was. Every trainee had one trainer assigned to them and only them. No one else had to share—so why did she? Was this Daegan's idea of a joke?

The feeling of betrayal hit Hannah like a tidal wave. While all the other trainees in Arcadia were with their trainer right now, he hadn't even had the decency to tell her she had been replaced.

She almost cheered when the boy threw a heavy punch that whacked Daegan in the face. Daegan held up an obnoxious hand and surrendered. As the boy raised his fists in triumph, she wished she could smack the smirk from his face. Daegan gave him a handshake that turned into a ridiculous man-hug, patting each other on the back. Hannah had seen enough.

She didn't know where she was running to. She didn't want to go to her room, nor the dining hall. Axis could help in the library and Caedric was a trustworthy shoulder to cry on, not that she wanted him to see her cry at all. But she kept running, eventually reaching a dead end. Her legs cried out with exhaustion, and she let her weak knees collapse to the floor.

After a minute, she rose to her feet and realised she was near where she had arrived in Arcadia all those months ago. It would be so easy to run away. She could tell the world about Etheria, break the Truce. There would be no sweeter revenge!

But then what? She would have an army of Trucekeepers looking for her, dead-set on wiping her memory—or worse. Who would be the one to silence her? Daegan? The new boy he was training? Maybe even her tormentors? No, she couldn't leave. Staying would be better than any of them getting the better of her.

She turned to head back but halted by a door she hadn't noticed before; one with a golden arch with intricate runes carved onto it.

She stepped inside, taking a moment for her eyes to adjust to the darkness. She was on top of a stone staircase that overlooked a large room held up by four tall pillars, each one adorned with a gently flickering fire lamp.

She crept down the stairs, drawn in by the secretive room. It was so large, yet so empty. Every room in Arcadia had a specific purpose, yet this one's eluded her.

A large clank of metal came from above, and she instinctively dived behind a pillar. She stood as still as a statue, acutely aware of her heart pounding, and prayed whoever had entered the room would not hear her.

The mysterious figure lingered by the door, peering out into the corridor before creeping inside and carefully locking it behind him. As he made his way to the middle of the four pillars, Hannah took a chance and peered around. She nearly coughed in shock as she saw the red eyes pierce through the dark. Shrouded in shadow, the figure grasped an ebony telum, which he waved with a sharp gesture.

The fire lamps roared, illuminating the room and the figure. This wasn't just a trainee snooping around.

Drakkar was up to something.

Chapter Twenty-Seven

A Closed Door

HANNAH leaned against the pillar and drew out her telum. She focused on her breathing the way Daegan had taught her. With a bloodied thumb pressed to her crystal, she imagined two glyphs in her head. She felt her blood flow through the crystal and her head became light—a familiar sign the spells had worked.

These were two useful glyphs Daegan had taught her for stalking Etheria; one enshrouded her in shadow, making her hard to spot amongst the dark corners of the room; the other muffled any sound she made. With any luck, she would see everything, while Drakkar stayed none the wiser.

Peering around the pillar, Hannah admired the wall Drakkar faced. Now lit up by the torches, she saw an enormous bronze circle against the wall with a small hole in the middle, hundreds of runes etched into the surface.

Drakkar approached the wall and drew out five blood crystals from a pouch. He held each one to the firelight to inspect them before placing one after another into the small hole. Each made a curious clicking sound, like a key in a lock.

Dissatisfied, Drakkar grunted and shook his head. He pocketed the crystals and climbed back up the steps, muttering to himself.

After the decisive clunk of the door as he left sounded, relief flooded her as she removed her thumb from the crystal. The concealing shadow dissipated, and her breathing and heavy heartbeat became audible again.

She approached the bronze wall, unable to recognise any of the runes. Curious, she placed her own crystal inside the hole. But, unlike when Drakkar did it, the lock-and-key noise her crystal made was different. Less like a failed key, more like an old, heavy door unlocking.

Heart beating fast once more, she stared at the wall and waited with bated breath for something to happen.

But the crystal did nothing.

Tempted though she was to investigate further, she retrieved her crystal. If Daegan found out she was here, he'd be furious—it wasn't worth it.

Her footsteps were heavy as she left, her head a rush with countless questions. *Perhaps Axis could help*, she wondered. But if she assumed that room was off-limits to a mere trainee, would she be in trouble for having been there in the first place?

For the entire climb to her room, she could think of nothing else. *Why did none of the crystals make the same noise as mine did? And where did he get so many?* She was so absorbed with her thoughts, nothing could have prepared her for the intruder in her room.

Daegan flicked through her books. 'I thought I told you to read this afternoon.'

Flustered, Hannah suppressed a touchy reply and composed herself.

'I thought you weren't seeing me today,' she responded as she busied herself picking up the books scattered on the floor.

'Where were you?' he asked, eyes still fixed on the book in his hand. 'Bearing in mind that any answer other than "the library" is unacceptable.'

Hannah shrugged. 'The library.' She didn't dare make eye contact.

'Hm.' He turned a page. 'Funny. I didn't see you there.'

'I—I went to the bathroom.'

Daegan slammed the book shut. 'I've been looking for you for an hour,' he snapped. 'You weren't in the library. You weren't in any bathroom—trust me, Aleesia checked every female bathroom in the castle.'

Hannah shuffled her feet and looked down.

'This means: one, you've been AWOL for at least an hour; and two… You just lied to me. Twice.' His voice became a growl. 'Tell me the truth.'

'I saw you…' she whispered.

'I'm sorry?'

'I saw you!' she snapped, louder than intended.

Daegan stared. 'I don't have the faintest idea what you're—'

'The boy!' she spat. 'I saw you with that boy. Training him.'

A silence fell over them. She made sure to look him in the eyes this time.

'Hannah,' Daegan replied, his face hidden beneath the brim of his hat. 'You're overreacting.'

'I had to work harder than anyone to catch up. But you know why it wasn't too bad? Because I had you.' Daegan refused to meet her gaze. 'Like everyone else, I had my own trainer. But *unlike* anyone else, I had the *best*.'

'I understand,' he replied, calmer than she had predicted, 'but it's harder than you think. Traditionally, Trucekeepers juggle their own duties with training. It's challenging now I'm the only Trucekeeper. Even the Truceleaders have had to step in to train—that used to be unthinkable! I'm sorry you're upset that you can't have one hundred percent one-on-one time with me, but, if I were you, I would see it as a compliment.'

Hannah couldn't believe what she was hearing. 'A compliment?'

'Most other trainees haven't had nearly the same amount of time with their trainer—Truceleaders have very little time to spare. You, however, are the only one to be given a traditional training… until recently. Because you show promise. I swear, Hannah, that having another trainee won't compromise the quality of your training.'

Hannah shuffled her feet awkwardly, her face hot.

Perhaps I did overreact…

'However,' Daegan continued, 'there's little point you being here if you don't follow simple instructions.'

Hannah didn't reply.

'I told you very clearly to study; to read your books, write notes. You could have done that lying in bed or dangling your feet out the window.'

How did he know I do that?

'I *did* the reading!' she argued, so convincingly she almost believed her own lie.

Daegan cocked an eyebrow. 'Oh, really?' He gestured for her to sit.

Hannah obeyed and silently gulped.

'True or false—dwarves and elves are sworn rivals.'

Hannah thought back to her fantasy film marathons with Luke.

'True,' she said confidently.

'False. It depends on their tribes.'

It took all of Hannah's self-control not to get riled up by his patronising tone.

'Zelom attacked us when we first met. His species of Etheria was a…'

'Zburător.'

'From?'

'Romania.'

'Attributes of?'

'Wolf and dragon.'

'And?'

'Shape-shifting abilities.'

'Good.' She could tell he was holding back a smile. 'Who accompanied Gilgamesh?'

Hannah knew this was before she even came to Arcadia. 'Enkidu.'

'What species of Etheria was he?'

'Supposedly a sasquatch,' Hannah answered, relieved she had at least read the parts that interested her.

'And what was the biggest mistake made by Gilgamesh and Enkidu?'

Hannah paused, her nose wrinkled.

Daegan rolled his eyes. '*Sapere aude*,' he muttered. 'Dare to know—knowledge is power for a Trucekeeper. What is a soucouyant?'

Hannah's eyes lit up. 'A vampire.'

She jumped as his fist crashed onto her desk.

'Be more specific!' he barked. 'Where do they come from? Why are they unique?'

'I don't know!' Hannah cried out.

'They come from the Caribbean. Seen either as a reclusive old woman by day or in their true form as a fireball by night. How can a Trucekeeper combat a soucouyant?'

'Stake in her heart?'

He shot her a poisonous look. 'You destroy the skin it disguises itself in with salt. Final questions—please get them right. Who was the leader of the Leviathans?'

'Thornwood.'

'Good.' Hannah detected a slight wobble in Daegan's voice. 'And what species of Etheria was he?'

'Half-vampire, half-warlock.'

Daegan nodded curtly. 'At least you listen sometimes,' he remarked. 'Which Trucekeeper was the one who largely brought us victory?'

This was the most uncomfortable pause yet. She scrunched her eyes and racked her brain but had no answer.

'I… I don't know,' she admitted.

Fire raged in his eyes. '*You* of all people should be able to answer that!' He rubbed the back of his neck and shook his head. 'I just don't know what to do. You have the determination, physical capabilities and even aptitude to become a formidable Trucekeeper. But you just waste your talents by arguing back, being lazy, not listening—and thinking only about yourself.'

Hannah wanted to argue back but didn't know what to say. As upset as she was, she knew he had a point.

'I don't know how many more chances you deserve.'

Without another word, Daegan threw the book at her and stormed out. As his footsteps retreated, Hannah sank to the ground; small, helpless and pitifully alone.

She was used to arguments—with teachers, other pupils, Zack, her aunt. But this was different. She had disagreed with Daegan before but nothing like this. The look of sheer disappointment in his eyes… He had worked so hard for her, and she repaid him with failure.

There was nothing else for her to do. It was time to leave.

Chapter Twenty-Eight

An Open Door

SHE tried not to overthink what she would do as she shoved what little belongings she had into a bag. She toyed with the idea of bringing a book on Etheria but decided against it. There was no sense in violating the Truce out of bitterness.

At the door, she took one last look at her room. Although the bed was uncomfortable and the noise of nocturnal Etheria woke her more times than she could count, she had been happy there. For a moment, she considered staying, but her mind was made up.

With her rucksack slung around one shoulder, she crept down the corridor, taking care that every step was silent. Trainees had to obey curfew or have permission to be out of their rooms at night.

'Hey!' came a quiet whisper from behind.

Her heart flipped, and her stomach turned into knots. She expected Nathan, Jason or maybe Amber. But as she turned, she found the boy who had trained with Daegan, still in stripy blue pyjamas.

She eyed him suspiciously as he peered out of his room. 'What do you want?' she hissed.

'Where are you going?'

'What does it matter to you?'

He beckoned for her to come closer. A small glow appeared at the bottom of the staircase—two dwarves on their nightly patrol. Still on the balls of her feet, she tiptoed into his room, a finger in front of her mouth. He nodded and closed the door, listening out for the patrol. It wasn't difficult to hear them; their footsteps were loud and clumsy. Even their rattling keys were enough to wake the whole tower.

Hannah shuffled. 'Thanks,' she mumbled. 'It would have been bad if, you know... they'd caught me.' She kept her head down.

'I doubt they would have done. I can see the patrol hub from my window. They stand around a fire drinking all night. Wouldn't notice an invading lakhe if it hit them in the face.'

Hannah frowned. *How had he learned about lakhes already?*

'Lakhe?'

'Nepalese,' the boy said, simply. 'Big, red, angry face; black mane; fangs. They're demons who live in forests. Sometimes protect townspeople, sometimes start fires.'

Hannah raised her eyebrows. 'How do you know all that?'

The boy shrugged. 'I'm new, but it's exciting... and I like to read.'

'How long have you been here?'

'About a week.'

Hannah raised her head and nodded. 'And you're already better than me. Just as I thought.' She slung her rucksack over her shoulder again. 'If you'll excuse me.'

The boy grabbed her wrist. 'You are, aren't you?' he asked, looking her in the eyes.

She paused, wondering if he thought she was an Etheria like Amber had and hating everything that made her different.

'You're really leaving Arcadia?'

'You know nothing about me.'

'I know you're crazy,' he said. 'You're leaving this? This insane, magical world that's been kept secret our whole lives?'

Hannah pushed past him and strode towards the door. She agreed; the world of Etheria was incredible. But Arcadia was not her home.

'You're Hannah, right?'

She nodded.

'Then I know something else.'

Hannah groaned, loathing her curiosity. 'What else do you know, boy-I've-never-met.'

'I know you're better than me.'

Hannah let out a small laugh. 'You must be joking.'

'I mean it.'

'Yeah, says the boy who knows whatever a lakhe is. I barely know the difference between a soucouyant and a vampire.'

'So, you struggle with memorising a bunch of thick books. Big deal. Have you seen the amount we're supposed to remember? It's nuts!'

Hannah felt reassured. *At least it's not just me.*

'What if I help you?' he asked guardedly. 'There's no point reading all those books if you just forget everything as soon as you read it. What if I help you?'

'What—you'll be my teacher? What are you, some sort of Etheria master?'

'I prefer the word "tutor." I've done it before—before I found out about the whole Trucekeeper thing. You wouldn't believe the money people pay for a tutor before exams—'

'Hang on. Let me get this straight—you'll study for yourself *and* teach it all to me?'

The boy nodded.

'What's in it for you? I don't have money.'

'Like I said, you're better than me.' He quickly carried on before Hannah could talk over him. 'I can remember things—I've got a good memory and a knack for theory. But *you're* the one who can fight.'

'Good one.' She took in his physique, examining his lean body and muscular arms beneath his pyjama top. She couldn't imagine him finding combat difficult. 'You seemed to hold your own against Daegan.'

The boy went pale. 'That was rehearsed,' he admitted. 'I'm not sure when you saw us, but he walked me through an entire routine, which we practised over and over. I eventually got it—after two hours.'

Hannah thought back. Daegan had looked happy but exhausted—almost fed up. Could this boy be telling the truth?

'And the crystal's tough, too. I can remember the glyphs fine, but—'

'You have to see the glyphs in your mind's eye,' Hannah said in her best Daegan impression.

The boy laughed, quickly biting his hand to be quiet. Even Hannah smiled too.

'That's what I struggle with. But he said you were a natural!'

Hannah couldn't help grinning. '*Daegan* said that?'

The boy nodded. 'So, what do you say? I teach you the book stuff, you teach me the fighting stuff?'

He held out his hand. Hannah felt the rucksack weigh her down and wondered what to do. Stay and see it through with whoever this boy was, or leave and find her own way somewhere else...

She nodded and gripped his hand.

'What have I got to lose?'

'I'm Niall. See you at breakfast tomorrow.'

She frowned. 'How come I've never seen you at breakfast?'

'I've been having it up here. There's nothing like breakfast in bed with your favourite Etheria book.'

'Daegan said it was breakfast in the dining hall or starve.'

'I've made friends with the brownies and hobs. They get anything for you if they like you enough. Obviously, I share with the brownies—they get upset otherwise.'

Hannah laughed. 'See you tomorrow, Niall.'

She tried to keep her cool as she tiptoed back to her room, unaware of him watching as she went.

As she tucked herself back in bed, she realised she was still smiling. Arcadia might have seemed lonely, but perhaps she should give it another shot.

Chapter Twenty-Nine

A Problem Shared

THE next few days in Arcadia were the best yet. Nathan, Jason and Amber looked bitter as Hannah walked into the dining hall with Niall. Hannah could see Amber eyeing Niall, desperate to think of a cutting comment.

Despite always having his nose in a book, Niall had somehow made friends with the other trainees in the short time he had been in Arcadia. As they sat down, he reintroduced Hannah to them. Although they knew her already, they saw her in a new light with Niall by her side. For the first time, Hannah enjoyed her time in the dining hall but kept in mind the option of breakfast in bed brought by hobs and brownies.

'I have a question,' Hannah said when she was sure the others weren't listening.

'Fire away,' Niall responded between sips of coffee. He was only half listening as he sketched a chimera in his notebook.

'What do you know about blood crystals?'

'Big topic. You need to be specific.'

Hannah looked around. 'Walls.'

'Again, more specific.'

'Do you know anything about walls that can be opened by blood crystals?'

Niall pulled a face. 'A bit. Like the door to Arcadia?'

'More like—imagine a bronze-plated wall with an enormous circle in the middle, all decorated with weird line patterns and runes. Oh, and in the middle was a hole for a crystal. Ring a bell?'

'Never heard of one with runes on it. Why?'

She leaned forward so only he could hear and told him the entire story about the room and what Drakkar had been doing.

Niall shrugged. 'It's probably nothing. Doesn't sound like anything to be worried about.' He carried on sketching.

'But you weren't there,' she insisted. 'You didn't see it.'

'Okay.' He reluctantly closed his notebook. 'Show it to me.'

Hannah hesitated. She had only met Niall last night—she wasn't sure if she could trust him yet. But there was no way she was going through extra books to find the answer alone.

He looked at the wall and shook his head. 'No idea. These runes...' He stroked them, his eyes narrowed as he inspected every inch, '... are a complete mystery to me, but there must be some explanation.'

'Exactly,' Hannah nodded, 'and that's what I want to find out.'

'No. I mean—Drakkar's a Truceleader, Hannah. He wasn't just given that position randomly. He's earned it. We should give him more respect, not all this suspicion—'

'But he was *acting* suspiciously. What do you expect?'

Niall paused. 'I just think we need to tread carefully. You can't go around accusing people with no evidence. Especially Truceleaders.' He gazed at the wall again. 'But I'll find out what I can.'

Hannah beamed. She didn't want to tell him yet that the only crystal that matched the door was hers—a crystal that wasn't even forged by her; a crystal that, according to all known rules, she shouldn't even be able to use. Everything she had ever wondered about who she was could be hidden behind that door.

Chapter Thirty

Let the Games Begin

AS always, Byron carried an air of disgust, seemingly revolted at being the messenger-boy. He came to each of the trainees to tell them their timetable for the day.

'Miss Moreland. Mr Adams,' he sneered. 'Daegan shall meet you both in room 219. Enjoy.'

Their eyes met across the table, and they smiled.

Lessons with Niall were much more interesting than when it had been just her and Daegan. They cracked jokes, and Niall answered the questions Hannah couldn't, and she loved showing off by taking them both on in a practice fight.

But try as he might, Niall still struggled with combat. Every swipe with his telum missed his target. Daegan was reluctant to give him an alternate telum, determined to stick to the standard dagger. But it soon became apparent that a change was in order.

As it turned out, there were more telums than just daggers. Hannah relished the chance to try out a bow-telum, the weapon of choice for Eldrin and Aleesia. She placed her blood crystal where her hand held the bow. Every time she drew back the string, she propelled a powerful spell that hit the target harder than a spell from a standard dagger-telum.

Niall found most luck with the staff-telum. It was like a spear but with spikes on both ends and able to separate in two. With extra lessons from Aarava—the resident staff-telum expert—Niall soon held his own against Hannah, though she was still far more proficient.

Niall was much more competent at magic. The staff-telum allowed him to cast spells effectively, and he used it to his strength. He mastered basic spells in half the time it took Hannah, although he still found it difficult to cope with how much blood the crystal drained.

'You'll get used to it,' Daegan urged them, 'but you need to practice. It can be your strongest form of defence. The Shield spell, for example, *will* save your life. It'll protect you from weapons and spells—you can even control the size and shape to contain Etheria within your own impenetrable bubble.'

'How big an Etheria?' Hannah asked.

'Depends on the strength of your spell. And the only way you get stronger is…' He waved his hands, gesturing for them to finish his sentence.

'Practice,' they groaned.

'Precisely.'

But despite being such an important spell, its glyph was the most difficult yet. It was complex, and the amount of energy it absorbed was immense. Niall mastered the glyph quickly but couldn't keep it up for much more than thirty seconds before dropping to his knees and downing aqua vitae.

'Trouble keeping it up?' they heard Amber chortle a short distance away.

Hannah, however, couldn't cast it at all, no matter how hard she tried.

'Focus your mind, Hannah,' Daegan told her. 'See it, move your telum in the shape if you need to—'

'Stop badgering on!' she snapped. 'I can't do it.'

Daegan hid his frustration, but Hannah couldn't. She spotted Amber casting it expertly and discretely shot a spark of fire that scorched her hair. She screamed so loud even the alicantos flapped their wings and flew from the forest trees. Natala, Limara and Mimi made jokes behind her back for weeks after, but Asti and Rideo joked about it to her sour face, both receiving a sharp punch.

The days bled into weeks. Before Hannah knew it, the frosty chills of the early morning thawed and gave way to warmer sunrises that basked in the warmth of the rising sun.

Her heart soared each day as she awoke to training, eager to outmanoeuvre Daegan and learn what she could from Niall. He hadn't been lying about his proclivity for glyphs. He was a natural, able to cast and sustain more advanced spells than Hannah could dream of. Every day was perfectly pleasant.

Until one morning, Amber had to ruin it.

'I mean, why *wouldn't* you choose Finias? It's superior to Gorias for sure,' she said as she droned on and on over breakfast. Fennrock could barely keep his eyes open, and even Luminon looked fed up with her pompousness.

'What's this?' Hannah forced herself to ask.

Asti and Rideo shot her a warning glance.

'Oh, you don't know?' she smirked, oblivious to the surrounding groans. 'The Games, silly.'

'Games?'

'Arcadian Trainee Games,' came Niall's voice as he settled down beside her and helped himself to the mountain of fruit from a horn on the table. 'Daegan didn't tell you?'

She shook her head, biting back a few choice words about Daegan and what he seemed to hide from her.

'Well,' he said through a mouthful of banana, 'they haven't

done it in a while—not had any new trainees, you see. But it's traditionally a game to see how their training is going.'

'It's rigged,' muttered Nathan, his face like thunder. 'They know humans don't stand a chance against Etheria. If Byron just listened to me and did what I said, then I—'

'A game…' Hannah mused, ignoring Nathan. 'Like a football match?'

'Like a race!' Natala beamed. 'You're split up into four divisions: Finias, Gorias, Falias and Murias. They're named after the four cities the Tuatha Dé Danann came from before they went to Ireland.'

Hannah narrowed her eyes. She thought back to where she had heard of them before.

'Aren't they Gods?' she asked. 'Caedric mentioned something about them.'

Nathan rolled his eyes. 'Ish,' he scoffed.

'We don't know for sure, but we've always been told they were a species of faerie,' Mimi explained. 'They brought four "treasures" from their cities.'

'The Stone of Fal from Falias,' explained Fennrock through mouthfuls of food, 'the Spear of Lugh from Gorias, the Sword of Light from Finias and the Cauldron of Dagda from Murias.'

Hannah let out a sigh. 'It's too early for all these names. What are they all?'

'Not that important,' Niall told her with a smile. 'There are four divisions they split us into, and each one has its own mascot as a symbol.'

'How do we decide which division we're in?'

A week later, the trainees were huddled around a towering rock, doing their best not to giggle at the increasingly frustrated Braddock. Fennrock shuffled his feet, embarrassed.

'*Any* spell?' Amber asked, doubt smeared across her face. 'How do we know which one to cast?'

Braddock buried his face in his hands. 'We've been o'er this again and again. Ye pick *one* spell. Any spell! Cast it at that stone—the sarsen rock that looks like it came straight from Stonehenge—and pick up what it drops.'

'I bet it's rigged,' Nathan muttered.

Braddock glared at him. 'Ye connect yer blood to yer crystal, yer crystal casts a spell. This monolith can tell more about ye from that than ye'll ever know about yerself. *That's* how it tells ye which division to be in.'

'But how will I know it gives me what I want?' she replied.

The other trainees groaned.

'You won't!' Taniiya cried from the waterside. 'It'll give you the one you're best suited to. Hopefully not the same as me,' she muttered.

Alice took a hesitant step back, her thumb dancing over her telum. 'Anyone else want to go first?'

Asti and Rideo needed no encouragement as they stepped towards the towering monolith. As one, they cast their own spells that slammed into the rock. Two stones the size of their palms dropped to the ground. After a high-five, they collected the rocks, but their faces dropped.

'You're not in the same division, are you?' Natala asked with a pout.

'Falias,' Rideo sighed as he held up his stone adorned with the image of a boulder.

'Gorias,' Asti said, holding up a stone with a spear.

One by one the other trainees cast their chosen spell at the monolith and collected a stone. Celeste and Luminon were also split up: Celeste joined Natala and Jason in Murias; Limara, Amber and Nathan joined Finias. Taniiya got her wish and joined Rideo and Mimi in Falias, gleefully splashing away from Amber.

After Fennrock was assigned to Gorias, Niall stepped up, casting the Ice spell and receiving a stone with a cauldron—Murias.

Hannah breathed a sigh of relief that Niall had gone first and thought of nothing more complicated than the Ice glyph—she could copy that without difficulty. With any luck, she'll be assigned to Murias too.

Heart beating against her chest, she placed her bloodied thumb against her crystal and aimed at the monolith. The blast of frost slammed into it, and a rock trickled to the ground. With trepidation, she bent down and turned the rock over.

A spear.

'Gorias,' she groaned and evaded Niall's disappointed expression.

'It's okay,' he said. 'You've got Asti and Fennrock with you. And at least you're not in Finias with Amber and Nathan.'

She cocked an eyebrow. 'That's true.' A smile crept onto her face. 'I'm just going to feel guilty about slaying you in the Games.'

Niall gave her a playful punch. 'You wish. Let's just agree not to let Finias win.'

Chapter Thirty-One

The Starting Line

'NO, it's like *this*.' Again, Asti took his fist from his hip, brought it up to his shoulder and thrust it forward, his smile broad and unrelenting.

Fennrock's true expression hid behind his red beard, but his eyes said it all.

'It's like a spear!' Asti explained, as if it were obvious.

'I *know* what it is. But we're *not* doing it,' Fennrock said.

'Aw, why not?'

'Because it's weird! Daft bloomin' satyrs. We can have a chant—if we *must*.'

'Nope.' Asti crossed his arms in defiance. 'Victory pose or nothing.'

'Well, that's an easy choice then,' Fennrock smiled. 'Nothing!' Hannah chuckled and Fennrock turned to her, a glint in his eyes. 'See? Gorias isn't too bad.'

Hannah nodded. 'I know. It's not you guys, honest. It's just…'

'You feel closest to Niall,' Asti finished for her. 'I get it. I'm kind of mad I'm not with Rideo. But guys—this is a dream team!'

'More than mine,' came a voice behind them.

Asti broke into an enormous grin and bounded towards Rideo. 'Regret your choice yet?'

'Duh.' Rideo gestured behind him to Taniiya and Mimi lounging in the lake and laughing. 'You're all land based. I'm in a team with a mermaid and a limnad. I'm the only one representing Falias on dry land.'

A cheeky grin appeared on Asti's face. 'Well, it's a race. At least those two are fast in the water. Have you ever seen a dwarf run?'

As Fennrock shot Asti a dirty look, Hannah took the opportunity to step back and allow Asti and Rideo to have their fun winding him up. She surveyed the surrounding scene, taking in the array of colours each team wore; Falias in yellow and orange, Gorias in light and dark greens, Finias in red and black and Murias in light and dark blues. Each trainee had a badge with the insignia of their division stitched to their coloured jerkin. Among the sea of blue, Hannah spotted the tall dark figure of Niall with a black cauldron stitched on his clothes. He caught her eye and made his way towards her.

'Nice headband,' he said.

Hannah beamed. Other than Niall, she never really knew for sure which of the other trainees liked her. But she took it as a good sign that Natala had made her a headband with green jewels to match Gorias' colours. In fact, it had meant so much to her that Natala became the first trainee Hannah had hugged and, since then, the other nymphs had been finding excuses to hug her too, as had Asti and Rideo.

'I hope your team's a damn sight better than mine,' he said. 'Jason will be useless in a race. He's barely moved, the lazy thing. And Celeste and Natala don't seem to get on. Look!'

Hannah looked to where Natala was fussing around Celeste, putting make-up on her. Celeste looked tense and on the verge of an outburst, but her face was straight, like a patient cat pausing before its attack.

'It's not just them. It's probably just an elf and nymph thing. Look at Limara and Luminon.'

They turned to look over at Finias where the two in question ignored each other even though they were inches apart.

'Good team, though,' Hannah thought aloud. 'They're all fit and fast. Perfect for a race.'

'But this isn't a normal race,' Niall reminded her.

That fact had been made very clear shortly after they were assorted into their divisions. It would be a normal race from A to B but with several routes they could take. Any route was feasible, be it on land or by water, but there wasn't an easy one. All included obstacles they would need to overcome using their gear or blood crystals, and there was a range of Etheria they could ride—if they could. Out of the fourteen contestants, there would only be points for the first twelve. The division with the most points would win.

Hannah stopped listening to Niall as he explained the history of the Arcadian Games. Instead, she caught sight of Drakkar and Nathan. As chief of Finias, it wasn't too surprising Drakkar was there, but there was something about the way they were talking. Drakkar's eyes shone, and Nathan smirked as if he had been told some wonderful news. A shiver crawled down Hannah's spine, and she fingered the handle of her telum. Part of her wanted to sneak closer to listen in, but she paused to look around. Daegan had noticed them too and was frowning with just as much curiosity.

When Braddock blew the horn, the trainees assembled at the starting line by the edge of the forest. It was a warm, calm afternoon. Etheria lazed casually around Arcadia's meadow, blissful and unaware of the excitement nearby. Everyone else was buzzing around the starting position. Faeries, dwarves, hobs and brownies, kobolds and coblynaus all gathered around, their voices humming in excitement and anticipation.

The Truceleaders were also there, with Caedric beaming down from a small stand erected by the starting line. As heads of divisions, Braddock stood in front of Gorias, Aleesia in front of Murias, Drakkar in front of Finias and, by the waterside, Aarava in front of Falias.

'Trucekeeper trainees,' Caedric called out. 'United we stand.'

The trainees and Truceleaders responded in unison. 'United we stand!' they cried. Their thumbs held down their middle fingers as they moved their hands to their chests, giving Caedric the Trucekeeper salute.

'Good luck, everyone,' Caedric said. 'On your marks!'

Niall winked at Hannah. She gave him an encouraging nod in return.

'Get set… Go!'

In a splash and a flash, all the trainees leapt forward, galloping across the meadow. Some took the path by the lake, some up a hill, but Hannah stayed hot on Niall's tracks as he raced towards the forest.

Shocked and disturbed by the sudden intrusion, the birds in the trees flapped and took flight as the handful of trainees shot through the forest, zigzagging between trees, giving little heed to the twigs scraping their faces as they soared past. An enormous oak tree loomed ahead of them. The two elves went to the left, followed by Rideo and Nathan. Hannah followed suit but hesitated as she saw Niall take the right-hand side. She faltered, looking both ways.

That's when she saw it.

It wasn't the worst sin to commit—and it certainly wouldn't have killed him—but as he ran alongside Rideo, Nathan discreetly aimed his telum at a puddle ahead of Rideo and blasted it with the Frost spell. It immediately iced over a split second before Rideo landed on it. The faun's hoof skidded, causing him to almost lose his balance. Hannah held her breath, terrified that he would lose his footing and snap his neck, but he stayed up and ran faster to get away from Nathan.

Hannah took one last look back at Niall but followed Nathan, her hand on her telum at all times.

Chapter Thirty-Two

The Running Cheater

AS far as Hannah knew, Nathan had no idea she was behind him, let alone that she had just witnessed his attempt at cheating. She hung back to avoid him spotting her but made sure not to let him out of her sight for a second.

As Hannah danced over roots, she thought about what Nathan could be up to. Was it something Drakkar had told him to do? She wouldn't be surprised. Or was he out for himself, determined to win no matter the cost? That seemed just as plausible.

Hannah's lungs were burning, desperate for a respite, but Nathan showed no signs of slowing down. Instead, he flicked his wrist and readied his shield gauntlet before diving forwards. Hannah's eyes widened and her mouth dropped as she saw him dive off a cliff.

Dust flew around her ankles as her feet skidded to a halt mere inches before a steep drop. Hannah peered down and saw a deep chasm, a river trickling beneath. She felt dizzy looking down, as if she were about to topple over to her doom. She rested against a tree as she regained her composure and took a deep breath.

It was obvious Nathan hadn't jumped to his death—*more's the pity*, she thought—but she was shocked how quickly he had reacted; almost as if he knew what to expect.

Attached to the tree on her side of the chasm was a thick rope that extended over the gap to the other side. In the distance she could see Nathan shooting down the rope like a zip wire, his shield sending sparks flying as it skidded along.

She took a moment to look around her, keen to spot another route. But there was none, and there was no chance she would let Nathan win without a fight. Flicking her shield into place, she too jumped up and grabbed the zip wire. Her breath caught in her throat as she shot down the rope at a shocking speed. As the chasm soared beneath her, she raised her eyes and spotted Nathan. She was almost there. Close enough to see him staring right back at her with a smirk. Close enough to see the sunlight glint from his telum as he slashed it against the rope.

Hannah had no time to think. Her survival instincts kicked in as she bloodied her thumb and pressed it to her crystal. She pointed her telum beneath her and cast a shockwave that propelled her up through the air, tumbling onto safe land. She rolled several times as she hit the ground and slammed into a tree trunk.

Groaning and clutching her side, she struggled to her feet, ignoring her body's pleas to stop. Already Nathan had made good his escape and was nowhere to be seen. Gritting her teeth and seething, she hobbled forwards, but it was no good. Exhausted and hurt, her legs buckled beneath her as she fell to the ground. She dug her fingers into the mud, frustrated at herself for going after Nathan in the first place. *If I'd just ignored him, I'd probably be fine. Why can't I just let things go? I just...*

A snout interrupted her bitter thoughts as it prodded her shoulder. Hannah looked up and life returned to her eyes. Although straight and serious, the cat-like face looked at her with kindness and proffered its horned head for her to help herself up. She stood back and admired its sleek torso and bizarre talons on its front legs. She had heard there were calygreyhounds in Arcadia, but she'd never seen one before.

Allowing her hand to slide from its antlers along its body, she paused, trying to read the Etheria's thoughts. It craned its neck towards her and, she thought, nodded. Cautiously, she swung one leg over and hauled herself onto its back, holding on tightly to the short yellow fur. The calygreyhound gave a short shiver before bending down and leaping forwards, bounding up the path that Nathan had disappeared down. As she swayed to and fro and hung on for dear life, Hannah grinned broadly; calygreyhounds were known for speed. Even from atop its back she could feel the power in its legs with every step. Nathan didn't stand a chance now.

After a few minutes of furious riding, she emerged from the trees, galloping alongside the edge of a cliff with Arcadia's lake beneath. She wondered for a moment if Taniiya or Mimi would be down there.

The calygreyhound interrupted her thoughts with a soft squeal. Hannah looked up and saw, in the near distance, another calygreyhound also with a rider. She leant closer to her mount, and it sped up as they closed the distance.

The long blond hair streaming behind the rider gave away who it was—Luminon. Hannah gave the calygreyhound an encouraging kick to its side, and it sprinted full pelt until they were side-to-side. Luminon glared at Hannah and jerked towards her, sending his calygreyhound smacking into hers. Hannah retaliated, and the two tussled as they rode at breakneck speed, each trying to unbalance the other.

Two other riders crashed through the undergrowth to the side, both Etheria snapping at each other. Hannah immediately identified the rider with flowing dark hair as Celeste atop a haetae, a large lion-like creature covered with scales and with a horn on its head. They were known for sensing human nature and able to tell good from evil. From the way it was attacking the rival rider, Hannah knew instinctively it was Nathan.

But it took a moment to spot his mount. For the longest time, it looked as if Nathan were riding on mid-air until it galloped into the sunlight, and the fur darkened. Similar to a chameleon, a parandrus could camouflage itself—certainly a useful characteristic for someone who wanted to sneak up on other racers to take them out. Like a cross between a deer and an ox, the parandrus' long shaggy hair bounced as it bounded along heavily, shoving Celeste and her haetae closer and closer to the edge of the cliff.

Seeing his sister in trouble, Luminon seemed to forget about Hannah in an instant and instead set his sights for Celeste.

But it was too late.

Nathan drew his telum and pointed it at Celeste. He unleashed a shockwave that propelled her from her mount and sent her toppling over the cliff edge into the lake below.

The two calygreyhounds skidded to a halt. Luminon and Hannah both looked over the cliff edge, eyes bulging and mouths hanging open. Hannah looked at Luminon, trying to gauge his reaction. Anger? Betrayal?

No—he gave Hannah less than a moment's glance, unable to hold the gaze for any longer, before directing his mount and riding sheepishly away.

Hannah's jaw dropped even lower. Angry at Nathan, disgusted at Luminon. Her fingers dug into her calygreyhound's tufts of hair as she readied herself to gallop to revenge.

But she paused.

No, she thought to herself. She looked down as her mind flashed back: to Zack holding Luke over the bannisters and her outburst to defend him; how she yelled at Daegan and was merely chastised. Her outbursts had never brought her anything but trouble. If she'd just helped Luke without attacking Zack, things might have been different. If she had thought before jumping into fights…

Grimacing, she swung herself off the calygreyhound and, without daring to look down, dove off the cliff edge.

Chapter Thirty-Three

A Change of Heart

HANNAH was relieved to discover the cliff wasn't as high as she had thought. Nevertheless, her body slapped the water with a thump as she plunged into the lake. She kicked her legs in a desperate attempt to break the surface, ignoring all the dangerous Etheria that probably lurked in the lake's deep.

She took a deep gulp of breath as her head emerged from the water and looked around. Panic struck her as she looked for Celeste amongst the rising and falling waves.

Seconds went by, and Hannah felt a shiver of fear crawl up her spine as she thought the worst. *She must be here*, she thought. *She must.*

Then she saw her, floating face up and unconscious, riding the waves. Hannah's heart flipped as she swam towards her, hoping and praying she was okay. She grabbed her body and held her upwards, her muscles screaming as she lifted her as far from the water as she could.

A rumble came from beneath her, the waves rippling as something disturbed the water and rocketed to the surface. Hannah kicked her legs and began swimming away from it, fearful of what might leap out of the water.

With an enormous splash, a mighty Etheria soared from the lake, its hooves walking on the water as its long, fishlike tail propelled its horse-like body forwards. Shocked, Hannah looked up to find Mimi atop a hippocampus.

'Hannah!' she cried out as she instructed the hippocampus to trot towards her. 'Gods, I thought I heard someone fall in. What happened?'

Still out of breath, Hannah could barely speak. 'Nathan,' she spluttered.

Mimi's face clouded into a visage of fury; a look Hannah had never seen on a nymph. 'Hop on,' she said simply as she dragged Hannah and Celeste onto the hippocampus.

Hannah was so exhausted she barely noticed the gallop to the finish line. Although the hippocampus tried several times to submerge itself into the lake, Mimi wrestled against it to ensure it stayed on the surface. She barely recognised the joyous uproar as they sailed through the finish line. She tumbled to the ground.

'Hannah. Hannah! Are you okay?' a voice said, filled with concern.

She blinked and looked up. Daegan stood over her, his finger to her pulse and panic in his eyes.

'Please don't give me the kiss of life,' she moaned. 'That'd be just… too weird.'

Daegan blinked in disbelief, and a small grin appeared on his face. 'Not sure who it'd be weirder for.'

Daegan hauled Hannah up and took her to the finish line to watch the others sail through. Fennrock was red-faced and embarrassed as he trotted through riding a defecating bonnacon, and Amber looked crest-fallen to be told that she had in fact not been riding a unicorn but a camahueto—a one-horned cow. Jason was the one who drew the most laughs though, as he ambled through the finish line, munching on berries he'd picked on the way.

'It was a race?' he asked. 'I thought we were just going for a stroll.'

Natala stormed up to him and slapped the berries from his hand. 'I swear, Jase, if Finias lose because of you, I'll…'

But they never heard what the nymph would do since, at that moment, Caedric bounded onto a podium to announce the results.

'Congratulations to all our trainees on an outstanding race. I am pleased to announce the results. In fourth place, with thirteen points, is Gorias.'

Hannah felt her heart sink and sat on the grass dejectedly.

'In *joint* second place,' Caedric continued, 'with nineteen points each are Falias and Murias.'

Niall screwed up his eyes in disappointment.

'Meaning that, with an impressive twenty-seven points, the winners are Finias—'

'Stop!' cried a voice.

Curious mutters surrounded Hannah as faces turned to look at who had interrupted them. Mimi dismounted her hippocampus and stepped forward.

'That—*boy*,' she said, stabbing a finger at Nathan, 'cheated.'

Curious mutters became shocked gasps as the onlookers settled in for what they thought was a brilliant twist. Amongst the Truceleaders at the front, Drakkar stiffened.

'Me?' asked Nathan, his face a picture of innocence. 'Says who?'

'Me,' she replied. 'And Hannah. And Celeste—*if* she could talk. But she's unconscious.'

'What's that got to do with me?'

Mimi's fist was shaking. 'You're going to stand there and deny it? Deny that you pushed her over a cliff and into the lake?'

Gasps emanated from the audience, some of disgust, some of joy from the entertainment.

'Whatever you say,' Nathan sneered. 'You *would* say that. You lost. I don't suppose anyone from *my* team witnessed my "error"?'

'I did,' came a quiet voice from the back. The crowd parted to reveal a sheepish Luminon shuffle forward, his eyes cast downward.

Nathan's eyes darkened, and his top lip tightened. 'Oh,' he said in a clipped tone. 'What did you see?'

'You used your parandrus to sneak up on her,' he said through gritted teeth. 'You shoved her closer and closer to the edge before you—you used your telum to…'

He couldn't finish his sentence, but he didn't need to. The Truceleaders had heard enough and, from their stony expressions, believed him.

'I don't know what would have happened if it weren't for Hannah,' he continued. 'I couldn't bring myself to jump in after her… But *she* did. She would have beaten me if we'd carried on.'

There was an agonising pause. The crowd shuffled their feet in an awkward silence as they waited for a verdict. Daegan stepped behind Caedric and whispered briefly into his ear. Caedric twitched his neck in a slight nod.

'Sophie,' Caedric said in a calm but terse voice. A ball of light hovered by his ear. 'Return to your hut and track this boy's crystal. See which spells he cast and where he cast them.'

The ball of light shot off in a flash as the Truceleaders gathered for an impromptu meeting. There was much nodding and agreement, but Drakkar stood as still as a statue, not daring to meet Daegan's eyes. Instead, he leered at Nathan who cowered under his gaze.

'Thank you,' Luminon whispered as he came towards Hannah.

Hannah blinked, unsure what to say. She wasn't used to kind words coming from Luminon. 'Er—sure. No worries.'

'I apologise that my sister and I can come across as somewhat cold. We're not used to humans. But you did a good thing today, and I'm proud to have you as a… colleague in Arcadia.'

His expression didn't match his friendly words, but Hannah knew he was sincere. He took her hand and shook it briskly before moving to attend to Celeste.

'Ahem!' came Caedric's commanding voice as he quietened the crowd with ease. 'After some last-minute changes and shockingly impressive mental arithmetic from Lord Byron…' Byron sneered at being mentioned in a jovial manner. '… I believe I need to announce some updated results. Due to events that have come to light, Nathan will be disqualified from—'

'What? That's not fair!' cried Amber. Astonished faces turned, stunned she had the gall to interrupt Caedric. But she was unaware of them, instead glaring at Hannah with tightened lips.

'As I was saying,' Caedric continued, 'Nathan will be disqualified, and Luminon's final position will be swapped with Hannah's.'

Hannah saw Luminon nodding emphatically.

'In which case, in fourth place is Finias, third place Murias and second place Falias… Meaning that this year's winners are Gorias!'

Hannah was only partially aware of the cheers emanating from both crowd and trainees, regardless of their division—with the obvious exception of Nathan and Amber. There were words of congratulations and slaps on her back, but Hannah said nothing. Instead, she just smiled and thought back to just a few months ago. She knew that if something like this had happened at Arningham School, she'd have flown off the handle and chased after Nathan where, inevitably, it would have ended badly.

She didn't know whether it was Arcadia or Daegan or something else, but she didn't want to give Daegan the satisfaction of admitting out loud that he was teaching her much more than just how to be a Trucekeeper.

Chapter Thirty-Four

New Friends

IT was a warm spring morning, and the trainees were lounging by the lakeside. Nathan and Amber kept a distance from the others, embarrassed and bitter about what had happened during the Games. Nathan still hadn't fully explained himself, preferring instead to sulk and scowl at anyone who brought it up. Some thought he was jealous he hadn't fit in, others wondered if he was just insecure and wanted to get rid of any competition. Hannah had different theories though, her mind repeatedly dwelling on what Drakkar might have whispered to him beforehand.

Byron seemed to appear from thin air, hidden from the sun by an umbrella gripped in his hand, to announce that they were to assemble by the forest at nine o'clock sharp.

'I bet they're deciding which of us are doing the Trials! I want to get my Trucekeeper badge!' piped up Taniiya, her tail splashing against the lake. Celeste took the brunt of the splashes, her hair dripping with water.

'Nice look,' joked Rideo, winking at her.

Celeste shot him a dirty look before casting a spell that dried it immediately.

'No,' Fennrock said. 'There's nae eclipse for another eight months at least.'

Taniiya stuck her tongue out at Fennrock who stuck his out right back at her.

'What do you think it is, then?' yawned Nathan, pretending not to care.

'Familiar sorting,' Niall said through a bite of toast. The trainees stared at him with blank expressions. 'Before the Leviathan War,' he explained, 'every Trucekeeper was assigned a familiar.'

'A what?' asked Jason, mouth full of croissant.

'A familiar. An Etheria you form a close bond with.'

'Oh, like a pet?' shrieked Amber.

'Kind of.' Niall shrugged. 'You've seen Caedric's, right?'

'Zephyr?' Limara asked.

'Exactly. That's his familiar from when he was a Trucekeeper. Back in World War Two, I think.'

'But if all Trucekeepers get them, how come he's the only one?' asked Jason.

'Sophie has a familiar too,' Natala pointed out.

'Oh, yeah!' Mimi said. 'Her unicorn, right?'

Natala nodded.

'But what about Daegan, Byron and that lot who don't have one?' Jason asked.

Niall paused. 'I… don't know,' he admitted, sounding almost ashamed.

'Ugh, so much for the bookworm,' Nathan scoffed.

'So much for the cheat.'

There was an intake of breath as the group of trainees stared, wide-eyed and excited for what would happen next. Nathan cracked his knuckles.

'Some of us have lived in Arcadia our whole lives,' Luminon interrupted. Ever since the race, he had been keen to keep the peace between the trainees. 'How come we've never heard of familiars?'

This prompted murmurs of agreement from the others.

'That's because he's making stuff up,' jeered Nathan.

Hannah gave Niall a look, and he nodded. They retreated up the lake, preferring to keep their distance from Nathan, Jason and Amber. Tensions had been high, and Niall was keen not to let it get too heated.

The sun was already high in the sky, and Hannah felt the prickly heat burn down on her. A humongous basajaun, sweating heavily beneath its fur-coat, dragged pillars of rock and hammered them together as they built an extension to the castle. The green-skinned leimakids skipped merrily as they chased the rabbit-like muscaliets, their bushy tails trailing along after them. The yales and enfields raced each other while a bull-like bonnacon and parandrus grazed peacefully in the meadow. Why Etheria lived elsewhere was a mystery to Hannah.

They were the first to arrive by the forest, waiting eagerly at the corner where the lake, meadow and forest converged. Daegan and Aarava looked exhausted as they waited next to a large cage covered by a blanket. Noises and incessant rattling emanated from the cage.

'What's up with you?' Hannah asked Daegan. 'You look like you've been up all night.'

'We have,' he replied curtly.

'Doing what?' asked Niall.

Aarava chuckled. 'You'll see. We have to wait for the others first.'

Slowly, the rest of the trainees arrived. Even Caedric made an appearance, quietly sitting to the side with Zephyr perched on his shoulder. Predictably, Nathan, Jason and Amber were the last to arrive, waltzing in like they were perfectly on time and oblivious to everyone's glares.

'Trucekeeper trainees!' Aarava announced, a grin on her face. 'This is a special day. Traditionally, every Trucekeeper would undertake their duties with a companion; an Etheria to help them see things from other Etheria's points of view, keep them company and help them out in the toughest of scrapes—more times than you can imagine.'

An excited murmur rippled through the trainees, the loudest from Amber jumping up and down, giggling.

Aarava continued. 'Sadly, the tragedy that occurred during the Leviathan War brought an end to the custom. To protect these species, we set them free. Since then, Trucekeepers have undergone their duties without their valuable aid.

'Today, however, is the dawning of a new age.' Aarava's grin was a full-on beam now. 'You're a fresh generation of Trucekeepers, the start of a new era for Etheria. It only seems fitting we reintroduce the tradition of familiars. Daegan—would you do the honours?'

'With pleasure,' he said, and with a smooth motion, ripped the blanket from the cage.

The clamour of excited whispering erupted into cheers.

'Quieten down!' called Aarava.

All the trainees craned their heads to get a glance at which Etheria were inside. Most were small, no bigger than a dog or cat. They looked energetic and eager to climb out to explore the new world around them.

'These Etheria are predominantly yokai. There are lots of different ones; kitsune, kamaitachi, mujina—even a furi. Now remember, these are not—I repeat—*not* pets. They are companions, assistants… Many of you may even see them as friends. If I see any of you putting them on a leash or dressing them up, you'll have your mind wiped by the Oblivion spell and be kicked out of Arcadia faster than you can say Basilisco chilote.'

Alice sighed with disappointment.

'The Choosing ceremony can be an ordeal for familiars. Some come from the wild, some from other settlements like Mu, Biringan City and El Dorado. Our work is highly valued, so these settlements take great pride in the Etheria they offer. Arguments often break out with several trainers wanting one in particular. Such a debacle will *not* happen today. You shall wait in line until a familiar has chosen *you*, after which you will leave. No fights. Understood?'

There was a mumble of agreement as the trainees jostled against each other in an attempt to form a straight line.

'Good luck.' Daegan smirked as he slid back the lock and opened the door.

In a flash, a mass of Etheria shot out of the cage, a few even flying. Cries of awe permeated the mass of trainees who were bubbling with excitement, Amber's shrieks the loudest by far.

Nathan was the first to be picked by a small monkey-like Etheria—a furi with red eyes and blue hair in a leopard-style pattern. For once, Nathan didn't sneer; his eyes lit up, and Hannah saw their immediate bond. Similarly, Jason had a mujina head straight for him that seamlessly shape-shifted into a woman, her luscious blonde locks flowing down to her chest, before changing back into a burgundy panda-like Etheria. The mujina climbed onto Jason's shoulder whose face was almost as red as his familiar's fur.

Hannah and Niall watched as others were selected. She recognised a yamabiko, a cross between a monkey and dog known to create echoes, attach itself to Fennrock. A tanuki couldn't decide what form to take but eventually relied on its native raccoon-like body and ran to Limara. There was even an adorable otter yokai, a kawauso, permanently drenched with water and riding a keukegen, a dog-like Etheria with hair so long it resembled a wig on legs. The kawauso dived into the water and climbed into Taniiya's outstretched arms while the keukegen settled by Asti.

Eventually an Etheria approached Niall—a small fox, with a golden tinge to its fur with dark red markings around its face and two bushy tails. It strode up to him confidently and elegantly, as though nothing would change its mind.

'I'm guessing that's yours,' Hannah whispered.

'A kitsune,' he said, kneeling to greet the approaching familiar. 'She's beautiful.'

The kitsune looked up at Niall with its black eyes, blinking once before purring and curling up in his lap. Niall cradled the fox in his arms, beaming like a proud father.

The sorting went quickly and soon most trainers had a faithful companion by their side. Only Hannah and Amber remained, a result that filled her with dread.

The last Etheria were the dog-like inugami, an interesting Etheria Niall had told Hannah about the other day—it could imbue its companion with magic and connect closely with them—and a kamaitachi, a small but excitable Etheria similar to a white ferret that flew through the air with claws and a tail that could become as sharp as razors.

Alice seemed to have forgotten the concept of Etheria choosing and enthusiastically beckoned towards the kamaitachi.

'Not the dog. He's ugly. I want the cute one!' she shrieked.

Hannah felt sorry for any Etheria stuck with her. The inugami was far from ugly, and Hannah resisted the urge to pick it herself to save it from a lifelong companionship with Amber.

The kamaitachi was intrigued by Amber's calls and looped in the air as it soared towards her, pausing in front of her disgustingly cheerful face. It gazed into her eyes, swooping left and right. After a moment's hesitation, Amber grabbed it from the air and clasped it, a chilling giggle falling from her oversized mouth.

To Hannah's delight, the kamaitachi took umbrage to this, soaring out of her arms and slashing her face. With a whip of its tail, it sliced a slight cut in her cheek. Amber turned pale and reached a trembling hand to her cheek. She screamed, and the kamaitachi let out a noise akin to a giggle before it flew towards Hannah.

Hannah held in her laugh as the kamaitachi hovered in front of her. It looked into her eyes and inspected her in the same way it did

Amber, but its decision was almost instant. The kamaitachi looped twice in the air and landed in Hannah's arms, closing its eyes with a faint smile.

Meanwhile, the inugami reluctantly trudged its way towards Amber. With a grimace, she reached out her hand to greet her familiar. The inugami responded by slobbering all over her.

Chapter Thirty-Five

Getting to Know You

HANNAH and Niall made their way to their favourite place in Arcadia, keen to spend time with their new familiars. It was a small mound with a steep incline, on top of which was a broad vista of the castle. From here she could admire the light grey medieval turrets, the dark Gothic spires and the marble white Ionic columns that bordered the walkway around the walls. Hannah was in love with the bizarre combination of architecture. Behind them was the forest and above were overhanging branches that cast a cool shadow. To the right, at the bottom of the slope, was the lake, the calm lapping waves at the shore soothing them.

'Chosen a name yet?' Hannah asked Niall, who was busy sketching a picture of the kitsune in his notebook.

'Mhm,' he replied. 'Kiko.'

'Kiko,' Hannah repeated. The kitsune gave a yap of approval. 'It suits her.'

'Thanks. What about you?' he asked, narrowly avoiding a falling apple slashed free from the tree by the kamaitachi's sharp tail. He landed beside Hannah and nudged the apple towards her with a friendly bleat.

Hannah stroked him, her fingers delighting in his soft fur. 'Thanks,' she said to him. 'I keep coming up with Dex.'

'Any reason?'

Hannah shrugged. 'It seems to suit him.'

They sat there for a moment in silence as they admired the view and petted their familiars.

'Why are you here?' Hannah asked suddenly.

'Want me to leave you alone?'

'No. I mean… what brought you to Arcadia? Why give up the life you had before?'

'You think we *give up* our lives for Arcadia?'

'You know what I mean. Tell me.'

'Not much to tell. My mum died when I was young. My dad… he had little an interest in me. He married a pretty, moderately famous model who shall remain nameless—'

'Oh, do tell!'

'Another time. Anyway, she had the money he had always dreamed of. And as soon as they returned from the honeymoon, they packed me off to boarding school. I hated it there, just like everybody seemed to hate me. I wasn't liked, appreciated… I wasn't even wanted. So I ran away. Now you know why Arcadia means so much to me. Here… I don't know how to explain it. I actually feel appreciated here, like it's my home. I can contribute to something here, make something of myself. Anyway, after I ran away, I came across Daegan.'

'Wait, he just found you and invited you to become a Trucekeeper?'

'No. I witnessed him kill an Etheria.'

'Wow,' Hannah whispered, 'but he hates killing.'

'So I've gathered.'

'What kind of Etheria?' she asked.

'A kapre.'

Hannah imagined one of the huge bestiaries she had gone through. 'Something about trees. They live in them, right?'

Niall nodded. 'Yeah. But they're *giants* that live in trees. Enormous trees, obviously. Apparently, this kapre had found an oak tree strategically situated by a public footpath. He'd been picking off hikers for the last few days.'

'That's what you get for exercising,' Hannah joked.

'I was just resting against the tree, no idea where to go. Daegan saved me.'

'He saved me too,' she said as she scratched Dex behind his ear. 'What from?'

'A zburător,' she said casually.

Niall's response was not nearly so casual. He sat up straight, disturbing Kiko from her peaceful nap.

'A zburător? And you *survived*?'

'Yeah...' She frowned. 'His name was Zorg... or Zoo—something weird.'

'Zelom?' he asked, eyes wide with fear.

'Yeah! You know him?'

Niall whistled and lay back. 'Not personally. I've read about him, though. Most Etheria know about him. He was one of the most dangerous Leviathans who ever lived. He almost single-handedly took out all the Trucekeepers. Seems like Daegan was the only one able to take him out.' Niall shook his head. 'One hell of a first Etheria experience... What were you running from anyway?'

'Nothing,' she sighed, waving her hand dismissively. 'Well, everything—but...' Dex sensed Hannah's waning mood and flew to her shoulder, nudging her face with his to comfort her. 'No family to speak of. Not really.'

'They died?' Niall's voice was gentle, understanding.

Hannah shrugged. 'No idea. All I know is that my dad's brother and his wife took me in when I was... I can't remember. It was great at first.' A delicate smile appeared as memories replayed in her head. 'I was sporty when I was younger; gymnastics, karate—even fencing. I loved that stuff.'

'Explains your knack for all this Trucekeeping.'

'My uncle used to take me to sports clubs. He would drive me there, sometimes watch me practice, then drive me back. It was our normal, happy routine. Then—it stopped.'

A lonely tear ran down her face, and Niall reached out a caring hand.

'It was icy on the roads. My aunt said we shouldn't go—missing one day wouldn't hurt. But I begged him and… we hit some black ice. We didn't see it, and we skidded and skidded. I didn't know where I was, which direction we were hurtling until…' Hannah hid the tears. She couldn't face Niall, not even Dex. She moved down to the shore, slipped off her shoes and paddled her feet in the shallow water.

'My aunt remarried this—person. Inevitably, a new baby came along. Actually, two—twins! Soon I wasn't a priority—I was a burden. At best, they ignored me; at worst, they hated me.' She kicked her foot, and small droplets splashed in ringlets on the lake's surface.

'There was nothing for me at home. As for school, it was just as bad. But I had Luke.'

Niall's head snapped up. 'Luke? Who was he—a boyfriend?'

Hannah stifled a laugh. 'Nothing like that.'

She sat down, still kicking her bare feet in the cool water and hoping a mermaid didn't play any tricks on her. 'We got into a fight with this guy, Zack. He was about to seriously hurt Luke… At least, that's what it looked like! I panicked. Luke told me not to do anything—he warned me. I should have listened to him. Anyway, Zack's injuries were pretty bad, so I got expelled… and then I was nearly killed, and Daegan saved me.'

Hannah felt better having told her story, as though a load had been lifted. She hadn't spoken about her family to anyone other than Luke. She carried on telling him the rest—regaining her memory and her time at Arcadia before he arrived.

By the time Daegan found them, they were back to their normal selves, laughing and playing with Dex and Kiko.

'Nice place,' Daegan commented. 'Magnificent view.'

Hannah and Niall barely acknowledged his arrival.

He chuckled quietly. 'That takes me back.'

'You haven't got a familiar,' Hannah said, receiving a prompt elbow from Niall.

'I did,' he murmured, 'but that was a long time ago. I just came here to tell you I'll be away for the rest of the day.'

'Who's the Etheria?' asked Hannah as she held a branch for Dex to play with.

'A bolla.'

'It's a young kulshedra—a sort of dragon, right?' Daegan nodded, and Niall continued. 'They sleep through most of the year but always wake up St. George's Day... because St. George cursed it to be blind all but one day. Yeah?'

Daegan nodded again, a glint in his eye. 'St. George was a wise Trucekeeper. One of my favourites.'

Hannah merely rolled her eyes.

'They're pretty rare nowadays. I have to make sure they don't go on murderous rampages on St. George's Day. A Trucekeeper's work is never done! I'll see you tomorrow. Study hard and *please* don't get into any trouble.'

'Speaking of trouble,' Niall said, inching closer to Hannah once Daegan was out of earshot, 'I've been doing some reading. *Runes and Crystals: A History.*'

Hannah groaned. 'Please, not now.'

'I only read one chapter, but I thought it might interest you. It might be about that wall you saw Drakkar fiddling with.'

Hannah's eyes lit up, and she leant forwards. 'Go on!'

'Oh, look who's interested now! Runes and blood crystals have a variety of purposes,' he explained. 'You already know about enchanting runes into crystals, but you can also use them on doors to strengthen them. These doors only unlock using a specific crystal as a key.'

'Sounds like our wall… or door, apparently. So, what is it?'

Niall puffed out his chest. 'A vault.'

Hannah stared at him, waiting for an explanation. 'Like a bank vault?'

'Kind of, but instead of stopping people breaking *in*, it's to stop people—or rather, Etheria—breaking *out*.'

'Like an Etheria prison?'

'Sort of, but not for any Etheria. A powerful, almost unkillable one—or at least hard to kill… Or maybe they just wanted to keep it alive for a rainy day.'

Hannah ran through her limited repertoire of formidable Etheria. 'So, what's inside?'

Niall shrugged. 'There are several powerful Etheria. But here's the catch—only the Trucekeeper who seals the vault can open it again.'

'So, if my crystal is the one that can open it…'

'You're only guessing that from a sound it made,' he reminded her, 'but yes—whoever had that crystal before you locked a powerful Etheria in that vault.'

'But why does Drakkar want to open it?'

'Food for thought!' mused Niall as he stretched out on the grass. 'Remember, it could be nothing but academic curiosity. He is a Truceleader, after all—you should trust him. Or maybe Caedric asked him to do something.'

'I told you what I saw in the Games. *He* was the one who told Nathan to attack the other players! We need to prove that he can't be trusted. Even Daegan was looking at him strangely.'

'You don't know that for sure! You need proof, Hannah. That's probably why Daegan hasn't said or done anything—he doesn't know either. Don't leap to conclusions.'

Hannah frowned, then stood up. Dex hopped onto her shoulder. 'I'll just go and ask him then.'

'What?' gasped Niall. 'How are you—'

'I'll catch up with you later,' she shouted over her shoulder as she hurried to the castle, Dex flying through the warm spring air after her.

Chapter Thirty-Six

Curiosity Killed the Cat

HANNAH'S confidence dimmed the nearer she came to Drakkar's office, nerves taking over. Her heart quickened, and her hand caressed the handle of her telum, wishing its blade wasn't so blunt.

Almost as soon as her knuckles wrapped on his door, it creaked open. Hannah had expected to see Drakkar but found no one, as if the door had opened of its own accord. She poked her head into the room.

'A door opening after a knock is a common method of inviting someone inside,' called a voice. 'So do come in.'

Hannah accepted the invitation. The door swung back. Dex only just managed to shoot through the crack before it slammed.

Hannah marvelled at Drakkar's office. It was crammed with books, cauldrons and vials, some of which were marked with ominous skull-and-crossbones. She batted Dex away from them as a shiver ran down her spine. Balls of colourful light shot over her head and disappeared, as though absorbed into Drakkar's outstretched hand.

'Ah. Miss Moreland—and her delightful new familiar. What brings you to my modest chambers?' he asked, his voice sounding like a rocking chair creaking in an abandoned house.

Hannah was keenly aware of his red eyes fixed on her. 'Magic,' she said. It was the only word that came to mind.

'That's a rather broad category, my dear. I can do many things, but mind reading takes a little more preparation.'

Hannah's mouth dropped open, terrified of the idea of Drakkar delving into her thoughts.

'Relax,' he assured her. 'It's harder to do with humans. I can't control your minds in the same way I can with some Etheria.'

'I, erm… I'm finding things difficult. Magic things, you know?'

'Yes, Miss Moreland. Please elaborate.'

'Well, the theory is complicated, and I'm struggling with basic blood magic. I'm anxious I'll fall behind. I was wondering if you could… help me?'

Drakkar gazed at her before sitting heavily into a well-worn armchair. He fumbled with his dark goatee and continued to examine her. Her eyes strayed from his to his desk and settled on an ornate picture frame. A slim, elegant woman gazed from the photograph, her mouth curved in a restrained smile. Drakkar's hand shot out and slammed it down, hidden from view.

'Have you spoken to Daegan about this?' he asked, as though nothing had happened. 'He is, of course, your authorised trainer.'

'He doesn't enjoy slowing down. And he's training Niall too who picks it up better than me.' At least that bit was true—just in case he *was* reading her mind.

Drakkar ran his long-nailed finger through his beard. 'You would like me to train you in magic,' he repeated.

Hannah nodded.

'Just the basics?'

'And more. I find magic… fascinating. I want to learn. Especially, you know, magical objects… and such.'

It was less eloquent than she had hoped, but Drakkar smiled approvingly. 'That could be a possibility,' he said as he sauntered to a glass tank in which Dex was playing amongst the purple plants. He picked him up by the tail and threw him towards Hannah. 'I need an apprentice. You could lend me assistance in return for extra tuition?'

Hannah nodded eagerly.

'I'm flattered, but it'll be difficult. Much of what I can do is... how can I explain it? Natural. Magic runs deep in my blood. Blood crystals and telums... They're tools used merely to channel my magic. You've heard of warlocks, I presume? The males of the sorcerer species?'

Hannah felt hypnotised but managed a frail nod.

'Let me quash any hopes—you cannot *become* a sorcerer. Others may use magic with crystals, but for us... Powerful magic is in our very blood. We're a race—descended from our fathers, warlocks, and mothers, witches.'

'But you can breed with other Etheria.'

He stared at her for a few seconds. 'True. I, for example, am the result of an illicit union between an elf and a warlock. One of my cousins—fascinating man—is a warlock with traits of both centaur and vampire. A truly formidable Etheria. Of course, if we wanted, we could rid ourselves of our physical form and live forever by possessing the body of another.' He chuckled quietly to himself. 'You would like training from a warlock?' he purred. 'One condition.' He raised a long, crooked finger.

'Which is...?'

'I need something. It may be difficult to acquire by myself.'

'What do you need?' she asked, repressing a resigned sigh.

'An Etheria,' he said as he withdrew his ebony telum from his sleeves. He pressed his thumb to the crystal, and a purple haze poured from the tip. 'A very particular one from Egypt.'

'Egypt?'

'Yes. I assume you've heard of a sphinx?'

Drakkar gestured towards the purple cloud he had created, beckoning for her to walk through. She held Dex tightly, no idea what to imagine from a portal. She was aware of nothing but being in his cool office one moment, and then in suffocating heat the next.

Chapter Thirty-Seven

Entering the Pyramid

HANNAH gasped as her body adjusted to the intense desert heat that suffocated her. Dex made a similar noise as he leapt from her shoulder and soared into the air.

An enormous sandstorm raged, vicious clouds of sand slicing her face. She flicked her left hand and raised her shield to protect herself. Despite the layer of sand flying around her, she recognised the Great Pyramid of Giza. She had always dreamed of going there since she was young. One Christmas her uncle had handed her a poorly wrapped present, grinning widely. She ripped off the paper and hugged him tightly, later devouring the thick encyclopaedia on Ancient Egypt. *If only he could have taken me here instead of...*

Drakkar stormed through the portal's purple haze, his eyes fierce and telum pointed directly at her. Hannah leapt backwards. A light shone from his telum, and she shut her eyes.

But she felt nothing.

The wind dissipated. She opened her eyes. The storm still raged, mounds of sand blowing viciously, but she didn't even feel a breeze.

'You needn't worry. A harmless spell to protect us from the sandstorm,' Drakkar explained.

'Why don't we come back when there *isn't* a sandstorm?'

'*I'm* the one who caused the damned thing. Look.'

Drakkar extended a yellowing finger to a group of tourists, looking up at the pyramids with the inevitable phone pointing towards the wonder of the world.

'Tourists,' he spat. 'We cannot allow them to see us emerging from a portal. The Truceleaders would be livid.'

'And how are we taking *that* home?' She pointed past the tourists to the Great Sphinx of Giza.

Drakkar sneered. 'We're here for the real thing, my dear, and it'll take a lot more effort to secure. Come.'

Hannah took a step forward to follow him but paused. Despite the spell he had just cast, she was still sweating; her head became fuzzy, and she felt tired. She groaned as a familiar feeling she hadn't missed rushed back and hit her like a roaring wave.

'You don't have any food, do you?' she asked Drakkar.

He whipped round, lips curled in a sneer. 'We're not here for a picnic!' he spat.

'I'm diabetic,' she explained. 'My blood sugar's low, and I—'

'The history of the sphinx…' he began, ignoring her and leading her past the Great Pyramid. 'Long before we built these monuments,'—he gestured towards the surrounding pyramids—'sphinxes were a wild breed of Etheria, freely roaming the wilds. Many humans, animals and Etheria became their prey. Since they can live well past a millennium and are not easily killed, one of the first acts of the Trucekeepers was to limit the breeding of sphinxes. They captured all females and moved them to Greece, where—as I'm sure you're aware—many Etheria originate. The now lost Garden of the Hesperides was an ideal place to monitor them. Since then, the male form of sphinx, the androsphinx, has thrived in Egypt. Though occasionally breaking the Truce, they were largely benevolent and found good favour with the residing Egyptians, hence the statue.' He waved towards the Great Sphinx as they moved further away from it.

'Time passed and, inevitably, a small group of female sphinxes found their way back to Egypt. Most were destroyed by Trucekeepers. Yet there was one that bred… Hortes was born shortly before her mother was killed. The Pharaoh, Menkaure, a well-trained Trucekeeper himself, volunteered to watch over Hortes, housing her in the pyramid that would one day house his own mummified corpse—this one.'

Hannah tried to ignore her hypoglycaemia, praying they wouldn't be too long. Instead, she admired the pyramid towering over them. Although the smallest in the necropolis, it didn't diminish its wonder.

'Since that time, all other female sphinxes have died. Hortes is the only one left. Hence her importance.'

'Fair enough,' Hannah replied. 'So, we get her to breed, yeah?'

Drakkar remained silent and continued to lead the way.

'Did Caedric authorise this?' Hannah asked nervously, already predicting the answer.

'No,' came his icy response, 'and I forbid you to mention this.'

Hannah steeled herself and kept her distance. 'Then you need to tell me more than just the history of sphinxes.'

For a moment, they stared at one another, each daring the other to look away first.

'Fine,' Drakkar huffed like a scolded child. 'Sphinxes are fascinating. They're very wise—they enjoy riddles and playing mind games, ready to attack the moment you lose. They're also gifted with clairvoyance, able to locate people, objects… occasionally they even predict the future to some degree of accuracy. Does that answer satisfy you?'

Hannah nodded morosely as he turned on his heel, an ill-tempered expression etched into his dark face.

'We're here,' he said at last.

Craning her neck upwards and shielding the sun from her eyes, she admired the pyramid, noticing a deep crack running down its wall where several stones were missing.

'Daegan tells me you're something of a history enthusiast. You know what this is?' Drakkar asked.

Hannah nodded. 'The Sultan of Egypt ordered the pyramids to be destroyed towards the end of the twelfth century—starting with this one. They gave up after eight weeks when they couldn't shift more than one or two rocks a day.'

'Impressive,' he sneered. With that, he climbed on one rock, then another before expertly scaling the wall.

'Wait, isn't this illegal?' she called out. 'Some guy got a lifetime ban from Egypt for doing this!'

'Ha!' Drakkar laughed as he hauled himself higher. 'The Cloaking spell and sandstorm should hide us from the authorities as well as tourists' prying eyes.'

Hannah unfastened the belt-rope she had stolen from Talos. She moved it from around her waist and secured it diagonally across her chest, prepared for whatever lay in the pyramid. A rush of giddiness washed over her as she placed her hand on the pyramid. She had dreamed of visiting the pyramids but never imagined she'd explore a secret entrance. If her career as a Trucekeeper didn't pan out, she made a mental note to publish a book—anonymously, of course.

She hauled herself up in time to see Drakkar dust away a small, circular groove in one rock. He slotted his crystal inside and placed a bloodied thumb to it. A familiar clunking sound boomed, and Hannah stepped back as rocks moved inwards. Her foot wobbled, and she lost her balance.

Drakkar grabbed her outstretched hand. 'Careful,' he warned her. 'This pyramid was built over four thousand years ago—no health and safety. If you get yourself killed in here...'

He never finished his sentence.

Hannah peered inside the newly formed hole, unable to see anything but darkness.

'Ahem, ladies first,' Drakkar muttered.

Hannah hesitated, but Dex didn't, floating down before Hannah had a chance to stop him.

Her heart skipped a beat as he disappeared from sight.

'Lost your pet?' Drakkar sneered.

Dex mewed to signal all was safe. Still reluctant, Hannah dangled her legs into the unknown abyss below. She paused.

'See you on the other side,' Drakkar hissed as he gave her a sharp push, and she tumbled into the darkness.

Chapter Thirty-Eight

Riddles in the Pyramid

HANNAH fell a few metres before thudding onto her back and sliding down a slope for what seemed an eternity.

Eventually, the slope levelled, and she slowed to a stop. In the pitch black, she couldn't see her hand in front of her face. She was keenly aware of the sudden rise in temperature. Her pores opened and sweat oozed down her neck.

She unholstered her telum, pricked her thumb and pressed it to the crystal, letting a ball of light illuminate the room. She breathed a sigh of relief as she saw Dex excitedly explore every nook and cranny. There was no danger, only an eerie statue of a pharaoh staring down at her.

Dex settled on her shoulder. She reached up a hand to stroke him, surprised by how damp his fur was. *Sweat*, she realised. She was astonished it was so humid—she had always imagined the inside of pyramids to be refreshing like caves.

Before long, the silhouette of Drakkar sliding down the slope came into view, his robes behind him fluttering as though he had sprouted wings.

'What took you?'

'Slow and steady wins the race,' he told her, avoiding her gaze. He cleared his throat and cast some spells. Several balls of light shot around the room, lighting it up properly, and a cool breeze of air washed over them.

'Much better!' he said, rubbing his hands and striding towards the statue.

As he dusted the pharaoh's stomach, Hannah took a chance to marvel at the detail the light revealed. There were hieroglyphics decorated on every wall, top to bottom.

'What do these say?' she asked Drakkar, tracing them delicately with her fingers.

'They tell the story of Menkaure. Maybe a few things about traps.'

'Traps?' Hannah frowned. Her knowledge of ancient Egyptians was hazy, but she wasn't aware of many traps. 'Aren't there mainly curses to keep away robbers?'

'Some are. Now if I can just find… ah!' His hand batted aside the dust that had settled over centuries and revealed another lock for his crystal. With the crystal inside, the room sprung to life. Fire raged in the torches on the walls and an ominous voice boomed.

'Who enters the resting place of the Pharaoh Menkaure?'

'Truceleader and Trucekeeper,' replied Drakkar, addressing the unmoving statue.

'What do you seek here, Truceleader?'

'Hortes,' Drakkar said, arm curling into his body as he bowed with his thumb holding down his middle finger.

Hannah scoffed.

'Don't underestimate the pride of some Etheria,' Drakkar whispered.

'The way to Hortes is only open to the worthy,' the voice said.

'Then let us prove ourselves,' replied Drakkar, head still bowed in respect.

'This is ridiculous,' Hannah whispered, arms crossed and eyebrows raised. Dex mewed in agreement.

'Solve the Riddles of the Sphinx, and you may pass,' the voice informed them.

'Wonderful!' exclaimed Drakkar. 'These are well-documented. Leave them to me.'

Hannah gave him a sarcastic smile before sitting on the slope and resting her head in her hand. All she wanted was for Drakkar to tell her about the Vault. This was more effort than she had planned.

'Truceleader, here is your riddle: Two sisters exist—one gives birth to the other, who gives birth to the first. Who are these sisters?'

With his chest puffed out, Drakkar replied, 'Day and night.'

After a second, a large rock to their left made a grinding sound as it raised to reveal a hidden passage.

'Trucekeeper, here is your riddle,' the voice said to Hannah.

She sat up, eyes wide.

'What?' Drakkar's voice quivered. 'Ask me! She doesn't know the answers! She—' His voice was silenced by whatever power the pyramid possessed. His lips moved, but no sound came out.

'Trucekeeper, there is a creature with one voice—it walks the earth with four feet, then two and finally three. What is this creature?'

Hannah's mind went blank. 'I… I don't—'

Drakkar furiously waved his arms at her to stop talking. She did so, fearing the consequences.

She paced the room, eyes closed and deep in thought. Hannah found riddles difficult even when her blood sugar was at a normal level. But right now, she felt like her brain was dragging, trying to find its way through a thick fog.

Okay—just one voice… that cut out a few possibilities: gorgons with snake-hair, chimera with different heads, three headed guard-dogs. That didn't narrow it down by much, though.

She considered the legs. She could think of several Etheria with four legs and just as many with two but struggled to think of three-legged Etheria. Jin chans, money-toads, yangwus, three-legged crows—but no Etheria changed how many legs it had.

So, what if it's not an Etheria, she wondered. Her mind went to tadpoles turning into frogs, caterpillars becoming butterflies… but no creature ever had three legs. Maybe some sort of monkey—able to move about on two legs, crawl on all fours and sometimes use its tail… Humans never really required a third leg, apart from when they got old and…

Her face lit up, and she laughed. 'Us… It's humans!' she cried out. Relief flooded Drakkar's face. 'We crawl on all fours as babies, then walk on two legs, and then use a walking stick… right?'

There was a long pause. Hannah worried the sphinx wouldn't accept her answer.

What if I'm wrong? Can I try again or…?

'You may enter,' the voice spoke, much to their relief. Another doorway slid open to the other side, just as dark and foreboding as the other.

'You may choose a pathway. One leads to Hortes, the other to inevitable death.' The voice faded, and there was silence, save for Dex's frightened mew.

'Inevitable death?' said Hannah. 'Cheery. Which do we take?'

Drakkar stared at both doorways, a look of concentration beneath his furrowed brow. 'I don't know,' he admitted through gritted teeth. 'This was never in the books!'

Hannah stood back and pointed her finger to one entrance, then to the other, moving her finger back and forth.

'… if it hollers let it go, eenie meenie minie mo,' she whispered under her breath.

'Incantations won't do anything here.'

'It's not an incantation. I'm taking this one.' She pointed to the left entrance.

'How can you be so sure?'

'I'm not,' she replied, painfully aware of her flawed plan. 'But let's take one each—if either of us thinks we're on the dodgy path, we run out and follow the other one. Sound like a plan?'

Drakkar resigned himself. 'I'll have it known that this is not *my* plan. But I agree with your course of action. After all, we have little choice.'

'Well, then…' She grimaced and cracked her knuckles. *No turning back now.* 'Come on, Dex.'

The kamaitachi made a loop in the air and followed her through the doorway into the unknown.

Chapter Thirty-Nine

Traps in the Tunnel

THE door thudded shut as soon as they were through, casting them into complete darkness. Hannah pushed her panic down, continuing her efforts to forget her blood sugar.

Get this done quickly, get back to Arcadia and everything will be fine.

With her telum, she created a ball of light that followed behind, illuminating her surroundings as the oppressive darkness loomed over them. Everything seemed safe as far as she could see, though she still expected the worst.

The ground beneath her feet, at first firm, became softer. Her body tensed as she stepped forward cautiously.

Her foot found ground and sank. Instincts kicked in. Her hand flicked down, and she raised her arm. Her shield assembled just in time.

Thud!

She lowered her arm—a short arrow stuck out, its head lodged deep in the shield. She tried not to think how she was going to explain this to Talos when she had it repaired.

'Nice choice, Hannah,' she grunted to herself. 'Good eenie-minie-mo-ing.'

Moving forward one step at a time, her foot tapped ahead, separating the safe spots from the dangerous. She kept her shield and telum at the ready, occasionally ducking and swinging her shield to disrupt an arrow's path.

Relief swept over her as she saw safe ground just ten yards away. She made a run for it, preferring to be on the other side of this trap. That's when her foot landed on a pressure pad, sinking slightly.

Her breath caught in her throat as everything seemed to go in slow motion.

An arrow launched.

By the time she realised, it was too late. She crouched, closed her eyes and braced for the inevitable, only vaguely aware of a gust of wind pass by her ear.

Then she felt nothing.

Cautiously, she opened her eyes, one at a time. The arrow lay on the ground, split in two. Dex hovered beside her, a mixture of pride in his mew as his sharp tail swished beneath him.

'Good boy,' she said, scratching his head.

She took a deep breath and calmed herself. *I really should have thought this through first.*

In the distance, she spotted an open archway. *The end—it must be!* She quickened her pace, her only desire to reach the warm arms of safety. Hannah barely noticed the horizontal wire tied from wall-to-wall as she ran through it. Even then, she was only vaguely aware of Dex's warning cry.

There was a sound like thunder and an ever-increasing vibration. Hannah slowed and looked above and below—nothing. To her right, nothing. But to her left…

There it was.

The rumbling became louder and louder. She pierced her thumb and shot a ball of light towards it and saw the enormous boulder tumbling furiously towards her.

Of course, she thought.

'Dex, move!' she shouted as she dived forwards, narrowly missing the boulder that hurtled past them. It crashed into the wall opposite, bricks and dust exploding in a cacophony of destruction.

She lay on the ground, cursing herself for being careless but proud of her quick reactions. But her brief respite was short-lived when a thick cloud of red mist crawled from the hole in the wall, quickly filling up the passageway. There was a grinding sound that came from the end of the corridor as a door began to slide down, blocking her exit.

She had been through so much already—she was damned if this gas was going to kill her now.

Hannah stumbled to her feet and grabbed Dex in her arms. She ran, legs burning from exhaustion, skin prickling and lungs burning as the gas caught up with her. She was desperate for rest and had to fight back the voice in her head telling her to give up.

She sprinted like lightning. The door slid closer and closer to the ground. A sliver of light was left. Still running at full speed, she threw Dex towards the narrow opening before leaping to the ground herself and sliding through. Her cheek grazed the closing door, and it slammed shut, shielding her from the gas.

She lay there for a moment, coughing out the dust in her lungs and relishing the feeling of being alive. Her body protested as she got to her feet and dusted herself down, still gasping for air.

She readied herself to cast another ball of light, but the room beat her to it. In an instant, the torches fixed to the walls burst to life, flickering with flames for what seemed the first time in a thousand years as the chamber awakened.

Chapter Forty

The Sphinx's Smile

HANNAH took time to admire the new room. Intricate paintings decorated every inch of the walls, flickering ominously in the firelight as if they were moving. Lining either side were statues of Egyptian Etheria with dozens of sarcophagi in between. Hannah shuddered to think what could be inside and instead focused on the statues.

She could see an ammit, an Etheria with a reptilian head, the body of a wild cat and a pair of stocky hind legs like a hippopotamus. It stood opposite a serpopard, a grotesque leopard with a snake-like neck and a head the cross of a feline and a king cobra—deadly venom to match. Next to them were statues of a vicious apep facing a griffin; beyond them a large bennu, similar to a phoenix, wings spread majestically as it faced a hawk-headed hieracosphinx.

Beyond these, intimidating eyes stared straight at Hannah. This statue was of a sphinx. Unlike the famous one outside, this one had wings tucked neatly atop its back and sported a feminine face.

A voice boomed. 'You must be truly special to have made it this far.'

Hannah looked around, eager to find the voice. 'Why, thank you. I certainly think so. Why not come out? Tell me that in person.' She sounded considerably braver than she felt, telum held tightly to stop her hand from shaking.

Between the sphinx's enormous legs, a gate slowly raised, and from the darkness, Hortes emerged. Her lion-like paws padded along the stone floor as she stepped out and stretched luxuriously, her impressive wingspan branching out. Her human-like face was sharp and angular with dark skin that matched the golden marks along her eyes. She fixed her gaze on Hannah.

In an instant, Hannah's knees wavered. She wondered how dangerous a sphinx might be. Weakness overtook her. She leaned against the statue of the ammit yet couldn't tear her eyes from the sphinx's hypnotic gaze. An enigmatic smile crept onto her face.

'Welcome, Trucekeeper,' she said. 'For a moment, I was worried you wouldn't make it. My name is Hortes.' The sphinx bowed, her curious smile unwavering.

Hannah shook her head to rid herself of the sphinx's effect.

'Why the riddles?' was all Hannah could think to say, 'if you wanted to be freed?'

Hortes continued smiling, her movements small and imperceptible. 'I can't let someone unworthy achieve a goal. Plus, when they get one wrong… oh, the failure is simply *delicious*.'

An icy shiver ran down Hannah's spine. 'You… *eat* people who don't get your riddles?'

'Of course—before I was locked up like a common beast. Since then, I've become *ravenous*.' The sphinx lowered her head and approached Hannah.

Where's Drakkar? If she took the dangerous route, how could he be taking so long in the safe one? Unless… Had he abandoned her? Hannah retreated quickly, but her back slammed into the door behind.

She was trapped.

Hortes spread her wings to their full extent. The tips glowed with a golden hue, and a hum engulfed the room. The ground tremored, as though the tomb itself were coming to life.

A crash came from Hannah's left. And another. Then three more to the right. Her eyes darted in search of the danger. One by one, the sarcophagi lining the walls smashed open. Grotesque remains of the corpses within climbed out and stretched. Grey strands of bandages hung down, decomposed flesh and brittle bones showing through the rotting wrappings. Their eyes glowed a cold shade of green.

She had ignored studying mummies—or the Cursed Dead, as Daegan had insisted on calling them. She made a silent promise never to dismiss another Etheria again… provided she survived.

Telum in hand, she pricked her thumb and pressed it to her crystal. A shockwave shot from the blade, and several mummies smashed against the statues, shattering upon impact.

More hands crashed through sarcophagi.

Hannah tried to remember Daegan's advice: *don't get surrounded; don't get ambushed from behind.* She kept her back against the wall and considered her options.

Great, she thought. *Just what I need when I'm low.*

A wave of mummies dragged their lifeless corpses to where she stood. Too many to fight one by one. She grimaced and tried casting the Shield glyph, hoping that she'd be able to hold them off until Drakkar arrived… if he ever did.

Nothing. She tried again and again, but the telum didn't respond. Dex tilted his head questioningly. 'Don't ask,' she told him.

Shielding her eyes, Hannah shot a bright light from her telum. The mummies didn't react. Hortes laughed.

Hannah fired a burst of flames and didn't hesitate to cast another Blast spell as bandages quickly caught light. The flaming Etheria soared into the murderous crowd, and a handful of others caught fire. They groaned gutturally, bodies writhing in pain.

After just a few spells, Hannah felt drained. Daegan was right—she wasn't ready just yet.

'You take the left!' she barked to Dex.

Dex mewed in response and got to work, his soft tail transforming into sharp steel that rotated rapidly and spun like a buzz-saw as his claws slashed left and right. His attacks cut through the mummies like a knife through butter.

Hannah charged towards the herd, her telum raised. A mummy lashed out and cut her arm. She kicked it and sent it flying into the swarm behind. She slashed her blunt telum and bashed another with her shield. A shockwave to her right, a slash to her left, a kick in front. The deadly horde thinned, but Hortes laughed once again.

'You think my army so pitiful?' she jeered, her wings spread open once more.

For a moment, Hannah didn't understand. Then she heard the menacing hiss. Where a statue had stood was now a living, breathing serpopard. Its jaw drew back, sharp teeth dripping venom as the head wriggled grotesquely on its snake-like neck.

Hannah's breath caught in her throat. Her hands shook uncontrollably; whether it was from fear or low blood sugar, she didn't know.

The serpopard's head dived towards her. She rolled to the side and threw herself to the ground as it swiped its claws, coarse hairs brushing against her cheek. She cursed herself; she was getting sloppy as her blood sugar got lower. She needed to get back to Arcadia—now.

Dex swooped in and swiped his tail in its face. The Etheria roared, and Hannah slashed her telum across its chest. Too blunt—it was barely injured, attention still directed at Dex.

Hannah thought back to Niall's Egyptian bestiary. Her mind was flooded with diagrams of Etheria, red circles highlighting their weaknesses. The serpopard's weak spot was at least easy to remember—its neck. But as she gazed up at it, she suddenly realised how difficult it was going to be to get anywhere near its towering neck.

Aiming the flap of the belt, she shot the rope towards a torch on the wall where it wrapped itself around tightly.

With the rope gripped in one hand, she plunged her telum into the serpopard's stomach, just managing to pierce the blade through the hard outer shell of its skin. The Etheria bellowed and leant over. Hannah seized the opportunity and drew the rope across the Etheria's neck before climbing onto its back.

She threw the rope to the kamaitachi who caught it in his nimble paws and brought the rope around the serpopard's neck. Together, they pulled with all their might. The serpopard roared against the rope and fell to the ground. It writhed, trying to escape, even going so far as to spit poison, but Hannah held tightly. Soon, its cries of pain diminished until it was silent and unmoving.

Hannah took a moment, eyes lingering on the creature. Mummies, Cursed Dead—they were less Etheria, more witchcraft. But this serpopard... it was the first time she had killed. She felt a hole in her stomach. Its last moments had been pain, maybe fear. She knew it had been her or it—and there was no way Hannah was going down without a fight. But now she understood why Daegan avoided it.

A hiss like gas escaping from a pipe brought Hannah back from her reverie. Beneath the statue of the sphinx was Drakkar, ebony-black telum held against Hortes' neck, around which he held a chain.

Hortes let out a growl of fury and whipped her tail. All remaining mummies collapsed, once more lifeless corpses. Hannah let the telum fall from her hand and sank to her knees, half delirious from exhaustion.

'What took you? Traps?' she asked between heavy breaths, struggling to stay on her feet, her head swimming.

'No traps on my end, but I wasn't expecting a labyrinth!' he growled.

Hortes' initial response was a mischievous chuckle. 'You seek to make me your slave?' she hissed.

Drakkar didn't reply, instead turning his attention to Hannah. 'You didn't get bitten or scratched by any of them, did you?'

'Why? Do they—'

Drakkar tutted. 'Yes. A wound from the Cursed Dead can prove deadly but not if treated immediately. Here,' he said, throwing her a small vial, 'drink this.'

Hannah downed the revolting liquid.

'Now point your telum at this vile creature,' he commanded. Hannah hesitated but did as he instructed, too weary to resist. 'If she makes any attempt to escape, kill her.'

He tugged at Hortes' chain, forcing her to follow as he produced a purple haze to walk through.

'Is it really a good idea to take her into Arcadia? She's dangerous.'

Hortes flashed a defiant smile. Hannah's glimmer of doubt grew, but Drakkar refused to answer.

'After you, my dear.'

Hannah made sure not to make eye contact with the warlock or the sphinx. She trusted neither.

Going through the portal was even worse the second time. Her stomach churned as if it were doing flips inside her body. She felt queasy and leaned against Drakkar's desk.

'So…' she said as Drakkar led Hortes to a cage in the corner of his office. He locked her inside, receiving a hiss of resentment. 'I believe I've earned something.'

Drakkar straightened up. 'What would you like? Money?'

Hannah shook her head. 'You said you would teach me about magic.'

Drakkar waved his hand at her. 'That is Daegan's responsibility.'

Hannah's heart thumped, and Hortes grinned, enjoying the show from her cage. 'No,' Hannah said.

'I'm sorry? You dare—'

'We had an agreement! I was to help you with whatever *that* was. In return you tell me what I want to know.'

'I hardly think—' he began.

'You promised.'

'Listen to me—' he tried again.

Hortes' chuckling was audible, as was Dex's concerned mews.

'I almost died getting you that sphinx, and you want me to keep it secret. You answer my question otherwise—'

Hannah saw Drakkar's hand squeeze his telum, his thumb digging into the pinhole and blood dripping to the floor. Hannah placed her hand on her own telum.

'Pray, tell me what this ridiculous question of yours is.'

'Vaults,' she told him.

His look of rage softened. He gazed at her as a small smile crept onto his face.

'And what do *you* know about vaults?' he sneered.

'They house dangerous Etheria, correct?'

Drakkar nodded. 'You seem to know about them already. What more do you need?'

Hannah gulped. 'The one in Arcadia—what's inside, and who locked it?'

Drakkar's poker face was rock solid; he refused to blink. Hannah couldn't read him.

'I'm afraid you're quite mistaken, Miss Moreland. There is no vault in Arcadia.' He pointed to the door.

Hannah's determination hardened. 'Stop lying. Who else knows about it?'

He didn't blink. He didn't speak.

'Tell me who locked it!' she pleaded, involuntarily drawing her telum.

'Quiet!' he yelled, drawing his own telum and shooting a pulse of energy. She only just evaded the tower of books that toppled over and thudded on the ground beside her. She scrambled to her feet, ready to defend against another attack—but none came.

'Get out,' he hissed, his words barely audible.

'But—'

'Out!'

Hannah jumped, fleeing through the door which slammed behind her, all hopes of discovering what lay beyond the vault now dashed.

Chapter Forty-One

New Toys

HANNAH was asleep as soon as her head hit her pillow, Dex curled up beside her. She had a vague memory of a brownie waking her with breakfast and an even foggier memory of it storming off in a huff but couldn't tell if they were just dreams.

Most of her dreams that night had been nightmares—barren deserts with hideous sphinxes and rotten corpses. She couldn't shake the image of mummies surrounding her, swiping at her with their jagged bones. The scratching, poking—she could feel it, as real as the attack itself. She screamed, desperate to escape.

She awoke with a start, beads of sweat dripping down her forehead. Dex jumped and gazed with concern. Hannah lay back and groaned. It was just Dex trying to wake her.

'Sorry, buddy.' She stroked him behind his ear. 'Nightmare.'

Dex mewed and proffered his mouth. Still half asleep, it took a moment to realise he held a roll of paper. Curious, Hannah took it from the kamaitachi and read the note.

Hannah,
I hope you spent all night studying and so have a suitable excuse for missing our lesson this morning.
Meet me by the armoury in Phulakopis at midday.
Regards,
Daegan
P.S. Your familiar's extremely useful to get hold of you.

Hannah felt her stomach churn in panic. She jumped out of bed, cursing herself as she threw on any clothes that came to hand, even forgoing her usual headband and using a hair tie from her wrist. She couldn't believe she had missed a lesson. Daegan would be furious.

She buttoned her blouse and rehearsed her excuse. 'Yeah, studying all night—like you said. All night... I lost track of time and slept in. I usually wake up on time but—God, he's going to kill me.'

She sprinted through the castle to Phulakopis and arrived at the armourer's hut precisely at midday, keeling over as she caught her breath.

'Next up—basic fitness. Looks like you need it,' came a voice from behind.

'Daegan,' Hannah gasped through heavy breaths. 'I'm... so sorry... up... all night... reading... I got to sleep late, and I just...'

Daegan waved his hand nonchalantly. 'Niall and I practised with his staff-telum. Don't make it a regular habit, and we'll forget about it this time.'

Hannah frowned. He was never this lax.

'You're in a good mood.'

He smiled conspiratorially. 'You noticed. Hannah—you'll remember today for the rest of your life.'

Her heart leapt. 'Sword?'

Daegan rolled his eyes. 'Yes. But that's not—'

Her feet launched her into the air. 'Finally!'

'I've trained you for a few months and seen your progress. There's only so much you can learn cooped up here. Caedric has given me a mission, one which I would like you to accompany me on.'

Hannah beamed, her infectious grin even tempting a smile from Daegan. 'You really think I'm ready?' she asked.

'Not to go out on your own. But with me, on a relatively simple mission—absolutely. Of course, you'll need a proper telum too—not just a training one.'

'How long will we be gone? What about Niall? Who'll teach him while we're away?'

'Slow down, Hannah. Niall's coming with us. He's proven himself too. He'll just observe, mind. He still needs more training first.'

The dwarves were busy slamming hammers on metal, shaping exquisite swords from adamant. One particularly rotund dwarf made his way to them and gestured to a selection of dagger-telums. They were an incredible assortment: curved, straight, some blades were thinner with different hues and patterns decorating the handles.

'Take your pick,' Daegan told her. 'Lots of blades that might suit you. Sabre clip, Turkish clip, spear point, khukri. And the traditional dagger, of course.'

Hannah looked at him joyfully. 'I can finally get rid of this ugly thing?' She held up the tattered training telum.

He snatched it from her and looked at it with distaste. 'You don't have any say over the sword we'll bind to your crystal, but you may pick whichever telum you'd like. Choose wisely—this opportunity doesn't come often.'

Hannah ran her finger across them, taking care not to cut herself on the razor-sharp blades. She took her time, eventually deciding to follow Daegan's lead and go for a dagger-telum: one with a silver blade and pearlescent white hilt with golden decorations.

'Nice choice,' Daegan handed the telum to her. She wasted no time in placing her blood crystal in the hilt.

The adjacent hut was very different. A contrast to the hairy dwarves, this one was spotlessly clean with a floral scent and populated by a handful of miniature faeries, wings fluttering as they reflected colours around the room.

'They're in charge of the blood crystals; maintaining them, enchanting runes, binding weapons—even tracking.'

'Tracking?'

'You're just a trainee so the faeries can see every spell you cast with your blood crystal—what you cast, where you cast it. So make sure you're not doing anything you're not supposed to be doing because they'll be able to look it all up!' he joked as he slapped her shoulder.

Hannah feigned an awkward laugh. Her heart flipped and sweat dripped. Would the faeries know about her trip to Egypt? She picked her nail as she followed Daegan, knowing that all it took was one curious faerie for her time in Arcadia to be over.

Chapter Forty-Two

Secrets in Crystals

'SOPHIE!' Daegan called out.

In a flash, a faerie grew from the size of a butterfly to a full-grown woman. She smiled, her eyes sparkling and face inviting. Hannah felt herself relax. With flowing dark hair and milky skin, she was one of the most beautiful Etheria in Arcadia, and Hannah struggled to look away from her magnificent wings.

'Long time, no see, Daegan. I gather from your crystal that the bolla didn't go down easily.'

'No,' Daegan sighed. 'That was a tricky one.'

'Not to mention the buckriders.'

'You've been following me… Don't trust me?'

'Depends what I'm trusting you with.' She leaned back and smiled, lips slightly parted.

Hannah had two questions running rings in her head but chose the less awkward one.

'Buckriders?'

'On the way back from the bolla,' he explained, 'there was a band of buckriders about to raid some villages nearby. They ride flying goats and cause havoc. I was in the area so killed two birds with one stone.'

'Well, what brings you down here?' Sophie interrupted. 'You never come down here now for anything other than work. How times have changed!'

Daegan flicked back his leather coat, and Hannah spotted it. It was more simplistic than Daegan's, with a wooden sheath, but its handle, guard and hilt golden. He presented the sword to the faerie.

'I'd like to bind this sword to Hannah's blood crystal. It'll be her first.'

Sophie drew it from the sheath. 'A fine blade,' she commented. 'Any ability?'

'It wards off evil spirits,' he answered. 'Ought to come in handy where we're going,' he whispered to Hannah.

Sophie finished admiring the blade. 'Very well.' She held out her hand to Hannah. 'Your blood crystal.'

She hesitated at first but relinquished her blood crystal. The faerie flashed them another smile before shrinking, both blood crystal and sword presumably shrinking with her.

'I hope the sword doesn't stay that size,' she grumbled.

'It won't,' Daegan assured her. 'But size isn't everything. In the meantime, Talos ought to be around.'

Once more, Hannah's paranoia escalated, as if butterflies were trapped in her stomach.

'Miss Moreland,' Talos greeted her, sounding more like a groan. 'A pleasure as always.'

'Always happy to see your face,' Hannah joked.

'Your superior informs me you're to depart on your first mission. As such, you are to take the standard Trucekeeper equipment. Please be careful and bring them as soon as you return—in one piece.'

'You mean me return in one piece, or the equipment? *I* plan on staying in one piece but can't make any promises about your toys.'

Hannah could just about make out the tut beneath his mask. She looked lovingly at the equipment and felt herself relax when she saw a belt-rope. *So he didn't notice me stealing the other one.*

'I believe Daegan allowed you to keep a shield gauntlet?'

Hannah nodded, deciding not to tell him about the damage sustained by the arrow in the pyramid.

'Very well. Good luck with the mission,' he said before scurrying off.

Daegan was in the middle of helping Hannah with the equipment—securing the shurikens in certain pockets, fixing the wrist-bow—when flickering wings approached them.

'Daegan,' came Sophie's voice. 'There's an issue with the girl's crystal.'

'Wait here,' he said to Hannah.

Hannah tightened the bow around her wrist and bit her lip, but she couldn't resist not knowing. Ensuring no one was looking, she sneaked to the faeries' hut and crouched by the wall.

'Can't you bind it?' Daegan asked.

'Binding a sword is never a problem—but binding two into one crystal is.'

'You mean there's already a sword bound to her crystal?'

'Yes. Presumably she doesn't know the rune to summon it, or she would have discovered that for herself.'

Hannah cursed. All this time she had wanted a sword bound to her crystal—and she had had one all along.

'Which sword?' Daegan asked, a hint of worry in his voice.

'Fragarach.'

There was a long pause.

'Fragarach,' Daegan repeated. 'You're sure?'

'Of course. We examined it. Exceptional penetration, ability to command truth, power over wind… It's Fragarach, no doubt about it. There was only one Trucekeeper who wielded Fragarach…'

'Astraea,' Daegan whispered.

Again, there was silence.

'Daegan,' Sophie whispered, 'who is that girl?'

'I don't know.'

'I think you do.'

They held each other's stare until Hannah could stand it no longer. She turned around the corner, acting as casually as she could. Daegan and Sophie continued to hold their stare.

'Any problems?' Hannah asked, praying they would be honest with her for once.

'It's nothing,' Daegan grunted.

'Shall I swap them, Daegan?' Sophie asked.

'I already told you which sword to give her.'

'As you wish.' Once more, she shrunk in a flash.

'What's Fragarach?' Hannah asked.

'Long story,' Daegan grumbled as he stormed out of the hut, leaving Hannah to sit and stew, angry at how many secrets people had in Arcadia—even herself.

Chapter Forty-Three

A Change of Scenery

HANNAH did her best to focus, but it was a lot. Sophie showed her a tile she had struck with her new sword, explaining how the shape of the crack was specific to the sword in her crystal and how it was the rune she would use to summon it.

She looked round her shoulder before passing Hannah a headband studded with blue jewels. 'I don't know if Daegan would approve,' she whispered, 'so don't say anything. He prefers Trucekeepers to look professional on a job, but I noticed you seem to like these. I just thought it'd look good on your trip.'

'There's not much Daegan *does* approve of,' Hannah sighed, smiling as she admired the headband. 'Thank you.'

Sophie nodded understandingly. 'He wasn't always like this, you know. The War changed all of us but him in particular. He lost a part of himself, especially when…' She trailed off.

Hannah stroked the blue jewels on the headband as she considered pressing Sophie for more, perhaps something about Astraea.

'Be patient with him,' Sophie said. 'I don't know what you're doing to him, but I'm starting to see a glimmer of the old Daegan coming back. When he substitutes the Latin nonsense for a jokey quip, you know you're getting through to him.'

Before Hannah had a chance to reply, Lena also came to give her a present, although it was considerably less exciting. 'You'll need this when you leave,' she said as she handed over her insulin pump, an apologetic smile on her face. 'You'll be fine once you get to Thule; it's another Etheria settlement, so the same principles apply. But until you get there, it'll be business as usual, I'm afraid.'

Hannah winced as she reinserted the needle for her pump. She had been without it for so long that it stung more than usual.

This trip had better be worth it.

With the headband secured on her head and her insulin pump attached, she rushed to the great hall to find Daegan and Niall waiting for her, both bundled in woolly coats so thick she could barely see Niall's notebook clutched in his arm. He had a big smile plastered on his face and looked resplendent with a silver scarf around his neck and faithful staff-telum strapped to his back.

'Here.' Daegan thrust a heavy rucksack into her chest and a thick coat like theirs. 'You're late.' He seemed in such a rush he hadn't even noticed her headband. Hannah hoped she'd get away with it.

Hannah heaved the coat and rucksack on and grunted. 'I can't believe there isn't a spell to make this lighter.'

'There is, but you need to get stronger.'

'What's even in here?'

'Basic essential provisions,' he answered. 'Including a tent. You'll have fun putting that up. No magic allowed,' he added with a wry smile.

Hannah avoided eye contact with Drakkar as he rounded the corner. It was too soon to see him and, judging by the sharp look he gave her, he felt similarly.

'Luck in your travels, Daegan,' Drakkar said, nodding. He nodded to Niall too, noticeably avoiding Hannah before producing a portal of purple haze from thin air.

Daegan led the way, followed by Niall and Kiko, leaving Hannah and Dex to bring up the rear. Drakkar gave her a warning look, and she could swear she heard him hiss, 'Be seeing you,' as she walked through the purple mist.

She would never get used to portals; the way they turned her stomach and made her head light—not to mention the drastic change in temperature. She held herself tightly and shuddered, blowing into her hands, rubbing them together.

Hannah looked around. Seemingly in the middle of nowhere, they were on top of a cliff with a sheer icy drop. To their right lay a dark forest with thick snow-capped trees.

'Hey,' Niall said, his voice soothing. 'You okay?'

'Cold…' was all Hannah could mutter. But there was something else; something she couldn't put her finger on. Something about Drakkar…

'Here,' Niall said, taking off his silver scarf. He wrapped it snugly around her, his fingers grazing her neck.

'W—w… what about y—you?' she stuttered, shaking with cold.

'I'll be fine,' he smiled. 'Besides, it suits you.'

Hannah smiled back, feeling a warm sensation as she did. She looked down and saw his telum pointed to her. Warmth flooded her body, and her muscles relaxed. He put a finger to his lips, silently reminding her that Daegan would disapprove if she hadn't cast it herself.

'Hurry!' Daegan called after them. 'We have a long walk ahead of us.'

Hannah groaned and trudged through the thick snow after him, each step sinking to her shins.

'Looks like Drakkar hates you,' Niall whispered. 'That look he gave you…'

'Tell me something I don't know,' she mumbled.

'So, what happened? I didn't see you for the rest of the day. Did he tell you about the vault? Was I right? I bet it's nothing to worry about.'

As they made their way through the heavy snow, Hannah told Niall everything that happened; Egypt, the traps, the mummies and serpopard, Hortes and how Drakkar denied any knowledge of the vault.

'Wow.' Niall whistled. 'He flat out denied it? Then maybe it's all okay. I told you!'

'We still don't know that. We need to know why he's so cagey and why he wants to open it.'

'We don't *need* to know,' Niall muttered.

'And who locked it in the first place?' Her mind darted back to Daegan and Sophie's conversation about her blood crystal.

'I'm surprised he's sentimental enough to have a photo of someone in his office. I wonder who she is… And I have to admit the sphinx is interesting…' Niall mused aloud. 'There's something he needs to know; something he has no way of finding out himself. Why else would he need a sphinx? Near omniscience… Whatever Drakkar wants, that sphinx is his key.'

'So, we need to get to the sphinx before he does. Right?' Her heart pumped faster, excited at the prospect of beating Drakkar at whatever game he was playing.

'I guess…' Niall replied. 'But,'—he gestured around at the snowy wilderness—'we can't do much from here.'

Hannah sighed dejectedly. 'Let's hope we get back before it's too late.'

Chapter Forty-Four

Briefing

AFTER four hours of intense walking, Daegan agreed to make camp in the forest. It seemed like an age of pushing their way past trees before they found a suitable space to set down for the night.

Daegan sat on a stump, sharpening his telum as he ordered Hannah and Niall to set up the camp.

'I don't suppose you can lend us a hand?' Hannah snapped as her tent fell down for the fourth time.

Daegan shook his head. 'I won't always be here to hold your hand, Hannah. Get used to doing things yourself.'

Hannah grumbled beneath her breath and started again. Luckily, Niall struggled less and gave Hannah a hand. After finally erecting the tent, they moved onto making a fire and preparing a meal. This they found easier, using her blood crystal to dry the sticks and start the fire. Naturally, Daegan didn't approve—'You can't always rely on magic,' he chastised—but by that point they were so cold they were just grateful for the warmth.

At least Daegan showed a glimmer of concern when Hannah tested and gave herself insulin before eating. It didn't take long for the meal to heat up, but as they wolfed it down, Hannah missed

Arcadia. She regretted how she took the meals for granted, not to mention the hobs and brownies that treated her and Niall to food in their rooms.

'I'm sure you've noticed we're not in Thule just yet,' Daegan said. 'Hence why we're camping here. I'm sure you understand the limits Drakkar's portals have. As convenient as they are, this is the closest we can get to Thule via a portal. That's why so many Etheria choose to come to Thule. It's well protected; not just because of where it is situated, but because of the protective charm that restricts even warlocks. Luckily, I know the quickest route—it's just a couple of hours away.'

'Why not head there now? Get it done with,' asked Hannah, shivering as she sipped at her warm soup.

'Not wise with some of the wild Etheria that roam here at night. Qiqirns, haietliks…'

Niall leaned over to her. 'I'll go through them tomorrow.'

'Not to mention we've had some trouble with Thrunters around these parts—led by a callitrix no less.'

'Aren't callitrixes Etheria?' asked Niall.

Daegan nodded. 'They give birth to twins—the mother loves one but not the other. And now one that *wasn't* loved now leads a band of Thrunters, determined to slaughter as many Etheria as he can. Simple revenge.

'Now, the reason we're here,' he continued, leaning forward, 'is to capture—*not* kill,' he emphasised, 'a saumen-kar.'

'A what?' Hannah asked.

Daegan rested his face in his palm and groaned. 'We went through this a couple of weeks ago. Niall—please.'

Niall straightened up, happy to oblige. 'Saumen-kar—very rare. Fascinating too.'

'The short version, please,' Hannah mumbled through a mouthful of soup.

'Saumen-kars aren't too dissimilar to yetis. These are the real deal—seven-foot-tall, white fur, black curled horns.'

'Sounds like a yeti.'

'But they're so much more!' Niall enthused. 'They either travel alone or in small groups, completely at one with nature. They're obsessed with humans—don't eat us though. One reason humans don't know about them is because they have telepathy and can make humans stray away or even forget they met them.'

'They sound easy-going. What's the problem with this one?' Hannah asked.

'The Queen of Thule has lost hers,' Daegan explained.

'The Queen? Does Arcadia have a king or queen too?'

'No,' Niall answered quickly, keen to show off. 'Etheria settlements all have their own culture and customs. Arcadia's more of a democracy, but Thule has a monarchy.'

'Okay. And the Queen of Thule has lost her pet?'

'More a partner... or companion,' replied Daegan.

'Like a *boyfriend*? Please tell me she's an Etheria too.'

'She is. Regardless, her saumen-kar has gone missing—a young one too. She wants it back; they can be quite dangerous when young.'

'I thought they didn't harm humans?'

'Not usually.' Niall shifted. 'But they can fly off the handle at a moment's notice. To calm them down, you could fight them—'

'—which is easier said than done—' Daegan interjected.

'—or tell stories.'

'Stories?' Hannah couldn't believe it.

'They love them,' Niall explained. 'It's one of the few things that calms them.'

'So, if it's about to kill me, I tuck it in with a bedtime story?'

Niall shrugged. 'If it listens.'

'I'm not sure we'll have a chance for that though,' Daegan warned them.

They fell into a silence, all three mulling over the stories they might have to tell the saumen-kar.

'Daegan. I have some questions.'

Daegan held back a sigh of weariness. 'Go on.'

'Faeries see what we do with our blood crystals, right? Can any other Etheria?'

'Oh, some. Not many. Depends on their senses.' He took a large gulp of steaming hot soup, savouring the flavour.

'Zburătors?' she asked.

Daegan's spoon stopped midway towards his mouth as he stared, suspicion beaming from his eyes. 'Yes, they can sniff out blood crystals,' he replied, his words slow and pronounced. 'What's this about?'

'Is that how Zelom killed so many Trucekeepers?'

Daegan glared at them both, curious about what they had been saying behind his back. 'Yes…'

'So, blood crystals connect to us; they read our mind, sense our feelings… is that why you appeared to me?'

Daegan sipped his soup. '*Felix culpa*,' he said quietly.

Hannah turned to Niall. He shrugged. 'Lucky accident, I think. Perhaps the crystal knew you were in danger,' he said. 'So Drakkar summoned a portal that—'

'That's not how it works!' Daegan exclaimed, dropping his bowl and resting his face in his hands. 'Gods, I don't want to explain this…' He got to his feet, gave them each a look and turned his back to them. 'We have a big day tomorrow. Don't stay up too late,' he muttered before he zipped up his tent and left them in the cold.

Niall and Hannah followed soon after. Hannah's tent was cramped but thankfully warm and cosy compared to the biting frost outside. As she climbed into her sleeping bag, she flexed every muscle, trying to bring life back her to her body. Dex nuzzled deep in the safety of the sleeping bag.

It wasn't long after they turned in that Hannah was awoken by a distant howling sound. Dex heard it too. His tail sharpened and prodded Hannah's chest.

Curious, she grabbed her telum and slipped quietly out of her tent while Dex took shelter in the warm remains of her sleeping bag. She stepped forward, bare feet nestling in the snow, fear coursing so furiously around her body that she barely noticed the cold.

She heard the sound again, this time more a low hum, and pressed her thumb to the crystal. Obediently, the telum produced a small ball of fire, which Hannah balanced on her hand. Loyal to its creator, the fireball didn't burn her, instead giving off warmth and light. She caressed it, ready to propel it at an enemy.

But no one attacked—neither human nor Etheria.

Save for the whistle of the icy wind blowing through the creaking trees and the gentle humming, there was silence. Hannah strained her eyes to make out a blue glow shining in the distance. Captivated, she stared for what seemed an eternity, the fireball growing smaller and smaller until it fizzled out.

She tried hard to get some rest, but her dreams were haunted by thoughts of qiqirns, saumen-kars and a mysterious blue glow that got closer and closer.

Chapter Forty-Five

Rotten Luck

DAEGAN woke Hannah and Niall at the crack of dawn. Hannah's immediate response was to roll over and go back to sleep, but Daegan zipped down the door to her tent. Freezing air invaded her tent, rudely awakening her.

After a disappointing breakfast that would have devastated Jason, they set off to Thule. Daegan had little care for Hannah's sore body and tired muscles, jetting off at the same pace as yesterday. He led the way while Niall and Hannah followed. Dex and Kiko were having the time of their lives; Dex's white fur and small body was perfect for hiding in the snow, and Kiko loved trying to sniff him out.

'Okay… erm—chimera,' Niall said, a cheeky grin on his face.

Hannah screwed up her eyes as she thought. She loved when she got an Etheria question right, but that was few and far between.

'I know it's a hybrid.'

Niall chuckled. 'Anything specific?'

Hannah shrugged. 'It's got a few tails?'

'Not tails…'

'Heads!' Hannah shouted. 'It's got multiple heads.'

'How many?'

Hannah groaned. 'Can't you just be happy I got the head thing?'

'You didn't. You said tails first.'

Hannah rolled her eyes. 'Three?'

'And what are they?'

With a shrug, Hannah said, 'Er... lion, snake and... I don't know, goat?'

'Spot on.' Niall gave her a nudge.

Hannah spent a second looking at Niall's cheery face, snowflakes nestling in the wisps of his peach fuzz, and smiled. She almost barged into Daegan who had stopped still.

'Look!' he whispered excitedly.

He was pointing to a bird in a tree. At first, Hannah assumed it was just an owl watching them go by. But the closer she looked, she realised it wasn't just an owl. It was three-feet-tall with long legs like a heron and thin, spindly arms beneath its wings—the strangest Etheria Hannah had seen yet. She couldn't help laughing.

'What is that?' she asked between loud giggles.

The Etheria scowled before flapping its wings and taking flight, soaring into the distance.

'Damn foolish girl!' Daegan growled.

'Was that a chickcharney?' Niall asked incredulously as he flipped to a fresh page in his notebook, his hand a blur as he sketched the Etheria that had disappeared.

'Yes,' replied Daegan, 'and thanks to *her*, we might have just jeopardised our entire mission.'

Hannah's laugh died down. 'Why's that? What even is a... what was it?'

'Chickcharnies are *unbelievably* rare Etheria. You might come across one in your entire life—two if you're lucky.'

'So what?'

'Chickcharnies kind of affect the future,' Niall said. 'Right?'

Daegan nodded. 'If a traveller comes across a chickcharney and treats it well, good fortune is supposed to be with him. But if he mistreats it, misfortune will follow.' He looked at Hannah, disappointment in his eyes. 'I thought I taught you better than this.'

Hannah shuffled her feet in the snow, all traces of laughter now distant.

'On the ground,' Daegan said suddenly.

'What?' *Is this some weird punishment?* she thought.

'On the ground!' he repeated, this time a shout. He flicked his wrist, and his shield gauntlet popped out. 'Now!'

Hannah obeyed and flung her body to the ground just in time to see a shadow leap over her. A toothy jaw narrowly missed where her head had been just a second ago.

She rolled away and saw Daegan, shield gauntlet at the ready, block the attack of a large dog and push it to the side. He stunned it with a spell and lunged, jabbing his telum into its body.

Hannah recognised the qiqirns as a shiver ran down her spine. They somewhat resembled wolves but were almost entirely hairless. Through the random tufts of hair, its naked skin was a deathly white. Cold mist floated from their mouths as their tongues flopped down, drool dripping to the snowy ground as a pained, high-pitched growl emanated from their throats.

Hannah grabbed her telum and stood, flicking her own shield into place. Niall did the same.

Another dived towards Daegan, who responded with a spell that propelled the qiqirn against a tree where it collapsed with a whine.

One growled and advanced towards Kiko, who growled in return and readied her legs to pounce. But Niall leapt over her and landed on the qiqirn, plunging the sharp end of his staff into its back.

Hannah heard a bark from behind and turned to see a qiqirn charging full speed towards her. Dex slowed it down, cutting its tail with his own. Distracted, it yelped in pain, and Hannah kicked its head before firing a Strike spell. The qiqirn refused to stay down and growled louder. Hannah raised her right arm and brought her wrist-bow out, aiming at the qiqirn's head.

As her finger toyed with the trigger, Daegan barged her out of the way before launching a throwing knife.

'I had that one!' she complained.

'Almost,' he conceded, 'but you can't waste your arrows here.'

'You're right,' Niall agreed, shaking the wet snow out of his hair.

Suddenly, hidden in the shadows, a figure emerged, crossbow in hand. It pointed at Niall.

Hannah screamed in warning. Niall snapped round, managing to block an arrow with his shield just in time.

As he staggered back, the figure dropped the crossbow, taking a spear in hand and charging. Daegan wasted no time in hurrying over but soon slowed to a halt.

Apparently, Aarava's extra lessons had worked. Niall let loose on his attacker, beating him to a pulp. Only when the figure was unconscious on the snow did Niall step back.

'Thrunter scout,' Daegan said as he inspected the unconscious man and saw a tattoo on his neck—an arrow in a circle.

'How did he find us?' Hannah asked.

'Oh, I think we know why. Bad luck. I wonder who we can blame...' Daegan looked at Hannah. Her eyes dropped. 'Take a second to compose yourself. We'll continue shortly.'

The rest of their journey seemed even longer. Eventually, their proximity to Thule was marked by a sudden snowstorm that became more ferocious the nearer they came. It reached the point where they held onto their familiars and attached belt-ropes to one another for fear of separating. Hannah could barely see Daegan, all vision lost in a blur of impenetrable snow.

All five were shaking vigorously by the time they reached the base of a cliff resembling an iceberg. Daegan reached out a gloved hand and wiped snow from the cliff. Carved into the ice was a hole for his blood crystal. Daegan removed his glove, pricked his thumb and touched his blood to the crystal. A door formed in the ice, slowly opening for them to escape the cold.

Chapter Forty-Six

A Thulian Welcome Party

IT wasn't much warmer, but the lack of wind and heavy snow made a difference. Hannah and Niall looked at each other and laughed at how much snow had accumulated on their clothes, each of them looking like a snow monster themselves.

Dex and Kiko shook the snow from their fur as Daegan approached two men. They each wore bulky armour coated with fur and held sturdy spears, in which Hannah noticed familiar crystals embedded.

'Wait—are there Trucekeepers here too?' she asked.

'No,' replied Daegan. 'Trucesentries. They guard Etheria settlements. Here, El Dorado, Biringan City, Hyperborea—all of them. You've seen some in Arcadia—they're Mantir's men.'

Hannah's mind joined the dots as she thought back to the friendly Minotaur giving orders to his ragtag band of soldiers.

'*Na-se bot davo-vi. Yan-sa ik davo-Kuni Kori,*' Daegan announced to the Trucesentries.

He continued to speak a language Hannah didn't recognise, but the Trucesentries understood perfectly, nodding and even laughing.

'Wow, Daegan's funny in different languages?' she whispered to Niall. 'At least it's not just Latin. He should try some of that charm in English one day.'

'It's Thulian,' he told her. 'We won't learn it for a while.'

The Trucesentries and Daegan shook hands amiably. Then, to Hannah's surprise, Daegan unholstered his telum and handed it over, crystal still embedded in the handle. He beckoned for them to do the same.

'W-wait…' Hannah stuttered. 'I only just got this.'

'Hannah…' Daegan said in a voice of warning. 'Please.'

Niall unholstered his telum and placed the long staff into the outstretched palm of one of a Trucesentry. Hannah scowled and followed suit, slapping her dagger into the sentry's hand.

'You'll get it back,' Daegan muttered, smiling.

'It's like going through airport security,' Niall explained. 'They can't risk a rogue Trucekeeper massacring somewhere like Thule.'

The two trainees, familiars in tow, followed Daegan and the Trucesentries down the steps carved into the ice. Once they rounded a corner, Hannah and Niall were treated to their first sight of Thule. They gasped at the azure beauty that lay before them, a snow-capped winter paradise.

Like Arcadia, it was as if a never-ending world had been hidden away, a haven for Etheria. Surrounding the outskirts were tall cliffs of ice leading up to the sky from which snowflakes floated down. In front of them, the steps widened to a grandiose ice staircase that led down to a path that wound through the middle of the hustle and bustle. On either side were buildings made from stone and ice, covered with a layer of snow. Behind these were frozen lakes, with Etheria fishing through a hole. An Etheria resembling a four-legged killer whale, an akhlut, was enjoying the feast of fish thrown up for him by the aglooik beneath while keeping the more mischievous qalupalik at bay.

There were Etheria Hannah recognised from Arcadia and some she had never seen before, better suited to the colder climate. Niall was having too much fun pointing out all the Etheria he recognised and jotting down notes in his book, though he received some disgruntled looks from the locals.

They passed the main square with an ornate ice fountain and saw a magnificent castle made entirely of ice. Hannah's jaw dropped; the towers climbed high into the sky, looking like giant icicles.

Suddenly, a large rock of ice narrowly missed her face, and she jumped back. Daegan stepped in front to protect her, more clumps of ice hitting his chest. Hannah peered over his shoulder and saw a crowd, presumably angry citizens, held back by exhausted Trucesentries.

'Get out of here!'

'You're not welcome here!'

'Down with the Queen! Down with the Queen! Down with the Queen!'

'What's going on?' Hannah whispered.

'I'm not sure,' he said, his voice rife with concern.

They followed the Trucesentries as they escorted them across the square, up the stairs and across the bridge into the castle. They barked orders in Thulian to more Trucesentries, and the heavy portcullis raised, the clinking of the chains louder than the busy path they had just passed.

They meandered through to a magnificent entrance hall lined with pillars on top of which blue flames danced. Even an ice chandelier dangled from the ceiling.

'Now,' Daegan warned in a hushed tone, 'let me do the talking. It's not that I don't trust you.' His eyes lingered on Hannah. 'There are certain things you do and do not say—especially to a queen. This is different, and we have to proceed with care.' He looked at them sternly. 'Understood?'

They were only half-listening, still in awe of the castle, but nodded in agreement, only snapping to attention when the enormous door in front of them opened.

They walked through to a throne room. A deep blue carpet led up to a pale woman lounging on a throne of immaculate ice. Trucesentries stood guard all around.

'Daegan, darling!' called out the woman.

She stood up and strutted to the rugged Trucekeeper. Daegan removed his hat and bowed.

The Queen proffered her hand, and Daegan kissed it lightly. There was a tense pause.

Then the Queen flung her arms around him and kissed him on the cheek.

Hannah saw Daegan give a small shudder and soon realised why as the lady went from Niall to Hannah, giving them each a tender handshake. Her hand was bitterly cold as though it had been dipped in ice water.

'Queen Kori.' Daegan bowed again.

'Oh, no need to be so formal,' Queen Kori replied. 'We know each other *far* too well for that,' she said with a wink as she lounged back on her throne, one leg kicking over the arm. 'Trainees?'

'Yes. Hannah and Niall.' Daegan gestured to each. 'Hannah's been with me the longest. She'll be taking part in the hunt. Niall is here to observe.'

'*Search*, Daegan—not hunt, Gods!'

Hannah was wondering why she made the distinction so clear when Dex jumped from her shoulder and flew to Queen Kori. Hannah held her breath and gave Daegan an apologetic shrug as he glared at her.

'Ah, how sweet!' shrieked the Queen. She stroked the kamaitachi who nuzzled against her cheek. 'The return of Trucekeepers *and* familiars—my, my!'

'It's been a while,' Daegan conceded. 'We thought a return to old traditions appropriate. Why not?'

'Why not indeed?' said the Queen.

A Trucesentry entered the room and bowed.

'Food?' asked the Queen.

The Trucesentry nodded, and she clapped her hands. 'Wonderful! You will join me,' she told the Trucekeepers, more an order than a request.

'We just popped by to get our briefing,' Daegan began. 'I think it would be better if we—'

'You will eat,' she insisted. 'Come.'

With that, the Queen rose from her chair and beckoned the Trucekeepers, who followed sheepishly.

Chapter Forty-Seven

The Etherian Queen

THE feast in Queen Kori's castle rivalled those in Arcadia. The dining hall was breathtaking; ice sculptures of Etheria surrounded them, and they were treated to live music by an orchestra of ahkiyyinis, skeletons who used their bones as percussion.

It didn't take long for Hannah and Niall to realise how famished they were and shovelled food into their mouths as soon as they sat down. Dex and Kiko had their own feast on the ground beside them. Daegan ate at a much slower pace, trying and failing to hide his embarrassment at the others eating with such reckless abandon.

'Of course, Thule's been dreadfully boring since the War ended. Don't you think so, Daegan?' The Queen didn't seem to care who was listening. 'Not that we miss the War per se, but we miss the excitement. You agree, Daegan.'

Daegan placed his knife and fork down, not daring to meet the Queen's gaze. He seemed exposed without his hat on. 'I'm afraid I disagree, your Highness.'

Hannah and Niall paused, mouths full, eyes fixed on Daegan.

'Oh?' she replied.

'There's no denying the excitement a war can bring, but when you find your friends are the ones paying the ultimate price… It's not something I would relish to repeat.' He cleared his throat and resumed eating.

Silence filled the hall. The Queen regarded him through narrow eyes.

'Your point is fair,' she mused.

An audible feeling of relief poured into the room, and the Queen continued to witter on. Hannah licked her lips and sat back, hands resting on her stomach. A pang of regret formed at the back of her mind; she had eaten so quickly she hadn't had a chance to enjoy it.

She inspected the Queen, particularly jealous of her ornate ice headband. She was fascinating to gaze at and made Hannah feel underdressed. It was no exaggeration to describe her skin as white as snow—whiter even. She even wore a white dress that flowed and fluttered in the breeze, a red sash tying it at the middle. Snowflakes fell from every gesture she made. Her blue lipstick, red nail polish and burgundy eye makeup stood out on her white skin, but her black hair made the strongest contrast, flowing down to her hips.

'What's happening outside?' Hannah asked.

Daegan glared.

'Your Majesty,' she added.

The Queen ignored Hannah's reluctance to address her by her title and dramatically waved her arms. 'Oh protests, protests. All subjects ever do is protest. Never be a queen, girl.' She jabbed at Hannah with a bony piece of meat. 'People always complain, and it's apparently all your fault.'

'Why are they upset?'

The Queen shrugged and took a large gulp of wine. 'They're happy my darling saumen-kar has gone missing. Damn peasants—I wouldn't be surprised if *they* orchestrated the disappearance. Something about not wanting to be sacrificed. I don't understand—it should be an honour!'

'Hang on. You sacrifice your people?'

'To my saumen-kar, yes.'

'Well, no wonder—'

A jolt of pain shot up from her shin. Daegan was glaring at her. His eyes alone threatened another kick. Nursing her leg, Hannah held her tongue.

'If you please, Your Majesty,' Daegan interrupted, 'would you mind briefing us? I'm in a rush to get back, you see. Being the only current Trucekeeper keeps me busy. I'm sure you understand.'

Queen Kori smiled and nodded. 'Being Queen means I too have to forgo some luxuries. The job is simple—retrieve my saumen-kar.'

'When was the last time you saw him?'

'In my room. Four days ago.'

'And do you know any cause he may have had to leave Thule?' Daegan asked.

The Queen shook her head. 'I hope it wasn't anything I…' she trailed off.

'Any distinguishing features? We don't want to bring back the wrong one.'

'His right horn,' she said. 'He was injured in a fight; he only has half a right horn.'

Niall nodded, jotting it down in his leather notebook.

'And no one saw him leave? Not even the Trucesentries?'

She shook her head. 'Saumen-kars' psychic powers can—'

'—Can make people forget they saw them,' he finished. 'I'm well aware.'

'I have to reiterate, Daegan. My saumen-kar is to be taken *alive* with no harm done.'

Hannah snorted. *We're Trucekeepers, not babysitters*, she thought. *We can't make any promises.*

Daegan flashed her a warning look.

'I'm sorry?' the Queen asked curtly.

Hannah held her tongue and stared at her plate, ignoring Daegan's kick from under the table.

But it was too late.

Queen Kori's eyes flashed a deep yellow and, suddenly, a sense of dread swallowed Hannah whole. She shivered as the Queen's eyes pulsed. Hannah couldn't tear her eyes away. She was on the verge of tears, ready to scream.

'It's not wise to upset a yuki-onna,' she snarled. 'If I wanted, I could keep you like this for the rest of your life.'

Hannah tried to respond, but all she could muster was a whimper.

'The saumen-kar is my beloved,' the Queen continued. 'He must not be harmed under any circumstances.'

As the Queen lifted her hold on her, Hannah felt the comfort of normality settle.

'I apologise, my Queen,' Daegan said, shaking with embarrassment or fury—Hannah couldn't tell. 'My trainee does not yet know her place.'

'See that she learns,' the Queen instructed.

The rest of the dinner was predictably awkward. Niall tried to cheer Hannah up but to no avail. Hannah was only trying to prove she could do whatever it took. Her appetite evaporated, and she poked at her food dejectedly until it was time to leave.

'I *told* you to let me do the talking,' Daegan hissed. 'I trained you better than this.'

'You'll need a guide,' the Queen declared.

'I hardly think that's necessary,' Daegan said.

'The wilds beyond Thule are perilous even on a good day.' She glanced at Hannah and added, 'It would be a pity if one of your trainees were to meet an unfortunate end.'

Daegan suppressed his reluctance and nodded.

'Gondei will meet you at the gates. Safe travels, Trucekeepers.

And Daegan,' she called from over her shoulder, gazing at him with half-closed eyes, 'do return before too long.'

The walk back through the crowded streets of Thule was a less wondrous experience. Hannah was already sick with this mission; she didn't want to save the saumen-kar for that Queen. She wanted to go home to Arcadia, wander through the forest with Niall, let Kiko and Dex play, skim stones across the lake to annoy the mermaids…

'Let's just head back,' she suggested. 'Let the Queen be deposed and beheaded.'

'Careful what you say,' Daegan told her, now more comfortable with his hat back on. 'A comment like that could cause more trouble than it's worth.'

'I believe I am to be leading your merry expedition,' chirped a voice as they approached the gate.

Hannah looked down and saw the strangest little man she had ever seen looking up at them, chest puffed out. At first, she assumed he was a Dwarf, but he looked different. Smaller and less rotund and muscular, this Etheria was nimbler with a mop of messy white hair. Beneath his large, radish-like nose was a bushy white beard that cascaded down his minuscule body and dangled by his enormous bare feet.

'You're a barbegazi!' Niall exclaimed.

The barbegazi bowed. 'Indeed, I am, kind sir. It is my honour to be your guide. Gondei—at your service.'

'Erm,' Daegan itched the back of his head. 'Pleasure, Gondei, but—'

'Likewise, good sir!' Gondei interrupted, his interminable grin already lifting Hannah's spirits.

'But… I don't think the Queen understands the dangers involved in—'

'Oh, I'm sure she doesn't. But I do! I've travelled with many great Trucekeepers over the years. Even your own Caedric would surely vouch for my usefulness. And the great Astraea!'

Hannah's ears pricked up again. *There's that name again!*

Daegan spoke quickly. 'Gondei, I'm going to cut this short. This might be dangerous. I cannot take responsibility for you. Do you understand?'

'I do, sir,' he replied, his confidence unwavering.

'And nothing I do or say can persuade you not to come?'

'I obey my Queen's orders, sir. However, on this mission your orders are Gondei's to obey.'

Daegan raised his hands in surrender. 'Fine,' he said, before beckoning Hannah to the side. 'We're about to leave Thule to begin the search,' he told her.

'Fine by me,' she replied. 'I'm keen to finish the job and get back to Arcadia anyway.'

Daegan nodded awkwardly, not really listening. 'I don't mean to fuss, but—'

'Is this about my diabetes?' She smiled slightly as Daegan nodded. 'It's fine, trust me. I've been dealing with it for years.'

'I know, but we're about to leave Thule, so you might get high or low. Keep an eye on it and let me know if there are any issues. We don't want to enter a combat situation with *that* as an additional problem.'

After a commanding nod from Daegan, the Trucesentries hauled open the door, and the harsh blizzard hit them once more. This failed to faze Gondei who slid out elegantly on his massive feet. There was a thud as the door to Thule closed behind them. Hannah, Niall and Daegan marched forward, trusting their lives in the hands of the barbegazi.

Chapter Forty-Eight

Snow Drops in Thule

THE barbegazi's feet were perfectly adapted to the snowy terrain, effortlessly sliding around as he guided the Trucekeepers, who instead sought the easiest route to traverse. He frequently whistled at them— only Daegan understood what he meant. They even had to do a light jog just to keep up with him. Daegan seemed unfazed, instead commenting on how Niall and Hannah had to improve their fitness.

'Sir!' Gondei called out as they neared the edge of a cliff. 'Are you equipped with climbing gear?'

Daegan nodded as he removed his belt-rope, urging Niall and Hannah to do the same. He gave them an all too brief tutorial on abseiling in icy conditions while Gondei found three sturdy boulders. His bulky muscles surprised Hannah as he pushed them to the cliff's edge.

'What about Kiko? She can't fly down like Dex.'

'No fear, boy,' Gondei said. 'I'll take good care of your pet.'

'They're not pets,' Daegan sighed, but Gondei paid no notice.

In a flash, he skied his way towards the edge of the cliff, picking up Kiko as he passed. Niall gasped as they slid over the edge. Kiko yelped with fear, her tails sticking out in terror.

They clambered towards the edge and peered over. The barbegazi landed with ease on the snow below, skidding to an elegant halt and letting Kiko down, her legs now shaking with fear as well as cold.

Biting back her nerves, Hannah followed Daegan's instructions, tying her belt-rope to a boulder and making sure it was secure.

'Now, when you're at the edge, just take a deep breath and—' Daegan didn't finish his sentence. Instead, he gave them a cheeky smirk and fell backwards. 'Just walk backwards!'

'Why isn't this something we learned back in Arcadia?' Hannah moaned.

Niall didn't reply. His eyes were glistening, tears threatening to break out.

'I don't like heights,' he whispered.

Hannah was stunned. Niall always seemed so confident, as if nothing could ever scare him. She lay a hand on his shoulder. 'It'll be fine. Your rope is secure, and we're all here to help you—even Gondei. Okay?'

Niall closed his eyes and sniffed before nodding.

They cautiously approached the cliffs with their backs, necks craning to see the edge behind them. Then they counted—five, four, three, two, one…

As Hannah leant backwards, her feet landed firmly on the cliff-face, her body now horizontal. She let out a giggle, surprised at how much fun she was having. She called out to make sure Niall was okay. He made no reply but nodded and audibly gulped. Sweat dripped down his face despite the freezing wind.

Daegan was already halfway down but still yelled words of encouragement. It was slow and arduous as they placed each cautious step against the ice, making sure not to slip. Occasionally they did; their bodies slammed into the icy wall, and snowflakes fell down. Dex hovered by Hannah's rope, anxiety emanating from his eyes. Hannah made sure his tail stayed far from her rope in case he accidentally cut it and sent her plummeting to her death.

By the time they were halfway down, Daegan had reached the bottom. Hannah heard a heated discussion and loud whistling.

'Why is he always doing that?' she snapped.

'It's how barbegazi communicate over long distances,' Niall explained.

Hannah wasn't keen on an Etheria lecture but knew it was good for him to distract his mind from the drop below.

'Whistles travel further than words. It's often mistaken for wind whistling through the mountains.'

'But what's he trying to tell us?'

'No idea,' Niall shrugged.

The whistling was ceaseless, but they ignored it, instead concentrating on walking down the cliff and landing in one piece. But the lower they went, the clearer they heard Daegan's shouts.

'Do you hear that?' Niall asked.

'Yeah, it's Daegan.'

'No,' Niall shook his head. 'That other sound.'

Hannah strained her ears, now aware of a distinct rumble coming from above them. Daegan's voice became clearer; Hannah made out one word, a word that sent a shiver down her spine.

'What's going on?' cried Niall, nerves burning.

'Okay, don't panic,' she said, working out how best to explain the situation. 'But... we have to hurry. Like, now.'

'Why?'

'Niall, just...' The rumbling sound intensified. 'Niall, I need you to withdraw your rope now!'

'What? Are you crazy? We're still so high—'

'We're low enough. There's deep snow. We have to chance it!'

'Why?' he screamed.

'Because there's an avalanche about to crush us!' she yelled, a light flurry of snow already falling; the deadly promise of something much more lethal.

But this didn't spur him into action. Instead, he froze in fear.

'Oh god, oh god, oh god,' he chanted under his breath.

Hannah shouted, tried to snap some sense into him—but her words fell on deaf ears and were carried away by the icy wind.

She ran sideways along the cliff-face, frantic to get to him. But she only got so far before she was hopelessly swung back the other way. She made a run for it again, this time making it further, but still swinging back. Hannah carried on like this, each time getting closer and closer as the rumbling grew louder and louder.

She was almost there. She swung back, unholstered her telum and sprinted. Niall was an arm's length away. She swiped and sliced his rope. He screamed as he hurtled to the ground, disappearing in a cloud of snow.

Hannah looked down, praying that she hadn't killed him, when she slipped and crashed into the wall. She flinched and lost grip of her telum, now lost in the snowy expanse beneath.

The rumbling rose to a roar. No more time—this was it.

Quick as a flash, Dex's tail whirled and sliced the rope, freeing Hannah as she felt herself being pulled to the ground. Wind roared in her ears as she fell, only letting out a grunt as she landed with a *thud*.

Her back screamed as it hit the ground, falling through the deep snow. She groaned as she opened her eyes. The immense heap of snow had toppled over the cliff and was heading straight for her.

Without a second to lose, Niall jumped on top of her and pointed his telum towards the snow. A transparent purple barrier spurted from the blade and encompassed them, covering them in a protective ball. The avalanche crashed against the shield, and Niall was thrown against Hannah, still holding his bloody thumb to the pulsating crystal. Hannah whimpered as the snow smacked against the Shield spell, burying them in a chamber of ice.

Chapter Forty-Nine

An Icy Grave

AFTER a while, the heavy thuds of snow piling on snow ceased.

There was silence.

Niall let go of his crystal and sat back, drained. The Shield spell dissipated, leaving them in a small, spherical cocoon surrounded by hard, compacted ice and little room to manoeuvre. For the next minute, they looked only at each other, lost for words.

They were trapped.

Niall coughed and rubbed his hands together. Every word from his mouth was mist in the cold. 'We need to get out of here. Any ideas?'

No longer dangling over a height, Niall was back to his normal self. Hannah wished she had even a glimmer of his positivity.

'We need to—I don't know… dig our way out?' she said, too stunned to think straight.

Niall slowly nodded. 'Could do. What with?'

Hannah sorted through her inventory in her head: shurikens, throwing knives—useless; belt-rope—broken; telum—lost. Shield gauntlet—

'Shield gauntlet!' she exclaimed, her negativity slowly ebbing. 'We can use that like a spade.'

Without a moment to lose, they both slammed the sharp edge of their shields against the snow, rewarded with a few chips of ice falling to their feet.

'It's too solid,' Niall said. 'No way we can smash through.'

'So, burn it,' she told him.

'What?'

'I dropped my telum. Yours is still strapped to your back. Cast a spell, melt the ice. If we soften it enough, we can break through and dig our way out.'

Though competent with magic, Niall was already drained from the shield and struggled casting fire. Only a slight jet of fire shot out, but it was enough for the snow to soften. Hannah laughed with excitement and chipped away, a chunk falling away to reveal a hole above them.

They continued like this for the next half hour, Niall softening the snow with fire and Hannah bashing away at it while he rested. A steady stream of melted snow poured to their feet until they were standing in a puddle up to their shins.

'Wait,' hissed Hannah. 'Do you hear that?'

They pressed their ear to the snow. A second later, an object smashed through, and the night sky above glimmered. Daegan was digging with his shield too, Gondei with his feet, and Dex and Kiko with their claws.

'Nice of you to drop in,' Daegan said as he helped them out.

'Oh, ha ha,' Hannah replied, gratefully taking hold of his hand.

So, that's a glimpse of the old Daegan that Sophie promised, she mused.

He hauled them to the surface and patted them on the back. 'I think we deserve a short break. Any shelter nearby, Gondei?'

'There's a village not a half mile away,' Gondei informed them, pointing in the distance.

'Right. Pick yourselves up,' Daegan commanded. 'We'll have a rest there and…' he glanced at their wet feet, '… perhaps a change of boots. Here.' He threw a white object, and Hannah caught it by the handle. She hadn't realised how empty she had felt without her telum. 'Don't lose it again,' he warned.

Although half a mile wasn't too far, it seemed the longest part of the journey to Hannah and Niall—uncomfortable, drenched and exhausted.

Suddenly, Gondei stopped dead, hands darting to his mouth. 'Oh… what could have happened?' he gasped.

Hannah looked up from her sodden feet and saw the village. Only it was no longer a village. Instead, there was nothing but rubble.

Wooden huts were smashed to pieces, charred, black and burnt to a crisp. Clothes and belongings were strewn about the ground, as were other sights they chose not to dwell on. Hannah surveyed the barren wasteland, a shiver running down her spine, this time nothing to do with the cold.

'Amka!' cried Gondei. He rushed to a small doll in the snow, its head limp as the stitching tried desperately to hold on to the body. 'No…' He turned to the others, tears streaming down his face. 'I knew this village. I knew Amka, the girl who held this doll so dear… She was my friend… I know I shouldn't have approached a human community. But they were so kind, so welcoming. I had injured myself nearby—my leg was broken. Cowering in the snow, I was sure I would die. Then a small girl approached me. I was terrified. I'd heard so many horror stories about humans. Besides, she'd seen me—I'd broken the Truce! But she took me into their village. The others—they helped me, nursed me back to health. Ever since, I've made sure to check on them, make sure they were safe and happy. But now…' He buried his face in the doll and wept.

Daegan ushered Hannah and Niall into a dilapidated hut and instructed them to light a fire before comforting the barbegazi.

Doing her best to ignore the heart-breaking sobs, Hannah took a moment to test her blood sugar before changing into a dry pair of boots and taking a spare belt-rope from Daegan's bag. She hoped he wouldn't tell Gondei off for interacting with a human village in the first place.

It took time, but somehow Daegan motivated Gondei to get moving again. With a determined fury, he sniffed and rifled through the snow. 'Qiqirns…' he whispered. 'But they're usually so docile. Surely they couldn't have—'

'Actually,' Daegan interrupted, 'it could be qiqirns. We ran into a pack on our way to Thule. They almost caused us a couple of casualties. Something's got them riled up…'

Niall's eyes lit up. 'The saumen-kar.'

'Don't be preposterous,' Gondei dismissed.

'They can impact the minds of humans, even many Etheria. It's not impossible for him to have infected their minds, made them vicious.'

Hannah thought how extraordinary, morbid even, it was for Niall to seem so excited by such a tragedy.

Daegan nodded at Gondei who looked at them dumbfounded. 'It's possible. We need to find this saumen-kar quickly.'

'Indeed,' Gondei fumed. 'I'll see if I can pick up any more leads. We'll soon be rid of these murderous isfetters,' he mumbled as he stomped into the village.

'Er, isfetters?' Hannah asked Niall under her breath.

'It's a word Etheria use. You know their obsession with ancient languages. It's a combination of the Egyptian word *isfet* and Norse word *vættr*. I guess you could translate it to "evil monster."' His eyes were alive with excitement.

Hannah couldn't help but laugh. 'You like this way more than you should.'

'Hannah. Niall,' Daegan said from the doorway. 'We've got a lead. Heading out in two minutes.'

Among the multitude of qiqirn tracks were also saumen-kar footprints, as well as a scent. Niall's theory seemed increasingly correct. He stayed quiet but still smug; Hannah could see it on his face. With Dex's keen eyes following the footprints and Kiko following the scent, they headed off with new determination towards the saumen-kar.

Chapter Fifty

Spirits in Forests

AFTER an hour of wading through the snow with Gondei mumbling what he was going to do to the saumen-kar, they reached a dark forest. The branches of the trees looked like veins pumping life through the heart of the forest itself. No light passed through the trees that shuddered audibly in the wind, sounding like a rocking chair creaking back and forth with no one inside.

Hannah shivered. 'Please tell me we're not going in there.'

'We are if that's where the tracks lead us,' Daegan said. 'Although, I'll admit, I'd rather not. I've heard tales of this forest before. Gondei—suggestions?'

'That blasted brutum could be in that forest. We follow the tracks,' he insisted, leading the way into the murky mass of trees.

The others followed more timidly. Dex held on to Hannah's shoulder, claws almost digging into her skin. She understood how he felt; the forest seemed alive, as if warning anyone who entered that they may never leave.

'Niall—shine a light with your telum,' Daegan ordered, doing the same himself. 'Hannah, summon your sword. This is where you'll need it.'

Hannah nodded, eagerly obeying his orders. A little too keen, in fact, pricking her thumb too hard and sending a spurt of blood onto the virgin snow. She pressed it to her crystal—nothing happened. She tried again, closing her eyes and pushing her thumb more forcefully against the crystal. Still, it remained untransformed. She sighed, embarrassed as they all watched, and reluctantly pulled out the tile Sophie had given her. She gazed at the shape of the gash the sword had made in the tile and felt the telum transform, the handle shaping in her hand.

Niall nodded his approval. 'Hey, Daegan—when do I get one of those?'

'Quiet!' he hissed. He crouched down and beckoned the others to do the same. 'Hannah, do you remember what your sword can do?'

'Yes, it can drive away ghosts… something like that?'

'It dispels *spirits*—don't just say ghosts. Keep it going while we're here,' he instructed. 'As long as you can.'

Hannah did as he said, following Gondei's lead with Niall and Daegan shining lights on either side. A strong vibration from the sword made her jump, nearly losing contact with the crystal.

'It's shaking… Did I do something wrong?'

'No,' he replied in a whisper, 'that means it's keeping something at bay. Something's following us.'

They looked around, surrounded by nothing but trees, snow and shadows.

Still, they continued, the hairs on Hannah's neck standing up. Whether or not the sword shook, she remained convinced something was behind her. But she heard nothing save for the quiet whistle of the wind, the creak of trees and footsteps.

She stopped dead.

'Do you hear that?' she asked.

'Hear what?' asked Niall.

Hannah's body went tense, listening. 'Those footsteps!'

Niall whipped around, telum at the ready for a fight—but nothing was there, save for their own footprints.

'I… I must have imagined it,' she muttered, brow furrowed.

'No, you didn't,' Daegan told her. 'Niall, cast the Tracker spell.'

The footprints on the snow lit up, revealing the steps they had all taken, each person's a different shade of red. Daegan inspected them; although similar sizes, he made out his own, Hannah's and Niall's; Dex was still clutching onto Hannah's shoulder, and Kiko and Gondei's footprints were unmistakable. However, sure enough, there was an extra pair glowing a bright scarlet, about half the size of Hannah's.

Daegan chuckled. 'Everyone step to the side,' he commanded. 'After you, Betobeto-san,' he said confidently, gesturing for something to pass. Nothing appeared, nothing jumped out—but the scarlet footprints continued, slushing through the snow as though some invisible being passed by.

'Betobeto,' Daegan explained. 'They're quite harmless. They follow travellers and try to synchronise their pace with them, getting closer and closer.'

'What happens when they catch up to you?' Niall asked, his voice a bizarre combination of dread and enthusiasm.

'Oh, nothing. They're really quite harmless. Let's continue.'

Daegan's words hadn't dispelled Hannah's fears, but the sword vibrating in her hand was a comfort. *At least it's working.*

'Must be the jumbees,' Daegan explained when she told him how the sword hadn't stopped shaking. She didn't appreciate the kapres huddled in the treetops, almost hidden save for their silhouettes and eyes shining in the dark.

Hannah pushed through, sword held aloft, determined not to look at any more Etheria as she passed. She swallowed any temptation to run.

She soon felt the familiar sensation of being drained; her head became light, and she stumbled slightly. Giving the crystal enough blood to summon the sword was shockingly similar to when her blood sugar went low.

A vague, sour aroma filled her nose. She tried to block it out, but soon her head went fuzzy, and, out of the corner of her eye, she spotted a man staring at her between the trees.

She looked over—nothing.

Suspicions cast aside, she faced the front and continued. But then she sensed it again, once more out of the corner of her eye; the same thing—a man, staring at them. She couldn't be sure, only spying it from her peripherals, but she could have sworn he had antlers and a rotated face, his eyes vertical.

She raised her sword, preparing to attack the lurking figure. But once more, there was nothing.

'What's wrong?' Niall asked.

Hannah didn't know how to respond, not even sure of what she had seen.

Daegan nodded. 'I saw them too.'

'What were they?' Kapres and betobetos she could handle, but whatever lurked in the corner of her eye was much more sinister.

'An ijiraq. Only one, mind you; ijirait often travel in packs. Niall, know anything about ijirait?'

Niall's eyes were still flicking from side to side. 'Bits,' he replied, distracted. 'They're said to be caught between the world of the living and the dead—'

'Superstition,' Daegan interrupted. 'Stick to the facts.'

'They're either helpful or deceptive. Some kidnap children. Their basic form is a deformed human with a lengthwise face and antlers. But you can only see them from the corner of your eye; when you turn to look at them, they disappear.'

'Top marks,' Daegan praised. 'Keep the sword aloft, and they ought to stay back.'

'I can't keep it up much longer!' she snapped. 'I feel like I'm going to pass out.'

'Worry not, ma'am!' cried Gondei, louder than appropriate for the forest. 'We are approaching the exit. The saumen-kar went this way!'

With a determined yell, Gondei slid across the snow at great speed, disappearing behind the trees.

The Trucekeepers, however, weren't nearly so keen to expel so much energy before a fight and went forward at their own pace, relieved to emerge from the forest unscathed.

Outside the forest, they found themselves in a field caught between the trees and a large lake. The snow was heavy, covering up any tracks. They followed Gondei who had slowed to a halt and was searching for any sign of the saumen-kar.

'I seem to have lost it,' Gondei told them apologetically.

Niall cast another Tracker spell, and once more, red footprints illuminated in the snow. They examined the tracks, noticing how they led to a pile of snow-covered boulders.

Daegan cautiously took off his belt-rope, eyes fixed on the pile of rocks.

As if on cue, the heap of boulders moved ever so slightly, as if they were breathing. Then they contorted as an arm stretched out and yawned. The hairs on Hannah's neck stood up again as she realised that the saumen-kar was just mere paces ahead of them.

Suddenly, the forest didn't seem so bad anymore.

Chapter Fifty-One

Shadows in the Snow

IT stood on its hind legs, at least twice the height of a man. It breathed heavily through its nose, searching for their scent.

'Crouch down,' Daegan hissed. 'Don't... move... a muscle. Niall—hide us.'

Obediently, they crouched, the faithful familiars hiding behind their backs. Niall whispered to Kiko who closed her eyes, concentrating intensely before opening them. Her eyes now glowed as white as the snow below her.

'What's she doing?' Hannah asked, waving her hand in front of the kitsune's face. Kiko didn't respond.

'Kitsunes create illusions, able to hide themselves. We'll get her to expand the illusion to cover us as well,' Niall said in a hushed whisper. 'We can't cast the Shadow spell on snow—we'd stand out like a sore thumb.'

It seemed to take her considerable effort, but Kiko kept up the illusion, and they remained invisible. The saumen-kar's eyes passed over them as it searched eagerly for the source of their scent.

Most of its body looked like an over-sized polar bear with thick white fur, albeit dirty and matted as if it hadn't washed in weeks. Its face was considerably more terrifying; a contrast to its white body, the face was a dark grey, one eye a searing bright blue and the other gleaming red. Its curved horns were as long as Hannah's arm and, sure enough, one was shorter than the other.

'That's the one,' Daegan said under his breath. 'Don't attack until he spots us. We need to surprise him.'

But Hannah wasn't listening. She was more concerned with Gondei, whose rapid breathing became heavier and angrier.

'Surprise him? We can't let that thing live another second.'

'Gondei,' Daegan cautioned. 'Don't let this get personal. We have an order from your Queen.'

'To hell with her orders!' shouted Gondei. The saumen-kar flinched, looking for the source of the raspy voice. 'He killed my friends!'

His shouts now an emotional battle cry, Gondei's long feet shot him at speed across the snow. Kiko yelped, and her eyes returned to normal as her illusion of invisibility faded. The saumen-kar spotted them, stamped its feet and roared. The roar shook the trees, snow falling from the branches.

Gondei bent his knees, speed increasing, and leapt, soaring through the air with a small dagger aimed at the saumen-kar's face. With little effort, the saumen-kar flicked the barbegazi, sending him crashing into a nearby tree. He slid to the ground and lay motionless.

Hannah's mouth dropped open as she ran to the barbegazi's aid. But the saumen-kar slammed his fist in front of her, blocking her way. The earth quaked, and she fell, rolling to avoid another slam. Kiko flicked her tail, and balls of fire soared towards the monster.

How come his familiar can do so much? she thought enviously.

Dex dug his sharp tail into the saumen-kar's shoulder. It screamed and tried to snatch him from the air, but Dex was too nimble, easily avoiding its hand and slashing with his sharp claws.

'Once upon a time,' Niall began, his voice almost drowned out by the saumen-kar's grunts, 'there lived a—'

The saumen-kar's blue eye became wide and bright as it searched for Niall. The three of them paused, hoping the fight would be cut short. But then its face contorted in pain, the red eye glowed fiercer and the saumen-kar roared once more.

'I don't think stories will pacify it,' Daegan said. 'Good try, but looks like we need to move to plan B.'

'The Queen seriously wants this maniac back in Thule? No wonder the people are rioting!' Hannah yelled.

'Ours is not to reason why,' Daegan responded. 'Get your belt-ropes ready. I'll try to bring this thing to the ground. When I do, bind its arms and hold tight!'

With the saumen-kar distracted, Daegan crouched on one knee and withdrew a green vial from his coat. He poured a viscous liquid onto a handful of throwing knives he held in his gloved hand.

'Sleeping serum,' Daegan explained. 'Once these hit the saumen-kar, it'll be easier to keep it on the ground—I hope. Niall,' he commanded, 'cast a shield to contain him!'

Niall clenched his staff and cast the same spell that saved them from the avalanche earlier. The saumen-kar charged, running into an invisible barrier and roaring in confusion.

'Now lower the shield!' he shouted.

Niall did so.

'Hannah—flash!'

A dazzling flash erupted from Hannah's telum, and the saumen-kar staggered, rubbing its eyes.

Daegan leapt forward and threw three knives in quick succession, each hitting their mark in the Etheria's chest. Furious, the saumen-kar responded with a roar and leapt forward, its immense body whacking Hannah and Daegan off their feet. Dazed, they lay in the snow, writhing in pain.

Together, they saw bright eyes staring down at them as it licked its lips.

'No!' Niall shouted as he came running towards them.

But he was too far. Hannah shut her eyes and braced for the inevitable.

The saumen-kar paused as a bark echoed from behind it. Its eyes grew wide, as if suddenly terrified.

The clouds darkened, and Hannah could swear she heard a rumble. A bolt of lightning accompanied a crack of thunder. An Etheria rocketed above them, colliding against the saumen-kar and biting its neck, shaking with sparks of lightning spurting sporadically.

The saumen-kar whimpered and fled with heavy strides as Hannah and Daegan lay on the ground, wheezing.

Daegan stumbled to his feet and limped his way to the Etheria that had just saved them—a wolf with a majestic blue-grey coat and jets of dark blue across its body. The occasional spark of electricity danced around it. It looked remarkably similar to the wolf painted on Daegan's shield gauntlet.

'It can't be...' Daegan gasped in wonder. 'Raji?'

The Etheria turned and rushed towards Daegan who flung his arms around it. The wolf rubbed its head lovingly against his shoulder and howled.

'What is it?' asked Hannah, brushing wet snow off her body. 'An amarok? How many types of wolves are there?'

'No way!' exclaimed Niall, carrying the still unconscious Gondei. 'Daegan... is that a raiju? I thought they were—'

'A myth?' Daegan chortled.

'Can someone explain?' Hannah asked, as she checked Gondei's pulse.

'A raiju is said to be the companion to a God of Lightning,' Niall told her. 'There was a rumour that that one raiju managed to reproduce and create a race. I never thought I'd see one. Daegan— you know her?'

'Know her?' Daegan looked at him incredulously. 'Of course I do. She's my familiar!'

Hannah couldn't believe it, looking from Raji to Dex. 'How is *that* your familiar? It's like a boss battle compared to my level one.' Dex mewed as though hurt. 'No offence, Dex.' She gave him a tickle under the chin, and he purred as though all were forgiven.

'Raji saved me before she was even my familiar. We formed a bond, and… well, they bent the rules, but Raji was allowed to stay with me. When she disappeared, I assumed she died in the War.' He ruffled Raji's hair; she closed her eyes in contentment. 'But no one gets the best of my Raji! Gods, where have you been?'

Hannah and Niall gave Daegan some space and checked on Gondei.

'He's still alive,' Hannah said. 'But he needs help. He can't stay out here.'

Niall nodded in agreement. 'I'll fire a flare with my telum. Thule ought to send someone.'

'In the meantime, we've got a saumen-kar to catch,' Daegan said.

Hannah couldn't suppress a grin as she saw Daegan next to Raji. It was amazing how perfectly they suited each other. Hannah never realised how empty Daegan must have felt without her.

Newfound confidence surging through their veins, they covered Gondei with a blanket and chased after the saumen-kar.

Chapter Fifty-Two

Monsters in the Snow

DAEGAN headed off first, Niall and Hannah trailing after him. Hannah couldn't deny the mission had become a lot more interesting with the raiju's arrival; it couldn't fail to disappoint. With the Tracker spell and Raji leading the way, it took no time to locate the saumen-kar again.

They crouched behind a mound of boulders and examined the area. It sat in a clearing surrounded by the forest and a pack of ravenous qiqirns. Hannah raised her wrist-bow and looked down the sights, aiming at the saumen-kar's head. Daegan slapped her hand away.

'What do you think you're doing?'

'Ending the problem before it kills us,' she replied. Again, Daegan slapped her hand away as she raised it once more.

'Raise that arm one more time, and I'll break it in two,' he growled. 'We do this *my* way. Understand? Because if you don't, you can wait with Gondei while Niall and I take care of this.'

Hannah avoided Daegan's glare and sulked. She wanted to argue back but knew it was useless.

'Do you understand?'

Hannah nodded. She didn't want to admit it, but she was scared. The saumen-kar had already proven how powerful it was. If their luck ran out, all it would take was one wrong move.

'Right,' said Daegan, a plan in mind. He once more poured the contents of a green vial on a couple of throwing knives. 'Niall— take Kiko and Raji to keep the qiqirns at bay. The saumen-kar has them under his influence. Use your Shield spell to create a barrier that will separate half of them from the fight. Kiko and Raji can take care of the other half. Hannah—you, Dex and I will take on the saumen-kar.'

Hannah winced. *Why pick me?*

'Dex will distract the saumen-kar while we weaken it and tie it down. Everyone understand?' There was a general murmur of agreement. 'Excellent. Remember: *coniunctis viribus*—we're stronger together.' He took a deep breath and lowered his hat. 'Let's get cracking.'

As they leapt over the boulders, the saumen-kar and its army of qiqirns growled. Daegan's telum transformed into Groundbreaker, shining a cautionary red. He slammed it on the ground, and the earth quaked. Qiqirns spread their legs as they struggled to keep their balance.

The Trucekeepers charged, telums at the ready. Hannah fired a shockwave at a band of qiqirns, propelling them into a larger group that Niall then contained with his Shield spell, cutting them off from the rest of the fight. They snapped their jaws and leapt against the barrier, but Niall held firm. Kiko and Raji corralled the others outside the barrier, avoiding their attacks and firing warning shots of fire and lightning.

Meanwhile, Dex seized the saumen-kar's attention, swishing his sharpened tail above its head and cutting its one intact horn in half. It roared in agony and rage, trying to grab the kamaitachi who expertly dodged out of the way.

'Kori's not going to like that,' Daegan cursed under his breath.

With a grunt, he threw two throwing knives; one the saumen-kar batted away, clinking to the ground, but the other lodged itself in its chest. It staggered back as it finally felt the effects of the poison.

'Now!' Daegan shouted in delight. 'Stun him!'

Hannah pressed her crystal and fired a flash that dazed the Etheria, ready to move on to the next phase.

But she was distracted as a qiqirn dodged a fireball from Kiko and galloped towards Hannah. She bashed its face with her shield and stuck her telum deep in its side. She withdrew the dagger, realising this was the first time she had used her new telum's blade. It cut like a dream and was infinitely better than the training one.

She heard a bark and saw another charging towards her. She pricked her thumb and placed it to the crystal. A blast from the telum threw the already dead qiqirn towards the approaching one, landing on top and knocking it out.

'Hannah! Where are you?'

Hannah turned back to Daegan who held on to his belt-rope, now tied firmly around the saumen-kar's right arm. It tried to pummel him with its left but couldn't reach. Hannah raced towards it and looped her own rope around its other arm.

'Hold tight,' Daegan warned her as he aimed his telum towards its legs and sent a gust that tripped the monster, its face landing in the snow. It groaned softly and lay still, resigning itself. 'Hold tight,' Daegan reminded her again as he handed his rope to her. 'I'm going to get the chains.'

'I can't hold them off for much longer!' Niall cried. The Shield spell kept the snarling qiqirns from them, but his arms were shaking and sweat dripped off his forehead.

'Just a bit longer, Niall!' Hannah called from across the clearing. 'Daegan's getting the chains, then—'

'Look out!' Niall shouted.

She whipped around. The saumen-kar's eyes snapped open and looked straight at her, both glowing a dark red. Its face contorted into a frown, and it howled as its colossal body picked itself up.

'Daegan!' Hannah called out. 'We've got a situation!'

She held on tightly as both ropes dragged her onto its back. Not knowing what else to do, she let go of the ropes, taking hold of its thick fur, and climbed onto its neck.

'What's plan B?' she shouted in a panic.

Daegan shouted something in reply, but Hannah wasn't listening. Instead, she focused on Niall. Exhausted from the spell, he staggered a few steps before finally fainting, his vulnerable body laying on the snow.

The qiqirns barked in delight and charged. Daegan shot spells, but nothing would stop the saumen-kar as it made its way towards Niall. As it stomped closer, Hannah realised precisely what it planned on doing.

'Niall!' she screamed. But it was no use. She raised her telum, aiming downwards.

'Stop!' she shouted at the monstrous Etheria. 'Stop now or I'll kill you, I swear!'

Her words fell on deaf ears. The saumen-kar continued striding towards Niall, as if in a murderous trance. With a grunt of effort, she closed her eyes, telum stretched out in front of her. She saw the Shield glyph in her mind, desperate to cast it. *I need it*, she thought to herself, thinking of nothing but the glyph. *I've never needed it so much before. I need to cast this.*

She opened her eyes a fraction, half expecting that she would have cast it through sheer desperation. But there was no shield; only a few metres lay between the unconscious Niall and the approaching saumen-kar.

'Niall! No!'

They were now above the trainee, small and insignificant beneath the colossal saumen-kar. Kiko bounded forwards, standing bravely in front of her beloved master. She bared her teeth as the monster raised its arms, ready to smash Niall to pieces.

Hannah screamed at the top of her lungs and plunged her telum down, burying it deep into the saumen-kar's neck. Blood stained the snow as it spurted from its neck. The Etheria whimpered, staggering to its knees. It jerked helplessly and groaned, reluctant to die. But soon it slowed and finally lay motionless.

'Hannah…' Daegan staggered to the pool of blood she stood in. 'What have you done?'

Chapter Fifty-Three

The Failure

'I—I killed him.'

Hannah's eyes were glued to the corpse before her, blood tainting the snow beneath. Her face was pale, mouth agape.

'He was going to kill Niall… I *had* to!' she said, more to convince herself than anyone else.

She couldn't read Daegan's expression. Fear? Disappointment? Hatred? He shook his head, and his legs collapsed as he dipped his fingers in the ever-growing pool of blood.

'He can't be dead,' he muttered to himself. 'I don't believe it, I…' Daegan withdrew his telum and pricked his finger, his thumb dancing above the crystal. A beam of light shone on the saumen-kar's lethal wound, and blood slowly disappeared. 'There must still be a chance. If I—'

Hannah left Daegan and rushed to Niall. He still lay in the snow, eyes closed and skin cold as ice. She felt his pulse—still alive.

Kiko nudged his hand to wake him—no movement.

Hannah propped him against a tree and built a fire to warm him. But as she grabbed his shoulders to haul him up, Kiko yapped and growled.

'What's wrong?' she asked.

Kiko growled louder yet and even leapt, biting at Hannah's hand in warning.

Hannah dropped her telum as she evaded the kitsune. When she looked down, she saw it; fresh blood clung to the blade, staining the snow beneath. Guilt washed over her as she looked at the Etheria she had murdered. Daegan was still trying to save him but to no avail.

'I… Daegan, look, I—'

'No!' Daegan barked as he seized her shoulders. 'Why did you do it? *Why*? You had specific orders *not* to kill the saumen-kar!'

'I had to!' she protested. 'It was about to kill Niall. He couldn't hold the shield. The crystal drained him, and he fell! He was about to be beaten to a pulp!'

'That's why he has Kiko! Was she there, ready to save him?'

Hannah thought back. She bit her lip and evaded his glare.

'Yes,' she reluctantly admitted. 'But—'

'No,' Daegan whispered venomously. '*Factum fieri infectum non potest.*'

'Will you please stop speaking in Latin?' she shouted.

Daegan's eyes went cold, and his face became red. 'You talk more about killing Etheria than saving them. You learn to fight, not defend. You think you're a Trucekeeper?' He spat at the snow, eyes covered by the hat pulled over his face. 'You're no better than a Thrunter.'

Hannah opened her mouth to protest, but no words came. She didn't know what to say; she barely knew what to think. No one had been there to judge her in the fight against the serpopard. The saumen-kar was different. Perhaps there could have been another way; a way to capture the saumen-kar and still save Niall. She admitted she had acted rashly, but it was no use apologising to Daegan.

It was too late.

'You're done,' he said. 'No trials, no Trucekeeper badge. You'll have your mind wiped and be dropped back to the cesspit from where you came. I'll file a report to the Truceleaders as soon as we get back.'

Hannah shook her head. 'I'm not going back.'

'What? Don't be stupid. You have a duty to—'

She'd had enough of the chastising. One mistake that she already sincerely regretted… She'd accept her punishment and leave, but there was no sense in going back to Arcadia just to be kicked out again.

Besides, she couldn't face having to tell Niall what happened. Nor could she stomach the smug satisfaction of Drakkar or Byron; Nathan, Jason and Amber's faces would be unbearable. Not to mention the disappointment of Caedric… and even Daegan.

Unable to bear the weight of her failure any longer, she turned from the bloodbath and made her way to the forest that surrounded the clearing.

'Where do you think you're going?' Daegan snapped. 'Get back here, Hannah!'

Dex chased after his master, hovering in the air in front of her. Hannah offered him her shoulder, but he gave a sad mew and flew back.

'No…' Hannah whimpered, betrayed.

She turned to see them all looking at her next to the still unconscious Niall, a range of emotions from disappointment to regret.

'I can't leave Niall here to run after you,' Daegan told her, 'and you can't enter that forest by yourself. It's too dangerous; you know that. Stop being a fool, Hannah, and come back.'

In a change of tact, Daegan tried to sound forgiving. But Hannah knew it was an act. Tears fell down her cheek as she ran from the clearing into the forest, ignoring the shouts of Daegan calling after her, once more running from her failure.

Chapter Fifty-Four

The Azure Tree

FEAR, anger, regret… She couldn't pin down the emotion that coursed through her body.

Hannah swiped at the branches in her way, pushing further and further into the dark forest. She wanted only to run from the guilt, the failure. She had tried to fit in, to make a difference, to make the most of her life. As ever, she had failed.

So, what now?

The forest was darker than it had been earlier. Eyes that stared down from trees gleamed menacingly. There were ruffles of unknown Etheria stalking her in the darkness. Hannah tried to rid her head of thoughts of jumbees, kapres, ijirait.

Tears trickled down her cheek as Daegan's words replayed in her mind. '*No better than a Thrunter… You're done…*' She was so caught up in her thoughts that the sudden noise took her by surprise.

She stopped dead, tears soon forgotten.

'Hannah?' a voice called out, like an echo. A voice she had nearly forgotten.

'Luke?' she replied.

Silence.

Then she heard it again, louder and clearer.

'Luke!' she shouted. Hannah set off, running towards the sound. She couldn't see him; she could barely see in front of her. Yet still she pushed forwards, weaving between the trees, slapping branches out of her way.

'Hannah?' Luke's voice echoed again.

She paused. It came from elsewhere, in a different direction.

Then she saw it.

Looming from the dark and hidden amongst the trees stood a figure. Towering over her, its rotting skin stretched thin across its body, bones protruding like a walking skeleton. Instead of a human skull, it was more like a stag's, with tall, sharp antlers. But more than all that, Hannah stared at its teeth, bared and dripping with fresh blood.

It glared at her, waiting.

She had read about this Etheria: a wendigo.

'Hannah, help me!' called the voice, straight from where the Etheria lay in wait.

She didn't need to be told the obvious—she needed to get as much distance from it as possible. Her hand went to withdraw her telum.

There was nothing there—just an empty holster. She cursed herself for dropping it earlier. Now she was stuck in this forest, alone and defenceless.

She looked back at the towering wendigo, daring it to make the first move. Then, in one smooth movement, she brought out her wrist-bow. The arrow hit its target, shattering through bones. The wendigo roared, the trees between them bowing and snapping from the full force of its yell. Hannah fled, the pounding strides of the wendigo booming as it bounded after her. She took a chance and threw a couple of knives behind her.

Nothing happened.

The wendigo's pace grew faster. It was catching up. She felt its breath burning the back of her neck.

This is it, she thought.

She closed her eyes, crying out as she fell to the ground on tired legs. Her lungs gasped for air as she braced herself.

But nothing came—no claws, no roars. Only silence, save for a low humming noise.

Hannah turned to find herself in a small clearing with a solitary tree in the middle. Its trunk was thin, resembling a silver birch, its branches devoid of leaves, and giving off a vaguely blue glow. She felt herself drawn to the tree, standing slowly and making her way towards it without her realising. But there was no voice, no sound other than the humming.

Every instinct told her to leave, to continue running. *But run where? Back to Thule?* She knew she wouldn't be welcome there. The Queen would demand her head. But she couldn't stay in the forest either; the wendigo was bound to still be looking for her.

She had nowhere else to go.

The closer she came, the louder it hummed. Heat beamed from the trunk, and her fingers singed as she made contact. A jolt shot through her body, as though fire coursed through her veins. She gasped, eyes shut tight in pain.

Then there was nothing. No hum, no pain, no sound; certainly no snow.

When she stumbled to her feet, she could scarcely believe what she saw. Below her was neither snow nor even a forest floor but the green grass of a meadow that spread far and wide. Above her, there was no longer a mass of branches but a starry orange sky.

Her newfound peace was soon cut short by a hissing voice. 'You've come here at last.'

'Hello?' Hannah tried to say. No sound came. 'Hello!' she tried again. Still nothing.

'I've been waiting for *such* a long time, Hannah,' the voice said, oblivious to her attempted reply. 'It must have been so difficult; training so hard… only for it to be in vain. You're not appreciated; you're misunderstood.'

'I'm listening,' she said, her words once again lost in the strange world.

'I could help you, help you find a place in the world. If only you promise to help me.' Hannah's eyes narrowed as her suspicions grew. 'Power and knowledge beyond your wildest dreams… The chance to prove yourself, overtake your peers—even your masters.'

Hannah dared to dream; she imagined returning to Arcadia, knowledge of every Etheria stored in her mind, and the ability to smite any who crossed swords with her. Nathan, Jason and Amber wouldn't stand a chance, Daegan would be sorry…

'Your fate is mere steps before you.'

The ground crumbled, and a vast hole bubbling with violet liquid appeared, black smoke rising from within.

'Step inside, Hannah. The Tunnel of Moirai awaits you.'

Every fibre of her being told her to ignore the voice, to turn and run. But run where? The tunnel was the only way forward. And that voice… it sounded somehow familiar.

She crouched by the surging purple liquid and extended her arm to touch the viscous liquid with just her fingertips. As soon as she made contact, the black smoke surged to life, twisting like hands that yanked her in.

There was a dazzling blue flash.

'The connection has been made. The revival can begin,' the voice echoed.

'What connection? What revival? Who even are you?' Hannah shouted, struggling to keep her head above the liquid.

Still, her words were unheard as the finger-like strings of smoke hauled her down. She kicked her feet frantically and tried to grab the safety of the shore, but it was just out of reach. She was sinking, as though sucked into quicksand.

'Her blood is the key. She is ours to control. The deception begins. The Leviathans will rise again.'

Leviathans?

'No!' she screamed.

Terror seized her body. She sunk lower and lower.

The voice repeated in a chant. 'The Leviathans will rise again; he is coming. The Leviathans will rise again; he is coming…'

She craned her neck upwards and took one last gasp of air before the tunnel heaved her downwards. The last thing she saw was the orange sky above, thousands of stars twinkling peacefully. They dissolved as a familiar purple mist loomed, and red eyes gleamed. Pain seized her body—and then she felt nothing.

Chapter Fifty-Five

Bad News

HANNAH awoke with a start, sitting up straight and gasping as sweat trickled from her forehead.

That voice… the one that had tricked her into the Tunnel of Moirai. The purple liquid and the smoke sucking her down to the abyss below… and those eyes—those unmistakable, crimson eyes.

She looked around, recognising the room's high arches and sounds from the window: voices and roars of playing, working, training. She was back in Arcadia, resting in the safety of the medical centre, somewhere she had visited several times after Daegan's training. Lying on the bedside table was her telum, the blade cleaned of any blood that had clung to it. She lay back and breathed a sigh of relief.

A nightmare, she told herself. *The tree, the voice, the tunnel—all a nightmare.*

She must have got lost running from the wendigo, passed out. Then Daegan would have found her and brought her back… but where was he? Where was Niall?

It then dawned on her—she didn't really know how she got home. She hid her face with a blanket and prayed Niall and Daegan made it back safely. But those red eyes haunted her every thought.

Unless it was a trap… Would Drakkar harm Niall and Daegan just to get at Hannah for asking about the vault?

'You're awake!' called a familiar voice.

Hannah felt like weeping as Niall came through the doors, an enormous grin on his face.

'Thank the Gods!' he said as he wrapped his arms around her.

She winced, suddenly aware of the bruises on her body. 'You're alive,' was all she could say. She couldn't help but laugh, unable to shake the giddy feeling of being reunited. Niall joined in.

But soon the memories of Thule came flooding back, and shame hit her like a brick wall. She stopped laughing, staring into the distance. Niall gave her shoulder a comforting squeeze.

'It's okay,' he reassured her. 'Everything's fine.'

She heard it in his voice, pitched slightly higher than usual; she could always tell when he was lying.

'What is it?' she said, her body tense.

Niall evaded her gaze. 'What do you want to know?'

Hannah stared at the ceiling, considering the blank spaces she needed filling in.

'Gondei… is he…?' She couldn't bear to finish the sentence.

Niall's eyes glistened with sadness. 'He, er… Yes. Shortly after he got back to Thule. They tried to save him but…'

The news was like a punch in the stomach. 'It was my fault,' she whispered.

'No!' he urged, clasping her hand in his. 'Listen, Hannah. I promise you—it was *not* your fault. Few of Gondei's size can square up to a saumen-kar and live to tell the tale. His death is not on your hands, trust me.'

'Was the Queen upset?' she asked.

Niall smirked. 'Big time. We're banned from Thule now, apparently.' To Hannah's surprise, he shrugged, as though visiting Thule had meant nothing to him. 'You missed the best bit. She launched an icicle at Daegan. It stopped in midair, just before it impaled him. Nearly hit him in the throat! You can still see the scar where it scratched him.'

Again, guilt reared in her mind, stronger than before.

'I bet Daegan was even angrier,' she murmured.

'I couldn't say,' Niall said. 'He said very little after you left. When I came to, we looked for you before heading back to Thule to let the Queen yell at us. Then I had an awkward wait for Drakkar to open the portal—Queen Kori didn't let me out of her sight. The crowds were cheering though!'

Hannah frowned. 'Daegan didn't come back with you?'

Niall shook his head. 'The Queen sent him to calm the lyngbakur.'

'The what?'

'Apparently Thule is actually on the back of a lyngbakur—a giant whale Etheria that grows an island on its back. Turns out the whole saumen-kar fight woke it, and it was about to swim away from land.'

Hannah had stopped listening a while back, her thoughts with Daegan. After all he had done for her, all he had sacrificed, she had let him down with one huge mistake. She didn't understand why he brought her back at all.

'How did he find me?' she asked.

'What do you mean?'

'In the forest. I ran pretty far...'

Niall frowned.

'After I... after the saumen-kar, I left, ran into a wendigo... then ran away from the wendigo, saw a blue tree—'

'Hang on,' interrupted Niall. 'I have *no* idea what you're on about. What wendigo? I don't even know what tree you're talking about.'

'But the... Where did you find me?'

'We didn't. We tried, but you vanished. We nearly lost hope until Drakkar told us he had already collected you.'

'But…' A million questions ran through her mind. 'But why did he save me?'

'Like I've been telling you—he's a Truceleader. He's on *our* side. I wonder how he knew you needed saving though.'

'No one asked him?'

Again, Niall looked sheepish and paced the room. 'No. The only thing the Truceleaders are questioning is what happens with you now.'

'What do you mean?'

'Daegan's writing a report, or so I've heard, about what happened on the mission, how you've been during your training period… They're deciding whether or not to kick you out.'

Hannah screwed up her eyes and pounded the bed with her fist as she thought over the last few months: her incessant complaints, reluctance to learn, brashness in combat lessons, rarely studying on her own…

'There's no way I'll come out of that in a positive light. I've been awful to him.' She stared at the ceiling, mouth curled downwards. 'How long have I got?'

Niall shrugged. 'Depends how much he has to write.'

'How is he?' Hannah asked, eyes still fixed on the ceiling.

'Not sure. He hasn't been seen since we got back.'

'When was that?'

'About a week ago.'

Hannah contemplated how she could have been unconscious for a week, half proud of being able to catch up on so much sleep.

'I'm glad you're awake,' he said.

'Hmm… Maybe I'll go back to sleep.' She sighed. 'I suppose I've got to face the music and—and take whatever punishment I get. I survived the Oblivion spell once before.'

'They'll take your blood crystal,' Niall reminded her. 'They'll destroy it in the Melissani Cave. Your memories would be gone— forever this time.'

There was a morose pause as she thought of all she would lose; all her friends, a place she'd been able to call home, her respite from constantly having to monitor her diabetes.

Hannah grimaced. 'Well… I might as well make the most of it!'

With that, she leapt out of bed, wiggling her bare toes on the cold stone floor and feeling a delightful shiver running up her spine and waking her body. She picked her blue headband from the bedside table and slipped it on.

'If I'm getting kicked out—and let's face it, it's likely—I might as well make the most of Arcadia.' She snickered at Niall's perplexed expression. 'Magic, Etheria… I'll never remember them, let alone experience them again. I want to make the most of it. *Now*!'

'By doing what?'

'I don't know,' Hannah shrugged. 'Magic? I won't be able to use that later.'

Niall shook his head. 'Not a good idea. Basic spells would probably be fine, but any more… it'd flag up, and the faeries would be down on you in minutes. You're under careful watch. Any misuse and they—'

'Okay!' Hannah thought again. 'A leaving party. An impromptu one… Do you think anyone would be up for that?'

All it took was a couple of choice words to a dwarf in the armoury and a kobold lazing by the docks and, before long, word that Hannah would be leaving soon spread far and wide.

Chapter Fifty-Six

The Farewell

HANNAH and Niall spread out on top of their hill, basking in the warm glow of the sun and enjoying the gentle sounds of Dex and Kiko playing, her sins in Thule seemingly forgiven. *I'm sure I have Niall to thank for that*, she thought.

It wasn't until late that afternoon, when the sun set, that Hannah realised the number of friendships she had made in Arcadia, even in passing. Countless Etheria made their way to the lakeside to say their goodbyes. Taniiya, Merla and Trisno relayed the message to a group of sirens, who sat upon rocks scattered around the hill. Their velvet blue feathers ran down their arms and curved around their slender, naked bodies. As they sang, Hannah listened, captivated; she understood why their voices had gone down in legend.

The dwarves were next to arrive, each with a barrel of ale and following Fennrock, apparently with a few tankards of ale in his belly already. He patted Hannah on the back and mumbled something incoherent about how much he would miss her. Large tears dripped down his cheeks, and Hannah distracted him with another tankard, which he happily accepted, finishing it all with one gulp. Celeste and Luminon joined as well, making polite platitudes and sitting to the side, talking only to each other and sipping wine from golden goblets. Though pompous, Hannah still appreciated the elves for coming, particularly the warm smile Luminon had given her.

Before too long, Lena and Sophie brought the faeries, and a crowd of nymphs danced from their dwelling in the forest as they followed them. Hannah spotted Natala and Limara, eager to start the party. Natala's familiar, a carbuncle, even made the jewel on its head shine like a disco ball.

Unsurprisingly, their arrival heralded the immediate coming of satyrs and fauns who were dragging caskets of skaldmead. Asti and Rideo pranced up to Hannah, playing their pipes, while others accompanied sirens with their instruments or danced with the nymphs. Word even reached the brownies and hobs who bore gifts of food from the kitchens. A basajaun constructed a bonfire, lit by a samodiva, and the satyrs, fauns and nymphs danced around it gaily.

Even the non-humanoid Etheria congregated, excitedly trotting or flying to join in the festivities. Bonnacons grazed at the foot of the hill with the tusked yales; griffins and hippogryphs sat lazily amongst the crowd, admiring the golden shimmering from the wings of alicantos and humouring the muscaliets and jackalopes that climbed over them.

Hannah surveyed the scene before her with a slight smile, though her eyes prickled with tears. She still couldn't imagine having to leave this place, a place that she'd learned to call home, where she was finally happy. *Make the most of it, Hannah*, she told herself.

The joyful cheers and songs suddenly diminished to an anxious murmur when they saw the Truceleaders. All seven stood in a line, eyes fixed on the party and shrouded in the darkness of the early evening. Whispers flitted from one hushed conversation to another as some prepared to run. Drakkar and Byron seemed to have a heated debate with Braddock and Aarava before Caedric, calm and confident with pipe in hand, approached the party without a word.

Hushed conversations turned silent, and even Hannah held her breath as he came nearer. Her hand twitched and grazed Niall's. Their fingers interlaced.

Voices started up again, more excited than before, and Hannah saw Caedric with Braddock and Aarava by his side, now lit by the light of the bonfire. Their broad smiles were unmistakable as they spoke to various Etheria and shook countless hands—even hooves and paws.

Hannah broke her hand away from Niall's as he approached.

'So,' he said, his smile unwavering. 'This seems somewhat premature—saying goodbye already?'

'Well, it's not like I'm likely to stay much longer...' She paused. 'Right?'

Caedric shrugged and puffed on his pipe. 'I don't know yet. It's not the first time you were convinced you were leaving Arcadia.'

Hannah held back a gasp. *How did he know?*

He looked behind him to make sure no one could overhear, before whispering, 'If it were up to me, you would stay. In the heat of the moment, you saved your friend's life. A noble sacrifice.' He straightened up and shrugged once more. 'Sadly, traditional Truce laws dictate that when a trainee is responsible for the failure of a mission, a vote must be taken to determine their future... Personally, I'm an advocate for updating outdated laws, but wisdom takes time.'

Graciously, he accepted a sausage roll from a hob and popped it into his mouth. He smiled as he saw Dex playing with Randy, Mimi's emerald ramidreju familiar, while Mimi herself entertained a crowd with a scandalous song-and-dance routine.

'You've certainly made an impact in Arcadia. Clearly you befriended many, Etheria and human alike. I'm sure the Truceleaders will take that into consideration.' He leant in closer.

'Nice move befriending the hobs and brownies, by the way. There's nothing quite like breakfast in bed.'

With that, he winked and returned to the castle with Eldrin, Aleesia, Byron and Drakkar, leaving Braddock and Aarava to enjoy the party. Soon they were dancing around the bonfire with the rest; music, laughter, food and drink aplenty.

At one point, Fennrock challenged Luminon to a race. They slung their bodies around surrounding Etheria; Luminon straddling a hippogryph and Fennrock what looked like an ordinary horse.

'On your marks,' said Asti.

'Get set,' Rideo continued, even louder.

'Go!' they shouted together.

Fennrock and Luminon sent their steeds charging towards the lake. Although initially neck and neck, Fennrock's horse bucked and sent him flying. He landed in the lake with an almighty splash. The sirens flew away with angry shouts, and with a mischievous giggle, the horse contorted and transformed into a small goblin who hunched over and rolled on the ground in stitches.

'Blasted brag! Evil little shape-shifting goblin!' clamoured Fennrock as he waded through the water, squeezing water from his beard.

Before much longer, the party shifted from the bonfire on the hill to the lake itself, where charming nixes were encouraging everyone to jump in.

Niall grabbed Hannah's hand and dragged her to join them.

'Oh no,' she warned him. 'I'm not a fan of water.'

'I don't care,' he said, the moon bouncing off his eyes. 'We're going in.'

Hannah's protests were ignored as a group of dwarves picked them both up and threw them in. Coughing and spluttering, they splashed to the surface, treading water against their heavy clothes. Catching each other's eyes, they couldn't help but laugh.

Their laughs gradually diminished though until they bobbed in the water and gazed at each other. The moon's reflection rippled on the lake's surface, lighting the couple as they moved closer.

Niall's intense gaze made Hannah's stomach do flips. The tension was too much. She didn't want to believe this could be their last night…

He leant forward, lips nervously brushing hers as they kissed. He leant back, trying to gauge her reaction. But Hannah jumped at him, arms flinging around his neck and legs wrapping around him under the water. They kissed again, more passionately, and held one another tightly, her mouth curling upwards in a smile.

They moved from the shallow waters to the foot of the hill, lying next to each other and continuing their kiss, oblivious to the Etheria's whispering and giggles. The party soon died down as they gave Niall and Hannah some privacy.

Bathed in the serene blue light of the moon, the two lay on the grass, gentle breezes swaying through the trees above and waves lapping against the lakeside. Hannah rolled on top, her legs straddled around him, and leant back, their lips breaking free. She looked into his eyes and he into hers, his hands running up and down her body.

'Hannah, I—'

Hannah shook her head. 'I know, Niall. It's just… If this is my last night here, let's not complicate matters. I may not remember, but you will. It's not fair to start something we can't continue.'

Clearly disappointed, he nodded. 'I just wanted to—I don't know…' He trailed off and picked at the grass.

'Let's just… lay here, you and me, until the sun rises,' Hannah sighed.

Niall stretched his arms, and Hannah fell into them. As they lay there, he pointed out constellations and told the stories behind them. Will-o'-the-wisps buzzed around them like a light show.

Hannah watched him as he spoke. She could give up the Trucekeeper equipment, even Etheria and magic, but the real tragedy would be to leave Niall.

Would he sacrifice Arcadia to be with me? she thought.

But no—she couldn't ask him to do that. He was in his element here, born to be a Trucekeeper. He was finally where he wanted to be, where he was be appreciated. She couldn't tear him away from that.

She did her best to soothe her nerves and not worry about a future she couldn't yet plan for. After all, any plans would be forgotten, too.

'Are you okay?' he asked, aware that she had stopped listening.

'Hmm? Oh, yeah…'

'What were you thinking?'

Hannah stroked his cheek. 'About how much I'll miss this.'

Her hand slid down and locked with his, as they held each other and fell into a deep sleep.

Chapter Fifty-Seven

Eyes from the Dark

THE soothing waves of the lake lapped against the shore. The nocturnal Etheria rustled in the trees and the forest. But Hannah was more preoccupied by the delicate snowflakes floating down. She caught one, holding it up to the light and admiring it. She looked down to see her bare feet, still wet from the lake, now sunk beneath a thick body of snow. Icy wind whistled through the trees, yet still she felt nothing.

She pushed through the snow, catching snowflakes in her open palms. She didn't know where she was or where she was going. Yet she continued, as though some invisible force drew her nearer to something.

There was a low-pitched hum. Hannah turned round, and there, in the middle of a snow-covered clearing, was the blue tree, shimmering.

'The connection is strong,' she heard a voice speak. 'Blood will be spilled. The vault will be opened.'

She scrunched her eyes shut and ignored the voice.

It's a dream. It must be a dream.

'Come, Hannah,' spoke the voice. 'You know where to come, where you must be, where your path lies.'

Her hand snaked its way to the tree, against her will. She struggled against it.

'It is done,' the voice declared, as her hand touched the azure blue bark of the tree.

There was a bright flash, and it was over.

With a start, Hannah awoke, her back straight and lungs gasping for air. She shook herself. *Just a dream*, she thought. *It was just a dream.* Niall was still by her side, fast asleep and breathing deeply.

Hannah sighed as she stood up, careful not to wake him, and tiptoed to the lakeside. She dipped her feet in, as she admired Arcadia at night for the last time. She turned to the castle, the majestic silhouette faintly visible in the night sky. It was as if the entire world were asleep, save for two lights.

Hannah frowned. One shone from Caedric's study—as rumour had it, Caedric never slept—but the other was a glow from the ground floor on the far side of the castle. The light was dim, as if whoever was inside didn't want to be discovered.

She racked her brain as she imagined the castle's layout, pinpointing the room in her mind.

Her heart plummeted as she realised.

It was from a window she had passed on her way down to the vault.

Drakkar—he's opening the vault. She was sure of it. Even the voice in her dream confirmed her suspicions. *'The vault will be opened...'*

She wasted no time in shoving her still dripping wet feet into her shoes before giving Niall a quick, tender kiss on his forehead. Her time at Arcadia was over, but Niall still had so much to offer—she couldn't put him in danger by bringing him with her. *This is my fight,* she told herself as she sneaked off, leaving Niall, Dex and Kiko asleep on their hill.

It only took a matter of minutes for Hannah to sprint to the castle. She took extra care not to make a sound and slipped through the castle doors, hurtling down to the vault. Only once she was at the window in the corridor did she pause to take her telum in hand. She looked at her blood crystal; using magic now might sway the Truceleaders in their voting… But she needed to know what she was walking into.

She steeled herself and pierced her thumb, pressing it to the crystal and casting the Tracker spell. A single set of red footprints lit up the floor.

Hannah breathed a sigh of relief, although wouldn't pretend for a moment that she could hold her own in a fight against Drakkar. She considered going to Niall for help, or even a Truceleader—but who knew how much of a head start he already had? She had to catch him in the act now, before it was too late.

Although heavy, she pushed the door open without too much noise. The fire in the torches flickered gently, some not lit at all. Hannah could only just make out the silhouettes of the pillars in the room.

Holding her breath and crouching low, she followed the glowing footprints down to the centre of the room where they ended, as though Drakkar had ceased to exist. She wondered if he could fly.

She looked around the room, in every dark corner.

Drakkar was nowhere to be seen.

A drop splashed on her cheek, like a raindrop from the sky. She wiped it away and gagged at the sight of her hand.

Blood.

Telum raised, she stepped back and gazed towards the ceiling. It was dark, but as she squinted, Hannah could make out a silhouette perched on the rafters, still as a statue. For a moment, she wondered if it was just a gargoyle, until its eyes fluttered open and shone red.

The last thing she saw was it spread its arms and jump down, the red eyes smashing her against the floor.

Chapter Fifty-Eight

The Warlock's Betrayal

PAIN shot through her back. Hannah came to, groaning and writhing in pain.

'You're finally awake,' came a voice.

She tried to sit up, but something held her down. Her wrists were shackled to the ground, two pearlescent rings around each wrist. She wrestled against them but ceased, screaming as a jabbing pain shot up her arm.

She lay back, trying to calm her breathing, and looked to the side. Against the wall, amongst the shadows, lay a small pile of unmoving dwarven guards, a small trickle of blood pooling on the ground.

A shadow crept over Hannah's face. Drakkar stood above her.

'Don't move,' he warned. 'It took a while to perfect, but those cuffs around your wrists are a spell of my own invention. The more the victim struggles, the more the cuffs hurt—to the point where it's nigh intolerable. Oh, the amount of Etheria I had to practice on to get it right…'

Hannah tested the cuffs but was punished with another shot of pain, worse this time. 'Is that why you needed that sphinx?' Hannah asked. 'To practice this spell?'

Drakkar laughed, flecks of spit shooting from his mouth. She grimaced.

'Of course not,' he replied. 'Sphinxes are far too rare to waste on something like that. I required our precious Hortes for a… different purpose.' He stared at her, eyes shining with unadulterated joy. 'A sphinx's knowledge is apparently infinite. There's nothing they don't know.'

'And what were you so desperate to discover?' she asked, wincing at the pain that blasted through her wrists.

'I needed to learn who locked this vault,' he answered, his crooked finger pointing to the bronze wall. 'She was reluctant to say at first. I persuaded her otherwise.'

'And? Who locked it?' She prayed he wouldn't know; that the sphinx deceived him.

'You know what a vault is, don't you? I'm sure your clever boyfriend told you,' he spat. 'It houses a dangerous Etheria, easier to trap than kill. I can only open it with the blood crystal of the one who locked it. So I needed to find out who locked it, and I needed *their* blood crystal.'

'Is that what you tried to get Nathan to do at the Games? Kill Celeste or steal her blood crystal? Something like that?'

'Not *just* Celeste,' he admitted. 'As many as he could. Caedric is a reckless fool to endanger the trainees in a race like that. It would be a perfect opportunity to get rid of a few Trucekeepers and secure some more blood crystals. Besides, that boy's easy to manipulate. He's jealous of you, you know. And of everyone else for that matter. He just wants to be appreciated.'

'You'd kill us just for crystals?'

Drakkar stared at her. 'I've killed many, many Trucekeepers over the years, with a little help from Zelom. None of their blood crystals worked. Not that I was surprised—their incompetence astounded me. It takes power and skill to lure an Etheria and lock it inside a vault; few have the ability. There may be others, but I only know of two to have succeeded for sure—Caedric… and Astraea.'

Hannah blinked. She tried to keep her poker face. *There was that name again.*

'Oh, you've heard of Astraea,' he said, seeing straight through her. 'I wish I was the one to have slaughtered her where she stood. Especially after what she did to Alna…' he trailed off, staring into the distance.

Hannah frowned. *Who's Alna? That woman he has a photo of in his office?*

'I did wonder if it was Astraea who locked this vault,' he said, 'but ever since she betrayed the Trucekeepers, her blood crystal has been missing… then you turned up. I didn't believe it when Daegan dragged you to Arcadia. I still can't believe you're able to wield Astraea's blood crystal. *That's* why I needed Hortes. I needed to know for sure that Astraea locked this vault and where the blood crystal to open it would be.' He paused, staring at her in disbelief. 'And you were the key all along, Hannah. Not that it's been easy getting you here. But you fell for my plan perfectly.'

'I didn't fall for any plan,' Hannah told him defiantly. 'Don't flatter yourself.'

'Oh, you did. I needed to form a connection with you—to lure you here.'

Hannah's ears pricked up. *Connection.* The blue tree flashed before her eyes.

'But more than that, I needed you to be disgraced. I needed you right here, right now—when *you* open the vault, it will seem a defiant act of bitter revenge by a disgraced Trucekeeper. There's no chance I'll be suspected.'

'What connection are you talking about?' She couldn't believe it. There was no way Drakkar had planned all this.

'Saumen-kars are very useful to sorcerers. Their psychic abilities make them especially easy to control.'

Hannah cursed herself. She should have realised it; the saumen-kar's glowing red eye had been a giveaway. No wonder it had paid no attention to Niall's story.

'It was me, Hannah. The poor saumen-kar never knew what happened. *I* controlled his mind, *I* made him run from the Queen. All it took was a subtle suggestion for Caedric to send you and Daegan there. *I* killed Gondei… *I* threatened Niall, *I* made you slaughter the creature—a necessary sacrifice. You ran away from Daegan, found the tree *I* cursed… and as soon as you made contact—that was it! An indelible connection I can use to manipulate you to—'

'No!' she screamed. 'It's not like you've succeeded yet. You haven't even opened the vault.'

'I can now. You're the key, Hannah. If Hortes was right, I have all I need right here.'

'But why? What's the point of opening it?' Hannah had no idea what to do or how to escape. All she could do was stall him.

Drakkar seemed to enjoy boasting, his red eyes shining even brighter. 'An Etheria with as much might as the one within will have unfathomable anger when released. Even the combined might of the Truceleaders wouldn't stand a chance, let alone the pathetic trainees.'

He gazed at her, grinning. 'I'm guessing your boyfriend never worked out what lurks within the vault in Arcadia?'

Hannah remained silent.

'Sadly, as time wears on, few humans bother to learn their history. So many clues to the secrets of the world lie within it. The Epic of Gilgamesh, for example.'

'I know it,' Hannah said, glaring at him.

Drakkar tilted his head. 'I'm impressed. But what you don't know was how Gilgamesh was a Trucekeeper himself, famed for defeating perhaps the most ancient and powerful Etheria we've ever known.' He cocked an eyebrow. 'Ever heard of Humbaba?'

Hannah suppressed a gulp as she remembered the nightmarish description she had read of him years ago back at Arningham. An enormous beast with lion's paws, a body of scales, talons, horns, a snake for a tail and a face made of entrails. She shivered.

'*Humbaba rig-ma-šu abubu. Pi-i-šú gira-um-ma na-pis-su mu-tú.* Humbaba's roar is a flood. His mouth is fire, his breath death. After mercilessly slaughtering Humbaba, Gilgamesh and Enkidu murdered his seven sons… They never stopped to consider his only daughter.' Drakkar gazed at the vault. 'And that's just the start. There's a book in the library—one the half-breed refused to give me. With it, I'll discover all known locations of the world's vaults. I can open them all… The Trucekeepers will be destroyed, and the Leviathans will reign supreme. From the waves we rise.'

Hannah gave a start. Her eyes widened and wrists struggled against the cuffs, sending agonising pain coursing through her arms. 'You traitor!' she shouted. 'How could you side with the Leviathans?'

He chuckled and stroked her hair. She shifted away, but he held her chin and slapped her with the back of his hand.

'I get it,' she said, trying a different tack. 'I understand why you're angry with the Truce. But this isn't the way. Arcadia is a special place, like Thule. Somewhere it doesn't matter who you are, how you look, where you're from, what you believe. No, it's not fair that Etheria are confined to settlements, your freedom restricted. But the Truce creates places like Arcadia. You may want more, but not like this. For a brighter future, we need to build—not destroy.'

Drakkar's eyes narrowed. 'I'm a Leviathan, girl,' he hissed. 'You'd never understand. Etheria should rule and roam this earth freely. Not humans… look at their incessant biological problems—you're a prime example of that.'

Hannah tried to wrench herself out of his spell, desperate to smack him in the face. But the pain shot through her body and forced her down.

'And the destruction you all cause, the way you ruin the planet with pollution and technology. Humans need to be expunged. Sigurd Thornwood will soon see to that.'

'Haven't you heard? Thornwood's dead. Surely you know—'

He cupped his hand around her mouth, shaking his head. He smelled like smoke and rotten fruit. She nearly gagged.

'Thornwood will rise again. Then, with the Trucekeepers dead and buried, we will emerge victorious. Surely Daegan told you there was a mole in the Truceleaders?'

Hannah resisted the urge to struggle and lay back, seething.

A silhouette behind her caught her eye. She craned her neck to see but stopped as Drakkar ran his clammy hands over her body.

'What are you doing?' she shrieked.

His smile grew to grotesque proportions as he withdrew her telum from her holster, drawing out the crystal and holding it to the light. 'And there's the rune Hortes assured me would be there. I must thank you, Hannah,' he said as he made his way to the vault. 'For the blood crystal, the sphinx… Though a human, you'll be a hero amongst Leviathans. It's a shame you won't live to see it.'

He gave her a repulsive smirk, but Hannah ignored him, instead arching her back and craning to see the shadow. Hidden behind the pillar, Hannah deciphered the outline of Niall, crouched with his finger to his lips.

Her heart leapt, and it took all her self-control to remain still. 'Hurry,' she mouthed.

Drakkar hovered the blood crystal above the hole in the vault. 'This is for you, Alna,' he whispered before he pushed forward, a click sounding. He emitted a spine-chilling cackle before returning to stand above Hannah. He twirled his telum in his hand, the light of the torches reflected off the sharp blade.

'The crystal fits,' he told her. 'There's only one thing I need now—your blood.'

Chapter Fifty-Nine

The Warlock's Duel

DRAKKAR bent down and sniffed from her chest to her head, finally resting his blade against her cheek.

'You like my telum?' he asked as it slid across her face. 'A gift, from Thornwood no less.'

She glared at him as the blade pierced her skin and tore down her cheek. The wound burned, but she held her breath, determined not to let him see her wince. Drakkar collected the blood on the edge of his blade and admired it.

'The fall of Arcadia will soon begin,' he announced.

'I think you've forgotten how many are prepared to fight for it,' she said with a wry smile.

Drakkar followed Hannah's gaze and saw Niall emerge from the shadows, his thumb already on his crystal. Two balls of fire shot from each end of his staff-telum. They rocketed towards Drakkar, who quickly flicked his telum. He redirected the fireballs that crashed into the bronze wall in a minor explosion. Another ball of fire erupted from Niall's telum, blocked by a Shield spell from the warlock.

With a grunt, Drakkar hurled a jet of lightning, hitting Niall's hand. His arm twitched, and his staff soared across the room.

Drakkar sent another stream of electricity. Niall dodged and ran, nimbly avoiding each spell, until he dived to the ground. He grabbed his telum and pointed it at Hannah.

His spell hit her cuffs, which snapped open, but as she leapt to her feet, Drakkar shot a torrent of lightning at Niall. He lay on the stone ground, screaming in agony.

Hannah grabbed her telum from the ground and plunged it into Drakkar's back. He let out a cry and turned, bolts of lightning scorching the walls.

'You'll pay for that,' he hissed, raising his own telum, her blood still stuck to the blade.

But with surprise in his eyes, he stumbled forwards as a Strike spell struck his back. Niall stood behind him, clearly in pain but ready to fight back.

'Get the crystal!' he shouted to Hannah.

Hannah sprinted to the vault as Drakkar launched a spell. Niall blocked it before shooting one back, a large icicle that Drakkar dodged. It hit the stone pillar behind and shattered into a hundred shards, melting before they even hit the ground.

Talented as Niall was, Hannah knew he wouldn't last long in a duel against Drakkar. Wiping her hands down her clothes to make sure she had no blood to react with the crystal in the vault, she reached forward. It obediently fell into her hand, and she slotted it back in her telum.

Niall was holding his own, either dodging or blocking Drakkar's spells, even shooting a few of his own from both ends of his staff with firm strokes.

Hannah charged forward, telum raised but stopped abruptly, as though running into a wall. She reached out and felt the Shield spell. She cursed as she saw Drakkar's shield run from one end of the room to the other. Hannah was blocked from the fight completely.

With a yell, she fired spell after spell. The barrier rippled but only thinned slightly—it was no use.

Then it happened, as though in slow motion. Drakkar launched a Strike spell that hit Niall in the stomach. He gasped and staggered backwards, propelled by another. His back slammed against the wall before he crumpled to the ground. Drakkar summoned a spear of ice that soared towards Niall, lying helpless on the ground.

Like a whip, something slashed the icicle, smashing it into oblivion.

A small mew reached Hannah's ears, and Dex danced through the air, evading the curses that Drakkar shot. He flew to a torch above Drakkar and slashed. Fire toppled to the floor, only narrowly missing the warlock.

Distracted by the kamaitachi, his shield faded. Hannah seized the opportunity and fired a spell that hit him in the shoulder.

'Filthy human!' he spat. 'I see Daegan trained you well after all. But you try to stop me, and you'll die in agony. You and your *pet*.'

He aimed up at Dex who whipped his tail. The steel-like fur took the brunt of the spell, but he fell out of the air with a cry.

Hannah screamed as she fired spell after spell; Flame, Strike, Ice, Blast, Bolt… all the offensive spells that had taken months to learn. She knew she couldn't win but forced the doubt from her mind.

Drakkar dodged and blocked with ease, firing his own right back. Hannah didn't find it as easy but dodged everything other than an icicle that scratched her arm.

With a grunt, she shot a stream of lightning. Drakkar matched her Bolt spell. Their streams met in the middle and merged into one. He gave a malign laugh and moved forwards.

Hannah gasped and nearly fell forward, her feet fighting to keep her up.

What's happening?

Through the crackle of lightning, fragments of what Daegan had told her flooded into her head. *Crystal convergence…* the crystals connect, a true test of strength. But she never thought it would feel like this; how much energy the crystal would drain. She dropped to her knee, struggling not to pass out, to give up, to let Drakkar win.

But she wouldn't let him. Not after how he'd manipulated her, tried to frame her, what he'd planned to do to Arcadia.

Her head became light and dizzy, and her heart thumped furiously as she began shaking, sweating.

No… The way the convergence drained her was just like battling her low blood sugar. Hannah fought against the feeling, the one she had experienced so often. Her breathing quickened as she panicked, losing consciousness fast.

But then she looked up.

Drakkar was struggling against the convergence too, his teeth bared in the effort. He wasn't used to this, the feeling of your own body betraying you, having to fight against it. She may not have been as powerful as him, but *this* she knew she could survive; she had done so for most of her life.

She screamed and heaved her arms up, as though trying to lift a boulder. The stream of lightning curved and eventually snapped like a twig. Both spells slammed into the ceiling and huge clumps of rock smashed to the ground.

Hannah fell to the ground, panting, fighting to stay conscious. She had used up too much blood in her battle against Drakkar.

'You fought valiantly, girl, but you never had a chance. A shame you're not an Etheria; you would have made a wonderful Leviathan.'

He raised his telum. Hannah glared at him, ready to meet her fate.

The room went dark. The ground rumbled, throwing up clouds of dust. A ball of lightning shot towards Drakkar before hovering in front of Hannah. It paused for a second and dissolved, revealing a wolf.

'Raji…' Hannah gasped.

Out of the corner of her eye, she saw Kiko run towards Niall and a flutter of white wings as a caladrius landed to nurse his wounds.

'Drop the telum, Drakkar!'

Hannah beamed at the sight that greeted her from the top of the stairs. Eldrin and Aleesia stood on either side of the group, bow-telums aimed at Drakkar; Aarava stood with her staff-telum, and Braddock gripped his battle-axe. And in the middle were Caedric and Daegan, dagger-telums held aloft.

Drakkar seemed unfazed, his telum still aimed at Hannah.

'We don't want to kill you,' called out Caedric, 'but we will not hesitate—'

Drakkar didn't let Caedric finish. His thumb slashed against his telum, and he cast a flash.

Hannah blinked away the sunspots in time to see arrows and spells soar, hitting the spot where Drakkar had been standing, the purple haze of his portal fading from view.

She jumped towards the haze, hoping it was still active, but it wafted in the air as it dissipated.

Drakkar had escaped.

Chapter Sixty

Unexpected Intruders

THE weakness from the fight had caught up with Hannah. She collapsed.

'Hannah,' came Daegan's gentle voice, his arm around her. 'Hannah, talk to me.'

She looked at him with tearful eyes. She didn't know what to say. Would they blame her for what happened with Drakkar? Would this see her kicked out of Arcadia?

'You're hurt,' he said. 'What did he do?'

'Convergence,' she muttered through her foggy head.

For a moment, Daegan stared at her in disbelief before clicking his fingers. A small yellow light spiralled towards them, growing to reveal Lena, Rod of Asclepius in hand. 'Lena, her arm,' Daegan instructed.

Lena tore the sleeve of Hannah's shirt to inspect her bloody arm which she touched with her staff. It lit up, and a soothing feeling burned through her as it cleaned and closed the wound.

'It ought not to be infected,' she said.

'It was just an icicle,' Hannah said.

'Wounds from spells can infect you,' she told her. 'Be careful. No more fights.'

Hannah shook her head and struggled to her feet, grimacing as she did.

'No,' she said through gritted teeth. 'We need to find Drakkar!'

'Hannah, Hannah,' Daegan said, arms on her once more. 'You're in no state to go charging off against a dangerous warlock. You told me you just survived crystal convergence. Do you know how rare that is for a human? And after such a short time training? You should be dead!'

'No, you don't understand.'

'Shh,' said Daegan. 'Lena will take you to the medical wing. You—'

'Axis!' Hannah blurted out.

Daegan and Lena shared an inquisitive look.

'Hannah,' Lena purred, peering into her eyes. 'What about Axis?'

'He's… he's heading for the library. There's a book Axis wouldn't let him have… Vault locations. He's going to open them…'

'Hannah, Drakkar isn't –'

'He's a Leviathan!' she shouted. 'He's opening all the vaults to destroy the Trucekeepers, bring back Thornwood… I don't know how, but—'

'The mole,' Daegan hissed. He jumped to his feet and abruptly barked orders. 'Aleesia, Eldrin, Braddock. Get to the library—now! Aarava, gallop to Mantir—we need a dozen of his best men to the library! Go!'

'Let's get you some rest,' Lena insisted.

'No,' Hannah and Daegan said together.

They looked at one another, both equally surprised.

'I've got to be there,' she said.

'I agree,' Daegan nodded. 'Lena, aqua vitae.'

Lena begrudgingly handed over a vial from her satchel. 'For the record, I do not condone going out into the field in this condition.'

'Noted,' Hannah mumbled. She took the vial and downed the familiar contents in one gulp. She coughed as it burned her throat like fire.

She took a moment to recuperate as Daegan had a hushed conversation with Caedric who nodded sagely.

'Lena, see to Niall. Hannah, let's go.'

Hannah was already feeling more like her normal self as she strapped the shield gauntlet Daegan handed her to her wrist. Together, they raced to the library, familiars faithfully following.

They didn't speak as they ran up the stairs, though Hannah was sure his thoughts were along the same lines as hers. She wondered if she should say something… but what? Apologise, make small talk, tell him everything Drakkar had just told her?

No, she thought, *there'll be time for that later.*

They heard the mayhem before they even reached the library but were still shocked by the sight that greeted them. Charging from a portal were more Etheria than Hannah could count.

Hannah even recognised a group of Pyres, the manic humans desperate to become Etheria, fire tattoos emblazoned on their necks. They wielded swords and surrounded Mantir and the nymph trainees.

An angry capcaun, a dog-faced ogre with four eyes, failed to evade Braddock's oversized battle-axe as Aarava and Fennrock seized the capcaun's arms and tried to hold it down.

Nathan, Jason and Amber were even there with Trucesentries, feebly firing spells at harpies that soared in the rafters, while Asti and Rideo dispatched them with ease.

A horrifying psoglav, a canine Etheria with teeth of iron, one eye and horse-like hooves, slashed at Eldrin and Aleesia who kept their distance. They elegantly jumped from one bookcase to another, firing spells and arrows from their bow-telums. Celeste and Luminon accompanied them, proving competent support.

'Hannah, help Eldrin and Aleesia with the psoglav. I'll take on the capcaun.' Daegan grabbed her shoulder. 'Good luck.'

With that, he ran off with Raji, spells erupting from his telum and bolts of lightning following the raiju.

Hannah dashed towards the psoglav, dodging sharp talons of rogue harpies. But beyond the elves and the psoglav, she saw Axis hunched behind a table. She was terrified, holding nothing but an ordinary bow in her hand.

Sliding across the ground and narrowly avoiding a fireball, Hannah skidded to a halt by Axis, who barely noticed her.

'I—I can't do it…' she whispered, shaking with fear. 'I'm going to die here.'

Her fingers pulled at her auburn hair. She cowered as another fireball exploded against a nearby wall. Hannah peered over the table. Drakkar, frantically looking through a bookshelf, was firing occasional spells to keep Trucekeepers at bay.

'It's Drakkar.'

'I know,' Axis muttered. 'What does he want? He barged his way in. I told him the library was closed. Then all those… *monsters*!' She covered her mouth, appalled at her language.

'It's okay, Axis,' Hannah reassured.

'They followed him and tried to… It was lucky the Truceleaders turned up. Hannah, what's going on?'

Hannah flinched as another spell slammed against the wall. She wasn't sure how much she should tell Axis; all she knew was that she couldn't let Drakkar get his hands on that book.

'Dex,' she turned to the kamaitachi. 'Distract Drakkar, but don't let him hurt you.'

Dex rubbed his head against Hannah's cheek, as if warning her to be careful too, before flying across the room to dig his claws into the warlock's robes.

Hannah turned to Axis. 'Remember the book Drakkar was asking for? The one you didn't let him have?'

'The Record of Vaults? Of course, I didn't give it to him. It's for the Trucemaster's eyes only—'

'Where is it?' Hannah snapped.

Axis bit her lip, unsure if Hannah could be trusted.

'I'm not going to read it,' Hannah reassured her. 'But we need to stop Drakkar from getting it. Tell me where it is.'

With a look of resignation, she nodded. 'You're right.' From her robes, she withdrew a bronze key and handed it to Hannah. 'It's in the chest behind that counter.' She pointed to the opposite end of the library. 'Keep it safe, whatever you do.'

Hannah gave her a supportive smile before pricking her thumb and pressing it to her crystal. Her legs pushed her forward as she darted over the counter and raced across the room.

A shrill squawk above made Hannah jump as a harpy, seizing the opportunity, dived down and snatched the key from her hand.

'No!' she cried out, grabbing onto the harpy's foot. It flapped its wings to gain height and shake Hannah off. Her fingers scraped against the sharp talons, but she held on and tried to wrestle the key from its foot. But it was no use; the harpy's grip was unbreakable.

Suddenly, the harpy stiffened, made a small cry, and fell from the sky. Hannah hit the stone floor with a thud, and the harpy landed on top of her. She heaved the carcass off, spotting a pristine arrow lodged in its neck. Aleesia, telum-bow in hand, gave her a quick salute before continuing to battle the psoglav.

Hannah made her way through the chaos until she reached the chest. Fitting the key in the lock, she flung open the lid and saw a solitary leather-bound book.

Someone shoved into her, slamming her head against the chest. Blood poured out of her nose as she looked up; standing above her, Drakkar clutched the book in his hands. He tutted as he tucked it under his arm, a repulsive grin on his face. His icy hands snatched her telum and removed the crystal, placing it inside his pocket.

'You found the book for me *and* sacrificed your blood crystal again. How kind! Once more, the Leviathans thank you for your service.'

Hannah was about to fight back, but there was no need. Her eyes looked past Drakkar who frowned and followed her gaze.

Hovering several feet above the ground and rising further was Axis, head tilted, arms stretched wide. Her eyes shone orange, and thick bursts of flame circled her body. She took a breath and brought her arms down, pointing straight at Drakkar and sending the bursts of flame hurling in his direction.

Instinctively, Drakkar created a shield into which the fireballs slammed. Hannah felt the intense heat even from behind it. Then Drakkar produced a portal and stepped out of the library.

Hannah staggered to her feet and dived into the receding purple mist.

But it was too late.

She gazed around, overwhelmed by the sight. Half the library was alight with flames from Axis, who Daegan was now trying to calm. Dead baykoks and harpies scattered the blood-stained floor. The psoglav too was huddled on the ground, close to death with arrows sticking in its body, while Aarava chained up the capcaun. A solemn Mantir placed coins on the eyes of his fallen soldiers.

They may have defended Arcadia against the invading Leviathans, but it didn't feel like a victory. All Hannah could think to do was comfort Axis, now returned to normal. Her auburn hair was a mess, and she could do nothing but cry as her beloved library burned to a crisp.

Chapter Sixty-One

What Now?

FIVE Truceleaders stood solemnly behind Caedric as he paced his study, teacup and saucer in hand. Zephyr plucked at his feathers as if Arcadia was as quiet as ever. Niall and Kiko stood with Sophie and Mantir, while Daegan and Raji stood just behind Hannah with Dex on her shoulder.

They stared at Hannah in silence as she shifted from one foot to the other and brushed a lock of hair behind her ear. It had been uncomfortable telling the entire room the story: finding the vault, Drakkar capturing Hortes, how the saumen-kar and tree had been a trap. Niall had jumped in to defend her, giving the story from his perspective: how Dex had woken him up and wordlessly encouraged him to go to the vault, how well Hannah fought against Drakkar.

Still, there was silence.

'Someone say something,' she pleaded.

'You're in no place to make demands,' Byron replied with his usual air of superiority.

Caedric put his tea on the desk and picked up his pipe. 'Did Drakkar say anything that may help us?' he asked in a tone calmer than she was used to. She couldn't look him in the eyes.

'Not much. He talked about my blood crystal and wanting to bring Thornwood back, something about Astraea and… I think her name was Alana?'

'Alna,' Caedric corrected as he nodded. 'Yes, I always thought that would cause a problem somewhere down the line.'

'Who was she?' Hannah asked.

'His wife.' He let out a puff of smoke that hung in the room.

Hannah cocked an eyebrow, wrestling with the image of Drakkar happy and in love—if either of those feelings were possible for him.

'She was killed during the war,' Caedric explained. 'By Astraea… It's no surprise he's fixated on her.'

'I did tell you he was the one to watch,' Daegan muttered through gritted teeth, his eyes avoiding Caedric's. 'All the signs were there. Plus, his history with Morgarr—'

'Drakkar's family does not speak for him, Daegan,' Caedric interrupted. 'You know as well as anyone how complicated families can be.' Daegan didn't reply. 'I wish you'd brought this to me sooner, Hannah.'

'What did you expect?' asked Eldrin in a pompous tone. 'She's not one of us. She's only *human*.'

Aleesia elbowed Eldrin and glared at him. 'I know what many in Arcadia may think about Hannah,' she said. 'Yet I'm willing to wager none of this is actually her fault. Any mistake she made, she tried bravely to undo. Did no one else see her in the library trying to stop Drakkar? She risked her life for us all.'

There was a quiet mumble as the room agreed.

'I'm not prepared to blame her,' said Aarava.

'Of course, she's not t'blame. She's only a wee lass trying t'do her best,' Braddock added.

Caedric nodded serenely. 'Hannah is not to blame,' he stated, choosing to ignore Byron's smirk. 'Drakkar was a master of manipulation. Until Daegan returned from a mission I sent him on, none of us in Arcadia knew there was a mole here. Even then, only he and I knew.'

'You never told us?' Byron spat. 'Why?'

'Honestly, Byron, it could easily have been you.'

'Preposterous.'

'Any of you could have been a spy. Though I had my suspicions.' He placed his hand on Hannah's shoulder. 'Hannah was a pawn used by a traitor. Let us not forget, if it had not been for her and Niall's brave efforts, the vault would now be open, and Arcadia would not still be standing.'

There was an uncomfortable silence. Hannah let herself smile, relieved Caedric understood her.

'Nevertheless,' he continued, his voice stern, 'we need to act immediately. You say Drakkar took your blood crystal?' he asked Hannah.

'And your blood on his telum,' Niall piped up. All eyes fell on him, and he stepped behind the minotaur.

'He slammed my face into a metal chest,' she told them. 'I couldn't—'

'For that, Hannah,' Caedric interrupted, 'you are not to blame. Perhaps it was an oversight on our part to let you go to the library.' His eyes flicked to Daegan, who straightened in defence. 'However, since he possesses your blood, crystal *and* the location of Astraea's locked vaults, we need to act fast.'

'Intercept them,' agreed Mantir. 'I can lead the full might of Arcadia's army to the vault.'

Caedric waved his hand in dismissal. 'Mobilising an army without being seen is a huge operation for which we don't have time to prepare.'

Aarava nodded. 'Besides, we don't even know which vault he'll open first.'

'Would Axis know the locations of Astraea's vaults?' suggested Aleesia.

'Sadly not,' Daegan told her. 'I asked her while Lena was attending to her in the medical wing. As librarian, she guards the Record of Vaults, but she would never read it. Only the Trucemaster can, and Axis has always been a stickler for the rules.'

'So, we donnae even stand a chance o' finding the damn traitor!' Braddock cursed, slamming the hilt of his battle-axe on the ground.

'We do,' countered Eldrin. 'A few years back, Caedric tasked me with the additional duty of Vaultkeeper. I had access to the Record.'

'You remember the locations?' asked Caedric, his eyebrows raised in surprise.

Morosely, he shook his head. 'I only remember two in particular.'

'If I might make a suggestion, Caedric,' said Byron, his voice still a sneer. 'Perchance it would be wise to send two groups of three to each vault.'

'Two groups of three Truceleaders?' Daegan asked dubiously. 'You forget, Lord Byron, that with Drakkar's betrayal there remains only six—and Caedric's position as Trucemaster dictates he cannot leave Arcadia.'

The lights dimmed, and Byron evaporated into smoke. He reappeared before Daegan, pointed teeth bared and hissing. 'Speak to me like that again, Trucekeeper, and your neck will be swiftly removed.'

Daegan hardly flinched, let alone reacted.

'If you had the respect to let me finish,' Byron continued, 'I was going to suggest that *you* join a group.' He walked with clipped steps back to the other Truceleaders, 'But not *mine*.'

'Okay,' Aarava took over, hoping to stave off the uncomfortable atmosphere. 'Can I suggest Braddock, Daegan and myself journey to one; Eldrin, Aleesia and Byron journey to another?'

Caedric nodded. 'Mantir and I will remain here and ready the trainees and army in the event of another attack.'

The Truceleaders nodded their agreement. 'United we stand,' they said, although with noticeably less enthusiasm than usual.

After giving Caedric the Trucekeeper's salute, all left to follow orders, leaving Niall and Hannah with their familiars, oblivious to the drama.

'What should we do?' asked Niall.

'You two,' Caedric replied over the rim of his glasses, 'do nothing.'

'But—' Hannah began to argue, but Caedric shook his head.

'I understand you were manipulated, Hannah, but it was still you who made the choices that led to this. You should have informed Daegan or me about your suspicions surrounding Drakkar.' He stood up, removed the pipe from his mouth and extended an arm which his caladrius flew to perch on. 'I don't blame you, Hannah. But I would prefer not to put you in harm's way and risk more blame latching itself onto you.'

No more was said on the matter, and Caedric left them. Niall paused before leaping into action. He flicked through the bookshelves that lined Caedric's octagonal room.

'What are you doing?' Hannah asked.

'Caedric knows everything,' he explained, his mind concentrating on the spines of the books. 'He's bound to have a book that'll help us.'

'Help us with what?'

'Come on! Only two locations? The fate of the Trucekeepers—no, the *world*—rests on the possibility of Drakkar going to two out of who-knows-how-many vaults!' He pulled a book from the shelf, grunting from its weight.

'It's too late,' Hannah told him. 'They've already gone.'

'Then we'll just have to go by ourselves.' His eyes darted across several pages as he thumbed through the book, lips tight as he concentrated.

'Caedric told us to stay in Arcadia.'

Niall slammed the book with a dusty thud. 'Yes, I heard,' he snapped, 'but if there's a chance in hell that we can do something—Hannah, they might be about to kick you out anyway!'

She hesitated and swallowed her temper. 'You're right,' she said quietly. 'If I'm able to do something other than sit here twiddling my thumbs and playing with the bagwyns and abadas while they all die, and the Truce is destroyed… how could I live with myself?'

Niall nodded. 'There's nothing here, though.'

Hannah kicked the tree in the centre of the study, which became a dark red in response. She turned to Niall, a helpless look in her eyes while his lit up, his mouth contorting into a grin.

'You have an idea, don't you?'

'Where's Drakkar's room?' he asked.

Chapter Sixty-Two

The Sphinx's Trust

THEIR feet skidded to a halt in front of Drakkar's office. Niall stepped forward, but Hannah stayed frozen.

'I'm not sure I should do this,' she murmured. 'Think of all I've done. Trying to help has made such a mess of things. The sooner I'm out of Arcadia, the safer you'll all be.'

Niall squeezed her shoulders firmly. 'Hannah, you did everything you could to protect those you cared about. Things didn't go the way you wanted, but this is how you can make things right. So...' He turned back to the door, as if there was no more to be said on the matter. 'Should we be on the lookout for traps?'

Hannah shrugged. 'No fireballs shot at me when I was here last. But I wasn't breaking in.'

'Okay... On the count of three?' Niall asked. After a moment, Hannah gave a half-hearted shrug and nodded. 'One, two...'

On three, Hannah turned the latch, and Niall kicked the door open, telum held out. There were no traps, no alarms, no one to greet them. It was empty.

'You don't have your crystal. Stay here,' Niall said as he stepped into the room.

'Nothing's attacking us anyway.'

The room was nothing like it had been. Last time, it was full to the brim with books, curious vials, strange-looking instruments and Etheria in cages. Now there were scarcely any instruments or vials, the bookshelves were bare, and there wasn't an Etheria in sight.

'Never saw him as a minimalist.'

'This isn't right.' Hannah shook her head. 'It was different. There was—there was so much crap! There's no way he got rid of it all.'

'Who knows what he can do?' Niall shrugged. 'Sorcerers would be great removal men.'

He laughed awkwardly and turned to Hannah. Her eyes narrowed as she chewed on her fingernail.

'It's enchanted,' she said.

'What do you mean?'

'We're not Drakkar. Maybe the room is enchanted to—I don't know—hide everything, create an alternate room. *This*,' she gestured at the naked room, 'is not his office.'

'So, we need Drakkar to get into his room? There's a flaw in this plan—'

'Not Drakkar,' she told him, her eyes glistening with a plan of her own. 'Tell me what abilities kitsunes have again.'

Niall whistled and ran a hand through his mop of dark hair. 'Where to begin? Well, there's the basic canine attributes—excellent smell, vision, fierce bite—erm… she's quick and strong. Sharp claws…' he trailed off.

'Go on,' coaxed Hannah.

'She'll be able to do more later in life. She's already growing her third tail! In theory, she'll be able to manipulate dreams; fox-fire powers will improve; she can create illusions like in Thule… possession, shape-shifting—'

'That one,' interrupted Hannah.

'Shape-shifting?'

Hannah nodded eagerly. Niall backed away and picked Kiko up. 'No,' he said, 'she's far too young.'

'Has she tried?'

'Of course not! She'll develop the ability at her own pace.'

Hannah took a deep breath. 'Look—Drakkar is dangerously close to strengthening the Leviathans to the point where the world could change—and with them at the helm, it won't be for the better. Kiko could be humanity's last hope for survival.' She knew she was exaggerating, but the point was still valid and, fortunately, enough to convince Niall.

'Give me a moment with her,' he sighed.

Hannah and Dex kept watch while Niall coaxed Kiko. The kitsune looked at him, eyes brimming with fear. Though she couldn't reply, she communicated everything in her look.

'She'll do it,' he said resignedly.

'She understands?'

'I think so...' Niall shrugged and gestured for Kiko to stand by the door.

He ruffled her head in encouragement and then, in a matter of seconds, the kitsune grew from knee-height to a head taller than Niall. Her burgundy fur flapped until it became burgundy robes; her head stretched and became grey; black eyes became scarlet. The resemblance was uncanny, and a chill ran down Hannah's spine. Even Dex hid behind her shoulder.

'Okay, let's do this,' Niall said, opening the door and backing away so only Kiko—or Drakkar—faced the door. There was a pause as Kiko stood, unmoving, before she took a wobbly step inside.

Niall and Hannah peered around the doorframe. To their relief, the room had returned to its previous state; mountains of books, vials and instruments populated the room, and cries of caged Etheria filled their ears. Kiko shrank and resumed her normal appearance as Niall hugged her. The kitsune closed her eyes and yapped in delight.

'This is more like it. Now where's he hiding that sphinx?'

Hannah bounded to his desk and found Hortes in a metal cage, a small bowl of untouched food by her paws.

'I don't suppose he sent you with a leash to take me for a walk?' Hortes purred with an undercurrent of vehemence. Hannah didn't blame her and knelt next to the cage. 'I haven't stretched my legs properly in… well, come to think of it, it's been at least a millennium.'

'Hortes,' Hannah said, 'I need to ask you a question.'

'Oh, this is interesting,' replied Hortes. 'Usually *I* ask the questions.'

'Are you loyal to Drakkar?' Niall asked.

The sphinx whipped her tail and growled. 'Does it look like I'm loyal to that warlock? He took me from one prison and locked me in a smaller one. He can hang for all I care.' Suddenly, her mouth curved upwards. 'Oh…' Hortes said seductively. 'I think I understand.'

'What do you mean?'

'As soon as you left Drakkar's company the day you—how are you phrasing it? Freed or kidnapped me?—he asked me questions.'

'What sort of questions?' Niall asked, kneeling beside Hannah, leaning forward so as not to miss a word.

Hortes smiled coyly. 'Something bad has happened.' Her eyes glowed white as her pupils disappeared. 'He tried to open the vault here.'

Niall and Hannah shared a look.

'What questions did he ask?' Hannah's patience was waning.

'Only two: what was locked within the vault? And who possesses the blood crystal to open it?'

'And?' Niall asked. 'What were the answers?'

Hortes ignored Niall, instead looking directly at Hannah. 'The answer to the first isn't necessary. And you know the answer to the second, so why ask me?'

'We need to ask you one more,' Hannah explained.

'Very well. Release me from my cage, and I'll happily oblige.'

Once again, Hannah and Niall exchanged a glance, both unsure.

'Okay,' Niall agreed. 'We'll release you. But make one wrong move…' He raised his telum to Hortes' head.

She smirked and bowed in response. 'Naturally.'

With a forceful swing, Hannah's telum hit the padlock. It clattered to the ground, and the door swung open. The sphinx proceeded from the cage, delighting in her newfound freedom. She stretched her front paws and arched her back.

'Now,' Hannah knelt beside the sphinx yet again, keeping more of a distance, 'where is Drakkar?'

'Oh, sweet girl,' Hortes said, her voice like treacle. 'Are you *sure* there are no other burning questions you're itching to ask?'

Judging from the smile on the sphinx's face, Hannah guessed that Hortes was already well aware of what she wanted to know. She had lots of questions: *How come I can use this crystal? Why does it unlock Astraea's vaults?* But she swallowed the temptation to ask.

'Another time,' she said offhandedly. 'What vault is Drakkar going to open first?'

Enjoying her freedom, Hortes paced around the office, inspecting every nook and cranny like a curious cat. 'He preferred to risk his life stealing the Record of Vaults than ask me for the locations himself. I suppose he feared I would lead him into a trap. It's a dense book written in ancient runes. It'll take him hours to translate enough to ascertain the location of just one vault.'

'Has he done it already?' Hannah asked, panic-stricken.

'Children, children. Relax. It has not yet been two hours since he took the book. You have time. Approximately… two hours and thirty-five minutes.'

'Where?' Hannah barked.

Like a flash, Hortes pounced, soaring over them and landing on top of a table with a map which she scratched at with a claw. Niall and Hannah leaned over the table and inspected the detailed map. Drakkar's scribbles meant nothing to them, but the sphinx's mark was clearly visible—a big X by the coast.

'Oakstone Castle,' Niall mused. 'That's not where the Truceleaders were going.'

'It's not too far from here,' Hannah told him. 'We ought to get there in…'

'Just under two hours,' Hortes finished for them, eyes sparkling with the love of chaos. 'If you leave right now, that is.'

Niall walked towards her, telum held in his shaking hand. 'Tell me,' he said. 'You can see into the future. Do we win?'

The sphinx stared, her enigmatic smile unwavering. 'There are many possible outcomes. It is impossible to determine what will happen… unless you leave now.'

Hannah had had enough of this. She couldn't afford to waste a second.

'Hold the fort, Niall.'

'Wait,' he grabbed hold of her arm. 'You don't think you're going without me, do you?'

Hannah stared at him with pinched lips and rubbed the back of her neck. 'I can't drag you into this, Niall. It's too dangerous, and I—'

'Don't make the same mistake again, Hannah. Remember what you told me—about your school: Zack and—Luke? You said you should have listened to Luke, that it might have helped things.'

She glared at him, her eyes flaring. 'Don't bring that up now. I opened myself up when—'

'How many times do you need to be told? You're not alone. Let other people help you.'

Hannah clutched her temples and squeezed her eyes shut. She knew Niall was talking sense, but if anything happened to him, she'd never forgive herself.

'Besides, Drakkar wouldn't have been able to manipulate you if you let others help you, if you'd trusted us enough to tell us about the blue tree. He definitely wouldn't expect you to chase after him with someone else. Wouldn't that surprise make beating him even better?'

Hannah grinned through gritted teeth. 'Fine,' she said.

Once at the door, she looked back at Hortes, now sat on her hind legs like a domestic cat.

'You can trust me,' Hortes said, already knowing Hannah's dilemma. 'I'll be here when you get back—assuming you survive,' she added with a cackle.

Chapter Sixty-Three

Journey from Arcadia

HER eyes glanced at the full moon as it shone through the branches of the forest outside Arcadia. Hannah couldn't believe how much had happened in just one night. And now, a few hours until dawn, she was racing through the forest to stop a dangerous warlock.

Hannah couldn't shake the feeling that Caedric was watching them. They had tried to sneak out unnoticed, but without Drakkar's portal, there was only one way out of Arcadia. It came as no surprise that Caedric had stationed guards there, but they were relieved to see a handful of trainees stood between them and the exit, leaning against the wall and casually bickering.

'I'm going to go explain,' she said, hidden behind a corner.

Niall grabbed hold of her. 'Like we said—we do this quiet and unnoticed.'

She shook his clutched hand from her arm. 'We can't sneak past without hurting them. And we're not doing that.'

Without giving him a chance to argue, she rounded the corner and approached the trainees. As predicted, they raised their weapons, an assortment of staff–, bow– and dagger-telums pointing at her.

'Relax. It's me,' she said, sounding more casual than she felt.

'We know,' Rideo said, a wobble in his voice.

'Caedric told us to keep a special watch out for you,' added Asti.

'No surprise there,' Hannah said. 'Listen—I know you've been given this job, but you have to trust me on this: we know where Drakkar is.'

A look went round the group, telums temporarily lowered.

'Caedric has told us to stay out of it,' Hannah went on, 'but we know where he's going, and we only have—Niall...?'

'Two hours, twenty-five minutes,' he said, wincing.

'Time is running out. We can't rush to Caedric to get permission and gather up a team and get there in time. We need to go *now*.'

Fennrock was the first to holster his telum, encouraging the rest to do the same. 'She's right.'

Nathan emerged from the group and stepped forward, teeth bared. 'No, she's not. She skulks around doing whatever she wants and gets away with it. Not this time.'

'What are you on about?' Limara asked. '*You* cheated in the race.'

'But *you're* the ones who were given a chance to help Thule and messed it up. Why weren't *we* picked?'

Jason nodded, a monstrous finger picking his nose.

'And *you* were the one who helped Drakkar in the first place,' piped up Amber as she stood by Nathan's side, smirking. 'We've heard the rumours about Egypt.'

Hannah said nothing but brushed her hand past her telum.

'*She* helped Drakkar?' Mimi roared. 'Have you forgotten what Nathan did in the Games?'

'Whatever,' Amber scoffed. 'You're nothing, Moreland. Time to go home.'

'Keep the telums up,' Nathan commanded, his eyes not leaving Hannah's for an instant.

'No,' whispered a voice.

Nathan's eyes darted to the side. It was just for an instant, but Hannah detected a note of fear. 'What?'

'I said no,' repeated the voice. Celeste stepped forwards, the tip of her dagger-telum lightly placed against Nathan's neck. 'Lower your weapons. Now,' she insisted.

Nathan whirled round, nostrils flaring and legs planted wide. 'You dare give *me* orders? Who do you think you are? Spend your whole life in Arcadia, and I'm still better than you. Don't forget who trounced you at the Games. I—'

No one saw the punch coming, least of all Nathan. There was a flash of movement as a fist slammed into his face, his cheek rippling and blood shooting from his mouth. Nathan toppled to the floor, silenced.

Jason stood back, hands raised in surrender, as Amber gasped, her telum clattering to the ground. All eyes turned to Luminon, who was rubbing his fist with a satisfied smile.

'Let us help,' Natala said as the trainees rushed towards them, Nathan, Jason and Amber now forgotten.

'The more you have, the better your chances,' Limara added as Mimi nodded in agreement.

'No,' Hannah answered. 'We can't ask any of you to risk your lives for us. I'm the one who put Arcadia in danger. I need to fix it. Just let us pass. If you want to help, hang around the faeries' hut. As soon as they track our Flare spell, tell Sophie we're at Oakstone Castle and to send back-up.'

The trainees wanted to argue, to persuade Hannah and Niall to let them come—but they cut them short. *This is my mess,* Hannah thought. *I can't put them in danger.*

Hannah and Niall raced through the forest faster than they thought they could. All they could think about was Drakkar and how every second that went by was a second closer to him opening the vault.

Hannah was impressed by how well she remembered the route from Arcadia's entrance to where she entered the forest all those months ago. It seemed like an eternity.

'Okay,' Niall said as they emerged from the trees. 'Quiet country road, no phones.' He was looking flustered. 'Any ideas?'

Hannah peered through the darkness, keen to find some method of transport other than running.

'Hortes said we could get there in time, but there's no way we could run fast enough. There must be something,' she mused as she looked around. She suddenly spotted an ivy-clad tree and recognised a shape hiding in the shadows.

'There!' she called as she rushed over and tore heavy branches from a mound.

Niall staggered towards her. 'Is that yours?' he asked incredulously as he spotted the car.

It was filthy with mud, and leaves stuck from every crevice, but it was their only way to catch up to Drakkar. To Hannah's relief, Daegan had left the keys inside, although she still had to smash a window to break in.

Thankfully, the car spluttered to life. Hannah flicked on the headlights and shifted the car into first gear. Although the engine didn't sound healthy, it only needed to take them so far. She shoved her foot down, and the car burst into action, damp mud spraying from the wheels as they shot down the road.

The first hour of the journey was uneventful. They tried to make small talk, if only to stave off tiredness and stay alert. Niall navigated, a task he seemed to enjoy as he decoded every road sign they drove past and kept track on a map he found under his seat. He even suggested playing a game. Hannah refused at first, but as the exhaustion became worse, she agreed, going through the alphabet and naming an Etheria for each letter. The gentle snores of Dex and Kiko in the back made it even harder to stay awake.

Suddenly, a sharp beep from the dashboard made them jerk in their seats.

'What is it?' Niall asked.

'Er… a few things,' Hannah replied. 'I don't know how Drakkar's doing with those runes, but I might need longer to decode this.'

Niall leaned to the side and peeked at her dashboard. She wasn't exaggerating—it was lit up like a Christmas tree.

'Low on fuel,' Niall explained.

'Along with God knows what else. What are those?' she asked, pointing to a multitude of flickering lights.

Niall mumbled something incoherent about the workings of the engine, but she knew he had no idea really. Dex had woken up, now resting on Hannah's shoulder, wide eyes still taking in the amazing machine he was riding inside.

Hannah saw a sign and recognised the nearby towns. An idea formed in her mind, and she turned off the road.

'Where are you going? You took a wrong turn.'

'New plan,' she told him as the car sped through the darkness.

Chapter Sixty-Four

Old Friends

HANNAH felt nostalgic as she pulled up to the house and killed the engine. The car sounded grateful to rest. The house hadn't changed since she left, but she still hesitated on the front lawn, a pebble in her hand. She flung it at a window on the top floor.

'Whose house is this?' Niall whispered.

Hannah sensed his jealousy when the window opened, and a boy with unkempt, mousy hair peered out, bleary-eyed from his interrupted sleep.

'Hi, Luke,' Hannah called, twisting her feet.

As soon as the boy registered who was standing in the front garden, his face lit up, and his jaw dropped. The window slammed, and numerous lights in the house flared to life. The front door was flung open, and he appeared, arms spread wide. She leapt into his arms, and they hugged, just long enough to give Niall cause to cough uncomfortably.

Hannah broke free, about to explain why she was there, but he spoke first.

'I fixed my ocarina,' he told her, beaming.

Hannah frowned. 'Okay… that's not—'

'Where the hell have you been?' he interrupted. 'I haven't seen you since Mr Barlow expelled you. You just stormed off. Then I hear you were attacked and were in hospital! But you ran away. We've been searching for you ever since.' Luke stepped back, looking at her coldly for a moment. 'The police questioned *me*. They thought I did something to you!'

Hannah's stomach twisted. 'I'm so sorry, Luke. I should have talked to you about it all or sent a message or something. I should have—' She stopped as Luke shook his head solemnly.

'What's done is done,' he said, forcing a smile.

She hugged him once more. 'I'm really sorry, Luke. But it's *so* good to see you again.'

'It's good to see you too,' he admitted, giving her a playful punch. 'It's late, though. Or early, I suppose. What time is it?'

Hannah grabbed his wrist. She didn't want him to know how early in the morning it was. *Knowing Luke, he'd probably want to go back to bed.*

Niall glared at Hannah's lingering hand on Luke's wrist, puffing out his chest and grabbing her arm.

She shot Niall a warning look in response. His expression immediately changed, now a picture of guilt and remorse.

'We need your help,' Niall said to Luke, avoiding Hannah's gaze.

'And you are…?'

Tension flooded the trio as the boys laid eyes on each other for the first time. They looked at one another, then at Hannah, then back at each other.

Niall was the first to break the silence.

'Niall.'

'Luke,' the other boy replied, reaching out his arm.

They grasped hands and squeezed for longer than was appropriate, seeing who would break the clasp first.

'How do you two know each other?' Luke asked.

'He's my—' Hannah stopped mid-sentence, unaware how to describe her relationship with Niall. Her mind went blank. Niall stared at her. 'He's my… colleague,' she finally said, wincing.

Neither Niall nor Luke seemed satisfied with her answer. 'I see… You have a job now?' Luke asked. 'What is it?'

'Long story,' she muttered. 'We need to get somewhere—fast. Our car broke down. Could you…?'

Luke looked dumbfounded. 'You're kidding. Yeah, no problem! Hop in the back of my taxi!' He tutted. 'It's the middle of the night, and you want me to drive you where exactly?'

'Oakstone Castle,' Niall said.

Once more, the boys glared at each other. Hannah wished Niall would hang back.

'Oakstone Castle,' Luke repeated. 'That's, what, an hour away?'

'Hannah, we're running out of time,' Niall muttered.

'What kind of work conference happens at this time of night?' Luke demanded. 'And at Oakstone Castle of all places. What is it— a school trip?'

Hannah took hold of Luke's arm, avoiding whatever look Niall was probably giving her. 'Look—I'm really sorry I disappeared. I didn't mean to. But I'm back now—'

'To stay?' Luke asked, his nervous smile full of hope.

Hannah felt her heart break as she looked into his puppy-dog eyes.

'Not right now,' she told him delicately. 'Things are different. But I'm here *now*. I'm sorry this isn't a social call, but you're my only hope, Luke. *Please.*'

He gazed at her longingly. He missed her; she knew that. She regretted not even writing him a letter.

'Let me get dressed.'

Niall barely looked from his watch, his foot tapping as he waited. Hannah wanted to snap, insist he change his attitude towards Luke who was helping them in their hour of need—but she knew it was no use. Niall was stressed enough as it was; having to rely on Luke was just making it worse.

Luke emerged, fully dressed in a baggy T-shirt with Beethoven on the front. 'You sit in the back,' he instructed Niall as he unlocked his car.

Niall opened his mouth to argue but just rolled his eyes instead.

Hannah held open a door and ushered Dex and Kiko in, hoping Luke wouldn't spot them.

'One second.' Luke checked his wing mirrors and ignored Niall's tut. He reached out and adjusted his rear-view mirror before freezing. 'Do you guys have a dog?'

Kiko sat in the back seat, an expression of wonder on her face as she looked around the car. Dex made a mewling sound as he flew from behind Luke's seat and landed on his lap, looking up at him. Luke froze, eyes wide with shock. There was a tense moment before Luke screamed as loud as a banshee and jumped from the car.

'Well, we have to tell him now,' Hannah sighed.

'And break the Truce? Are you mad?'

'I won't break the Truce if I cast the Oblivion spell,' she snapped.

Niall paused, lost for words. 'You'd wipe the mind of your own friend?'

Hannah looked despondently to her old friend, patting his lap to rid himself of any more creatures.

'I guess I'll have to.'

It took longer than they hoped to calm Luke. He was in a state, panicking about the creatures that might make a mess in his mum's car, mumbling something about insurance.

Ensuring there were no onlookers, Niall removed his telum and pointed it at Luke's head. Before Hannah could say anything, a small glow emanated from the tip, and Luke was silenced. He looked at Hannah and smiled, his eyes empty.

'Should we get going?' he asked and skipped to the car.

'Daze spell,' Niall explained. 'I read about it. It clouds someone's mind, calms them down. Even more effective on humans. It ought to wear off in about half an hour though.'

Hannah opened her mouth, but no words came out. Niall avoided her scowl as they climbed silently into the car and continued their rush towards Oakstone Castle.

Chapter Sixty-Five

The Race to the Vault

'HANG on,' Hannah said halfway through the journey. 'When did you get your driving licence?'

Luke shrugged, the cloudy smile from Niall's spell still affecting him. 'I failed my test last month. I'm retaking it again tomorrow.'

Hannah shot a venomous look at Niall who rolled his eyes. 'This is your fault!' she hissed.

'Forget all that,' Luke said. 'I want to hear what's happened to you.' He looked at Hannah earnestly.

'Don't,' Niall said from behind.

'I… I'm afraid I can't tell you,' she replied.

He laughed, his eyes flitting from the road to Hannah. 'Seriously?'

She made a concerted effort to keep a straight face. 'I might as well,' she said to Niall in the back. 'He's seen Dex and Kiko anyway.'

Niall remained silent while Hannah gave Luke an abridged version of what happened. Zelom, Daegan, Etheria, Drakkar, Thule, Arcadia… Luke listened attentively, not making a sound until she finished, and he started to sound more like his normal self.

'Wait… you're telling me all these mythical creatures and monsters—'

'Cryptoetheria,' Niall corrected.

Hannah shot him another glare. 'You can call them Etheria,' she reassured Luke.

'Okay,' he said, still trying to process everything. 'So, all these Etheria I've heard about… they're *real*?'

'Yes. Well, most of them.'

'Right. And Gods…?'

An impatient tut came from the back seat.

Luke cocked an eyebrow as he looked at him in the rear-view mirror. 'I'm sorry if you don't remember what life was like before… what was it, Arcadia? But I'm sure you thought the whole idea of Etheria being real was pretty wild too.'

Niall remained silent. Hannah grinned.

'So, Gods aren't real?'

'We don't know,' Hannah said. 'Some Etheria believe in Gods, but it's not like they're just walking around Arcadia like everything else.'

'But vampires, elves, dragons—even griffins and stuff—they *are*?'

'Yeah! And that's just the tip of the iceberg.'

Luke let out a howl of excitement. Hannah tried not to dwell on the fact that she would have to erase his mind as soon as they were done.

'This is amazing!' he cried. 'And those little guys in the back…?'

'Dex and Kiko. Yeah, them too. Kiko's a kitsune, and—'

The delicate white ears of the kamaitachi propped up when he heard his name and hovered by Luke's side, nuzzling his cheek.

'Hiya,' Luke greeted him, taking one hand off the wheel to stroke Dex.

'—and Dex is a kamaitachi.'

'He flies,' Luke said, stating the obvious with wonder in his eyes. 'He's cute. I can't believe you get pets!'

'They're not pets,' Niall reminded them. 'They're familiars.' He gave an apologetic nod and sat back in his seat. 'Just clarifying.'

'Can I be one? A Trucekeeper?' Luke asked out of nowhere.

An awkward silence overcame the car. Neither Hannah nor Niall knew how to respond.

'Maybe,' she replied, unsure. Though deep down, she knew Daegan was unlikely to agree.

'By the way, do you need to test?' Luke asked.

Hannah felt her stomach twist into knots. She cursed under her breath.

'I'm sorry. I should have reminded you,' Niall sighed from the back.

Hannah resisted the urge to react; she knew he didn't mean to sound patronising. 'I didn't have a chance. How was I supposed to ask Lena for it? They'd know we were leaving. Besides, it's too late to head back now. And I'm pretty sure what we're doing is a little more important.'

'Hannah,' Luke said, 'if you don't have your equipment, you really ought to—'

'Normally, I'd agree with you, Luke,' said Niall.

Luke looked just as shocked as Hannah.

'But right now, we're in a bit of a hurry. Hannah knows her body. If her levels change, she can duck out and I'll deal with it myself.'

Hannah stared at the ground, hoping it wouldn't come to that. There was no way Niall could survive by himself.

Luke glanced in the rear-view mirror and opened his mouth, ready to reply. But after a small touch on his shoulder from Hannah, he stopped himself. 'So,' he said, in an effort to change subjects, 'I didn't have time to talk to you—after Mr Barlow, you know.'

'Talk to me about what?'

'You know…' he said as he shifted in his seat, eyes still fixed on the road, 'us in the cupboard…'

Hannah heard Niall sit up and evaded the topic. Once more, the car settled into an awkward silence for the rest of the journey, with directions being the only words uttered as they raced to the vault.

Chapter Sixty-Six

Warnings

THE ruin of Oakstone Castle loomed above them, the oppressive silhouette hidden amongst the starry night sky. The calm waves lapped against the beach at the bottom of the cliff beside the castle. But any onlooker would notice the shimmering purple light that flashed as the warlock appeared.

Hannah leant against Luke's car and stared through a pair of binoculars while Niall sharpened the ends of his telum. Luke had parked as close as he could and now sat in the car, drumming his fingers on the dashboard, nervously humming the tune to Beethoven's Fifth.

'We're too late,' Hannah sighed. 'We should just charge in now.'

'I'm not sure that would be a good idea,' Niall said, pointing to the field illuminated by moonlight.

Hannah hadn't noticed them before but now spied a handful of creatures the size of large dogs scattered throughout the field. They crawled through the grass as if patrolling. Even from a distance, Hannah could recognise the malnourished dog-like Etheria with hostile eyes and spikes on their back—chupacabras.

Above them came the unmistakable flapping of bat wings and sharp talons gleaming in the light—a wakwak.

'At least we can hear the wakwak,' Niall said. 'The closer it gets to you—'

'—the quieter it is,' Hannah finished. 'Yes, I know. But what are those over there?' she asked, her finger shaking as she pointed.

Niall was quiet for a second as he racked his brain. 'Tatzelwurms!' he finally exclaimed. 'Lizard-like creatures—heads like cats, bodies like serpents.'

That seemed to be an accurate description as Hannah gazed at them, sliding gracefully through the tall grass, long snake-like bodies slithering beneath the vicious cat-heads. A shiver shot down her spine, and she fingered the hole in her telum where her blood crystal used to be.

'You got a plan?' she asked.

Niall was busying himself with the Flare spell. With any luck, it should flag up in the faeries' hut, and the trainees would be on-hand to explain.

'Sort of,' he admitted, 'but it's far from perfect. Best not to fight them, even one by one. We cast Shadow and Muffle spells to sneak past—but without your crystal you'll have to keep close to me. And if they catch us…' Niall trailed off, not wanting to think how long Hannah would last without magic.

'I've still got my telum and shield,' she told him. 'I'm pretty sure I can do more damage with that anyway.'

'What do we do about *him*?' Niall gestured towards Luke, sitting patiently in the car and playing his ocarina.

Hannah paused. She didn't want to seem ungrateful, but he wouldn't last a second against a weak Etheria, let alone a Leviathan hellbent on starting a war.

'Luke,' she said in as breezy a manner as she could muster, 'we're off. Thank you *so* much for the lift, but—'

'Woah! Nope—nuh-uh. You're not getting rid of me again,' he said assuredly. His hand reached through the window and grabbed hers. She felt a jolt of electricity shoot up her arm. 'I've only just got you back again. There's no way—'

'Luke—this warlock, the Leviathans—they *hate h*umans. We're the reason they have to hide. They won't hesitate to kill you.'

'I'll help,' he insisted. 'I can be a fearless warrior,' he joked as he flexed his biceps.

'No,' she insisted.

'But I—'

'No!' she shouted, louder than she had intended.

She paused, straining her ears to see if anyone had heard. But there was silence. No sound other than the waves in the distance.

Too quiet… They could no longer hear the wakwak's wings.

'Get down!' Niall shouted.

Hannah's body hit the floor, narrowly missing the sharp talons of the wakwak as it soared past. She rolled under the car, cursing herself for losing her blood crystal.

'What's going on?' shouted a panicked Luke.

'Wind up the windows and lock the door! Stay inside!' she shouted, as she flicked her hand, and the shield clicked into place.

She rolled out and jumped to her feet, blocking her face from the diving wakwak as it slammed into her shield.

'Ideas on how to take it down?' she asked Niall who was shooting spell after spell from his telum, each one dodged by the agile wakwak.

'They're weak against fire,' Niall grunted. 'But I can't hit it!'

'Dex! Distract it!' Hannah ordered the kamaitachi.

Eager to help, Dex soared upwards. His soft white tail sharpened and sliced through the wakwak. Scarlet feathers fluttered to the ground, and the wakwak screamed.

Niall saw his opportunity. 'Kiko—fire!'

In a flash, a multitude of flames hurtled towards the wakwak who flapped and squawked as the flickering flames pummelled it. Powerless, it fell to the ground, landing with a thud on Luke's car bonnet.

Niall sprang forwards, telum bared to pierce into its chest. Hannah released her shield gauntlet and held it over the wakwak. The blade slammed into it with a loud clang.

'What are you doing?'

'What Daegan would want,' Hannah said as she dragged the unconscious wakwak from the car and laid it amongst the tall grass by the road. 'It's not a threat anymore. No need to kill it.'

Niall took a breath and rubbed his nose. 'Of course. You're absolutely right. I… er, I've got some spare rope. I'll tie it up— make sure it doesn't cause any more trouble.'

As Niall saw to the wakwak, Hannah turned her attention to Luke, still at the wheel and white as a sheet. He reached out a shaking hand to wind the window down as she walked towards him.

'See why you're better off here?' she asked.

Luke tried to reply, but his words came out as worried stutters, forcing him to nod and hold back his whimpers.

'Keep quiet. If anything happens, honk the horn twice or drive away as fast as you can.'

'Thanks for the lift, Luke,' Niall said, grabbing his hand and shaking it stiffly. 'Have a good night.'

Hannah shook her head in disbelief. *It's like he's saying goodbye to a taxi driver!* But she was pleased Niall had stopped being so antagonistic towards him.

Luke reached out. 'Don't go,' he pleaded. 'It's not worth risking your life.'

Hannah wanted desperately to do what he wanted—to stay with him and ignore the danger. But she couldn't. She had made a home in Arcadia, and she would be damned if she would let Drakkar tear it apart.

'I'm sorry, Luke. Keep hidden and stay safe.'

Luke nodded his understanding. He wound the window back up before sinking so low in his seat he was totally hidden and continued humming to himself.

Chapter Sixty-Seven

Field of Leviathans

HANNAH instructed Dex to fly high in the air to keep away from the Leviathans and alert them if they were spotted. The kamaitachi gave a mew of understanding and propelled himself into the night sky.

'Before we go,' Niall said as he turned to her, 'I just wanted to check you were feeling okay.'

Hannah cocked an eyebrow. 'Yeah, I'm fine. Why?'

'I don't want you going low or high and passing out on me in the middle of a fight with a—'

'I'm fine,' she repeated, a sharp edge to her voice. 'Trust me, I can tell when I'm going high or low. I'll be okay.'

Niall seemed to accept her answer, but she wasn't sure if she believed herself. She just hoped she'd be able to hold on long enough with no issues.

'Ready?' Niall asked.

With a breath to steady her nerves, Hannah nodded. Niall cast two spells in quick succession, covering them in a blanket of shadow and quietening their footsteps. Confident they were well hidden, they made their way to the edge of the field.

The Leviathans were hardly the most diligent of patrol guards, sauntering from one side of the field to the other. Niall suggested waiting a while to choose the best moment to cross the field, but Hannah needed only to remind him of the time pressure. The light from Drakkar's telum was moving from one side of the ruined castle to the other, before going up a floor and repeating the process. Before too long, he would find the vault, and it would be too late.

Steeling themselves, Niall picked up Kiko, and they ran, flying across the field as fast as their legs could carry them before skidding to a halt and crouching by a clump of tall grass.

'Why are we stopping?' Hannah hissed.

Niall gripped her shoulder and pointed.

Just a few feet ahead of them was a chupacabra, quietly growling. They held their breath, terrified that the fearsome creature might hear the slightest noise. It sniffed once. Then again, an intense intake of breath. It focused its gaze on the grass they hid behind.

Hannah tensed.

'It can smell us!' she whispered, her hand gripping Niall's like a vice.

The chupacabra made another low growl, louder this time, as its paws padded towards them, its dribble now growing with the promise of fresh meat. Hannah's lip wobbled, and her other hand gripped her telum, knowing full well it wouldn't be enough without her crystal.

A cry from the air seized the chupacabra's attention. Distracted, it looked at the sky as a creature hovered below the moon, curved tail glistening. With a yell, Dex dived, his tail cutting a handful of spikes from the chupacabra's back, causing it to yelp and flee.

Niall raised his telum, letting his blood drip onto the crystal, and cast another spell as the cries of the chupacabra melted into a muffled silence.

Wasting no more time, they sprinted to the castle, only sliding to a halt once they were safely behind a large boulder.

They looked at the towering ruin, the light from Drakkar's search climbing higher and higher.

'It doesn't look like he's found it yet,' Niall whispered.

'Have any Trucekeepers taken down a sorcerer before?' she asked tentatively.

Niall gave her an impatient glance. 'Yes… but never less than a group of at least *three*—trained and experienced. But, hey—they didn't have the element of surprise.'

Hannah could sense that even Niall didn't believe his own optimism but appreciated the attempt to inspire confidence.

She handed her belt-rope to Dex who tied it securely to the topmost peak of the tallest tower. While Hannah scaled the wall, Niall used his belt-rope to strap Kiko to his back before grabbing hold of Hannah's and following behind, all the while complaining of his fear of heights. Hannah was surprised he only complained and didn't require coaxing like in Thule.

She leapt over the wall and landed on the ground, relieved she was still close enough to Niall for the Muffle spell to still work. She suppressed a shiver as she spotted piles of bones that peppered the room, trying to ignore the thought that something lived there and lay in wait for them.

'There!' hissed Niall, pointing downwards.

Hannah followed his hand to see a dim light through a hole in the ground.

'He's one floor below.'

'What's our plan of attack?'

They looked at each other and saw the same feeling in both their eyes. Neither relished standing up to a warlock, but Niall mustered something that resembled an encouraging smile.

'We've got this, okay?' Hannah said. 'We've had Daegan train us. Remember? The guy's a badass. How could we lose? Besides, it's one telum against two. Well, without my crystal I guess it's one telum against one, plus a dagger.'

'We're just trainees. Trainees still die, Hannah. Even during their Trials. Drakkar won't hold back.'

'Then neither will we,' she told him.

They stared at each other, daring the other to break first. Neither did.

'Right,' Niall said. 'Here's the plan…'

Chapter Sixty-Eight

Castle of Flying Daggers

NIALL'S stealth charms wore off while they huddled there, but it didn't matter—their element of surprise would soon be gone anyway. There was no way they could take Drakkar out without him fighting back. With nods of understanding, they straightened up and braced themselves, hoping beyond hope their plan would work.

With careful steps, they crawled to the hole and dropped down, bending their knees as they hit the ground to cushion their landing, just as Daegan had taught them. With barely a sound, they were mere metres behind Drakkar who extinguished the light from his telum, somehow still wet with Hannah's blood.

She wished they had broken into Talos' workshop to steal the wrist-bow; a well-placed arrow in the back of Drakkar's neck would have ended it there and then.

He paced towards the end of the room where, lit in a flood of silver moonlight, was the vault. Drakkar reached into his pocket and pulled out a gem that glittered—Hannah's blood crystal. He held it in his bony fingers, caressing it, and placed it into the vault's lock.

'Wait,' Hannah whispered carefully.

Niall was shaking with impatience. 'I can't. He's about to open the vault.'

'We need to—'

'Go with the plan *now*,' he hissed as he pressed his red thumb to the crystal and unleashed a wave of bright red energy that flashed across the castle.

It struck Drakkar in the back who staggered forward. He whipped around, spitting furiously.

There was no time to waste. As Niall charged forwards, he closed his eyes and cast a blinding light before letting out a cry as he jumped, telum raised, blade aimed at Drakkar's chest.

But the effects of the flash were short-lived against the warlock. His sight recovered quickly, and with a quick spell, he halted Niall's attack mid-air, slamming his back against the bronze door of the vault—right where he needed to be.

He struggled to his feet, too swift for Drakkar to react, and retrieved Hannah's blood crystal.

'No!' roared Drakkar as Niall threw it across the room.

He shot a Blast spell at Niall, smashing his head against the vault door once more. Blood dripped down the back of his neck as Drakkar raised his telum above his hand, ready to end the trainee's pitiful life.

But the warlock grunted as a Strike spell hit him from behind. He turned to find Hannah, telum aimed at him, ready to duel.

She fired a Blast spell, which Drakkar redirected with his telum.

Hannah felt her heart sink.

She tried again. Drakkar merely sidestepped, evading it with ease. He returned the same spell, and Hannah's feet left the ground. Her body rolled as it hit the stone floor.

'Haven't you noticed yet, girl?' Drakkar growled. 'Warlocks are the living embodiment of magic. You really think those spells affect me the way it does lesser Etheria? Or humans?'

Drakkar grunted in amusement as he saw Niall, thumb pressed tightly on his blood crystal, as he created a shield between Drakkar and the vault.

'Lower the shield, boy. I can smash through it anyway. Do either of you really want to do this again?' he asked them.

'Blood magic can still hurt you,' Hannah responded.

'Not nearly enough,' he growled.

'What about Etheria magic?' Niall sneered.

As if on cue, Kiko sent a hailstorm of fireballs that slammed into Drakkar. He cried out and created a shield, unable to hold off the rally of fire. Kiko's eyes shone pure white as she concentrated entirely on the attack. Hannah found a crack in his barrier and shot a spell, hitting him in the side. As he stumbled, Drakkar lost contact with his crystal. His shield dissipated, the rally of flames free to slam into him.

But it still wasn't enough.

Kiko's eyes darkened, and the fireballs ended. Drakkar patted his burgundy robes, putting out the flames, before looking up, pure fury pouring from his eyes.

'When I took your blood…' he hissed. Hannah stroked the scar on her check, still raw from the blood he had stolen. 'I should have just killed you!'

He screamed as his hand arched backwards and thrust forward. Hannah saw his telum shoot through the air, flailing madly, soaring straight towards her heart. Quick as a flash, her knees buckled, and she threw herself to the ground, watching the blade fly past her and miss by inches.

A horrifying sound reached her ears as the knife stuck into something behind her.

'Hannah…?' came a soft, pained voice.

Standing behind her was a boy with a knife impaled in his chest, blood pouring down his front. The boy whimpered as he fell.

Hannah let out a piercing shrill as she saw Luke dying right in front of her.

Chapter Sixty-Nine

The Opening

HANNAH knelt beside Luke, a ruby puddle pooling around her knees, Drakkar's telum still sticking out of his chest.

'Oh no… no, no, no. Please, no. Luke?'

In an instant, Hannah's world turned upside down. She no longer cared about Drakkar or the vault. Luke had nothing to do with this. He would die, and it would be her fault.

'I told you to stay in the car. What were you doing?'

'I…' Luke spluttered, choking his words out with difficulty.

'Shh, don't speak,' Hannah said.

'I heard a noise,' he croaked. 'Just… wanted to make sure you were safe.'

She blocked out Drakkar's roar of anger and focused instead on trying to stop the bleeding. 'It'll be okay, Luke. Alright? We'll get you to a hospital. We'll get you patched up. You'll be okay.' But she didn't even believe herself. If the adamantine metal of telums was enough to hurt Etheria, there was no telling how lethal it was for humans. His wound already looked worse than a normal stab wound.

A surge of electricity sounded from behind, accompanied with a cry of pain. Hannah wanted to ignore Drakkar; she wanted just to pick Luke up and race him to hospital. But how would they treat a wound from adamant? She would break the Truce just by explaining…

'Face me, girl!' Drakkar yelled.

With a look of thunder, she turned to the warlock, her hand shaking as she saw his threat. Blue jolts of electricity coursed around his body, his magic now bursting from within, no longer channelled through the telum. Drakkar held Niall securely with one arm with his telum to his throat, a trickle of blood already dripping down his neck.

'One friend has already died tonight. Don't let it result in two,' he warned. 'You know what I want. I want this vault, one that Astraea sealed with your blood crystal. I want it opened *tonight.*'

Hannah looked from Luke to Niall to Drakkar, weighing up her options. She could always blast the ceiling, let it crumble on top of him; Drakkar would have to let go of Niall to save himself. But what about Niall—would he survive that?

Then she felt it. The familiar feeling in her head, fatigue coursing through her body. This wasn't just exhaustion from the blood crystal—her diabetes was affecting her too. There was no way she could continue fighting Drakkar like this. There was no point in trying any form of attack like this—she'd be too slow, and Drakkar would slit Niall's throat without hesitation.

'Come on!' he snapped. 'Do it quickly, and at least this one will live.'

With a sigh of defeat, Hannah plucked her blood crystal from her telum.

'No, Hannah! Don't do it!' Niall yelled, immediately silenced as the blade was pushed more firmly against his neck.

She manoeuvred her way around the holes in the ground, her feet shaking with trepidation. She kept her distance as she passed Drakkar, his eyes fixed firmly on her as she approached the vault.

There was a click as she placed her blood crystal in the vault.

She took a breath.

'Do it,' Drakkar hissed.

Hannah grimaced as she pricked her finger and reached out a shaking finger. Her heart thumped against her chest, the blood coursing through her body.

There was a rush as she touched the embedded crystal, unlike anything she had felt before. It was so much more intense than the draining feeling when she cast spells. She could sense her very energy surge from her body and through the crystal, the increasing heat becoming unbearable. Her finger was scalded, and her body went limp. It took all the energy she had left to stay standing.

Suddenly, the blood crystal turned ice cold and dropped to the floor. Hannah reached out a weary hand to retrieve it, stepping back as she heard a rumble. The vault scraped against the stone wall as the door slowly raised, revealing a dark cavern.

They stared into the abyss and waited, breaths bated in anticipation. For a while, nothing happened. Hope sparked in Hannah's mind.

Perhaps there's no Etheria in the vault at all. Maybe Drakkar was wrong.

But the low growl and hiss from within killed her hope, and her fear rose. From deep within the vault approached a fierce Etheria, a growl coming from not one but two heads. As the moonlight hit the creature, Hannah's breath caught in her throat—it was all she could do to stop herself from screaming.

This was an Etheria Hannah recognised and one she had hoped never to encounter.

Its paws stepped into the light, claws digging into the floor. Then a head emerged, a lion's, but twice the size and with a darker mane. It continued forward, and another head appeared from its back, a goat's with sharper, protruding teeth. The straggly short brown hair ended halfway down its body and turned into emerald-green scales that ended in a long tail with a snake's head; it hissed, purple venom dripping from its fangs that smoked as it hit the floor.

Hannah cursed as a shiver ran down her back, the chimera growling and gazing at them hungrily.

Chapter Seventy

The Chimera

EYES wide with wonder, Drakkar let go of Niall. His staff-telum clattered to the ground, and he clambered away, grabbing his telum as he crawled as far from the warlock as possible.

'What did you do?' Niall asked her. 'A chimera… There's no way we can beat that.'

Hannah said nothing, unable to snatch her eyes from the beast before them.

Drakkar's reaction to the chimera was the opposite. He looked at it lovingly, his eyes dimming as if relaxed; he looked almost happy.

'Isn't it beautiful?' he exclaimed.

The chimera snarled as Drakkar approached and snapped its mighty jaws in warning. Undeterred, he raised his hand and stroked its mane. The Etheria did not lose its menacing look, though ceased its growl.

Drakkar turned to face Niall and Hannah, his hand still running through the chimera's hair.

'The Truce shall die, along with mankind,' he told them with an air of finality. 'From the waves we rise.'

With that, he reached his hand outwards and, obeying his silent command, his telum slid out of Luke's chest and flew across the room to his outstretched hand. Blood oozed from Luke's wound.

Telum in hand, Drakkar pressed his bloody thumb to his crystal and plunged the blade deep into the chimera's neck. It roared in agony, and a bright white light engulfed the castle.

Hannah blinked, furiously trying to quell the black spots that clouded her vision. When she could finally see again, she opened her eyes. The warlock had vanished, and the chimera lay on the ground.

'What happened?' she asked Niall. 'He—he's gone. The chimera's dead! We won!'

She leapt into the air and hugged Niall, burying her face in his neck and laughing with joy.

Niall didn't hug back. Instead, he tapped Hannah's shoulder and pointed towards the chimera.

Drakkar was nowhere to be seen, but the red eyes that now shone from all three heads of the waking chimera told the whole story. The chimera stood and stretched, getting used to its body, its movements choppy and unrefined. As the heads turned to stare at Hannah, she understood—she recognised those eyes.

'He... Is he...?'

'He absorbed himself into the chimera,' Niall confirmed.

'But *how*?'

'Sorcerers can give up their physical bodies to possess another Etheria. That's how many remain immortal.'

Hannah felt her heart sink. A warlock was one thing, but a warlock inside the body of a chimera was something else entirely.

'Can he still use his magic?' she whimpered.

Niall shook his head. 'I don't know. Not yet—he's not used to the body. But the longer we wait, the more powerful he'll become.'

Hannah stared at the ground, a sinking feeling in her stomach. They'd tried so hard, done all they could—and she was getting weaker and weaker by the minute, pulled downwards by her low blood sugar. Niall gripped his staff and pricked his thumb, watching the blood drip down the staff. He looked at Hannah, and she saw it in his eyes—resignation, sacrifice.

'Shall we?' he asked.

They flicked their left hands, and their shields clicked into place. Dex and Kiko joined them at their sides. The chimera lowered, hissing and growling as it readied itself.

Hannah took a deep breath and readied her telum, trying to focus through her fuzzy head.

'Flash it,' she ordered Niall.

The chimera tensed its legs, ready to pounce.

Dex, Kiko and Hannah shielded their eyes as Niall let loose a flash of light. The chimera stumbled, and the Trucekeepers began their last stand.

'Dex—distract the tail!'

'Kiko—burn it!'

The familiars followed their orders; the snake-head hissed as Dex slashed with his razor-sharp tail; the chimera jumped backwards as it avoided Kiko's jet of flames.

The goat-head reared back and opened its mouth. An even larger stream of fire erupted towards Kiko who narrowly avoided the attack.

Meanwhile, Niall and Hannah concentrated on the lion-head, fiercely snapping and snarling as they fired their spells. They did little damage, serving only to infuriate the already vehement beast. After their ordeal with Drakkar, they knew they couldn't rely on magic for long—not without any aqua vitae and not with Hannah's blood sugar as low as it was.

'I can't keep this up!' Hannah shouted.

'Keep a distance!' Niall reminded her, his voice just as tired.

But that wasn't how Hannah fought. Pushing through her exhaustion, she leapt forward and bashed the head with her shield.

The chimera simply hit her back, and she fell to the floor, winded.

Hannah and Niall looked at each other. They knew what they were thinking; they didn't stand a chance. Hannah screwed her eyes shut as the chimera reared up on two legs and roared. Two heavy thuds hit the ground, and the castle shook.

Hannah looked up, mouth falling open, eyebrows raised in shock. Facing the fearsome Leviathan was an equally enormous Etheria, covered with thick dark hair, bloody claws and yellow eyes.

The werewolf caught their eyes and sneered. 'Looks like you could do with some help,' he said, his voice like a deep bark.

The chimera pounced at the werewolf who lunged to the side, digging a bloody gash into the lion's face with a swipe of his paw. It roared in response.

'Hannah—we should go,' Niall said. He pulled her to her feet and dragged her towards the stairs.

Her eyes went from Niall, to Luke, to the werewolf and chimera…

'We can't,' was all she could utter. 'I can't leave Luke, and I—'

'We'll take Luke,' he snapped.

He doesn't understand, she thought to herself. *They couldn't just open the vault and leave this werewolf to deal with their mess—whoever he was.*

'Get—out—of my—home!' barked the werewolf as he threw the enormous chimera against the vault door. The castle walls shook as loose bits of rock fell on the stunned chimera.

Hannah looked from Niall's defeated eyes to just behind him. Her face lit up.

'I think we can win this,' she insisted, fully aware of how bemusing her sudden smile must have been as she saw what was headed their way.

Chapter Seventy-One

The Battle of Oakstone Castle

A gust of wind blasted them, accompanied by a rumble of thunder and a flash of lightning.

Niall gasped as a griffin glided through the crumbling wall, and a rider leapt off. Though cloaked in silhouette, there was no mistaking the rider as he adjusted his hat, and his faithful familiar landed beside him.

'Daegan!' cried Hannah.

Daegan shot her a look, one Hannah couldn't decode. She rushed to fight by his side, but he had other ideas. 'Ansel,' Daegan shouted at the werewolf, 'take the children to safety.'

'You must be kidding!' the werewolf shouted back. 'I've only just started!' He ducked under the chimera's claws and whacked it with his elbow.

'Now! Raji—take care of the chupcabras and tatzelwurms outside. Make sure Ansel gets them away safely.'

The raiju nodded its understanding and soared through the hole in the wall in a stream of lightning.

Ansel grumbled as he dodged another attack and retreated, letting the griffin take on the chimera. 'You've got some nerve talking to me like that,' he snarled as he passed Daegan, 'after what you did to me last time we met.'

Daegan ignored the werewolf and instead dived into the battle.

With impossibly large strides, the werewolf hurried to Luke and hoisted him over his shoulder.

'Be careful!' Hannah cried. 'He's human! He's been stabbed by an adamantine telum.'

'You don't say,' grunted the werewolf. She glimpsed his blood-stained teeth. 'Come,' he said, trying to corral them down the stairs and out of danger.

'No chance.' Hannah barged past him. She couldn't leave Daegan—not now.

'Oh, no you don't,' he responded. He picked her up by the hem of her shirt and brought her back. 'I've been given strict orders to get you out of here—'

'I don't have to listen to you,' Hannah snapped back.

Ansel was unfazed.

'Are you even with the Trucekeepers?' she asked.

A grunt came from the werewolf's snout, and he shrugged his shoulders. 'On and off. Looks like they might need me if this goes south.' He stole a glance behind him. Daegan shielded himself from the chimera's jaws. 'Are you coming or not?' he asked a defiant Hannah.

She knew the wise thing to do; she knew what Daegan would want her to do.

But when have I ever done what I was told?

She ran towards Daegan. 'I have to help!'

'Suit yourself,' Ansel growled as he hoisted Niall up.

'Put me down!' Niall screamed, kicking desperately. 'Hannah!' he called after her. 'Don't risk it!'

The werewolf had had enough. He ignored Niall's pleas and leapt to the field, with Dex and Kiko following behind.

Daegan glanced briefly at Hannah. 'Forget something?' he asked as he jumped back and unloaded all six of his adamantine arrows into the chimera. It roared, though only slightly injured. 'I told Ansel to get you away.'

'He took Niall and Luke—'

'Your boyfriend? What's he doing here?' he asked, shooting a spell from his telum.

'He's not—It doesn't matter,' she snapped. 'I'm staying. Let me help you!'

She could tell Daegan was reluctant, but she knew he needed the help. Even the griffin, currently battling the goat-head, was struggling, several of its feathers alight and burning.

'Have you tested?' he shouted through a spell.

Why does everyone keep fussing about my diabetes?

'I'm fine!'

Daegan sighed heavily and threw her a vial.

Aqua vitae! She beamed at Daegan as she downed the vial in one gulp. The liquid trickled down her throat, and she felt a surge of energy course through her body as the liquid revitalised her.

'It won't be enough, but it'll help,' he shouted from over his shoulder. 'You distract the head—I'll deal with the tail.'

Daegan pressed his thumb to the crystal and summoned Groundbreaker. He swung it downwards. The ground beneath the chimera broke away, and it jumped backwards, narrowly avoiding a hole that opened.

Daegan slid under the chimera, slashing at its stomach, before jumping to his feet and bringing the sword crashing down. The blade struck the snake, and with a final hiss, the lifeless head fell to the floor.

The lion-head roared, louder than before, and snapped. Hannah raised her shield, but sharp teeth broke through.

The tail shook like a hose as dark venom sprayed manically from the cut tip. Daegan only just evaded it, most landing on the wall where it steamed and burnt into the centuries-old construction. Hannah avoided it too as it whipped around, but the griffin wasn't so lucky. It squawked in agony as the venom seared through feathers and skin.

The tail whipped again, heading towards Daegan. Hannah didn't think twice and cast a Blast spell. Daegan went flying, narrowly missing the venom, and only just landing on his feet.

'Get out of here!' he called to the injured griffin. Fortunately, the tail had run out of venom, but the griffin was in bad shape. 'Fly back to Arcadia and take the wounded boy with you!'

Seizing the opportunity while he was distracted, the chimera slammed into Daegan.

'No!' Hannah screamed as she watched him plunge helplessly through the hole in the floor.

She dashed to where he had fallen and skidded to the ground. Peering through the dark, she could only just make out the vague silhouette of Daegan lying on the ground.

He wasn't moving.

Her breath caught in her throat. *He can't be dead*, she told herself. *There's no way.* She turned back to the chimera; it stood with all four legs tensed as it readied itself to pounce. Hannah did the same, lowering herself into a crouch. With a roar, the chimera leapt forwards, its teeth surging towards her. Hannah reacted immediately and threw herself into the hole, her hands grabbing hold of a ledge and swinging her body down.

Her landing was far from elegant, as her knees buckled, and she fell on all fours. She scampered to where Daegan lay and checked his pulse. She let out a shaky laugh, relieved to feel his heart still pumping, and shook him.

A thud slammed onto the ground behind her. As she turned to face the chimera once more, she felt small and hopeless.

'It's just you and me now, Drakkar.'

It growled angrily in response.

'You've lost. You might kill me, but there are others—they've all seen you; they've all survived. They'll tell the Trucekeepers, and they'll come down on you like—'

Her self-indulgent speech was cut short. Fed up, he pounced and pushed her to the ground, the lion-head baring its teeth.

Winded, she writhed on the ground, her entire body screaming, begging for it all to stop. But she wouldn't let herself give up now—not with the chimera approaching Daegan with a low growl.

The goat-head reared back, wisps of smoke and flame teasing the eruption soon to come.

Hannah didn't think twice. As she charged forwards, she knew there was only one way to protect Daegan. She couldn't attack the chimera—not the second before it burnt him to a crisp; there was no time. She had no idea if it would work; it never had before, and she was already so weak from the fight, from being outside Arcadia.

But there was no other way. Daegan's life rested entirely in her hands.

She leapt in front of Daegan, telum outstretched and eyes closed, bracing herself for the inevitable, for the flames.

But no flames came, only a vague heat.

Hesitantly, she glanced up and gasped as she saw a shield emerging from her telum, barring the flames from her and Daegan.

Finally! she thought, her face beaming as relief flooded her mind.

The jet of flames hit the shield like a ton of bricks. It took a lot for her to keep it up. Every second that passed became harder and harder; she could feel the heat from the flames threatening to burn her to a crisp; her head was light; she lost sensation in her body. Any help the aqua vitae had given her had been used up. She couldn't keep the shield up. There was a point where she would have no energy left, and the shield would fall.

This is it, she thought, silently regretting not being able to see Luke again, or Niall, or Dex and Kiko... or Daegan.

The incessant flames came to a halt. Hannah's thumb left the crystal.

'Just do it,' she panted, resigning herself to her fate.

The chimera stepped back and made a sound. Hannah frowned. It was neither a growl, nor a hiss, nor a snarl. What came out was a whimper as the chimera's two remaining heads looked through a hole in the wall. Whooshing sounds came from above, and several arrows with orange tips flew over her head. Each one pierced into the chimera.

Inches in front of Hannah, a figure crashed through the night sky and landed deftly.

Hannah's immediate reaction was to summon what little energy she had left to crawl away, scared Drakkar had sent for Leviathan reinforcements.

But the figure stepped towards the chimera, a telum in the right hand that transformed into a sword glowing red; in the left, the figure unsheathed another sword. Hannah felt herself relax. Whoever the figure was, they paid her no attention.

With three deft, expert moves, the figure blocked the chimera's attack with a shield gauntlet and propelled the Etheria backwards. Then, jumping forwards, it slashed outwards with both arms. Both remaining heads toppled to the ground, its eyes now dark and dim. Hannah watched with astonishment as the remains of the chimera lay lifeless at the feet of its killer.

The figure didn't dwell on the victory. Instead, it approached Hannah.

She looked up at her saviour. Her cascading blonde hair fell past her shoulders, and her dark outfit held much of the equipment Talos gave Trucekeepers—but there was some she didn't recognise.

A flood of questions entered Hannah's mind.

Who are you? Are you a Trucekeeper? How did you become such a badass?

In the end, she simply resorted to, 'Thanks.'

The woman smiled, her piercing green eyes inspecting the helpless girl on the floor. She said nothing but offered a hand, which Hannah gratefully accepted.

Once on her feet, the woman picked up Hannah's telum and took out the blood crystal, which she admired fondly. Then, to Hannah's dismay, she clasped her fingers around the crystal, gripping it tightly. Shining, shimmering powder fell from her hand, and when she unclasped her fingers, nothing but dust fell from her open palm. The remains of Hannah's blood crystal fell in a pile on the ground.

Hannah fell back to her knees, fingers feeling through the crystal dust, hoping for a large shard that might still work.

But there was nothing. She had destroyed her blood crystal.

Hannah didn't know whether to feel angry or heartbroken. 'Why?' she whispered.

The woman gave no reply, but she jumped through the hole from which she came. A gust of sea breeze sent her hair flying in mad wisps like snakes as she fell.

Hannah rushed to watch her crash into the sea below, but she landed on a blue Etheria resembling a winged stag, which flapped its enormous wings and propelled the two of them across the sea, vanishing into the distance.

Chapter Seventy-Two

The Truceleaders' Verdict

A mermaid momentarily disturbed the calm waters of Arcadia Lake, soaring out and plunging back in with barely a splash. The kobolds in the port were half-asleep as they smoked on the decks of the moored ships. Etheria in the meadow grazed on the grass as the alicantos played with the sarimanoks in the air, a cascade of colour adorning the sky above.

Dex snored lightly, nestled beside Hannah who sat atop the mound by the lake. She had considered staying in her room and sitting on the windowsill—after all, that view was arguably better. But after everything she had been through, she didn't want to hide away. She needed to show her face, prove that she hadn't been defeated.

Then again, the fate of her life at Arcadia was being considered at that very moment in the Truceleader Halls. She had asked Daegan if she could sit in, even make a case for her defence.

'I'm sorry, Hannah. As with many of the Trucekeeper's traditional rules, I can't bend this to suit your whims. Relax. I'll tell you the verdict myself when it's over.'

Since then, she had awaited him with a strange mix of emotions. On one hand, she couldn't wait to see him climb the hill to give her the news; but on the other, that news might not be the outcome she hoped for. She was desperate to stay; it seemed a lifetime ago when she first joined, but things were different now. No longer quiet, solitary and angry, feeling as though she didn't belong—Hannah was happy, with more friends than she could imagine in a place she could finally call home.

And now all this was in the hands of seven people.

She tried to distract herself, but even the sounds of life from around the castle brought back unwanted memories, the faeries' hut especially. After all, it had been Sophie who had noticed their Flare spell. As promised, the trainees told her everything, after which she rode her unicorn familiar to tell Daegan, who rushed to their aid.

Hannah looked down at the blood crystal she was playing with in her hand. She held it to the light and admired the dark blue tinge that shone through as she thought about all that had happened since the battle at Oakstone Castle.

Lena had got to work on Luke immediately, only just managing to save his life. Ansel had disappeared soon after, not even staying long enough for Hannah to thank him; he only muttered something about how Daegan owed him one. And of that, there was no doubt—if it weren't for the werewolf, Luke would be dead. She had asked Daegan who he was and how he knew him; Daegan simply smiled and explained he was a good friend from the old days— whatever that meant.

She had also miserably explained to him how the woman who saved her also destroyed her blood crystal. Daegan seemed very interested in the woman, asking Hannah more questions than she could answer: What did she look like? What weapons did she have? Did she say anything? Was she a Leviathan or Trucekeeper? Pyre or Thrunter? There was a limit to what Hannah could say about the woman, but she answered honestly.

But as grateful as she was for the woman slaying Drakkar, she didn't know if it was worth sacrificing her blood crystal.

Still, Daegan was kind enough to take her to the Cave of Melissani for another one, her own this time.

She had entered the cave with trepidation, heart beating out of her chest. The gnomes guarding the entrance did little to calm her nerves, keen for a fight. But once past the small and ineffective guards, getting her own blood crystal was surprisingly easy.

There were Etheria who lived there, mining minerals such as crystals and adamant. Ever since the Leviathan War, they hadn't had many visitors; the bluecaps whizzed about like excitable blue flames; beardless karzeleks, smaller than dwarves, eagerly welcomed Hannah, the latest hero of Arcadia. They guided her away from the mischievous knockers to veins of ore, and warned her where not to step for fear of cave-ins.

She kept Dex very close, just in case he strayed where he ought not to; she had heard that the Etheria who dwelled there didn't appreciate intrusions.

The coblynaus were hard at work mining and barely noticed Hannah, only looking up when they heard her gasp. The area of the cave with the largest ores to mine was enormous. Its ceiling was as high as a cathedral with stalactites and stalagmites like mountains, shining and shimmering as they reflected a rainbow throughout the room. An oread nymph called Lea handed Hannah a pickaxe and told her to swing at the huge clusters of crystal. She did so, and a small clump fell into her hand.

Back outside Arcadia Castle, the dwarves in the blacksmith's hut chipped it into shape, and Hannah took it to Sophie to enchant a rune into it. She felt a little sour that this was something other trainees had done long before, finally understanding why choosing a rune was such a challenge. Flicking through all the possibilities, she didn't understand why some like Nathan, Jason and Amber had chosen such negative runes; Nathan had reverse Ansuz, Jason had reverse Algiz, Amber had reverse Teiwaz. Not one of them was complimentary, but Hannah supposed they had to be honest if they wanted to get the most out of their blood crystals.

She narrowed hers down to a few possibilities; some positive, some not so much. Sophie agreed with one of them and snatched her blood crystal to enchant it with the rune of Thurisaz. Hannah looked through the book to see what it said:

Those with the Thurisaz rune tend to rush into dangerous situations. However foolhardy this may be, those suited to the Thurisaz rune tend to prevail since they fight for others and refuse to give up, no matter the cost…

It was more complimentary than Hannah had intended. She couldn't help but blush slightly.

She tested the new blood crystal by casting a Strike spell on a wooden dummy. The jet of orange light struck the dummy, chips of wood flying off, sending it crashing to the ground. She looked at the crystal in wonder, not even feeling half as drained as she had done casting spells with the other crystal. *This is the one.*

She replaced the crystal in her telum and stretched out, basking in the heat of the sun and waiting for news. Before long, she saw the unmistakable figure of Daegan, hat stuck to his head even in the hot summer weather.

'Well?' she asked, eyes still glued to the lake. She didn't dare look at him. If the news was bad, she didn't want him to see it affect her.

To her surprise, he removed his leather coat and sat down next to her, head raised to bask in the sun.

'How's Axis?' she asked, still pretending not to care about the verdict.

'Better now. She's still with Lena in the medical wing. In a bed near your boyfriend, actually.'

'He's not my boyfriend.' She had reminded Daegan countless times, but either he failed to remember or found it funny to antagonise her.

'Caedric is working with Lena to determine what happened to her in the library. He's keen on discovering who her father actually was after that fiasco. We've seen nothing like it.'

'Any word about the woman from the castle?' she asked.

Daegan tensed up. 'Not yet. I'm working on it though.'

'By the way…' Hannah coughed and picked at her nail. 'I never apologised—for what happened at Thule. I just wanted to—'

'It's fine,' said Daegan. 'Water under the bridge now. And I should be thanking you; I heard about your Shield spell at Oakstone.'

Hannah shook her head. 'I can't believe I actually managed to cast it. I tried so many times before, but…'

'You finally listened to me, I suppose. I told you right at the beginning you needed to understand what you were fighting for. I assume that was the moment it all clicked for you; that we're here to protect and defend, not attack.'

There was an awkward pause. Hannah knew Daegan was waiting for her to ask him about the inevitable. From his cheeky smile, she could tell he enjoyed toying with her.

'Okay—just tell me,' she sighed.

'You can relax,' he told her. 'You're staying.'

'Good,' she replied, feigning cool disinterest.

Daegan cocked a curious eyebrow. 'Well, don't thank me straight away! I had to defend you in there, you know.'

'You did?'

Daegan nodded. 'I know I'm bossy and a little stubborn, but I do always try to protect you, Hannah.'

Hannah smiled. 'Who was against me staying?'

'Byron mostly. And Eldrin a bit.'

Hannah had given up long ago caring about the Truceleaders she knew didn't like her. 'No surprise. They hate me.'

'They don't *hate* you, Hannah. They're just harder to impress.'

'Diplomatic way of putting it,' she muttered. 'What were their objections? Be honest.'

'What you'd expect, really. They didn't appreciate your reluctance to take orders and your reckless enthusiasm to charge into dangerous situations.'

'Don't some see that as bold and brave?' she asked with a coy smile.

'Only when you have the means to handle the situation you charge into,' he replied, smiling back. 'But I told them that, despite the brashness, you've shown exceptional progress in all aspects of training—even magic—and they agreed: Aarava, Braddock, everyone. And I added how you don't rush into things for the hell of it; there's always a purpose and—and this is what they liked the most—you always did it for others: for friends, for Arcadia, for the Truce. And after all, isn't that what being a Trucekeeper is all about?'

Hannah snorted. 'That's a good line. I'm sure they loved that!'

'Yes, I suppose they did,' Daegan chuckled. 'I meant it though.' He turned to her, only fleetingly making eye contact. Hannah could tell being so open made him feel awkward. 'Byron and Eldrin were wrong. Despite what happened with the saumen-kar… you accept when you're in the wrong now, you don't run away at the first opportunity anymore. You were prepared to face your punishment—and still are—and you did your best to fix your mistakes. Plus, you work well with others. I still remember that bitter girl who first came to Arcadia and hated everyone.'

'I didn't hate *everyone*,' Hannah said. 'Just most people.'

'My point exactly. And now?'

Hannah turned away, keen to hide her blushing cheeks. She wasn't used to such high praise.

'You've made an impression on Arcadia—on everyone here. I'm proud.' Daegan nodded, blushing slightly himself. 'You still have a lot to learn though.'

'Did you get to vote on whether I stay?' she asked.

'No… I'm not a Truceleader, I'm afraid—just a humble Keeper,' he reminded her.

She frowned. 'But Drakkar's gone. Isn't there a space in the Truceleaders that you could fill? There always have to be seven Truceleaders at a time.'

Daegan shrugged. 'Mantir would have a better shot than me. But they've already got someone from outside Arcadia anyway.'

'What?' Hannah was shocked. 'That was fast. Who?'

'Well, he hasn't arrived yet. He's an elf—'

'Another one?'

'—from Hyperborea. His name is Ronan.'

'I thought only giants lived in Hyperborea?'

Daegan grinned proudly. 'You've done your reading! Originally, there were just giants. Now it's expanded to a settlement similar to Arcadia. There are more than you may think.'

'What's he like?' she asked tentatively, scared they might have another Drakkar on their hands.

'I'm sure you'll find out. So,' he sighed, 'you're in and due to complete the Trials in a few months.'

A gentle whistle came from Hannah's pursed lips. 'Really?'

'Of course. You're ready to get a badge of your own.' He patted her lapel. 'You'll be more than ready by the time it comes. Of course, because of all this, if you fail, they won't let you retake—at that point, they'll expel you from Arcadia. That's your punishment—one chance.'

Daegan's words worried Hannah. She had heard various things about the Trials; some said it was easy, some said the opposite. If the latter turned out to be true, there would be little point in celebrating now.

'I'm not worried,' Daegan said, as he noticed her change in expression.

She couldn't suppress her joy any longer and jumped at him, trapping him in a hug. Daegan stiffened up, predictably awkward, but still brought his arm around to fulfil his part of the hug.

'Hope I'm not interrupting anything,' said a voice behind them.

Hannah relieved Daegan of the hug and saw Niall above them, beaming.

Daegan huffed in amusement. 'Look at you two with your scars.' He pointed to the scar on Hannah's cheek and the one on Niall's neck, both caused by Drakkar's telum. 'Almost as handsome as me. You're looking more and more like Trucekeepers every day!'

'We don't have as many as Aarava,' Niall said. 'I heard the news!'

'How? I only just found out.'

'You really think there are any secrets in Arcadia anymore?'

With an awkward cough, Daegan stood up. 'You have a point—there aren't many secrets kept in Arcadia…' He gave them both a disapproving look that made Hannah blush. She hadn't thought of what Daegan would think about her and Niall's kiss. 'Be careful you two,' he said, like an awkward father. '*Ubi amor, ibi dolor*,' he said as he picked up his coat, nodded his hat to them and turned to leave.

'Oh—one more thing, Hannah. The boy in the medical wing. Wipe him.' With that, he gave them a brief salute, middle finger held down, and walked off, whistling to himself.

Hannah's spirits were quashed. She looked worriedly to Niall. 'Do I have to?'

Niall nodded sadly. Hannah knew he was jealous of Luke but appreciated his remorse. 'The Truce insists any human who isn't a Trucekeeper must have knowledge of Etheria erased.'

'He can't *become* a Trucekeeper?'

Niall shook his head. 'From what I heard, the Truceleaders have already voted against it.'

Hannah kicked a nearby rock, sending it flying into the lake. The splash woke Dex who just yawned in response.

'I still can't believe you knew where to find me,' she said. 'When you saved me from Drakkar.'

'Where else would you have been? I knew you weren't going to give up on him.' He paused, shuffling his feet. 'Look, I wanted to apologise—for not believing you about Drakkar. I've got an issue with authority.'

'That makes both of us,' Hannah chuckled.

Niall smiled. 'I'm the opposite. I trust too much, I suppose. I've always assumed the world is a happy, innocent place.' He shrugged. 'I guess I was wrong.'

Hannah turned to face him and grabbed his shoulder. 'No,' she told him, looking at him sternly. 'Don't you dare give up on that, Niall. That's what we all hope for, that's why we're Trucekeepers. We dare to dream of peace, of a better world—that's what we fight for. I don't want to live in a world without that dream.'

'Hannah…' Niall said tenderly, his body pressed to hers. He stroked her arm and felt her tense up.

A million conflicting thoughts ran through her panicked mind. She stepped back and bit her lip, avoiding Niall's gaze.

'What's wrong?' he asked.

'Niall, I…' she trailed off, still unsure what she to say or how she even felt. 'I've been reading some articles from the Truce,' she started. 'Unlike me, I know. But there was one that stood out.'

'Oh, yes?' Niall said tersely. 'You mean the one that says Trucekeepers shouldn't fall in love? That they should be solitary, dedicate their lives to protecting the Truce. That one?'

She nodded, gulping. 'That's the one. I—'

'What are you doing, Hannah?' he asked. 'Was it all a mistake? Do you feel nothing?' He bowed his head. 'Is it Luke?'

'It's not like that,' she promised. 'Luke and I…' She drifted off, preferring not to talk about Luke. 'Forget about him.'

'With pleasure. He's about to have no memory of me anyway.'

She scowled. 'Niall, believe me when I tell you nothing would make me happier than the two of us. But we can't—at least not now. If I fail the Trials, I'll be kicked out of Arcadia. I need to train—with no distractions.'

'I won't distract you,' he pleaded.

'It's more than that. We're so alike, which I love, but when we're together, I can be brash, reckless—more than I am already. With the way I feel about you… it's dangerous. Look what happened with the saumen-kar; Drakkar played us. *Us* led to him nearly starting a war!'

Niall looked at her, speechless, though with understanding. He nodded.

'I'd better see to Luke now. Watch Dex for me.'

With that, she trudged down the hill towards the castle and away from Niall, now alone on their hill.

Chapter Seventy-Three

Memories

IT had been awkward picking Luke up from the medical wing and pretending everything was fine. Aside from a strange scar that resembled a blue star on his chest, Lena had done a brilliant job saving him; Hannah reminded herself to thank her for that at some point.

'We're twins,' Hannah joked as she pointed to both of their scars.

'It's amazing, isn't it?' he asked, eyes fixed on the faerie deep in discussion with a wounded Trucesentry.

'What, Lena?' Hannah asked, feeling a twinge of jealousy.

'Yeah… I mean, not just her. Her, for sure. Wow. But— everything! That white bird—'

'Zephyr.'

'Whatever it is, I want one! And her… She's a faerie. Hannah, faeries are *real!* Who would have thought?'

'Have you met the minotaur who lives here?' she asked with a wry smile.

Luke's eyes lit up. 'No! Seriously? Do you guys—do you keep him locked in a labyrinth?'

Hannah burst out laughing. 'No. But there's a vampire we probably should.'

Luke's pale face turned even paler. 'Is he dangerous?'

Hannah paused, unsure how to reply. 'Probably not.'

That did little to reassure him, but a little colour returned to his face. 'So long as he doesn't sparkle in the sunlight… Give me a tour? If these guys exist, I'm dying to find out what else does. Have you ever heard of Pheme's trumpet?'

Hannah perched on the edge of the bed. 'Maybe later.'

'Oh,' he exhaled. 'I know that voice. That's the "I'm-about-to-let-you-down voice."'

'I don't have an "I'm-about-to-let-you-down voice!" I just… You haven't seen your parents in a week. There might be a search party looking for you. You should go back, let them know you're safe.' She stroked the star-shaped scar on his chest. 'After all, you did nearly die.'

It took a long time to get him out of Arcadia and through the forest outside. He moped the entire way, moaning that he wanted to see if elves were like the ones in fantasy films or like Santa has.

It took even longer to hitchhike a ride to the nearest town, made harder by Luke's protests that they didn't know whose car they would get into. Normally Hannah would agree, but with her telum by her side—and having just taken on a chimera—she felt invincible.

Once they made their way to a town, they found a coffee shop and sat down on a sofa tucked away from prying eyes. They avoided the gaze of unhappy baristas no doubt considering throwing them out unless they bought a drink.

'You don't have any money, do you?' she asked him.

'I left my wallet in my car—which I would like back one day,' he reminded her. 'Can't you just, I don't know, magic some money?'

Hannah smiled and shook her head. 'You've got a lot to learn,' she said, immediately regretting her choice of words.

'So, when *can* I learn?'

Hannah looked at him blankly. 'Learn what?'

'You know,' he nudged her. 'When can I start training to be like you?'

'Like me?'

Luke looked around to make sure no one was listening, but everyone around them had earphones plugged in, tapping on laptops. 'A Trucekeeper,' he whispered.

'Erm…' *Do I be honest with him?* 'Soon.'

'Awesome! And can I get one of those pets?'

He was so full of excitement, Hannah couldn't bring herself to upset him. 'A familiar? Sure.'

He gave her an awkward thumbs up. 'What are the options? Do you get to choose, like one out of three? Or—'

'You know what?' Hannah said. 'I'll write you a list when I get back from the bathroom.'

Luke nodded, his eyes alive with the possibilities. Hannah stood, her knees shaking, but his hand on hers made her freeze.

'I'm just excited to have you back,' he told her earnestly. 'I've been a mess without you. It's going to be so… You know?'

She forced a weak smile and stood behind him, making sure no one could see her and checking once more for any CCTV cameras. She removed the telum from her new holster, nestled discreetly under her left arm inside her jacket.

With a solitary tear running down her face, she pricked her thumb and pressed it to the blood crystal. She hesitated, not wanting to think of the Oblivion glyph. As soon as she did, his memories would cease to exist. He'd be scared, confused… and the memories of the Etheria he loved would be gone. Was that really the reward he deserved? She had heard horror stories of previous Trucekeepers who had got the glyph wrong, some completely obliterating the targets' minds, sometimes even killing them.

She replaced her telum in her holster and wiped away the tear with resolve.

'Luke, I've got—I've got to go. You know, time to save the world again!'

There was no disguising the disappointment on his face, but he nodded his understanding. 'Of course. I've got to go home anyway. Tell my folks I'm okay. Just… don't forget me, alright?'

'I could never do that,' she promised.

Once he left, she collapsed on the sofa, her face in her hands and already regretting her decision—she had exposed the world of Etheria to a Human and let him go without erasing his mind. She had violated the Truce, gone against strict orders. If any of the Truceleaders found out…

'Buy you a drink?' asked a gruff voice.

'No,' came her automatic reply, not even bothering to look up.

Whoever it was sat opposite her, regardless. She slapped the sofa in frustration, keen to be left alone.

'I said, no—'

She halted her words upon seeing a smiling Daegan sipping a frothy cappuccino. 'What are you doing here?'

'Don't tell me I need to train you in manners too,' he quipped.

He slid a latte in an overly large mug across the table to Hannah and sat back, sipping his own.

'Almond milk,' he said with a knowing smile. 'Lena told me you didn't bring your insulin pump—*again*.'

Daegan looked out of place in the real world, provoking curious glances from laptops. But he seemed blissfully unaware, sitting back and enjoying his coffee.

'I'm not used to seeing you like this,' she told him.

'Drinking coffee?'

'In the real world.'

'What about when we first met?'

Hannah smirked. 'You saved my life at a random bus stop, then drove me into the middle of nowhere. It's not like we got pizza.'

Daegan licked his lips and rubbed his stomach. 'Tell you what, I could do with a pizza right now.'

'What are you doing here?' she asked, preferring to cut to the chase.

Daegan looked a little hurt. 'I'm here for you. It's difficult, wiping the memory of a friend. Believe me, I know.' He paused as he took a long sip, his eyes examining Hannah shifting in her seat. 'You did do it, didn't you?'

Hannah avoided his eyes, scared he would see the truth inside them. She nodded.

'Good,' he said. 'I trust it wasn't too draining to cast with the new blood crystal?'

Hannah stroked the crystal and smiled. 'It works a lot better.'

'So it should. I know you find your diabetes frustrating, but your body is so used to the process of giving blood that, in theory, the faeries predict your magic should be more powerful than the others', especially with the right crystal. Gods, imagine… For a trainee to survive crystal convergence *and* conjure a strong Shield spell at the end of a long battle?' Daegan shook his head. 'Don't always dismiss the hand you're dealt. Sometimes your worst weakness can become your greatest strength. You've got the makings of a powerful Trucekeeper.'

Hannah grinned, looking forward to using that to put Amber or Nathan in their place one day. 'I still miss my old one though.' She pouted. 'I guess now the crystal's gone…'

'It was our only lead.' Daegan nodded. 'Our only chance of finding Astraea. We have no option but to give up. For now, at least.'

Hannah pushed her coffee to the side and leaned forward. 'Speaking of old crystals, I have to ask. Other than making their way back to their owner, blood crystals only perform whatever abilities you tell them to, right? They won't act on their own accord. So how come you appeared when I touched Astraea's blood crystal that first time?'

Daegan too leaned forward, looking around to make sure they could not be overheard.

'Because you touched it with your blood—'

'But you didn't appear at other times. Why?'

Daegan's face matched Hannah's serious expression. 'Remember this is top secret,' he prefixed, 'but that blood crystal used to belong to another Trucekeeper, Astraea—that much you know. She…' He trailed off. 'She went rogue during the War. I was assigned to that crystal as soon as we found out—meaning that as soon as she used it again, I would disappear from wherever I was and reappear next to her. But it wasn't her I found—it was you.'

'Please,' she implored him. 'Just tell me the truth. You were expecting to find Astraea, a rogue Trucekeeper—a powerful one who locked away a chimera! I'm pretty sure I'm not her. So, tell me: Who was Astraea, and why could I use her blood crystal?'

Daegan looked into Hannah's eyes. 'She was your mother.'

Hannah felt as though the world had been ripped from under her feet. Her head felt light, as if she were falling, plummeting to an unreachable bottom.

'What—How… How can you be sure?'

'Well, you look like her for starters. Your green eyes, in particular. Not the blue parts so much though.' Daegan shifted in his seat and looked away. 'And you remind me of her. The way you act just like her is uncanny. Besides, you can use her crystal too.

'Listen—Astraea was an exceptional Trucekeeper,' Daegan continued. 'One of our best. During the Leviathan War, we sent her on a mission. She was to infiltrate the Leviathans—gain their trust, become one of them. One of our Trucekeepers, Morgarr, defected to the Leviathans. She was instructed to use him as her way in. But as time wore on, we feared she had betrayed us. I was closest to her, so it was decided that I should be assigned to her crystal. As soon as she used it again, I was to arrest her or, if she resisted arrest...'

'Did you kill her?' Hannah coughed out the words, not quite able to believe what she was hearing.

Daegan shook his head. 'No. She went missing. We presumed her dead. At least, that's what the rumours said. Most blame Morgarr—they say he discovered she was a spy and... Anyway, I suppose I forgot I was assigned to her crystal at all. We searched for her—*I* searched for her. I've spent Gods know how long ever since. But I got nowhere—until I found you.'

Hannah sat back and rubbed the scalding hot mug with her thumb. She felt sick. This was too much to take in at once.

'That's why I never got my own crystal,' Hannah mused aloud. 'You thought that if I used hers, she might reappear.'

Daegan nodded. 'Or at least help us get closer to finding out what happened to her. Caedric took some convincing. He knew the dangers of an untrained Trucekeeper having a crystal like that, one which was the key to several vaults. But he knew how important it was to me—to the Trucekeepers—to find out what happened to her.

'There are lots of differences in families,' Daegan went on. 'There's no end to fathers being different to sons, daughters being different to mothers. But there's *one* thing they have in common— they all share the same blood. You could use your mother's blood crystal because her blood runs in your veins. That's one reason the Truceleaders want to monitor you, even though they were scared at first. You're the missing link. Astraea was one of the greatest Trucekeepers, and I've always doubted that she really betrayed us. I wanted answers.'

'But what answers can I give? I'm just as clueless—no, I'm *more* clueless than even you are!'

'How old are you, Hannah?' Daegan asked candidly.

Hannah didn't understand. He knew perfectly well how old she was. 'Sixteen.'

'Exactly. The War ended about sixteen years ago, a little less in fact. I'm positive that you're evidence she didn't die—you're proof she survived the War, even for a short while. She disappeared somewhere for whatever reason, and then you were born. If only we knew who your father was.' Daegan shifted uncomfortably and took a long sip from his mug.

Hannah's heart sank. She slammed the mug on the table, hot coffee spilling over.

'So now you just want me to stick around to lure her back? I'm your pawn?' It took all her self-control not to yell in public.

'No,' Daegan replied, unperturbed by her small outburst. 'Maybe to the likes of Byron. But to me? To Caedric?' His smile meant well, but it came across as more patronising. 'That may have been the reason at first, but things changed. Finding out what happened to Astraea or bringing her back—that would have just been a bonus. We see so much of her in you. You've proven that already. I know you doubt you belong in Arcadia sometimes, but you really do.' Daegan smirked. 'After all, it's in your blood.'

Hannah shot him a piercing look. *Too corny.*

But the way he smiled and sipped his coffee, his strange clothes standing out in the otherwise normal coffee shop—it all made her grin.

'I seem to remember you didn't even want me around at first,' she said. 'You didn't seem keen on training me.'

Daegan winced. 'It's not that I didn't want you around. I just wanted you to be safe, keep you out of danger.' He shrugged. 'But I misjudged you. It turns out you don't need protecting.'

'So…' she sighed, sitting back down with a satisfied smile. 'What now?'

'I was hoping you'd ask that,' he said, sliding a beige paper folder across the table.

'What's this?'

'Information. I doubt you've come across this Etheria before. Even Niall hadn't.'

Hannah opened the folder and skimmed the first page.

Adze—vampiric Etheria; native to Africa.
Known to suck blood of humans. Ability to possess.
Often found in the form of a firefly or human.

'We're going to reason with him,' Daegan told her. 'Caedric thinks, and I agree, that Drakkar will be just the first of many attempts by the Leviathans to ignite a war. It would be useful to have an Etheria this powerful at possessing, wouldn't you say? They would be a perfect spy, especially easy to escape as a firefly if they were found out.'

'And if the adze is already with the Leviathans?'

Daegan's half-smile stayed fixed on his face. 'Then we'll do what we must. After all, you need to get your practice in. We need to train you for the Trials.'

'Well,' she said, handing the folder back and cracking her knuckles, 'let's get to it.

Acknowledgements

Writing acknowledgements is a bit like writing a birthday card—there are heartfelt thoughts and feelings you want to say but don't quite know how to get it across... So I'll just dive into it.

My thanks go to my father and his knowledge of Ancient Greek—the whole name 'Etheria' is down to him.

Thanks also to some of my ex-pupils and the select few in the Dungeons & Dragons club who read the opening chapters and gave their very honest feedback. Thank you also to my family, particularly Ma, Uncle Jack and Jerome for being some of the first I sent the whole thing to.

I'll never hear the end of it if I don't mention my beautiful wife Sophie for her unending patience, tolerating me blabber on about characters, mythology and plot ideas. Her support is everything to me, and so much of her is found in this book, from a faerie to Hannah herself. Sophie's diabetes inspired the magic system and blood crystals, but more than that, she gave me the bravery to go the whole way and make Hannah diabetic. She's promised to read it when it's finally printed (so now you don't have an excuse!).

Thanks also to Nik for designing an excellent book cover and my editor Kayla for all her efforts in making the book what it is today. And a nod to my own familiar—my dog Halie who kept me company throughout the editing.

My largest thanks go to my mum...doesn't it always? At this point, she's read the book more than I have! Thank you for the tireless work and support in writing, perfecting and promoting the novel. You're the real Trucemaster.

And finally, an enormous thanks and appreciation to the world's cultures for their tales and creations I admire so much. Really, this book wouldn't exist at all without them. It's a testament to the unending storytelling tradition of humanity. I thank the thousands of years of imagination and sharing it with the rest of the world.

About the Author

Matt Twinley is the author of *The Blood Crystal*, the first book in his young adult fantasy series *The Trucekeeper Saga*. After graduating the University of St. Andrews, Matt flitted from job to job, working as a wine merchant, audio transcriber and English teacher, all the while wanting to be a writer; he penned plays for schools, blog posts, film reviews and several projects he swears will never see the light of day. It was only while daydreaming in class as a teaching assistant that he planned his first book.

Matt lives in Surrey, UK with his wife whose Type 1 diabetes inspired the magic system featured in *The Blood Crystal*. He can usually be found hiding indoors scribbling away at a new story, researching something bizarre or lost in a video-game, film or book. If you find him outside, he's either at a restaurant, bookshop or cinema—otherwise he's lost.

www.ingramcontent.com/pod-product-compliance
Lightning Source LLC
Chambersburg PA
CBHW051159190726
48288CB00006B/1719